Tamara McKinley is the author of more than eleven novels. She was born in Tasmania, but now lives in Sussex and Cornwall and writes full time. Her novels are both contemporary and historical, following the lives of Australian pioneers and those who came after them.

OCEAN CHILD

Tamara McKinley

Quercus

First published in Great Britain in 2013 by

Quercus Editions Ltd
55 Baker Street
7th Floor, South Block
London W1U 8EW

A CIP catalogue record for this book is available
from the British Library

ISBN 978 1 78206 772 6
EBOOK ISBN 978 1 78206 664 4

10 9 8 7 6 5 4 3 2 1

Printed and bound in Great Britain by Clays Ltd, St Ives plc

Typeset by Ellipsis Books Limited, Glasgow

In loving memory of Daireen McKinley,
who loved me as a daughter.

There are many faces of love – each demanding their own loyalties – each shaded by circumstances, experience and expectation.

But when love is true and steadfast, it demands the greatest gift of all – to be returned.

1

England, February 1920

The soft, downy warmth intensified and Lulu Pearson moved restlessly in an attempt to escape it. But the smothering heat seemed to press harder, covering her eyes, her nose and her mouth. With a whimper of distress she discovered she had no strength to push it away, and as her damaged heart hammered and she fought to breathe, she knew she was about to die.

The pressure was even greater now, the blood singing in her ears, the fear giving her strength to fight this awful thing. But as she flailed and thrashed and tried to cry out, her heart struggled – thudding away inside her, weakening her with every tortuous beat.

She heard voices. Was aware of a sliver of light. And suddenly she was free.

Rearing up in the bed with a great gulp of clean, life-giving air, she opened her eyes. The room was in darkness, and this was not the little house in Tasmania. Her heart continued to struggle as she fought to regulate her breathing and calm the terrible fears this recurring nightmare always elicited. She was no longer a child – she was safe.

No one would have guessed he was sixty-five, for his step was robust, his figure sturdy, the walking stick more of an affectation than an aid. He fitted into the country scene and, as it was a role he'd played over many years, he felt comfortable in the tweed jacket, plus-fours and walking boots. It hadn't always been so, for he was a city man at heart, but, like a good actor, he'd grown into the part and enjoyed these annual visits to Sussex.

Camouflaged by the dappled shadows of the trees, he ate the last of his sandwiches and watched the rider slowly descend the far hill towards the livery stables. She had been gone for over an hour, but he hadn't minded the wait. The weather was clement, if a little chill, and he was being generously paid. He tucked the sandwich wrapper in the canvas bag, brushed crumbs from his moustache and raised his binoculars.

He knew Lulu Pearson intimately, yet they had never met or spoken, and if things went to plan, they never would. His occasional surveillance had begun many years ago, and as time had passed he'd seen her grow from coltish childhood into the beautiful young woman who now moved with lithe grace about the stable-yard. Her hair was her crowning glory, usually falling almost to her waist in curls that sparked gold and chestnut in the sun, but today she had pinned it into a thick knot at her nape.

As she left the stables he got to his feet and began the long, uphill walk home. With the canvas bag and binoculars swinging from his shoulder, he headed back towards the village and a welcome pint of beer.

The effects of Lulu's nightmare had been dissipated during her gentle horse-ride, and although the arrival of that strange letter this morning still puzzled her, she felt exhilarated. It was wonderful to be in the fresh air after all those hours in her studio, and now she was eager to return to work. The clay model was almost finished, and she wanted to make sure she'd captured the right sense of power and movement before she judged it ready for the foundry. Yet her great-aunt Clarice would be expecting her home for afternoon tea and, despite her enthusiasm for work, the prospect of a blazing fire, buttered crumpets and Earl Grey tea was enticing.

She put all thoughts of Tasmania and the mysterious letter aside. It was a perfect English winter afternoon, with the sun shining from a cloudless sky, frost glittering in the shadows beneath the trees and the air crisp with the promise of snow. It was on days like these she was thankful she hadn't followed the fashion for short hair, and as she tramped slowly homeward she took out the combs and pins and let her luxuriant locks fall over her shoulders and down her back.

No doubt Clarice would make a fuss about her being out so long, but her troublesome heart was beating steadily enough, and it was liberating to have only the sky and silent landscape for company after the smog and noise of London. She'd enjoyed the independence of driving the omnibuses during the dark days of the Great War, and the thrill of earning her own money and sharing a flat with other girls, but the Downs soothed her.

She smiled at the thought, for she had once believed she could never belong anywhere but Tasmania. She'd been so young when she'd arrived here – her accent and family circumstances setting her apart from the other girls at boarding school – her damaged heart making it difficult to join in their boisterous games. A stranger in a strange land, she'd felt bewildered and lost, blindly clawing her way through those emotional early years until she made friends and felt easier in her new life. The landscape had helped, for although the trees were different, the hills more gentle, the rivers less wild, it contained the essence of that Australian island she still called home.

She climbed the stile and sat to catch her breath after the trek up the hill. The light was extraordinary, and her artist's eyes drank in the scene as if parched of beauty. The South Downs undulated around her, offering glimpses of church spires and tiny hamlets, of the tapestry of ploughed fields, hedges and

3

black-faced sheep. A solitary walker traversed the hill to the west, his sturdy figure silhouetted against the sky until he slowly faded from sight – leaving her truly alone in these magnificent surroundings.

A shaft of sunlight illuminated the house far below, and she eyed it fondly. Wealden House was far removed from the tin-roofed wooden cottage in Tasmania. It was rambling and old-fashioned, the signs of age and neglect veiled by distance and the protective cover of wisteria and Virginia creeper. Smoke drifted from several of the tall chimneys, and the sun glinted on the many windows beneath the peg-tiled roof. The formal gardens were divided by hedges and connected by a cobbled path seeded with scented herbs. There were arbours entangled with honeysuckle and roses, a croquet lawn and tennis court, and a pond which reflected weeping willows and dormant rhododendrons. At the southern boundary lay the kitchen garden and greenhouses, and to the north a wide gravel driveway swept up from imposing gates through banks of azaleas to a large porch and an oak front door.

Lulu clambered off the stile and, on reaching the five-bar gate at the bottom of the hill, remembered that first spring sixteen years ago. It had brought the English bluebells; a great carpet of them spreading from beneath the ancient oaks and ashes, providing a wonderland for the little girl who had never seen them before. Then the daffodils, wild anemones and buttercups had come – a new carpet of yellow and white beneath the delicate froth of apple and cherry blossom.

She closed the gate and dug her chin into her collar as she walked into the shadows that now crept across the ragged lawn. The frost glittered like crystals in the grass, but there was already the promise of new life in the tiny green shoots of snowdrops and crocuses that poked their heads through the weeds. Each season had its own beauty, and if she hadn't been so cold and hungry, she would have fetched her sketchbook and tried to capture the scene.

Entering the kitchen, Lulu kicked off her boots and made a fuss of the elderly Labrador stretched before the range. This was the warmest room in the house, for even the blazing fire in the drawing room couldn't cope with the draughts that whistled under every door and down the stairs.

The housekeeper crashed through the kitchen door and folded her meaty arms beneath her vast bosom. 'About time too,' she muttered crossly. 'I've enough to do without trying to keep my crumpets warm.'

Lulu bit her lip against the giggle and continued to pat the dog. 'I'm so sorry, Vera,' she managed. 'Am I terribly late?'

Vera Cornish sniffed and tugged at her wrap-around floral pinafore, but her dour expression softened as it always did with Lulu, and she sighed. 'Tea's at four, as you well know, Missy, and without a house full of servants, it's the devil's own job to keep up with things.'

Lulu apologised again, but the silence that fell between them seemed to emphasise the emptiness of the cavernous kitchen – reminding them both of the time when the cook and housemaids chattered with the gardeners around the scrubbed table. The delicious smell of baking remained, but the clatter of pans and the tramp of many feet on the flagstones were gone, leaving only ghostly memories. The Great War had changed everything.

Vera clucked with annoyance and grasped the tea-trolley. 'Wash your hands,' she ordered. 'What with 'orses and dogs, you'll be eating more than your peck of dirt, and what with your 'eart and everything . . .' The rest of the sentence was swallowed up in the screech of wheels and the clatter of china as she thrust the trolley out of the room ahead of her.

Lulu was still smiling as she washed her hands under the kitchen tap and padded down the chilly hallway in her thick

5

socks. Vera's disgruntled exterior hid a soft heart, and Wealden House just wouldn't be the same without her.

She checked the mail that had come by second post, and entered the drawing room. There was a letter from Maurice, but she was in no hurry to read it.

'How many times have I asked you to change before coming in here, Lorelei? The stables cling to you like a noxious scent.' Clarice was fragrant with French perfume, her expression stern and her ramrod poise uncompromising as she waited for Vera to position the trolley to her satisfaction. With an imperious nod, the housekeeper was dismissed.

Lulu and Vera were used to this rather haughty demeanour and ignored it. Clarice enjoyed playing the *grande dame,* but there was no malice behind it, and as her aunt didn't like tacit shows of affection Lulu resisted kissing her and sank onto the sofa nearest the fire. 'Sorry,' she murmured, running her fingers through the tangle of her hair, 'but I couldn't wait for tea. I'm ravenous.'

Clarice poured from the ornate silver pot as Lulu took a hot buttered crumpet from the chafing dish and bit into it. 'Plate, Lorelei, and napkin.'

She took both and munched the heavenly food as the heat from the fire began to thaw her. Clarice had always refused to shorten her name – she thought it rather common – and although she liked to maintain the impression that she was a harsh taskmaster, it was an act Lulu had seen through long ago – and yet, when truly riled, Clarice had a glare that could stop a rampaging bull at fifty yards. Today, however, the blue eyes glinted with humour.

Clarice was seventy, or thereabouts – it was a closely guarded secret, and Lulu had never dared probe – but she had the complexion, vitality and sharp wit of a much younger woman. Her short silver hair had been freshly set in rigid waves, and there were pearls in her ears and in a rope that encircled her neck and fell in loops to her waist. Rings glittered on her fingers, and bracelets jangled on her slender wrists. Clarice was the widow of a long-dead diplomat, and the strict code of conduct and appearance he'd enforced was still rigidly adhered to. She had no intention of letting standards slip while she could draw breath.

'It is rude to stare, Lorelei.'

'I was just thinking how lovely you look this afternoon,' she replied truthfully. 'That soft grey really suits you.'

Clarice smoothed the low-waisted dress over her knees, the heightened colour in her cheeks showing her pleasure at the praise. 'Thank you, dear. I wish I could return the compliment, but you look like a ragamuffin in that get-up.'

Lulu took in the grubby jodhpurs, the moth-eaten sweater and worn tweed jacket. 'The horses don't mind, and they're comfortable.' She flicked the curls out of her eyes and picked up another crumpet.

'I do so envy your youthful appetite,' sighed Clarice, 'and the way you never seem to put on weight. If I ate half what you do, I'd be the size of a house.'

Lulu hid a smile. Clarice was as slender as willow, and always had been, if the old photographs were anything to go by, yet her appetite was robust.

'Still,' added Clarice, 'it's good to see you eating again. It shows you're in good health – but I worry that you try to do too much.'

'I can't spend my life sitting about and feeling sorry for myself,' Lulu replied through the crumpet. 'Exercise and fresh air cheer me up no end.'

'That's all very well, but you know what the doctor said. Your heart isn't strong, and it doesn't do to overtax it.'

'I know when I've done too much,' she reassured her, 'and although I tire easily, I've learnt to deal with it.'

Clarice eyed her over the teacup and changed the subject. 'Did you find Maurice's letter?'

Lulu nodded, but her thoughts had returned to that other letter which had arrived this morning. As it was from Tasmania, and the contents made little sense, there was no point in discussing it with Clarice – who had made it quite clear over the years that she didn't want to talk about Australia, or anything connected with it.

'Maurice must be very lonely to write to you every day. What *can* he find to say?'

Lulu brought her thoughts back to the present as she sipped the fragrant tea. She didn't really want to discuss Maurice and spoil the mood of the day, but Clarice was awaiting a reply. 'He keeps me up to date on his latest painting, the people he meets at the gallery and his general health.' She didn't mention the rambling pages of introspection, the endless picking away at his fears, and his inability to settle on anything for long – it was too disheartening

'I realise he had a bad time in France, but that is no excuse for idleness. It's time he bucked up his ideas.'

This was a conversation they'd had before, and Lulu took her usual defensive stance. 'Maurice tries his best,' she murmured, 'but it's difficult to find work when he can't cope with crowds and noise.'

She had a sudden memory of Maurice cowering in a corner during a violent thunderstorm, whimpering in fear as each bolt of lightning lit up the London house they shared. She'd known then that the battlefields and trenches still haunted him, and as the terrible storm had raged overhead she had taken him into her bed. Their lovemaking had been frantic, clinging to one another in a kind of desperation as if the heat and touch of another body could reassure and heal – blot out the memories. But of course it had only been a fleeting release, for the memories were still raw.

'I do hope you haven't got too involved. He obviously relies upon you, and although you have your art in common, there is very little else to commend him.'

Lulu reddened under Clarice's penetrating scrutiny. There was little doubt Clarice suspected her intimacy with Maurice, but she needn't have worried. It had been short-lived – a mistake they had both soon acknowledged. 'We've agreed to be friends, nothing more,' she replied. 'There's never really been anyone special since Jimmy.'

Silence fell, but for the hiss of flames on damp logs. Lulu's gaze settled on the photograph that stood on the grand piano. Jimmy looked handsome in his uniform – and unbearably young, with his wide smile and honest brown eyes. They had known each other for years and were planning to marry, when war was declared in 1914 and he enlisted. He had been killed within weeks of landing in France.

Unwilling to dwell on such sadness, Lulu loaded up the trolley and headed for the door. 'I'm going to have a long soak in the bath before I check on the sculpture.'

'Don't forget we've been invited to cocktails and dinner tonight at the brigadier's to discuss the Easter fete. If you're not coming with me, you'll have to make do with cold cuts and soup. It's Vera's night off.'

The brigadier was a bluff, red-faced old buffer who had been pursuing Clarice unsuccessfully for years. Lulu had long decided there were better ways to spend an evening and declined the invitation.

With the tea things washed and set to dry on the drainer, she fed the dog then slowly went upstairs. After her bath, she snuggled into her fleecy dressing gown and sat at her dressing table, where she could glean the meagre heat from the fire that was doing battle with the draught from the ill-fitting window.

The mysterious letter had been forwarded from her address in London, and was lying beside her. Although she'd read it several times this morning and almost knew it by heart, it intrigued and unsettled her. Tugging the single sheet from the envelope, she smoothed it open. The handwriting was bold and masculine – the contents completely baffling.

Dear Miss Pearson,

As I have been training your colt, Ocean Child, for over a year now and have had no word from you, I thought you should be kept informed of his progress. Perhaps your agent, Mr Carmichael, has done this already, in which case I apologise for contacting you.

The Child is proving to be an exceptional two-year-old, having won most of his trials – these are races to test young horses over different distances, and there is no betting or handicapping involved. Although he has yet to be fully tested over longer courses, I have high hopes he will prove to be a stayer. He has a good temperament, is not distracted by noisy crowds and has become a firm favourite in the yard, especially with Bob Fuller, the young jackaroo I employ to ride him.

The Child is still too young for more important races, but he's muscling up nicely, and I've been working him hard with regular spells of rest in between. In another six months or so, I plan to enter him into some of the smaller steeple-chases to see how he fares.

I hope you don't mind me writing, but as there has been no word from you, I feel it is my duty as trainer to keep you informed.

Yours sincerely,
Joe Reilly

Lulu frowned. 'I don't know who you think I am, Mr Reilly,' she breathed, 'but you've obviously got me confused with someone else.'

Her smile was wry as she put the paper back in the envelope. The nearest she would ever come to owning any kind of horse was the sculpture awaiting her attention in the studio. What an extraordinary mistake to make for a man who obviously knew his business. Surely he must have realised she couldn't possibly be the owner? After all, she lived on the other side of the world – why on earth would she have a horse in training so far away?

'Ridiculous,' she hissed, as she tightened the belt on the dressing gown and reached for her writing box. Her reply was polite but short, and when she'd sealed the envelope she dressed and went down to the village post office.

He had been drinking a welcome beer in the village pub and was enjoying an evening pipe when he saw her walk down the lane. Following her to the tiny shop that seemed to provide everything, he hovered by the open door and eavesdropped on her conversation with the fat, garrulous woman behind the counter.

Satisfied he'd heard enough, he headed for the station and the last train home. The letter from Australia had obviously arrived. All he had to do now was inform his employer and await further instructions.

As she strolled back to the house, Lulu wondered what Mr Reilly's reaction would be to her letter. Embarrassment probably, she concluded.

She skirted the side of the house and followed the path to the semicircular summer house which she'd turned into her studio. Nestled against the high brick boundary wall, its deep windows looked out over the lawn and offered a sunny spot even on the coldest day. She had fallen in love with it the day Clarice had first brought her to Sussex. Ten years old, and trying to come to terms with the sudden changes in her life, the summer house had become her refuge.

Great-Aunt Clarice had understood her need for solitude while she sketched and painted, or moulded clay figures, and those early years, which might have been interpreted by some as lonely, had brought a slow, steady awakening in Lulu – a realisation that now she could dare to dream – that under Clarice's loving, watchful eye she was free to blossom. It was the greatest gift anyone could bestow, and she adored Clarice because of it.

Stepping inside, she lit the gas lamps, dug her chin into her coat collar against the cold and began to peel off the damp cloths that kept the clay pliable. She examined the three-foot high sculpture and smiled at the irony, for her current work was a colt. A leggy, unbroken creature with a stubby tail and short mane, he seemed poised to break free from the restraints of the armature that held him to the wooden turntable. She absorbed the lines and curves, the promise of growing muscle and strength she'd managed to capture, and the feeling of constrained energy and movement that had been so difficult to attain. It was a fine piece, maybe the best she had done.

She regarded the colt, her thoughts dwelling on the strange letter. Perhaps it was an omen – a sign that he was somehow linked to the one in Tasmania. It was a ridiculous idea of course, one that Clarice would scorn – and yet, as she assessed the clay colt and her thoughts raced, she realised how very auspicious this moment was. The piece had yet to be titled, but because of Joe Reilly's error in sending that letter, she now had a name.

Her imagination took flight as she hastily reached for a lump of clay and began to soften and mould it. It might be difficult to do, but it was a chance to stretch her ability and enjoy the challenge. The real Ocean Child would race over Tasmanian tracks, grow old and end his days at pasture, but hers would stay forever young and dance in the shallow ripples and waves of a bronze shoreline.

Joe Reilly had finished mucking out, the yard was swept and hosed, and Bob Fuller, the jackaroo, had just left to exercise Ocean Child up on the gallops. It was still early, but the kookaburras were already laughing in the nearby trees and Joe could hear the haunting single note of a bellbird not far away.

He dug his hands in the pockets of his moleskins and proudly surveyed the yard. It looked very different to how it had been when he'd returned from Europe, and although it had taken time, energy and most of his savings, it had been worth it.

Where the stables had been falling down and infested with rats, they now rose sturdily on either side of the paved yard, their newly tiled roofs and fresh paint gleaming in the autumn sun. The repairs to the barn, tack room and feed store were almost finished, the fences replaced and the paddocks clear of harmful weeds.

There had once been over thirty horses at Galway House, with stable hands and jackaroos to look after them. But that was in the good years – the years before war and influenza had intervened. He remained optimistic, however, for there were already five recent arrivals to the yard, with enquiries about two others, and he'd had to take on a couple of hands to help. The stock markets were still jittery, but the world had begun to shake off the gloom of the past years and there was a sense of excitement in the air as they entered a new decade, reflected in the jazz music that was becoming so popular, and in the way people were prepared to spend their money on pleasures again.

His gaze travelled beyond the yard to the hills where the gallops ran for four miles along their crest. He had heard Tasmania being compared to England, and now he understood why, for this corner of the island was as green and lush as the Sussex countryside surrounding the military hospital where he'd recuperated.

The two-storey homestead stood squarely among the trees and faced the short driveway and double gates. Its rear aspect was of the fast-flowing river that ran in a tree-lined gully at the bottom of the valley. The wrap-around veranda was cluttered with the usual chairs, tables and his mother's tubs of flowers. The shutters and screens were mended, the lawn had been cut and the trees were in full leaf. It was the home he'd once thought he would never see again, and he felt a glow of appreciation and love for the old place.

The Reillys had lived at Galway House for four generations, their name synonymous with well-trained and successful race-horses. Joe had willingly followed in his father's footsteps, and had been looking forward to marrying his childhood sweetheart, Penny, and taking over on his father's retirement. Then war intervened. His father had died shortly after Joe had been shipped out, and as the memories of Gallipoli and Fromelles came unbidden, his fingers automatically traced the scars that puckered the flesh above his left eye and cobwebbed his cheek.

Penny had promised in her letters that she would love him regardless of how badly injured he was – that they would marry and take over the yard as planned – and yet on his return home he'd seen her flinch from his kisses and had noticed how she avoided looking at him. She had done her best to hide her revulsion, but the girl he'd loved since boyhood could not accept the changes in him and, knowing she was too kind-hearted to do it herself, he'd broken off their engagement. The relief in her eyes had torn him apart, the scars a tacit reminder – if he ever needed one – that war had changed everything.

He shook off the gloomy thoughts, whistled for the two dogs, cranked up the flatbed truck and headed for the gallops. He was one of the lucky ones who'd made it home. At thirty years old he was fit and healthy and his business was on the up. He loved his home and his work, had embraced the isolation and peace they gave him, and was content.

Bob Fuller was walking the Child to rest him, but even from a distance Joe could see the tow-headed youth's excitement. He'd barely climbed out of the truck before Bob was chattering at him.

'He's a little ripper, Joe. Didn't turn a hair when I asked more of 'im.'

'I hope you didn't overextend him.'

'Fair go, Joe. Look at him! He's not even blowing.'

The boy's enthusiasm was catching, and Joe returned his grin as he assessed the colt and realised he still had plenty of running in him. Ocean Child was a chestnut, with pale mane and tail and a white diamond blaze on his forehead. Still youthfully leggy, he nevertheless had an air of confidence about him that boded well, for he'd proved over the past year that he was undeterred by noise and strange surroundings.

Joe ran his hand over the well-shaped hindquarters and down the sturdy legs. There was good muscle and bone there, the pasterns just the right length. His chest was in perfect proportion and would widen and muscle up as he matured, and the eyes were intelligent.

'You're a beaut and no mistake,' he murmured as he stroked the neck and looked into those golden eyes. 'Give him another short run so I can see how he's moving, then spell him. He's had enough for today.'

He leant against the railings, hat in hand, dark hair tousled by the breeze as he watched horse and rider canter away along the dirt track. The Child was certainly moving well, and seemed eager for the exercise, but unformed muscle and growing bones needed time and patience to build to their full potential, and he'd seen the tragic results when other trainers pushed too hard.

He watched keenly as Bob brought the Child around and galloped back towards him. The colt's neck was stretched, ears pricked, each leg placed with confidence as he opened up his chest and raced along the track. Joe's pulse quickened. Ocean Child was one hell of a good horse, and if he lived up to this early promise, Galway House might have a real winner.

The morning passed quickly as everyone went about their usual work, and Joe had just sat down to deal with the account books when he was interrupted by the arrival of his mother. 'Our visitors are here,' she said breathlessly. 'I bet you'd forgotten they were coming.'

Joe had indeed, but whenever he was with the horses he forgot most things. 'Sorry,' he murmured, reluctantly closing the ledger. He smiled as he ran his fingers through his hair. 'I don't suppose you could deal with them, Ma? I've got a lot to do this morning.'

Molly Reilly was short and plump, with a bustling presence and a mop of rather wild greying hair. She had struggled to keep the yard going after her husband's death, but despite her determination and energy had found it an impossible task. Joe understood that her relief at his survival was tempered by the knowledge that he now found socialising extremely distressing.

'You can't hide in here for ever,' she said with a briskness that belied the concern in her eyes. 'This is business.'

He noted the determined tilt to her chin and knew there was little point in arguing. Towering over her as he took his battered hat from the nail on the wall, he rammed it on and tugged the brim low so it shadowed the damaged side of his face.

'What are they like?' he muttered as he ambled along beside her.

'Rich.'

'That's a good start.' A smile twitched his lips. His mother had her own endearing way of cutting straight to the point. 'Anything else?'

'They've got two horses at Len Simpson's yard in Melbourne, but they've had a falling out with him and want to move them.'

'Sounds like they could be trouble. Len's a good bloke.'

'My thoughts exactly, but we can't afford to be picky.'

Joe had been weaned on stories of difficult owners and their high, sometimes impossible, expectations of their horses. It seemed the more money they had the more awkward they were. He tugged the hat brim and steeled himself for the meeting. His mother was right – they needed the money.

A showy black car sat on the driveway, chrome headlamps and wide running board glinting in the sun. Joe took in the two people waiting on the veranda. The man wore tweeds and had a cigar clamped between his teeth. The young woman was wreathed in furs against the chill wind, and Joe could only think of the word 'glossy' to describe her.

'Alan Frobisher,' the man said, shaking his hand, 'and this's my daughter, Eliza.'

Joe glanced at the girl, who was eyeing him with open curiosity. He dropped his gaze as he swiftly shook the cool, slender hand, then stepped back and tugged furiously at his hat. He was aware of her continued scrutiny as they headed back towards the stables, and was so disconcerted he became tongue-tied. His mother had no such inhibitions and was chattering like a sparrow as they toured the yard.

They had inspected everything and were now standing by the paddock fence. Joe began to relax as the women went off to the house and he was left alone with Alan. 'How did you hear about us in Queensland, Alan? You've come a long way.'

'A bloodstock agent called Carmichael,' he replied. 'I understand he's recommended you before.'

Joe's interest was piqued. 'He sent me Ocean Child, but we've never met, only communicated by mail. What's he like?'

Alan shrugged. 'I've only spoken to him on the two-way, but the Victorian Breeders Association recommends him.'

Joe nodded. It seemed the elusive Carmichael did all his business at a distance, for no one had yet admitted to ever having seen him. 'May I ask why you want to move your horses?'

The other man looked away. 'There was a difference of opinion,' he muttered. 'Things got awkward.'

Joe waited for him to continue, but it seemed Alan had decided he'd said enough. Whatever had proved awkward would remain between Alan and his previous trainer – and yet Len Simpson was well-regarded in racing circles for his easy-going temperament. Joe couldn't fathom what had gone wrong. 'Len has a fair reputation,' he said, 'so if he took them on, I'd be glad to. But I'll have to contact him and make sure he has no objection.'

'Fair enough, but he won't object. Speaks very highly of you, which is why I took Carmichael's advice.' Alan turned from his scrutiny of the grazing horses and smiled. 'I think I've seen enough, Joe. Let's do business.' His expression became quizzical as his gaze settled on Joe's face. 'France, I suppose.'

Joe nodded.

'At least you came home,' the older man muttered. 'So many didn't.' They began to walk towards the house. 'Don't mind Eliza, mate – she's still young and, without a mother's guiding hand, hasn't really mastered the art of discretion.' He shot a glance at Joe. 'I saw how she was staring, and I apologise.'

'I'm used to it,' Joe lied tactfully.

'Once she gets to know you she'll forget about the scars, you'll see. Eliza's a little headstrong at times – it's what comes of losing her mother at such a young age, I reckon – but she's a born horsewoman, and once she's fully engaged with her animals she's a very different person.'

Joe felt a chill of apprehension and he drew to a halt. Perhaps the differing opinions and awkwardness stemmed from a meddling Eliza – if so, he could not do business with Alan no matter how much he needed his money. 'I run a tight yard here,' he warned. 'The owners are welcome to visit any time as long as we're not preparing for a race, but I don't encourage them to linger or mess about with the horses. It upsets the rhythm of the stables.'

'Too right, mate. Any time you feel we've outstayed our welcome, just tell us. You're in charge.'

'As long as you understand that?' He sternly held the other man's gaze.

Alan's expression was solemn. 'You have my word, and I'll make sure Eliza keeps her distance too.'

'I thought you lived in Queensland?'

'We do for now, but I'm thinking of buying a place in Deloraine.' He must have noted Joe's alarm at this news, for he chuckled. 'No worries, mate. We won't get in your hair. Just give us a winner now and again, and we'll be happy enough.'

As he stood on the veranda and watched the Frobishers drive away in a cloud of dust Joe was still not convinced about the contracts he'd just signed. 'Len didn't give much away, but he assures me the horses are promising and that Alan pays his bills promptly.' He gnawed his lip. 'Alan seems a nice enough bloke, but that girl could be a menace if they move over here,' he muttered.

'She's just young and rather full of herself. I shouldn't let her worry you.' Molly waved the cheque under his nose. 'They're paying top money, Joe, and Eliza hinted they might recommend you to their friends. I realise you find her a little daunting, but if you remember you're in charge, things will work out. You never know – this time next year we could have a full yard.'

Joe didn't want to dampen her enthusiasm, so kept his opinions to himself. 'Has the post come yet? I'm waiting for that money order from Hobart.'

Molly reached into her cardigan pocket. 'Sorry, I forgot all about it in the excitement. Nothing from Hobart, but there's a reply from England.'

He tore it open and scanned the single page. It didn't take long, but the contents drained the colour from his face and he sat down with a thump.

'Whatever is it?'

'Trouble,' he said tersely, as he gave her the letter. 'I knew I shouldn't have trusted that Carmichael.'

'But this makes no sense,' breathed Molly, as she scanned the note and sank into the chair beside him.

'Worse than that, we have a horse without an owner. A promising two-year-old I can't race, and can't sell on until this is cleared up. What the hell am I going to do?'

'At least the fees for the next two years have been paid upfront, so we won't be out of pocket,' snapped Molly. She shoved the single sheet back into the envelope. 'Get hold of Carmichael and demand an explanation, then send her the papers and a stiff letter ordering her to stop playing games.'

Joe retrieved the letter that was in danger of being mangled and tucked it into his pocket. His expression was grim as he glared into the distance. 'I'll do that, but Carmichael's not an easy man to pin down. There's something fishy about all this, Ma, and I aim to find out what the hell's going on. No one plays me for a fool and gets away with it.'

2

The men from the foundry drove away, and in the silence following their departure Lulu admired the bronze. *Ocean Child* stood on a black marble plinth, head lifted as if scenting the sea at his feet, stubby tail and mane ruffled by the salt wind. He was everything she had hoped for, and although she knew it was her best work, she was still anxious for Maurice and Clarice to like it.

'It's very beautiful,' said Maurice, 'but I dread to think how much it cost you to have it cast in bronze.'

'Bertie paid,' she explained. 'He'll get the money back when he sells it.'

Maurice's gaunt face twisted in disgust. 'Agents are leeches – always taking their money first. No wonder we artists are so poor.'

'That's not fair,' Lulu scolded. 'Bertie's a benefactor, not an agent. He doesn't charge commission, as you well know, and I'm lucky he's seen fit to sponsor my work.'

Maurice sniffed and tightened the scarf around his neck. Although it was April, it was cold in the summer house, and his coat was too thin to counter it. He shrugged bony shoulders and dug his large hands into his pockets, dark eyes trawling over the sculpture in undisguised admiration. 'No doubt he's already got a buyer lined up,' he muttered. 'You always were his favourite.'

Lulu was exasperated. This was an old gripe and she was sick of hearing it. Bertie Hathaway was rather daunting, for he was a very rich man who was used to getting his own way. Maurice's relationship with him was tenuous to say the least, and she suspected Maurice was a little jealous of his patronage of her. This was not helped by the fact that Bertie had yet to show any enthusiasm for Maurice's work. 'He's offered you space at the exhibition in June,' she reminded him.

Maurice gave a deep sigh and buried his long nose in the scarf. 'He wouldn't have if you hadn't persuaded him.'

She wanted to tell him to stop behaving like a petulant child, but knew from past experience that any kind of criticism would leave him depressed for days. 'The offer to exhibit your paintings in London is there if you want it,' she said instead. 'It could be a marvellous debut.'

'I don't know if I'm ready to exhibit yet. All that noise and fuss – you know how it affects me.'

She took in his mournful expression and held her tongue. She had met Maurice at art school, had formed an immediate friendship and after graduating it had seemed logical for him to move into the upstairs flat of Clarice's house in London and share the attic studio. But the Maurice that stood before her had been psychologically damaged by his ordeal as a war artist, and there was little trace of the gregarious man he'd once been. 'Why don't you go indoors and get warm?' she said softly.

'Are you coming?' His dark eyes were pleading.

She shook her head. 'I'm waiting for Clarice, but she shouldn't be too long.' She watched him walk towards the house, noted how thin he'd become over the past few months, and how his walk was that of a much older man. He wanted so much from her, and her soft heart filled with the pity he would despise – yet even that was wearing thin from his constant neediness.

'Good, you're alone.' Clarice stepped into the studio and firmly closed the door. She pulled the fur coat a little more snugly around her slender figure and shivered. 'Maurice gets me down when he's in one of his bad moods.'

There seemed little reason to reply so she pointed at the sculpture. 'What do you think?'

Clarice studied it from every angle in silence. Then she reached out and ran her fingers over the muscled hindquarters. 'It's perfect,' she breathed. 'You've captured his youth, the promise of what he'll become, and the energy he possesses.' She turned to Lulu, her eyes suspiciously bright. 'I never realised how very talented you are, my dear. Congratulations.'

Lulu's emotions were in turmoil. To see Clarice so moved was more than she could ever have hoped for. She threw her arms around her great-aunt and gave her a hug.

Clarice remained stiff in the embrace, her hands fluttering as if she wasn't quite sure what to do with them. 'I'm delighted you're so happy, dear, but please mind the coat. It's my only mink, and although it's a bit moth-eaten now, I wouldn't want make-up all over it.'

Stung, even though the rebuff was gentle, Lulu stepped back and tucked her curls behind her ears as tears pricked.

The soft hand patted her cheek. 'You're a clever girl, and I'm very proud of you, Lorelei. But just because I'm a firm believer in never letting my emotions get the better of me, it doesn't mean I don't love you.'

Lulu nodded, her unshed tears making it impossible to speak. Of course she was loved – the signs were all around her in the home Clarice had provided, in the studio, the clothes in her wardrobe and the flat in London. Yet Lulu yearned for something more tactile. There were times when all she needed was a cuddle, a kiss, some outward show that her aunt cared – but she knew it was a forlorn hope, and silently berated herself for being as needy as Maurice.

Clarice seemed to realise the inner battle Lulu was having and changed the subject. 'I like the way he's dancing in the waves. Is there a particular reason for that?'

'He's called Ocean Child.'

'What an intriguing name,' murmured Clarice. 'What made you think of it?'

Lulu remembered that she hadn't told Clarice about the letter. 'It was rather strange, actually,' she began. 'I got this very odd letter from Tasmania and—'

'Letter from Tasmania?' Clarice interrupted sharply. 'You didn't tell me.'

'It was ages ago, and I got so involved in my work I forgot about it.'

'Who was it from?'

'A man called Joe Reilly at Galway House. He's a—'

'I know what Reilly is,' Clarice interrupted again. 'Why is he writing to you?'

Lulu noted the alertness in Clarice's demeanour, the intense gaze, the stiffening of her slender shoulders, and was confused by this strange reaction. She told her the contents of the letter. 'It was obviously a mistake,' she finished, 'and I wrote to tell him so. I haven't heard from him again.'

'Good.' Clarice sniffed delicately into a lace-edged handker-chief.

Lulu was curious. 'How do you know him?'

Clarice dismissed the man with the wave of an elegant hand. 'I met members of his family years ago through my late husband's interest in horse racing.'

'Don't you ever wish you could go back for a visit?'

Clarice drew the fur collar to her chin, her expression formida-ble. 'I can think of nothing I would like less.'

'Perhaps one day I'll be able to afford to return,' she said wist-fully.

'There's nothing for you in Tasmania,' snapped Clarice. 'Don't start that nonsense again, Lorelei. Your life is here, and a good English education has rid you of that *ghastly* colonial accent. You wouldn't fit in over there any more than I did.'

Lulu bit her lip as she remembered those awful elocution lessons. Her accent had been the last bit of Tasmania she'd held on to – but it seemed that too had to be expunged.

As if she could read her thoughts, Clarice looked at Lulu almost accusingly. 'Childhood memories can be very unreliable. Much like your upbringing before I took over,' she added in a mutter. She shivered and moved towards the door. 'I'll freeze to death out here. I'm going inside.'

Frustrated by Clarice's continued refusal to even discuss Tasmania, Lulu turned off the lamps, locked the door behind them and followed her down the path towards the house.

Clarice avoided the drawing room, where Maurice was no doubt ensconced by the fire reading her newspaper, and made her way slowly up the stairs to her bedroom. She was in no mood for polite conversation, and was certainly not prepared to continue any discussion on Tasmania.

She eyed the miserable fire in the hearth and gave it a vigorous prod with the poker to stir it into life. With the heavy velvet curtains drawn against the draughts, she poured a glass of sweet sherry, sank into the armchair by the fire and mulled over the events of the evening.

Hearing about the letter from Reilly had come as a terrible shock, and even though Lorelei seemed to have dealt with it sensibly, Clarice had a nasty feeling that wouldn't be the end of it.

Drawing the cashmere shawl around her shoulders, she took a sip of sherry and set the glass aside. Despite the passage of time, and her own best efforts to dissuade her, it seemed Lorelei was still drawn to Tasmania. Reilly's letter had stirred her up again, but worse, had brought memories back to Clarice she'd thought long buried.

As she sat in the flickering light of the fire she tried to recapture the faces of those she had once loved. Time had smudged their features and silenced their voices – they had become ethereal, elusive shadows – but they still haunted her.

It had all begun that January, when she and her husband had arrived in Sydney. She could remember that day so clearly – even now – for she had dreaded it. And as the shoreline had drawn closer her emotional turmoil had increased. She had prayed fervently that marriage to Algernon and the passing years would have stifled the forbidden love that had once consumed her, proving it to be only a transitory infatuation of youth – but within hours of landing she had been put to the test. And found wanting.

Sydney, 1886

As the mariners clambered up the rigging to furl the sails, Clarice was forced to accept that her expectations for this long voyage had been too high. She had hoped the exotic places they visited and the star-filled nights at sea might rekindle ardour in Algernon and bring them closer. But Algernon seemed impervious to her needs, blind to her thwarted desires, and determined to maintain a distant courtesy which prohibited intimacy. Her marriage was a sham and, at thirty-six, her future was bleak.

News of Algernon's posting to Australia had come as a terrible shock, and although it would mean she would be reunited with her elder sister, Eunice, she'd recognised the danger of coming face to face with the man she had once loved. She had tried to dissuade Algernon, but the position in the Governor's Office would bring a knighthood a step closer, and that being his driving ambition, he'd refused to countenance her pleas.

She stared at the glittering water in the vast harbour without really seeing it, tucked a strand of fair hair behind her ear and dabbed her eyes with a lace handkerchief in an effort to control the emotions Algernon found so abhorrent.

Her marriage to the widower Algernon Pearson had been

arranged by her father, who was closer to him in age than she was, and at first she had refused to consider such a match. But at twenty-five, and considered plain, she'd had little choice. The man she loved had married another, there were no other suitors and her father had been insistent.

It had not been the love match Eunice had made, but Algernon proved to be an attentive, erudite man, and after months of courtship she'd reluctantly agreed to marry him. Their wedding night had not been the ordeal she'd expected, for Algernon was a man of experience and had shown surprising consideration and enthusiasm in his lovemaking.

That had all changed as the years passed and there were no children. He began to spend more hours at the Foreign Office, and when he did come home, he slept in another room. An air of weary acceptance seemed to hang over him now, his disappointment in her almost tangible.

'Open your parasol, and put on your gloves. The sun will darken your skin.'

Clarice was startled by her husband's voice and, feeling guilty about her unkind thoughts, quickly complied.

Algernon stood beside her, hands clasped behind his back, the straw hat placed squarely over his grey hair. He regarded the shoreline with little interest and seemed impervious to the debilitating heat, even though he was wearing a tweed jacket over his starched shirt and woollen trousers.

'No doubt there will be a reception committee to welcome us,' he said. 'As British aide to the governor I would expect certain standards – even here.'

Clarice saw his nostrils flare above the trim moustache as if the very smell of Australia insulted him. Algernon's standards of conduct, dress and manners were impossibly high – which was why, despite the temperature, she was tightly corseted, her long skirt and petticoats clinging to her legs as her hands sweltered in cotton gloves. Eunice had written to warn Clarice of the dangers of wearing too many clothes; now she could feel the perspiration running down her spine and see it beading her décolletage. She just hoped she wouldn't faint. What Algernon would say to that didn't bear thinking about.

She glanced at the gathering on the quay and silently prayed for an official welcome. Algernon would plunge into a sour mood for the rest of the day if there was not. 'Eunice wrote that Sydney is quite sophisticated for such a new colony, and that Governor Robinson is looking forward to your arrival.'

The nostrils became pinched. 'Your sister would hardly have the ear of the governor,' he replied disdainfully. 'Enough prattle, Clarice. I wish to concentrate on memorising my speech to the welcoming committee.'

Clarice had heard it many times and thought it pompous in the extreme, but as her opinion didn't count she turned her attention to the harbour as the *Dora May* was towed in by a flotilla of small boats. Now they were nearer, she could see the elegant houses and gardens, the stately red brick of government buildings and churches, and the broad, paved roads. It appeared far more civilised than some of the ports they had visited on the way.

Her pulse quickened as she searched the crowded dock for that familiar, once-beloved face, dreading seeing it, but unable to resist trying – but too many people waited there and her disappointment was tinged with relief.

The press of passengers on deck soon became claustrophobic, and the combination of heat and her own thudding heart overwhelmed her. Her head felt as if it was stuffed with kapok, and there were bright pinpricks of light darting before her eyes. Seeking air, she began to fight her way through the mass.

'Clarice? Where are you going?'

His voice sounded distant, and as darkness closed in she began to push harder. If she fainted, she would be trampled. She had to find shade and room to breathe.

She finally stumbled free of the crush and sank thankfully on to one of the hatches. A tarpaulin had been strung above it to provide shelter and Clarice sighed with relief as, at last, her head seemed to clear and the draught of her fan cooled her.

'Get up,' Algernon hissed, his large hand encircling her wrist. 'You are making a spectacle of yourself.'

'I feel faint,' she replied, wresting her hand from his grasp. 'Let me recover.'

'You cannot sit here like an untidy bag of laundry!' he snapped. 'Go to our cabin where you will be out of the public gaze.'

She tried to rise, but the dark clouds returned and her legs threatened to give way. 'I cannot,' she whispered. 'Please find me some water.'

Algernon glared, realised they were being watched and immediately became solicitous. 'See to my wife's needs,' he ordered a nearby maid, 'and be quick about it.'

Clarice didn't care if the whole world was watching as she rested her head in her lap and tried to regain her senses. The cloth was cool as the girl mopped her brow and neck, and helped her to drink water from a cup. Pulling off the hated gloves and taking the cloth, Clarice discreetly dabbed the perspiration from her chest and face.

The water, shade and cooling fan began to ease her discomfort at last, and she eyed the clearly disgruntled Algernon, who was pacing the deck and checking his pocket watch. 'If I could have your assistance,' she murmured, 'I am still a little unsteady.'

His expression was grim. 'This simply won't do, Clarice. The governor will be expecting us to disembark first,' he said. 'Now we must go ashore with the common herd and make our own introductions.'

Clarice grasped his arm, opened her parasol and let him lead her to the gangplank. Her legs trembled still, but her head was clearer and Algernon had yet to notice the absence of her gloves. She pasted on the smile that she knew was expected of her, lifted her chin and prepared to greet the governor.

They reached the stone wharf, but it seemed to move beneath her feet, and she clung more tightly to Algernon's arm.

'I don't see the governor,' he muttered crossly, as he freed himself from her grip and tugged at his jacket lapels. 'Neither is there any sign of a welcoming committee.'

'There's just me, I'm afraid, Algy. The governor's tied up in some debate over irrigation.'

Clarice almost fainted again. Lionel Bartholomew stood before them, resplendent in military uniform, his fair hair and magnificent moustache brushed to a gleam, blue eyes alight with mocking humour. He'd hardly changed in the last ten years and was still the charismatic, handsome Lionel who made her heart pound, and her senses sing.

'General Bartholomew.' Algernon sketched a stiff bow, his dislike clear in his expression. 'I am disconcerted the governor could not spare a few minutes to welcome me after such a long journey.'

'He's a busy man,' said Lionel, without a hint of apology.

Clarice's pulse raced as he took her hand and looked into her eyes. 'Welcome to Australia, Clarice,' he said softly.

As he kissed her hand she breathed in the long-remembered scent of him and trembled. 'Thank you,' she whispered.

'We should be on our way,' said Algernon. 'Take us to our accommodation, Bartholomew, and see that our trunks are delivered before nightfall.'

Lionel's smile didn't falter, but his eyes lost their good humour. 'My man will take care of your luggage,' he replied, 'and as your accommodation is not quite ready, I have arranged for you to stay at my home.'

Algernon's protest was forestalled. 'We have been in the sun long enough, Algy. Clarice is not looking at all well.' Lionel tucked her hand under his arm and led the way to his carriage.

She could feel strength beneath the fabric of his sleeve and found it hard to breathe in such proximity. 'Thank you, Lionel,' she managed, as they reached the welcoming shade of the trees and she reluctantly freed her hand. 'I *am* finding the heat intolerable.'

His gaze swept over the draped skirt with its soft bustle and many petticoats, and the tightly laced bodice. 'I'm surprised your sister didn't warn you to dress more appropriately,' he said, his expression concerned.

Clarice blushed and swiftly glanced at Algernon who was still looking grim. 'I dared not follow her advice,' she murmured. 'Algernon would not approve.'

Lionel's moustache twitched and his blue eyes narrowed. 'Unless he wants a wife who faints every five minutes, he doesn't have a choice.' He helped her into the carriage, adjusted the fringed canopy and took a bottle out of a basket stored beneath the seat. ' Lemonade,' he said, offering her a glass. 'It might chase away the heat until we get home.'

Clarice's blush deepened as their gazes held before he moved away. She sipped the lemonade, her heart drumming so loudly she wondered that Algernon couldn't hear it. The passion she'd thought dead had been revived by Lionel's kindness, his smile and the touch of his lips on her hand – but it was a dangerous, frightening passion that must never be reciprocated or permitted, for its very rebirth was an act of betrayal against her sister Eunice – his wife.

Clarice opened her eyes, determined to dismiss the memories. She regretted not being able to show her deep affection for Lorelei, but past events had proved beyond doubt that emotions were dangerous when given free rein. They weakened resolve and laid bare the soul to hurt and betrayal.

Yet, in the silence of her bedroom, she felt the stirrings of the old passions which had led her on the path to perdition and the ache in her heart for everything she had lost. 'Damn you for stirring up the past, Joe Reilly,' she muttered, 'and I pray this is an end to it.

Lulu's nerves had got the better of her, and she'd felt unwell all day. As the time approached for the guests to arrive at Bertie's London gallery, she'd had to lie down in his office for a while and take one of her pills. It was terrifying to reveal her work to such a knowledgeable crowd, and this exhibition was not only the culmination of a year's work but the largest Bertie had staged for her. She dared not let him down.

Lulu had dressed carefully in a shift of shimmering peacock blues that enhanced her eyes. Her hair tumbled down her back and framed her face, held in place by a blue silk scarf artfully tied around her head so the fringing fell to one side. Clarice's white fox stole was draped over one shoulder and her only piece of jewellery was a silver armlet.

The Kensington gallery was alive with the sound of many voices, the popping of corks and the clinking of champagne glasses. A haze of cigarette and cigar smoke was interlaced with exotic perfumes as white-coated waiters glided silently between the clusters of people gathered to discuss the art and catch up on the city gossip. Jewels sparkled and silks whispered beneath feathers and furs as the guests drifted and mingled.

Feeling much better, she ignored Clarice's disapproving glare, took a glass of champagne from a passing waiter and raised it in salute to Bertie, who was on the other side of the room chatting with Lulu's best friend, Dolly Carteret.

At forty-two, Bertie Hathaway cut a splendid figure in the

beautifully tailored tuxedo. He was tall, handsome and broad-shouldered, with the assured air that came from great wealth and a clear understanding of his lofty position in society. His fortune was inherited, his wife the darling of London society and his connections impeccable. Clarice had gone to school with his grandmother, and Dolly had attended the same finishing school as his sister. Dolly was engaged to his younger brother, Freddy; their marriage would unite two of the wealthiest families in England.

Hitching Clarice's white fox fur over one shoulder, Lulu sipped the champagne and turned her critical gaze to the bronzes that were displayed on plinths about the room. It was interesting to see them from a fresh perspective, and she was delighted at how well they looked in this large white space.

The women and dogs she had sculpted exuded effortless elegance in their elongated, sleek lines, and she was thrilled at how well the greyhound had turned out. But it was *Ocean Child* that was attracting the most attention, and she could see why – for he looked magnificent.

Her gaze raked the room. There was still no sign of Maurice, despite the fact he'd promised to come, and that made her cross. Bertie had reluctantly agreed to show some of his paintings as a favour to her, and the least Maurice could have done was put in an appearance.

'Well done, Lulu. I told you it would be a success.'

She turned and smiled as Bertie refreshed her glass. 'Thanks. It's a marvellous evening, and I'm so grateful for everything you've done.'

Bertie's smile didn't quite reach his dark eyes. 'It's a shame Maurice didn't turn up, but it was only to be expected, I suppose. I have to say, his stuff isn't really to my taste, and I suspect I'll find it hard to shift.'

They regarded the rather menacing oils on a nearby wall, and

Lulu experienced a familiar pang of unease. The torture in Maurice's soul was all too clear in his art. It lay in the dark paint, the twisted figures and haunted eyes – even in the erratic, angry strokes of his palette knife – but the world had moved on from such horror. Bertie was right; they would be difficult to sell.

She sipped her champagne and leant closer to him. 'Has anyone actually bought anything of mine, or are they just here for the champagne?'

His black brow lifted quizzically. 'My dear girl, what a thing to ask.' He led her towards a private corner where his assistant hovered with the order book. 'I've got something to show you.'

Lulu was in a daze as he went through the book. Each of the eight sculptures had a limited edition of six. She would keep one of each, but nearly all of the rest had been placed on order. She leant against a convenient pillar and stared at him, unable to speak.

He smoothed back his hair, his smile almost smug. 'After tonight, Lulu Pearson, you will be the toast of London.' He raised his glass to her and drained it. 'I'm delighted for both of us,' he said, 'and as I've already received several enquiries about commission pieces, I hope you haven't planned on going anywhere for the next year or so.'

The supper party at Bertie's Knightsbridge mansion was a glittering success, and as Lulu stepped out of the taxi she realised dawn was already lightening the sky. Clarice had retired to her hotel room some hours ago, but Lulu had stayed on, elated with excitement and champagne. Now she was weary and longing for bed, fully aware that there was always a price to pay for overdoing things. Her heart was thudding quite painfully as she looked up to the windows of the upper floor. All was in darkness. Maurice was either still out, or more likely asleep.

She clung to the handrail as she went down the concrete steps to the garden apartment and stood for a moment to catch her breath before opening the door. Dropping her bag and borrowed stole on the table in the narrow entrance hall, she eased off her satin shoes and padded into the kitchen to make cocoa.

As she carried the cup down the passage she noticed a glimmer of light coming from beneath her bedroom door and frowned. She could have sworn she'd turned everything off before she went out. Opening the door, she almost dropped the cup at the sight of Maurice sprawled in the chair before her gas fire. 'What on earth are you doing in here?'

He uncoiled from the chair and ran his fingers through his already mussed hair. 'I thought I'd wait up,' he muttered. 'Sorry if I frightened you.'

'Thanks, but there was no need.' She had meant to ask him to return her key, but somehow she'd kept forgetting, and now was not the time to get into a wrangle over it.

'How did it go?'

Despite her weariness she couldn't help but grin. 'Brilliantly – and you'll never guess . . . Bertie sold one of your paintings.'

'Really?' Maurice's face was suddenly wreathed in a smile. 'Which one?'

Lulu sank on to the bed and eyed the pillows with longing as she tried to remember the title of the landscape. '*Storm over the Somme*,' she replied through a vast yawn. 'I'm sorry, Maurice, but I've had it. I must sleep.'

'I know it's late, old thing, but you can't possibly want to sleep after such good news. This could really be the start of something for me, don't you think?'

Lulu suspected Bertie had bought the painting himself out of kindness, but would never reveal her thoughts to Maurice. The poor chap needed bucking up, and the sale of just one of his works had done that already – but it was rather galling that he hadn't even asked about how her work had been received.

'Perhaps it will ensure your presence at the next exhibition,' she said drily. 'Bertie wasn't at all pleased by your absence.'

He ran his fingers through his hair again and shrugged. 'You know how it is. I just couldn't face all those people.'

'I know,' she sighed, 'but if you really want to make it as an artist, you're going to have to find some way of dealing with that fear.' She looked up at him as he paced the small room. He was obviously elated at the news, but she just didn't have the energy to cope with it now. 'Go to bed, Maurice, and let me sleep. Otherwise I'll be fit for nothing.'

'But I need to talk, Lulu. This—'

Her patience snapped. 'Go away,' she said sharply. 'I've had an exhausting day and I need to sleep. We'll talk later.'

'Oh, well, if you're going to be like that.' He dropped his chin and headed for the door.

Lulu sank against the pillows and closed her eyes. She regretted her spark of anger, but was feeling too exhausted to even apologise. At least he was leaving.

Maurice had his hand on the doorknob when he changed his mind. 'There's a letter for you, by the way. I put it on the mantelpiece.'

Lulu watched him through her lashes as he hovered by the door, obviously hoping for some response. As she remained silent, he shrugged again and closed the door behind him with a none-too-gentle bang.

She lay there watching the flickering shadows from the gas fire being swallowed up by the light seeping through her window. Her heartbeat was uneven and a tightness in her chest made it difficult to breathe – but as she relaxed into the soft bed she felt the restriction ease and her pulse slowly return to normal. This was definitely a case of having overdone things, and Maurice was the last straw.

*

Lulu had fallen asleep almost immediately. Now the sun was going down again, the cocoa was cold and it was almost time for dinner. She sat up, realised she was still wearing her clothes from the previous night and decided to have a bath. Clarice was expecting her for dinner at the hotel.

Feeling refreshed and relaxed after her bath, she returned to the bedroom to dress and caught sight of the envelope Maurice had left on the mantelpiece. The writing was familiar. 'It looks like Mr Reilly is apologising for his mistake,' she muttered with a wry smile.

She thought about ignoring it until she returned from dinner, then decided not to – it might be interesting to read what his excuse was for making such a silly error.

Dear Miss Pearson,

I was disconcerted by your reply, and wondered at first if perhaps I had been given the wrong details. But Mr Carmichael assures me you are the owner of Ocean Child, and the papers to prove it are enclosed.

I have made further enquiries into the purchase of Ocean Child and into the character of your Mr Carmichael, and can find nothing untoward in either. Yet your denial of ownership places me in a very awkward position. Please examine the enclosed documents carefully, and if you still maintain you have no knowledge of this purchase then I will have to consult a solicitor. My racing license is at stake if there is the slightest doubt regarding the ownership of Ocean Child, and although he is one of the most promising horses I've trained, he cannot be entered into races or sold on until this question is cleared up.

I would appreciate an early answer.

Joe Reilly

Lulu read the letter again before going through the documents he'd sent. The sales certificate and registration papers looked important, with seals and stamps and gilded lettering, but as she'd never seen anything like them before she couldn't tell if they were genuine.

She examined the signatures of the auctioneer, the representative of the Victoria Turf Club and the mysterious Mr Carmichael, then stared out of the window for a while, deep in thought. She was bewildered, but had to admit to a growing sense of excitement. It wasn't every day a girl was given a racehorse. Perhaps she had a secret admirer – for what other explanation could there be? Shadowy possibilities came and went and she couldn't quite dismiss them even though she knew she was fantasising.

As Lulu dressed for dinner, she came to the conclusion there was only one person who might know the answer, and as she was leaving London early next morning, there was no time to waste.

Clarice was waiting for her in the hotel lounge, resplendent in black silk and pearls, a glass of sherry on the low table before her. She looked up as Lulu joined her. 'This is a pleasant surprise, Lorelei. I wasn't sure you'd come after such a long night.' She signalled to a passing waiter, who brought another sherry.

'I've had a good rest,' murmured Lulu, as she sipped her drink and tried not to show just how much she hated sweet sherry.

'It was a very successful night, my dear. I think you can safely say you have made your mark on London, and dear Bertie is delighted. Have you seen the papers?'

Lulu's mind was on other things, but she took the newspapers, dutifully read the reviews of the exhibition and the gossip columns, which waxed lyrically over Bertie, his supper party and the high-society people who had attended.

'Ghastly photographs, of course, but then what can one expect from the press?'

Lulu smiled. 'Dolly is as glamorous as ever, but I look like a startled rabbit, and far too pale.'

'You had me and Bertie worried, but you rallied, just like I knew you would. Breeding always tells, my dear – it is our family's strength, and thankfully you seem to have inherited it despite everything.'

Lulu pretended to sip sherry, her thoughts far from Clarice's opinions on class and breeding.

'You don't seem very excited by all the fuss,' said Clarice. 'If anything, you appear distracted.'

Lulu put down her barely touched drink. 'There is something on my mind,' she began, 'but I'm not sure where to begin.'

'At the beginning, dear. You know I can't concentrate on prattle when I'm looking forward to dinner.' She pulled a compact from her handbag, eyed her reflection sourly and applied a defiant dash of lipstick.

'I've heard from Joe Reilly again.'

'To apologise, no doubt.' Clarice sniffed.

Lulu shook her head. 'He's still insisting I own the horse and has even sent proof.'

The clasp on Clarice's handbag was shut with a snap. 'Probably forgeries. The racing world is rife with corruption. Let me see those.'

Lulu saw the complacency ebb from Clarice's face as she carefully read each document and, by the time she'd come to the last, her lips had formed a thin line. She was frowning, and a small pulse jumped in her jaw as she set the papers aside. Making no comment, the sherry forgotten, she stared into some distant place beyond the hotel lounge.

Lulu knew better than to badger her with questions, but this silence was frustrating.

'It is obvious Mr Reilly is convinced you own the animal, and one has to have a certain amount of sympathy for him,' she said finally. 'As for this Mr Carmichael . . . I'm not sure where he fits into this at all.' She drifted into silence again, her expression unreadable.

'It's all quite exciting though, isn't it?' Lulu blurted out. 'I mean, it's not every day one is given a racehorse.'

Clarice's expression was brittle as she emerged from her thoughts. 'It's a Trojan horse, Lorelei. Not to be trusted.'

'But aren't you just a little curious as to who gave it to me?'

'No,' she snapped. 'And neither should you be.'

'It could be a gift from a secret admirer.'

'Don't be ridiculous.'

'How can you dismiss the idea out of hand like that?'

'Because secret admirers exist only in trashy fiction. This so-called gift came long before your name was bandied about in the press, and I hardly think it possible you would attract that sort of attention in Tasmania.'

Lulu could see her logic, but was prevented from replying by Clarice abruptly rising from her chair and leaving the lounge. It took Lulu a moment to gather her things and catch up with her in the crowded lobby. 'You can't really expect me to just forget about it?'

'We will not discuss it here,' she said flatly. 'In fact, I'd prefer not to discuss it at all.' She pressed the brass bell for the lift.

'But we must,' persisted Lulu.

Clarice did not reply, and they rode up to the fifth floor in silence.

Lulu had only witnessed Clarice like this once before – and had hoped never to experience it again. It had been the day she'd been rescued from her mother's house, and the memory of that awful argument between the two women was still sharp. She had cowered beneath the kitchen table, unnoticed, helpless and without a voice as they tore into one another with lacerating words made more powerful by their calm, almost flat delivery. She had been left fighting not only for breath but for some sense of worth in the light of her mother's calculating coldness.

'I'm not angry with you,' Clarice said the moment the bedroom door closed behind them, 'but with whoever is playing this nasty game with you.'

'It's an expensive game,' retorted Lulu.

Clarice walked across the room to the window and looked out to the rooftops and spires of London. 'I agree,' she said finally. 'There can be no doubt this horse exists, but it's the reason behind it that worries me.'

'So, you believe Mr Reilly is telling the truth, and that he really is training it?'

'The Reillys have a good name in racing circles. If he's anything like his grandfather, Joe can be trusted to tell the truth.'

'I didn't realise—'

'Why should you? I knew them long before you were born.' Clarice turned from the window, her demeanour stiff and unapproachable. 'It seems Mr Reilly is just as much a victim as you in this disgusting charade.'

'What about Carmichael? Did you know him too?'

Something shifted in Clarice's eyes, but it was fleeting, and Lulu couldn't identify it. 'Never heard of the man.'

'Reilly says in his letter that he's checked him out. So he must exist.'

'I have little doubt of it,' Clarice murmured.

The hint of sarcasm in her reply told Lulu she knew far more than she was saying. But Clarice was unpredictable in this mood – one wrong word and she might clam up all together. 'What do you think I should do?'

'I will contact my solicitor and get him to validate the documents. If they prove to be genuine, then my advice is to write to Joe Reilly and instruct him to sell the horse. By doing so, it will free both of you from this mischief-making once and for all.'

41

'But then I'll never discover who gave it to me and why.'

Clarice studied the diamond rings on her fingers, then looked up with a troubled expression. 'It is sometimes better not to know.'

Realisation hit with such force Lulu had to sit down. 'You think my mother's behind this, don't you?'

Clarice snorted in a most unladylike way. 'I might have done if I didn't understand Gwendoline so well.' She stood and rummaged in her handbag for her address book. 'Gwendoline's spite is deeper than her pockets – she'd never pay for anything unless she could guarantee a profitable return.'

Lulu was deep in thought as Clarice telephoned her solicitor despite the late hour. The question was burning to be asked, but how would Clarice react? She gathered her courage and blurted it out as Clarice put down the receiver. 'Could it have been my father, do you think?'

'I knew you'd bring him up,' Clarice sighed. 'As Gwen has kept his identity a secret, he's unlikely to know you even exist – let alone give you such an expensive present.' Clarice began to root about in her handbag again.

Lulu wasn't really fazed by her answer. Her father's identity had always been a closed book as far as her mother was concerned, but over the years she had found it exasperating not to know who he was and had often fantasised about him. Lulu sighed. There were so many things her mother and Clarice had left unexplained, and these missing links in her life always left her feeling incomplete. Now there was yet another mystery, and Clarice seemed determined to close the door on this too. It was time to stand firm.

'I don't really want to sell the horse,' she said evenly. 'This whole thing is intriguing, and I simply can't walk away from it.'

Clarice stiffened.

'I had a very successful night last night,' Lulu continued. 'I can afford to go to Tasmania and solve this mystery for myself.'

'Don't you *dare*.'

Lulu blinked. 'Why ever not?'

'You're far too sickly to travel. The doctor won't allow it.'

'I've made the journey once before, remember, and I'm stronger now – much stronger.'

'Look at you.' Clarice waved a distracted hand. 'A light breeze would blow you away, and you're far too pale. I will not permit it.'

Lulu kept her nerve. 'I'm twenty-six,' she reminded her, 'old enough to do as I please.'

'Your age is not the issue here,' Clarice said firmly. 'It is your health that concerns me, and as I am your legal guardian I have the right to forbid you to take such risks.'

'Forbid is a strong word, Aunt Clarice. Why are you *really* so adamant I shouldn't go back?'

'There is nothing for you in Tasmania.'

'There's a horse, and a mystery.'

'There is also an unbalanced mother who hates you and untold memories which are best kept buried.' Clarice was clearly struggling to remain calm. 'Nothing good will come of this, mark my words. Sell the horse, be thankful for what you have here and let sleeping dogs lie.'

Lulu regarded her steadily. 'There's more to this than you're telling me. Why not explain? Then perhaps I can make my own judgement.'

Clarice held her gaze. 'There is nothing to explain.'

'I'm not a child, Aunt Clarice. If you have any idea of what this is about, then you should do me the courtesy of enlightening me.'

The blue eyes regarded her steadily. 'You have asked my opinion and I have given it to you. Perhaps you should have the good grace to accept that I know as little as you, and have only your welfare at heart.'

43

'What is it you're afraid of, Aunt Clarice?'

'I'm not afraid of anything,' she said, lifting her chin defiantly. 'I just don't want you getting excited and hopeful over something that is probably nothing more than a cruel hoax.'

Lulu could feel her chest tighten, and made a concerted effort to relax. 'Even if it is a hoax, then surely I have a right to know who's behind it,' she argued, 'and the only way I can find out is if I go home.'

'That is *not* your home. Why do you persist in this childish nonsense? You're an English girl now. *This* is where you belong.' Clarice was breathing heavily, clearly furious at having her authority questioned.

Lulu was shocked at her vehemence. This was a very different Clarice to the rigidly controlled woman who had raised her – but the uncharacteristic show of emotion merely reinforced Lulu's determination to speak her mind and face up to her for once.

'It's where I live, certainly, and you have made it my home. But you always knew I wanted to go back for a short visit at some stage.' Lulu began to pace, avoiding meeting Clarice's furious glare. 'It's not that I don't have the money to go—'

'You silly girl. This isn't about *money*. If I'd thought it wise, I'd have given you the fare long ago.' Clarice grasped Lulu's arm and forced her to stand still and face her. 'Forget this foolishness, Lorelei. You're on the brink of tremendous success with your sculptures – don't spoil everything you and Bertie have worked so hard for.'

Lulu's resolve wavered. 'I realise this is bad timing, but I haven't agreed to the commission pieces yet. As for the others, I'm sure Bertie will oversee the foundry for me and make sure they are delivered.'

'How can you even contemplate throwing everything away after all I've done for you?'

Clarice had never used that as a weapon before. It had to be a sign she was getting desperate – but why? 'It isn't that I'm not grateful for everything you've done, and I love you for it. But I've never made a secret of wanting to go back, and now I have a reason, and the means to do it. I'm not throwing anything away, merely postponing it. But I do need your blessing. Please.'

Clarice's expression hardened. 'You will never have it.'

Lulu had to sit down again. Her heart was struggling and it was difficult to breathe. 'And if I go without your blessing?'

'You will no longer be welcome at Wealden House.'

A long silence followed, broken only by Lulu's ragged breathing. She was the first to break that silence. 'What are you afraid I'll find?'

'Trouble,' Clarice snapped. 'It's why I rescued you from your mother in the first place.'

'But we've already agreed Gwen probably has nothing to do with this.'

'Nothing is certain where she's concerned.' Clarice seemed to be back in control of her emotions. 'It would be a tragedy if you got entangled with her again,' she added softly.

Lulu felt a rush of love for her aunt and took her hand. 'You don't need to protect me any more, Aunt Clarice,' she said. 'I'm a grown-up now and perfectly capable of dealing with Gwen.'

'I doubt it. She can be a formidable enemy, and you are simply not strong enough.' Clarice moved her hand from Lulu's grasp and rang for the porter.

Lulu wanted to protest that Gwen no longer had the power to terrify and belittle her, but the fearful memories silenced her, and she wondered if she could indeed face her again.

'If you go, then you know the consequences.'

Lulu stared back at her. 'You can't really mean to banish me from Wealden House.'

'I do not make idle threats, Lorelei.'

Lulu tried to make light of it. 'You're being rather melodramatic, don't you think?'

'Sometimes only drastic action will do, when faced with such an impossible situation.' Clarice began to put the last of her things into a case.

Lulu rose from the chair and touched Clarice's arm. 'Talk to me, Aunt Clarice. Tell me the *real* reason you don't want me to go.'

'More than enough has been said this evening.' She turned from Lulu and looked at her watch. 'Where *is* that porter? I'm going to miss my train.'

'I thought you weren't leaving until tomorrow morning? What about dinner?'

'I have no appetite for *dinner*,' she said coldly. 'If you want something to eat, call room service. I'm going home.' She put on her hat and coat and picked up her gloves.

'You can't just walk away like this, Aunt Clarice. It's not fair.'

Clarice's gaze was arctic. 'Don't you *dare* talk to me of fairness, Lorelei Pearson. I gave you my name and my home. I've lavished you with every luxury I could, from a first-class education to an apartment in London, and you repay me by deliberately going against my wishes.'

'I am merely asking for your blessing,' Lulu replied as she blinked back the tears.

'You don't have it.' Clarice snapped the lock on her case and glared at her. 'I'm warning you, Lorelei: if you decide to go to Tasmania, then you will find Wealden House closed to you.'

The conversation was brought to an abrupt end by the arrival of the porter. Lulu followed Clarice out of the room, noting how the elder woman's every move spoke of her fury and disapproval.

As they waited for the concierge to hail a taxi, Lulu began to wish she had never heard of Joe Reilly or of Ocean Child. She loved Clarice, and had no wish to cause her distress, but despite everything she had done for her over the years, there were questions about her past that had never been satisfactorily answered – and it seemed to Lulu that the only way to discover the truth was to return to Tasmania, thereby risking the only maternal love and secure home she had ever known.

The last train for Sussex was preparing to leave Victoria Station as the railway porter helped Clarice into the empty first-class compartment and put her bag on the overhead rack. Doors slammed like rifle fire, the guard's whistle echoed through the cavernous station and the great steel wheels began to turn as she took her seat.

As the smoke and steam billowed past the window and the train slowly gathered pace, Clarice leant back and tried to quell the rising anxiety. She had broken every one of her rules by reacting so harshly to Lorelei's innocent questions – but she hadn't been prepared, had had no time to formulate the answers that might have satisfied the girl and turned her from the destructive course she seemed so determined to follow.

What a fool I've been to ignore my instincts, she thought. Joe Reilly's first letter was a warning, and I should have done something about it. Now I've merely made things worse by speaking without thought and losing control of the situation.

She turned to the window. It was dark outside, the June night broken only by intermittent grey veils of smoke coming from the engine, and as Clarice stared at her reflection she saw the guilt in her eyes and the pallor of a woman tormented by regret and indecision. She shouldn't have threatened banishment – it was too harsh – and she knew Lorelei would be trying to make sense of what lay behind her position.

Clarice closed her eyes and willed her thoughts into order. Reilly had no reason to lie about the horse – therefore the documents would prove to be genuine – but did he know more than he was saying? Was he deliberately shielding the person who had given Lorelei the horse, and if so, why?

She pulled off her gloves, and her hands trembled as the memories of those years in Tasmania flooded back. She had used them to reconcile with her sister Eunice, to heal the wounds and make reparation, for Clarice had destroyed the ties between them and she'd needed Eunice to forgive her before it was too late. The bitterness Clarice still felt was for the part she had played in weakening Eunice's ability to overcome the tragedies and shame that had finally overwhelmed her – and should her suspicions as to the identity of the mysterious Mr Carmichael prove correct, then he too must share the blame.

Eunice's daughter, Gwendoline, should also bear that guilt, but Clarice knew her niece far too well, and doubted she felt anything. Clarice sighed. She had never taken to Gwen, even as a child, and over the years her low opinion of the girl had been sadly justified. Gwen had been a spoilt brat and, as she'd matured into womanhood, had proved to be vindictive, grasping and utterly selfish.

Clarice listened to the regular clatter of the wheels as the train steamed through the night – but far from soothing her, they seemed to taunt her with their whispering. She stared out of the window, seeing nothing but haunting scenes from the past.

Drawing the mink coat around her, she shivered. She had to find a way to stop Lorelei, protect her from her mother's spite. Gwendoline knew far too much and would have no compunction over exposing the secrets Clarice had worked so hard to bury – in fact she would relish the chance to wreak revenge.

Clarice battled to control her emotions as she sat in the empty carriage. Lorelei might consider the old scandals unworthy of such shame and discomfort – but to Clarice they remained as potent as ever and she knew she could never speak of them. But her continued silence came at a price – a terrible price she had never imagined she would have to pay – yet pay it she must, for Lorelei had to be stopped.

3

Dolores Carteret lived in a large house in Mayfair. It was owned by her parents, but as it was empty for most of the year she had decided it was silly not to move in permanently and take advantage of its proximity to all London had to offer. She had always felt restless in the country and, following her London debut, she discovered the city suited her vivacious personality, which made her a firm favourite with the social set.

Lulu waited impatiently on the doorstep. The day had begun badly, with a heated argument with Maurice over the wisdom of digging into the mystery of the horse. His opinion on the matter mirrored Clarice's, but Lulu suspected his was rooted in his own need for her to remain close, and she'd left the house feeling quite battered by it all.

She rang the bell again. Where on earth was the maid?

The door opened a crack and Dolly's wan face peered around it. 'Hello, darling, come in.' She flung the door wide, unconcerned that the pedestrians of Mayfair could see her silk underwear beneath the diaphanous peignoir. 'You must excuse my dishabille, but I'm not feeling quite the ticket, and simply *couldn't* get out of bed.'

Lulu hurried past her into the house so she could shut the door. 'You'll cause an accident one day, receiving visitors in that get-up.'

Dolly's green eyes lacked their usual sparkle, but she managed a wry chuckle. 'I *do* so hope so, darling, otherwise life would get *frightfully* tedious, don't you think?' She didn't wait for a reply, but threw her arms around Lulu and gave her a hug. 'Lovely to see you, darling, and congratulations on a terrific success. Bertie is absolutely *thrilled* for you.'

Lulu drew back from the embrace and noted her friend's swollen eyelids and pale complexion with some alarm. 'What's the matter, Dolly? You don't look at all your usual self.'

Dolly shrugged and refused to meet her gaze. 'It's nothing. Just a rather tedious little problem that will no doubt sort itself out.'

Lulu took her hands and forced her to stand still. 'You've been crying, Dolly, and you never cry. What on earth is going on?'

The tears welled in the green eyes and she angrily wiped them away. 'It's too silly, really,' she muttered, 'nothing for you to worry about.' She grabbed Lulu's arm and dragged her into the drawing room. 'Never mind about me, Lulu – you look absolutely done in. What *have* you been up to?'

Lulu was used to the rapid-fire questions, the emphasis on at least one word in every sentence and the sheer energy Dolly generally exuded – but today she was obviously weighed down by something, and knowing Dolly, it probably meant a man was involved. They had been friends since boarding school, and Dolly's life was a continuous drama of one sort or another, and although Lulu didn't really approve of her scandalous behaviour, and found the dramas exhausting, Dolly's heart was warm, her friendship generous and unquestioning. It was difficult not to like her. 'It has been a long day,' she said with a sigh.

'I've given the servants the day off, so I'll get dressed and organise some tea. Sit down and rest. Then you must tell me *all*.'

Lulu sank into a soft armchair and closed her eyes against the sun that was streaming through the deep bay windows. For all her vivacity and brittle patter, Dolly was a stalwart friend, and although some might call her flighty and unreliable, she possessed an admirable sense of loyalty. It had been Dolly who'd first called her Lulu, been the first to comfort her when she was homesick and feeling adrift at boarding school, and the first to make sure she was included in the parties and games and invited to the country-house weekends. She was the only person Lulu could trust to give her honest advice.

She must have dozed off, for when she opened her eyes the tea was on the table and Dolly was sitting in the opposite chair smoking a cigarette, dressed in an emerald-green silk shirt and wide-legged trousers, quietly watching her .

'Sorry,' she muttered through a yawn. 'I was obviously more tired than I thought.'

Dolly's lovely face was clear of make-up, her dark hair falling in a glossy cap to her narrow jaw making her look much younger than twenty-six. 'We've been friends for years,' she murmured, wielding the long cigarette holder and flicking ash into a crystal dish, 'and I can always tell when something's bothering you. What's happened, Lulu?'

Lulu sipped the tea. It was warm and soothing, and just what she needed. 'If I'm to tell my story, then I think it's only fair you tell yours,' she said firmly. 'Come on, Dolly, what's happened?'

Dolly gave a dramatic sigh. 'It's nothing, Lulu. You know me, forever lurching from one disaster to another. I'll get over it.' She blew a stream of smoke into the room. 'But I get the feeling that whatever's ailing you is far more important, so come on – spill the beans.'

'It's a long story,' she began.

'I have all day – all night if that's what you need.'

Lulu eyed the numerous invitations on the mantelpiece. 'I see you're due to attend a gala dinner party at the Ritz tonight, so I won't keep you long.'

51

'You're *far* more important than some stuffy old dinner at the Ritz with Freddy. You will stay for as long as you like.'

'Won't Freddy mind?'

Dolly dismissed her fiancé with a wave of her elegant hand. 'He'll understand.'

Lulu felt sorry for Freddy. Dolly ran rings around him, and he was a nice man who didn't deserve to be treated in such a cavalier fashion.

'Don't look at me like that, Lulu. Freddy is quite capable of breaking off the engagement if he doesn't like the way I treat him, so there's no need for you to rush to his defence.'

Lulu accepted she'd never mastered the art of the enigmatic expression, so she gathered her thoughts and told Dolly about the letters, the colt and Clarice's reaction.

Dolly's eyes widened as the story unfolded.

'I've just come from Clarice's solicitor,' said Lulu finally. 'He confirms the legality of the papers. It seems I really do own Ocean Child.'

'My dear, how *exciting*,' Dolly pulled a face, 'but *ghastly* of Clarice to be so *tedious* about it all. What are you going to do?'

Lulu's hands fluttered. 'I don't know,' she admitted, 'and that's why I'm here to ask your advice.'

Dolly stubbed out her cigarette and fiddled with the ivory holder. 'It's a tricky one,' she mused. 'Clarice is obviously determined you shouldn't go, which is a mystery in itself. But I doubt she'll really carry through her threat to banish you.'

'I'm not so sure. You didn't see her last night, Dolly – she was positively radiating fury, and for a woman who is usually so in control, it was quite frightening to witness.'

'I can imagine,' Dolly replied. 'She always struck me as *terribly* stiff and unapproachable, and although she's always a *marvellous* hostess when I visit, I feel she only tolerates me because of my parents.'

Lulu grinned. 'She doesn't approve of any of my friends, so you're not alone. It helps that your parents are frightfully rich and well-connected of course. Aunt Clarice can be the most awful snob.'

Dolly grinned. 'Thank goodness they are, otherwise I wouldn't be able to live in Mayfair on my measly trust fund.'

'Your *measly* trust fund is worth hundreds a year,' she remarked evenly. 'It's your spending that stretches it to breaking-point.'

Dolly shrugged off this gentle reproach and leant forward, her expression thoughtful. 'What is your head telling you to do about the horse, Lulu?'

'To sell it, make things right with Aunt Clarice and forget any of this happened.'

'And your heart?'

'That I should go home to Tasmania and find out what is going on.' Lulu sighed. 'If I do that, then Clarice will never forgive me.'

'She will,' Dolly said comfortably. 'All parents forgive eventually. They have to, you see, because we are so much a part of them they simply can't bear to let us go.'

'So speaks the indulged daughter,' Lulu replied drily.

'I agree.' Dolly flicked her fringe out of her eyes and gazed out of the window, her expression suddenly sad. 'Pa can never say no when I want something, and he's usually *frightfully* good when I get into a bit of a scrape and need rescuing.'

'Clarice is very different to your pa,' Lulu reminded Dolly, 'and of course she's not my mother, so her threat must be taken seriously.'

Dolly fitted another cigarette into the holder. 'If some secret admirer had given *me* a horse, then I would be on the next ship out of here. But you're far too sensible to do such a thing without giving it a great deal of thought first – and, as you say, your circumstances *are* different to mine.' She blew a stream of smoke towards the ornate ceiling rose. 'And of course there's your health to consider.'

'I've had the lectures about my heart condition,' said Lulu, raking her fingers through her hair, 'and frankly I'm getting rather tired of hearing them.'

'It is a factor, Lulu. You cannot ignore it.'

'I know,' she admitted, 'but it didn't do me any harm when Clarice brought me here all those years ago – and the doctor says I'm getting stronger each time he sees me.'

'That's excellent news.' Dolly cocked her head, her gaze steady. 'Have you spoken to Bertie about this conundrum?'

'There's no point until I've reached some sort of decision, and if I decide to stay, then nothing will have changed. I'll take on the commissions, bank the money and start on next year's exhibition pieces.'

'You don't sound terribly *convinced*, darling, and Bertie will positively blow a gasket if you don't keep him up to date with your plans. What does Maurice have to say? I'm assuming you've talked it over with him.'

'We had the most awful row this morning,' she confessed. 'He told me I was mad to even contemplate it, and had a long list of reasons why I should stay in England.' Lulu's smile was wry. 'I got the distinct impression his advice was more geared to his needs than mine. But then, that's Maurice.'

Dolly's expression hardened. 'It might be good for him to stand on his own two feet for once. All the while you're close at hand he simply leans on you, and I've often thought how wearing that responsibility must be. Rather like having a demanding child.'

'I know you think Maurice is a parasite, and in a way he is, but I remember how he used to be and simply can't just brush him aside like you do Freddy.'

'Why are you so concerned about Freddy all of a sudden?' The green eyes flashed. 'Is there something going on between you?'

'Don't be ridiculous, Dolly. You're clearly in a very odd mood today, and if you're determined to start a fight, then I'm leaving.'

'Don't go.' Dolly reached for her hand. 'I'm sorry, darling, I didn't meant to be so sharp.' She tilted her head, the green eyes pleading. 'Forgive me?'

'I always do,' she murmured, 'but there are times, Dolly dear, when you would test the patience of a saint.'

Dolly smiled and shrugged before digging her purse from beneath a stack of newspapers and discarded letters. She pulled out a coin. 'I want to conduct an experiment,' she said mysteriously. 'It's one that I've used many a time when I have a tough decision to make, and it rarely fails me.'

'My decision can't be made on the toss of a coin,' Lulu protested.

'We'll see.' She threw the coin in the air and trapped it on the back of her hand. She looked at Lulu, her gaze steady. 'Now, I want you to really concentrate, Lulu, and treat the toss of this coin as a decision you cannot back out of – the result is final and there is no alternative.'

Lulu thought it was nonsense, but decided to play along. Yet, as she focused her thoughts, she was surprised at how keenly she willed the coin to provide the solution. 'All right – heads I go; tails I stay.'

'Ready?'

Lulu nodded, her eyes fixed firmly on her friend's hands as they opened to reveal the coin.

'Tails it is.' Dolly regarded her solemnly. 'What is your immediate reaction?'

'Disappointment,' she admitted, 'loss, regret – a terrible sadness.'

'I thought so – and that initial reaction is telling. You knew all along that you have to go – call it curiosity, homesickness, the need to be independent, whatever – but until this moment you've been afraid to admit it.'

'What about Clarice, Bertie and Maurice?'

'It's not their decision to make. You have spent your life trying to please everyone – now it's time to follow your instincts and please yourself.' Dolly crossed the room, sat beside her and took her hands. 'I so clearly remember that little girl with the funny accent whose face lit up as she talked of kookaburras and bell-birds, and the scents of eucalyptus and pine. It was what made you special.'

Lulu had never felt particularly special – merely different – but it was nice to hear.

Dolly opened Lulu's hand and pressed the coin into her palm. 'Take it with you to Tasmania. You might find you have to use it again.'

'Do you really think I dare risk everything and go?'

Dolly nodded as she closed Lulu's fingers over the coin. 'If you don't, you'll regret it for the rest of your life.'

Lulu realised Dolly was right, but doubt still niggled. 'It is a long way,' she murmured, 'and I shall be quite alone. What if I am taken ill?'

'Ships have doctors, and I'm sure Australia does too,' retorted Dolly impatiently.

Lulu eyed her sharply. 'What's eating you today? Come on, I've told you my problems. Now you must tell me yours.' She sat back and folded her arms. 'I'm staying here until you tell me every-thing.'

Dolly left the couch, picked up her silver cigarette case and walked to the window. She smoked for a while in silence, then sank on to the window seat. 'I want your word this will go no further, Lulu. I can't risk anyone finding out.'

'You have it.'

'There's this man . . .' she began.

'There usually is,' said Lulu.

'I know, I know, but this time it's a little more serious than usual.'

Lulu watched the different expressions flit across Dolly's face and realised her friend was deeply troubled. 'Go on,' she prompted gently.

'I won't tell you who he is– suffice it to say he's a friend of Bertie's. They were at Oxford together.' She rose from the window seat and began to pace. 'He's much older than me of course, and frightfully sophisticated, and *honestly*, Lulu I *knew* I shouldn't have flirted with him so outrageously, but I simply couldn't help myself.'

'Oh, Dolly,' sighed Lulu, 'please tell me you didn't sleep with him.'

She stubbed out her cigarette. 'I didn't *mean* to,' she insisted, 'but you know how it is after a night of champagne.' She gave a great sigh and threw herself into the chair. 'I woke up the next morning in a seedy hotel room in Fulham of all places, with little memory of what had happened, but he'd left a note on the pillow, thanking me for a most entertaining and satisfying night.'

Lulu perched on the arm of the chair and took her hand. There was very little she could say, for it was clear Dolly was distraught. 'You're not . . . you know?'

Dolly's laugh was bitter. 'No, thank God.'

'Then why are you so worried? If you're not planning to see him again – and I'm the only one who knows – you can put it down to experience and try to forget about it.'

'I wish it was that simple.' Dolly chewed a fingernail. 'He's threatening to tell Freddy and Bertie if I don't agree to meet him again.' Her lovely eyes were awash with tears as she looked up at Lulu. 'I'm going quite mad with worry, Lulu. What am I to do?'

Lulu was shocked. This was far beyond her experiences, and she couldn't think straight. 'Is he married? Perhaps a discreet anonymous note to his wife . . . ?'

Dolly shook her head. 'She's as bad as he is.' Her voice broke on a sob. 'He's even suggesting a ménage a trois, with her – can you believe it? I feel so dirty – so used, and I simply don't know which way to turn.'

Lulu tried desperately to think of a solution as she held her sobbing friend, but nothing came to mind.

Dolly eventually stopped crying, withdrew from Lulu's embrace and blew her nose. 'Pa usually sorts things out for me, but of course I can't possibly tell him about this. He'd never forgive me.'

'Are you so sure about that? He's forgiven you before, and he's an influential man who just might be able to put a stop to this.'

'I couldn't bear to see the disappointment and disgust on his face – too shaming.' She shook her head. 'No, this time it's up to me to find a way out of the mess I've made.'

Lulu returned to the couch as Dolly crossed the room and poured them each a strong gin and tonic. They sat in silence as the grandfather clock in the hall ticked away the minutes.

'I've just had a *brilliant* idea,' shouted Dolly, leaping to her feet. 'Why don't I come with you to Australia?'

Lulu was speechless with shock. She loved Dolly, and treasured her friendship, but she could be overpowering and inclined to run wild – as this recent escapade had proved. Six weeks together on a liner would test their friendship to the limit. 'You wouldn't like being cooped up on a ship for so long,' she said hastily.

Dolly's eyes were alight with excitement. 'I *adore* life at sea,' she breathed. 'The starlit nights, the dancing on deck, all those *lovely* officers.'

'That's what I'm afraid of,' said Lulu drily.

'Oh, *darling*, don't be so *stuffy*. Anyone would think you were Clarice's age, the way you go on.'

'Someone has to keep a clear head about this. We could be away for months, and you'll miss the London season. You also seem to have forgotten about Freddy.'

Dolly slumped into the chair. 'The season has become tedious with its endless round of Ascot, Wimbledon, Henley and so on – and I certainly don't want to run the risk of bumping into that man again.' She shuddered. 'Freddy poses a *bit* of a problem, I suppose, but maybe the separation will do us some good.'

'Don't you think it would be kinder to break off the engagement, Dolly? You obviously don't love him.'

'I suppose I should,' she muttered, 'but I rather like having him around. He's sort of safe and familiar, and he does make me laugh.'

'Not exactly the recipe for a long and happy marriage.'

'We're getting sidetracked,' said Dolly impatiently. 'I need to get out of London until things cool down. You're going to Australia. It makes perfect sense that I come with you. What do you say?'

The misgivings were legion, but Lulu saw the plea in her friend's eyes and knew she couldn't refuse. 'All right,' she said reluctantly, 'but I want your solemn promise that you'll learn from all this and try to behave.'

Dolly dragged her from the couch and gave her a hug. 'You won't regret it, I promise.' She grinned like a schoolgirl. 'Let's go into town and do some shopping. We'll need a whole new tropical wardrobe for a start, and you'll have to advise me on what I'll need for Tasmania. Gosh, I haven't been this excited for years. What an adventure!'

Lulu slumped back into the chair as Dolly raced out of the room to change her clothes. She was already regretting her decision, and the thought of shepherding Dolly through the minefield of ship's officers, fellow passengers and Tasmanian horse trainers and the racing fraternity filled her with dread. The peaceful homecoming she'd envisaged was wrecked before it had even begun.

The warmth of the day had diminished as the sun went down, leaving a chill in the air that promised heavy dew by morning. The three-storey terraced house was in darkness, and Lulu breathed a sigh of relief. She was exhausted after the long shopping expedition with Dolly, and the last thing she needed was another confrontation with Maurice. Yet, just as she was about to put the key into the lock of her garden apartment, the door was flung open.

'Where have you been?' Maurice's hair was ruffled, his eyes wild in his gaunt face.

Lulu tamped down her impatience as she pushed past him. 'With Dolly,' she said shortly. 'Not that it's any of your business.'

'What did the solicitor say?' Maurice followed her down the hallway.

Lulu dumped her shopping bags and keys on the table and took a deep breath. 'The papers are genuine,' she replied, turning to face him in the narrow confines.

'So you'll be selling the horse?'

'No, Maurice. Dolly and I are going to Tasmania.'

'But you can't!' he exploded, his fingers raking through his hair. 'I need you here.'

Lulu's energy was rapidly ebbing. 'We had this argument this morning,' she said quietly, 'and I don't wish to continue it. I have made my decision, and neither you nor Clarice will stop me.' She reached out to touch his arm, but he shrugged her off. 'I'm sorry, Maurice,' she murmured, 'but I have to do this. Please try to understand.'

'I don't understand at all,' he said plaintively. 'You're being selfish, Lulu. You know I can't function properly without you.'

'Of course you can,' she said flatly, 'and if you stopped thinking about yourself for a minute you might realise that it's you being selfish – not me.' She turned and headed for the kitchen, all too aware of his heavy tread behind her.

The silence was oppressive as she waited for the kettle to boil, but she was determined not to be cowed by it. There had been enough drama for one day, and she simply didn't have the energy for more.

'I'll come with you,' he declared into the silence. 'It wouldn't be safe – two girls on their own without a chaperone.'

Alarmed, Lulu gathered her wits. 'You know that isn't practical, but bless you for thinking of it,' she said quickly. 'We both know you hate being on the water, and as the journey will take at least six weeks, it would prove far too much for you.'

His chin sank to his chest and she reached across the table for his hand. She was too kind to point out that he couldn't afford such a trip, but perhaps she could persuade him to make the best of her absence. 'Why don't you consider taking in another artist to share the studio while I'm away,' she suggested. 'That would give you a bit of income as well as company, and before you know it, I'll be back.'

'Bertie suggested I should go to the artists' colony in Newlyn to get a fresh perspective on things.' He eyed her through his lashes. 'He was here this morning.'

Lulu went cold. 'And, of course, you couldn't help but tell him about my plans?'

He shrugged. 'I didn't think they were secret,' he said defiantly.

She snatched back her hand. 'You really are the limit, Maurice. You knew I wanted to tell him in my own time.'

'Well, I saved you the bother, didn't I?' He looked away. 'He's not exactly delighted you're leaving him in the lurch, but then you don't seem to care what any of us feel.'

She looked at him suspiciously. 'You haven't rung Clarice as well, have you?'

He shook his head.

'Then I'd be grateful if you left me to do it. It's really none of your business, and Clarice needs careful handling.' His expression remained mulish. 'I'm sorry, Maurice, but I can't live my life with you in my pocket – not any more. It's time for us both to stand on our own feet and get on with things.'

'Easy for you to say,' he muttered. 'Some of us don't have your advantages.'

'Don't do this, Maurice,' she warned. 'You're a talented artist with a private income as well as your army pension. You have a home, and a studio. If you don't like my suggestion about lodgers, then go to Newlyn.'

'I won't know anyone there. I was hoping you might come with me.'

Lulu's emotions were in turmoil as she looked at the bent head and narrow, slumped shoulders. 'Oh, Maurice,' she sighed, 'you know I can't.' Receiving no response, she stood and folded her arms. 'Newlyn could be a new start – a chance to broaden your talent, and get well again in all that lovely sea air and sunshine. Give it a try, Maurice, please.'

He shrugged and refused to look at her.

Lulu's patience finally wore too thin. 'It's late, and we both need a good night's sleep. Go to bed, Maurice and perhaps tomorrow you'll see things more clearly.'

He scraped back his chair and stood before her in abject misery. 'Don't go, Lulu, please.'

Her soft heart melted and she hugged him. 'I need to go back home, Maurice. I've waited so many years to face the demons that have haunted me, and now I have the chance I can't walk away from it.' She could hear the rapid thud of his heart through his shirt, felt his arms tighten around her as if he would never let her go.

'Home,' he murmured into her hair. 'Such an emotive word, isn't it?'

She nodded, afraid to speak in case it broke the spell.

'Home means peace, comfort and kind memories,' he murmured. 'I can understand why you need to go.'

Lulu almost smiled at that. Home meant different things to different people, and a great many of her memories were dark and painful.

He held her at arm's length, his expression enigmatic. 'We all need to go home sometime,' he said quietly.

Lulu's pulse raced as she looked up at him. 'Does that mean . . . ?'

He nodded, kissed her forehead and stepped back. 'Your heart is obviously still there, so you must go, Lulu.'

'And you? What will you do?'

His smile echoed something of the young man he'd once been. 'Oh, I'll think of something,' he murmured. Pulling on his moth-eaten jacket, he headed for the front door. 'Goodnight, Lulu. Sweet dreams.'

She closed the door behind him and leant against it with a sigh. It felt as if she was in the middle of an emotional tug-of-war, but at least Maurice seemed to have accepted her decision. Independence was far harder to attain than she'd ever thought possible, and she could only pray that Clarice and Bertie would be as understanding.

The telephone rang an hour later, just as Lulu was about to get into the bath. Clucking with annoyance, she wrapped herself in a towel and answered it.

Bertie's voice rasped down the line. 'We have things to discuss.'

'I was going to call you tomorrow. I'm sorry you heard it from Maurice—'

Her apology was drowned out by his tightly controlled, angry voice. 'Come to my house tomorrow. Twelve sharp, and don't be late.' He disconnected the call.

Her hand trembled as she replaced the receiver. Bertie was a man who didn't appreciate being thwarted. His powerful presence was daunting enough at the best of times, but when crossed, he was truly terrifying. Lulu clambered into the bath and burst into tears. She was sick of being bullied.

The bright sunlight streaming through the windows seemed to mock her. Lulu hadn't slept well and had little appetite for breakfast. She dressed in a cotton frock and cardigan, and tried hard to boost her courage for the forthcoming meeting by adding a dash of scarlet lipstick and a dab of her favourite perfume. She had to remain focused – had to stand her ground and try to come to a compromise with Bertie – otherwise her career would be over before it had really begun.

Haynes, the butler, opened the door to Bertie's mansion, his expression haughty as usual as he showed her into the panelled library and quietly closed the door.

Lulu was too restless to sit down, and she glanced repeatedly at the ormolu clock on the mantelpiece as the time ticked away. It was past noon. Bertie had obviously decided to keep her waiting, thereby making her even more nervous.

She eyed the walls of books, the large oak desk and the deep leather chairs. It was a man's room, redolent with cigars and whisky, the few paintings depicting hunting scenes, the plaster busts of long-dead poets and statesmen adding an almost museum-like quality. The heavy oak door muffled any sound from the rest of the house, but the tick of the clock seemed to emphasise the silence. Restless and uncomfortable she went to the window and stared out at the garden. This was worse than being in a dentist's waiting room.

'You have a lot of explaining to do.'

She whirled to face him, her heart thudding. The aura of tightly controlled anger was almost tangible as he closed the door behind him and made his way to the desk. 'I'm sorry,' she began.

His dark gaze never left her as he lit a cigar and leant back in the chair. 'Really?' he drawled. 'Is that an apology for not coming straight to me – or because you've been caught out?'

Lulu perched on the edge of a nearby chair, her handbag grasped on her knees. 'Maurice shouldn't have told you,' she said, 'I was going to . . .'

'It's a good thing he did. Otherwise I would have been made to look a complete fool.' His dark brows lowered. 'And I don't appreciate being made to appear foolish, Lorelei.'

'I never meant—'

'I'm glad to hear it. Perhaps now you have come to your senses and given up on this mad idea of going to Australia, we can discuss the commissions.'

Lulu licked her lips. Her mouth was so dry she could barely speak. 'I haven't given up on it,' she managed. 'The commissions will be dealt with, but after I return.'

Bertie rose from his chair, his towering figure blocking out the light from the window. 'You're supposed to be a professional,' he roared, 'and professionals don't run off to Australia and leave their clients in the lurch.'

'I'm sure they'll understand,' she said hastily. 'The pieces you sold can be dealt with by the foundry, and I'll do all preparatory drawings for the commissions before I leave and—'

'It's not good enough,' he snapped. 'Those commissions were ordered in good faith. I will *not* have you letting me down like this.' He glared down at her as she bit her lip. 'I am a patron of the arts,' he growled, 'and you – you are just one of hundreds of artists scrabbling for success. You should be grateful to be in such a good position.'

'I am,' she said stoutly, 'and of course I realise I wouldn't have come so far without your sponsorship.'

'Then you'd better explain yourself, Lorelei,' he snapped.

His use of her full name was warning enough to tread very carefully.

He sat in stony silence, his dark gaze never wavering from her as she told him everything.

'England is your home – your birthplace,' she continued. 'Imagine you've been forced to leave it – made to adapt to a different life, forced to change everything, even the way you speak. I have to go back, Bertie – not just because of the colt – but because I need to find who I am, and where I came from, so I can put the missing pieces together and finally be whole.'

He stubbed out the cigar and rose from the chair, hands in pockets as he turned his back on her and stared out of the window. 'You have put up a fine defence,' he muttered, 'and I can understand why you feel as you do.' He turned towards her and rested his large hands on the back of his chair. 'But you are on the brink of great success here. Do you really want to risk everything on a whim?'

'It's not a whim.' Lulu stood so she didn't feel at such a disadvantage. 'I've wanted to go home ever since I landed here.' She looked into his eyes, silently pleading for him to understand and give her his blessing. 'My work is important to me, Bertie. I have no intentions of letting this chance slip away.'

'Mmm.' He dug out his pocket watch, flipped open the casing and stared at the dial for a length of silence. 'These are wealthy, influential clients who don't appreciate being let down. Neither do I.'

'You have my word that I'll fulfil my promises,' she said evenly.

Bertie took a deep breath, closed the watch and returned it to his pocket. 'Have you spoken to Clarice about this?'

'Briefly.'

He raised an eyebrow. 'I take it she doesn't approve either.'

Lulu shook her head. 'It seems I can please no one.'

'Perhaps you should heed our advice,' he said. 'It's time you grew up, Lorelei, and faced your responsibilities. Neither Clarice nor I deserves to be treated like this after all we've done for you.'

She balled her fist as the anger shot through her. 'Do you know what, Bertie? I'm sick of being grateful,' she retorted. 'What you and Clarice have done has always been appreciated – and I know how lucky I am – but I'm not prepared to live the rest of my life feeling beholden to everyone. I'm fully aware of my responsibilities and mature enough to know my own mind. This visit home might be inconveniently timed, but there it is. I'm going, and no one will stop me.'

His dark eyes held a twinkle of amusement as he strode across the room and opened the door. 'I'm going to my club,' he said. 'The chauffeur can drop you home on the way.'

Elated by her ability to stand up to him, she was nevertheless terrified that she'd gone too far. 'There's no need,' she muttered.

'There's every need,' he drawled. 'If Maurice is ever going to produce something worth selling, he needs to go to Newlyn. It's time that young man stopped feeling sorry for himself and woke up to the real world.'

'The world in his head is very real,' she replied. 'Please don't bully him.'

The black eyebrow rose. 'I hardly think you're in the position to tell me how to speak to Maurice. You don't seem to realise just how much work goes into sponsoring you, and frankly, if I have any more nonsense, I'll wash my hands of both of you.'

Lulu meekly followed him as he strode into the hall and ordered the butler to have the car brought round. During the silent short drive to her flat she could think of nothing to say, but her thoughts were in a whirl. As the car came to a halt, she gathered her courage. 'I won't let you down,' she promised, 'and neither will Maurice.'

Bertie's stern expression softened. 'You're a talented artist, and I'd be a fool to risk you being snapped up by someone else. Take your holiday to Tasmania, Lulu, but on your return I expect great things from you.'

The relief was immense. 'Thank you. You won't regret it.'

'Let's hope not.' He frowned as he eyed the house. 'Perhaps I ought to come in and have a word with Maurice. Newlyn could be the making of him, you know.'

She stepped out of the car and searched in her handbag for her keys as Bertie joined her on the pavement. 'I expect he's in his studio. The light is just right at this time of day.'

The door opened on to a square hall tiled in black and white diamonds, and the elegant staircase curved up towards the attic studio. Sunlight poured in, sending splashes of colour across the hall from the stained-glass window above the door.

Lulu stepped inside and froze. The silence was profound – as if the house was holding its breath – but in that silence she could sense an ominous foreboding. She took another step into the hall, the hairs on her arms and neck rising with some unidentified fear.

There was a long shadow cast across the hall. Lulu followed that shadow fearfully, her gaze travelling upward.

Maurice was hanging from the top banister rail.

Lulu's screams echoed in the white space.

'Call an ambulance,' shouted Bertie as he pushed her aside and raced up the stairs, digging frantically into his pocket for the penknife he always carried.

Galvanised into action, Lulu reached for the telephone.

Alerted by her screams, the chauffeur came hurtling into the hallway. He rushed to take Maurice's weight as Bertie began hacking at the dressing-gown cord.

Lulu urged the ambulance people to hurry before racing up the stairs. One look at the colourless face and staring eyes was enough. Maurice had been dead for some time.

'We must try and resuscitate him,' she shouted as the two men laid him on the floor.

'It's too late,' Bertie said, pulling her away from the inert figure. 'He's gone, Lulu.'

'No, he can't have,' she sobbed. 'There must be something we can do.'

His hands were gentle but firm as he drew her into his arms. 'He's already cold,' he murmured, as she collapsed against him. 'He must have done it early this morning.'

'I should have known,' she continued. 'Why didn't I see it coming? Oh, God, Bertie, what have I done?'

'Maurice's mind was always fragile – it was sadly inevitable that this would happen some day. I suppose the thought of you leaving him behind was just too much.'

'It wouldn't have happened if I'd been more caring,' she muttered bitterly through her tears. 'I should have listened to him – really listened and not . . .'

'Hush now, Lulu. It was not your fault.'

But it was – it was – and as the minutes ticked by Lulu became ever more convinced that her actions and harsh words had led to this tragedy. She replayed the scenes of the previous day. The signs had all been there, but she'd been blind to them – not wanting to see.

Her heart was struggling and it was hard to breathe – but her own discomfort was nothing compared to the mental torture Maurice must have experienced to do such a terrible thing. The guilt was overwhelming – surging through her in wave after wave until she thought she would go mad.

The police arrived at the same time as the doctor. Lulu sat in Maurice's kitchen, listening to their voices and the tread of their feet as Bertie took charge in his usual, calm and orderly manner. She was numb with shock, unable to think straight or speak coherently. Maurice was dead – and already the house echoed with the void he'd left behind.

'I've given them a statement,' said Bertie some time later. 'Come, Lulu, I'll take you back to my place.'

Lulu let him lead her down the steps to the car, but she moved like a sleepwalker, seeing nothing, feeling nothing, needing only to curl up and blot out the memory of Maurice hanging from the banister railing.

He'd followed Lulu and Bertie across London, struggling to keep up on his rather rickety bicycle. Now he was one of many bystanders on the other side of the street, watching as the police arrived and the ambulance came to take away the blanket-shrouded body.

He gnawed his lip as Bertie escorted a distraught Lulu down the steps and handed her into the car. He could only guess at what had happened, and he wondered if this tragedy would bring an end to his employer's plans. It was certainly unforeseen – and something he must report immediately.

Lulu remembered very little of what happened over the following week. She was aware of Clarice's arrival, of Dolly's frequent visits and Bertie's ordered handling of Maurice's inquest and funeral arrangements – but she felt as if she was an onlooker in a drama over which she had no control.

It was the eve of the funeral and Lulu was sitting on the window seat in Bertie's mansion, staring out across the manicured lawn.

'I thought I'd find you here,' said Bertie, closing the sitting-room door behind him. 'It's my favourite view too, you know. Very soothing.'

Lulu nodded, but she hadn't really noticed the view at all.

'I thought you should have this,' he said, taking an envelope from his jacket pocket. 'The police brought it back this morning. It's addressed to you.'

Lulu's hand was shaking as she took the last letter Maurice would ever write. 'I can't bear to read it,' she confessed.

'I think you'll find it gives you comfort. Hopefully it will ease the guilt you feel. It's a guilt we all bear, you know, so you are not alone in this.'

Lulu took the single sheet from the envelope and, after a deep breath, began to read.

My dearest Lulu,

Please forgive this final selfish act. But I too need to go home. I have yearned for that elusive death which has taunted me for so long, and now have the courage to leave this torturous world and find peace in endless sleep.

Shed no tears for me, darling girl, for I am at last content – and when you reach the tranquil shores of your homeland, know that I have reached mine. Go with my blessing and my love,

Goodnight, sweet Lulu, goodnight.

Maurice

Lulu's tears fell unheeded as she carefully folded the letter and held it to her heart. Maurice was at last at peace – and so was she. The healing could now begin.

Eight painful weeks had passed since Maurice's death, and as Lulu climbed down from the train she adjusted the hat Dolly had given her to boost her spirits. Dolly had offered to come with her, but Lulu had managed to dissuade her. Yet, as she stood alone on the platform watching the train chuff down the track, she experienced a moment of panic and wished she wasn't quite so alone.

Silently berating herself for being pathetic, she waited until the smoke cleared, tucked her handbag under her arm and left the country halt. Facing Clarice was going to take nerve and stamina, but face her she must. Dolly was right – it was time to take control of her life and step out of Clarice's shadow.

Walking down the dusty road she passed the familiar village shops and returned the friendly greetings of people she had known for most of her life. The ancient church was somnolent in the August sunshine, the flower borders of the village green blazed with colour and the pond's tranquillity was disturbed by squabbling ducks and moorhens. She absorbed the sights, sounds and scents of the village that had been her home for sixteen years, for after today she might never see it again.

The thought saddened her, and she paused for a moment to watch a group of children throw bread to the ducks. Then, realising she was wasting time, she continued on to Wealdon House. She reached the iron gates and, after taking a deep breath, headed for the front door.

Her key turned in the lock and she stepped into the gloomy hall. The house was quiet, its chill greeting her after the warmth of the August sunshine. She pulled off her lacy gloves, touched the hat for luck and headed for the drawing room.

Clarice was in her usual chair, the Labrador at her feet, afternoon tea on the trolley beside her. She looked up and smiled. 'I expect you're hungry after that journey,' she said, 'but you're so late the tea is probably stewed by now, and Vera's out for the afternoon.'

Lulu hesitated before lightly kissing the soft cheek. 'If it is, then I'll make more.' There was no response to her kiss, so she petted the dog and sat down.

Clarice busied herself with the tea things. 'You look well. New hat?'

'Dolly gave it to me.' She set it aside with her handbag and gloves.

Clarice looked disapproving. 'I might have guessed,' she muttered, as she passed Lulu a plate of egg-and-cress sandwiches. 'It's no doubt very fashionable, but looks more like something the gardener would put over seedlings.'

'That's why it's called a cloche,' Lulu explained. 'I think it's rather fun.' Her nerves were on edge. She bit into the sandwich, found she had no appetite, and set it aside.

'I hope you're planning to stay for the weekend,' said Clarice. 'Bertie is calling in for drinks tomorrow afternoon on his way back from a shooting party at the Grange.'

Lulu eyed her aunt guiltily over the teacup. She had sworn Bertie to secrecy, and if Clarice had even an inkling that Bertie already knew her plans, then she would never be forgiven. 'I don't know if I can—'

'Well, of course you must,' interrupted Clarice. 'I can't possibly entertain Bertie on my own, and I expect he's keen to discuss the commissions with you.' Her gaze was direct. 'I understand you haven't been in touch with him since Maurice's funeral.'

'I've been busy,' she mumbled.

Clarice put the cup and saucer down with a clatter. 'Busy? What can possibly be more important than showing courtesy to the man who not only made you a small fortune, but who took over the whole ghastly business with Maurice?'

Lulu's pulse was racing, and it took a great deal of effort to meet the stony gaze and remain outwardly calm. 'I know I've been lax,' she admitted, 'but I just couldn't face anyone for a while. I was planning to call him tonight.'

The gaze didn't falter. Clarice was waiting for a more satisfactory answer.

Lulu licked her lips and decided the best way to approach

73

this was head-on. 'I had some important decisions to make, but Maurice's suicide made them even more difficult.'

Clarice's expression hardened. 'As you planned to call Bertie tonight, you have obviously reached a conclusion,' she said.

'I must go to Tasmania, Aunt Clarice. Don't you see? I'll regret it for the rest of my life if I don't.'

'You'll regret it more if you do, Lorelei.'

'I'm sorry you feel so strongly, Aunt Clarice. But I've made up my mind.'

Clarice's expression softened and she leant forward. 'Then change it, Lorelei. This is your home, and I deeply regret the ultimatum I made all those weeks ago. You have become the daughter I never had, and I'm so very proud of what you've achieved. Stay, Lorelei, please.'

'I can't.' Clarice's warmth brought treacherous tears and she was finding it hard to see. 'It's too late.'

'It's never too late, my dear. Send a telegram to Mr Reilly and have done with it. All this has been a terrible strain on your health – on mine too.'

Lulu looked at her in alarm.

Clarice raised an unsteady hand to her chest. 'The doctor is quite concerned about my blood pressure, you know.'

'You didn't tell me.' Lulu edged forward in her seat, her concern sharp.

'I didn't want to worry you, but I had quite a nasty turn after I returned from the funeral, and had to stay in bed for several days.' She gave a weak smile. 'Dr Williams wanted me to go into the cottage hospital for a rest, but of course I refused. One is never as comfortable as when one is at home.'

Lulu was horrified. 'I'm so sorry. I never realised how badly all this must have affected you.' She reached for Clarice's hands and looked into her face. The shadows under her eyes could be the result of sleepless nights, or of something more sinister. 'If I've been the cause—'

'It's not your fault,' she interrupted. 'Not really. I allowed myself to get overwrought, and at my age that is never wise.' She gave a deep sigh. 'One forgets just how old one is, you see.' Her demeanour was utterly weary, her voice so soft Lulu could barely hear her. 'It seems I am sinking into a general decline, my dear. Frightful nuisance of course, but it comes to us all eventually.'

'Please don't talk like that. You have years ahead of you if you follow the doctor's advice and take it easy.'

Clarice shook her head. 'I doubt it, but I will certainly do my best to remain active for as long as possible.'

Lulu eyed her sharply. There had always been something of the actress in Clarice, and until this moment she had enjoyed rude health, and taken pride in never consulting the doctor. 'This high blood pressure seems to have come on very suddenly,' she said thoughtfully.

Clarice lifted a fluttering hand. 'It's what happens when one gets old,' she murmured, 'and no doubt these fearful headaches are all a part of it.'

If it wasn't so tragic, Lulu would have smiled. Clarice never had headaches. 'This all sounds very worrying,' she said. 'I'd better ring the doctor. Headaches and high blood pressure are serious matters.'

Clarice made a show of rousing herself as Lulu stood up. 'There's no need,' she said hastily. 'He was here this morning, and is quite satisfied with my progress.'

'I'd still like to speak to him – just to reassure myself.'

'Please don't disturb Dr Williams on a Friday afternoon,' Clarice said hurriedly. 'The poor man works so hard and has little enough time with his family.'

Lulu perched on the edge of the seat again and held her gaze, certain now that Clarice was play-acting. 'As long as you're sure the doctor has everything under control,' she murmured.

Clarice poured another cup of tea, her gaze averted. 'He has

75

given me a tonic and a few pills to perk me up, but I don't really need them – not when I have you to keep me cheerful while I recuperate.'

'I'll stay for the weekend, but after that it might be an idea to ask one of your friends to keep you company.'

Clarice forgot she was supposed to be at death's door and sat bolt upright. 'Why should I do that when I have you?'

'Because I'm leaving for Australia at the end of the month.'

'You can't. You don't have a passport.' Triumph lit in her eyes.

'I had my wartime identification papers. They were enough to get a passport.' She saw the light flicker and die and felt a stab of remorse. 'The tickets are paid for, Aunt Clarice. We leave on the SS *Ormonde* on the twenty-eighth.'

'We?'

'Dolly is coming with me.'

At that, Clarice seemed to rally her fighting spirit. 'I might have known that *flapper* would be involved in this. Empty-headed fool – she doesn't have the slightest inkling of what she's doing by encouraging you in this madness.'

'She had less to do with encouraging me than you did,' replied Lulu, who was feeling strangely calm now she knew Clarice had been play-acting.

'I have *never* encouraged you,' Clarice said fiercely.

'And that's precisely why I have to go.'

' But why, Lorelei? Why are you so determined to hurt me like this? Wasn't Maurice's suicide enough to dissuade you?'

'That jibe was unfair,' she said softly.

'I was just trying to make you see how important it is you stay here.'

Lulu ached to see the bewilderment and regret in her eyes. 'I love you, Aunt Clarice, and always will. But if you refuse to talk to me I have no choice but to seek out the truth for myself.'

The colour had gone from Clarice's face as she stood up. 'And what if this precious truth you so earnestly seek is dark and ugly and destructive, Lorelei? What then?'

'A dark, ugly truth is better than a lie, Aunt Clarice. At least one knows where one stands.'

The silence was heavy between them. They were at an impasse, neither one willing to back down, the last gauntlet thrown – or so Lulu had thought.

'If you go to Tasmania I will disinherit you.'

Lulu could only stare at her in shock. 'That is your privilege,' she said, gathering her wits. 'But as you said before, this has nothing to do with money. It's more to do with some secret you've been holding on to for years. Surely it must be such ancient history that it cannot hurt either of us now.'

Something shifted in Clarice's eyes, but it was fleeting and, if anything, seemed to stiffen her resolve. 'Maybe it is to you,' she said, 'but to me it is still raw.' Her faded blue eyes regarded Lulu with weary acceptance. 'Past sins cast long shadows, Lorelei, and, as no doubt you have recently discovered, they often demand a heavy price from those who invoke them.' She took a deep breath. 'My time in Tasmania was not happy – and neither was yours. I am merely trying to save you the heartache I know is waiting for you there.'

Clarice moved away to stand before the French windows. 'If you go, then you know the consequences,' she said sadly. 'I have said my final word on the matter.'

Lulu stared at the rigid back, the determined tilt of the old woman's head, and knew it was over. 'In that case I will collect some of my things and leave,' she said softly. 'I'll arrange for the rest to be sent to London and, as I assume the flat is no longer mine, I'll stay with Dolly until we sail.'

'You may keep the flat. I have no wish to see you homeless.' The voice was soft and unbearably weary.

'Thank you.' Lulu waited for Clarice to offer at least a crumb of hope that a way might be found to heal this awful breach – but the spine remained rigid, the head turned away.

'Gwendoline is unstable and probably dangerous,' Clarice said flatly. 'She will no doubt tell you things that will destroy everything you believe in – perhaps even threaten your very life. She is quite capable of that, as I'm sure you remember, so be very careful.' Clarice crossed the room and, without a backwards glance, closed the door behind her.

Lulu stared after her, Clarice's warning ringing in her head. As she sank back into the chair and burst into tears, she wept not for the lack of love from her mother, but for all she and Clarice had lost.

Clarice had shut herself away in her bedroom so she wouldn't see Lorelei going back and forth with suitcases and boxes. But even the solid old door couldn't smother the sound of her footsteps on the landing, the click of her door, the opening and shutting of drawers, and Clarice found she was listening to every movement – waiting for that awful moment when the house fell silent and she was abandoned.

Almost an hour had passed when she heard the light footsteps going down the stairs. She opened her door a crack and listened. Lorelei was ordering a taxi, saying goodbye to the dog and collecting the last of her things from the drawing room. Clarice's regrets were legion. She hadn't meant things to go so far – hadn't wanted to banish or disinherit her, just protect her.

'Protect yourself, you mean,' she muttered crossly, 'and your pride. God forbid I should damage that.' Yet the twin necessities of pride and reputation had been instilled in her since birth. They were all she had left – the things she had fought so hard to keep when it seemed the world was against her. But were they worthy of the sacrifice she was making?

She took a deep breath and banished the doubts. 'The sins of the older generations lie heavy on the young,' she murmured, 'and Lorelei cannot understand that unless she discovers it for herself. Perhaps I have protected her too well, but unwisely.'

Clarice's soft words echoed in the silent room. Lorelei had proved over the past weeks that she was strong enough to follow her own path in life and overcome whatever lay ahead. It was time to let her go. But oh, how it hurt. How lonely this old house would be without her laughter and youthful company.

She blinked away the tears – they were for the weak and solved nothing. She moved silently along the landing and forced herself to peek into Lorelei's room. The dressing table was cleared, the bed stripped of all but the eiderdown, and a stack of boxes was piled in a corner. The wardrobe door stood ajar, and she could see the empty hangers and shelves. It didn't take long to erase the essence of the person who had lived there for sixteen years, but the memory of her perfume lingered – as if awaiting her return.

Clarice closed the door and continued her battle to regain the stalwart strength she had learnt to call upon in such times. She had to believe Lorelei would return – and even if that home-coming was marred by the girl's new-found knowledge, Clarice would welcome her and try to put things right between them.

The guest bedroom at the front of the house was ghostly in the gathering dusk, with dust sheets draped over the furniture, but it had deeply set mullioned windows, and a clear view of the drive.

Clarice tweaked the curtains just enough to watch the taxi arrive, its tyres crunching the gravel as it approached the front door. She watched as the driver placed the cases into the trunk and opened the door – and drew sharply back as Lorelei looked up. She didn't want the girl to see her.

As the taxi spluttered down the driveway Lorelei turned and looked out of the back window. Her face was pale in that halo of beautiful hair, her eyes as wide as a startled fawn's. Clarice would hold that image of Lorelei in her heart until she returned.

Tears rolled unchecked down her face as the taxi drove through the gates and out of sight. She had loved and lost many times throughout her life, and had never known the joy of motherhood. And yet now she was experiencing the agony of losing a beloved child – and discovering it was the hardest loss of all.

4

Joe stood on the quayside and watched as the SS *Rotomahana* steamed in and dropped anchor. She was a regular visitor to Tasmania, carrying cargo and mail and a few passengers over the Bass Strait from Melbourne twice a week.

'D'you reckon she'll be coming with her horses, Joe?'

'Reckon she might,' he murmured. He glanced at the youth by his side and hid a smile. Bob Fuller was seventeen and in the throes of first love.

Bob dug a comb from the back pocket of his moleskins and tried to tame his wild hair. It didn't make much difference, but he smiled with satisfaction, tucked the comb into his pocket and carefully replaced his broad-brimmed hat. 'She's a dinkum sheila, and no mistake.' He sighed, as he searched for her among the alighting passengers. 'But I bet she's got the blokes in Brisbane lining up.'

'She probably has,' replied Joe, 'but a girl like Eliza's too rich for our blood, mate. Better to find a good Tassy sheila that won't expect fancy dinners and expensive presents.' He saw the youth flush and knew his gentle advice had not been too welcome. Bob had met Eliza Frobisher fleetingly on her one and only visit to Galway House, but it was enough to convince the youth he was in love – hence the clean moleskins and shirt and the attention to his hair.

'Yeah, I suppose,' muttered Bob, 'but a bloke can dream, can't he?'

'Why not? It's a free country, mate,' replied Joe. 'C'mon, we've got two horses to collect.' Joe led the way up the ramp and into the darkness of the hull where the livestock was penned for the rough crossing.

'Mr Reilly? Over here.'

It took a moment to adjust to the gloom before he could see her. He crossed the distance between them in a few strides, his gaze taking in the businesslike shirt, breeches and polished riding boots. She wore no make-up today, and it was quite a shock to realise she couldn't be much older than Bob. 'G'day, Miss Frobisher.'

She shook his hand. 'Dreadful crossing – poor Moonbeam didn't like it at all.' She barely gave the lovesick Bob a glance before turning her attention to the skewbald filly which was sweating up and restless in the narrow stall. 'Perhaps your boy could walk her for a bit to calm her down while you deal with Starstruck?'

Joe nodded to Bob, who had turned the colour of beetroot. 'Take her along the towpath. That should settle her,' he said quietly.

'Rub her down first,' ordered Eliza. 'I don't want her catching a chill.'

The light of love fled from Bob's eyes as he grabbed the cloth and bent to his task. The skewbald seemed to appreciate his firm but gentle handling, and quietened as he rubbed her down, placed a blanket over her and led her to the ramp.

'Bob has handled horses most of his life,' Joe said firmly when he'd gone, 'and I'd appreciate it if you remember that in future.'

Her caressing hand stilled on Starstruck's chestnut neck, and her brown eyes widened. 'The boy looks half-witted,' she replied, 'and I was concerned for my filly.'

'Bob's got all his wits, and knows what he's doing,' Joe retorted. 'Shall I unload Starstruck?'

'Of course.' She patted the Arab's neck and stepped back as Joe put on the halter and led him out of the stall.

The thoroughbred colt stood over sixteen hands, was positively bursting with energy, and threatening to bolt after being cooped up for so long. Joe wrestled with him, got him down the ramp in one piece and held tightly to the cheek-strap and leading rein as the animal snorted and stamped.

'I hope you're not expecting my horses to travel in that.' An imperious finger was pointed at the much-patched and welded horse float hitched to the back of the truck.

'It might be old, but it's up for the job, and as I'm not planning to ride your horses back to Galway House there really isn't any alternative.'

'Oh, yes, there is,' Eliza said firmly. She turned on her heel and marched back into the hold. 'Come on, Mr Reilly. We're wasting time.'

Joe had had about enough of bossy Miss Frobisher already, and was tempted to tell her to take her blasted horses back to the mainland. With a sigh of exasperation he tied Starstruck firmly to the truck and patted his neck. 'Looks like we're both under orders, mate,' he murmured. 'I wouldn't misbehave if I were you.'

Starstruck's golden eyes regarded him knowingly as he tossed his head and bared his teeth in a horsy grin. Joe was still smiling as he went to see what alternative transport Miss Frobisher had in mind.

'It's a good thing I had the foresight to bring this,' she said, as she pulled the tarpaulin off the float with a flourish.

Joe stared in admiration. Like its owner, the float was glossy and superior, and the only time he'd seen something similar was at Carrick races, and that had been owned by a Sydney man. He walked around it, appreciating the plump new tyres, the gleaming paint and the heavily padded lining that had been fixed to the inside to protect its cargo. It was wide enough for two horses and far outclassed his.

'You'll find it easy to manoeuvre. Turns on a sixpence.' She folded her arms and glared as if daring him to argue.

He tugged his hat brim. 'Better get it hitched up then.' He grasped the tow bar, discovered the float was indeed light to handle, and soon had it firmly fixed to the truck. He assessed the arrangements, hoping the colt wouldn't kick in the sides trying to reach the filly. 'Will Starstruck play up if the filly rides with him?'

'They're both too young for that, and they're used to travelling together.'

Starstruck seemed to have decided to behave and daintily tripped up the ramp and began pulling at the net of hay Eliza had put in as Joe tied the halter ropes to the conveniently placed rings. Bob returned with the skewbald, and the filly happily joined her stable companion for breakfast.

Joe eyed his battered old float and realised it looked even more dilapidated beside its shiny new rival. Perhaps Miss Frobisher had a point after all, and he should think of buying a newer one.

'Are you going to tie ours on the back?' Bob was already hunting for some rope.

'No, he is not,' said Eliza. 'It will scratch the paint, rattle about and unsettle my horses. You'll have to leave it here.'

'Fair go, Miss Frobisher!' spluttered Bob. 'Some bludger might steal it.'

Her gaze was withering. 'I doubt *anyone* would want that heap of junk.'

Joe could see Bob was set to argue and hastily interrupted. 'I know the harbourmaster,' he said quietly. 'He'll keep an eye on it until I can get back.' He wrestled the heavy old float off the quay, parked it in the long grass by the harbourmaster's house and went in to speak to him and collect the mail.

He returned to find Eliza leaning against the truck smoking a cigarette, an overnight case at her feet, while Bob stood with his back to her, hands in pockets, staring moodily at the men unloading the *Rotomahana*. Joe's smile was wry as they clambered into the truck. At least Bob had been cured of love-sickness by a closer acquaintance with the glamourous, but tricky, Miss Frobisher. Perhaps now he could get a sensible word out of him.

The atmosphere in the truck was heated despite being winter, and Joe suspected it had more to do with the proximity of the fragrant Eliza than the weather. She was wedged between him and Bob, who was making a show of ignoring her by studying the view from the window that he'd seen a thousand times before – but Joe could tell that the boy was all too aware of the occasional brush of her arm or thigh as the truck bounced and rattled along.

The drive home took them down paved roads at first, but as they drew nearer to Galway House they had to negotiate the baked mud of the country tracks that bore the evidence of farm vehicles and mobs of sheep and cattle.

'Doesn't Tasmania have *any* decent roads?'

'Not much point,' Joe replied. 'Up to a few years ago there were no cars on the island, and even now most people get about on horseback.'

'God,' she sighed, 'how primitive.'

There was no point in arguing, so Joe concentrated on avoiding the potholes and ridges and sighed with relief as he finally turned in through the five-bar gate and headed for the stable-yard.

Eliza's critical eye examined the two horses as they were led down the ramp, then inspected their stalls and pronounced them adequate before heading for the house with her bag.

Joe kept his mouth shut, turned the animals out into the homestead paddock to spell them after the long journey and leant on the railings to watch them. They were good looking, especially the Arab, which was firm in the bone and looked as if he could run like the wind.

'I've given over the guest room to Eliza' said Molly, who'd come to stand beside him. 'She's decided to stay for the rest of the week so she can make sure her horses are settled before she catches the boat on Friday.'

Joe grimaced. 'She's a spoilt brat – barely out of the nursery, and yet she's the rudest, bossiest female I've ever had the bad luck to meet. She's already upset Bob by treating him like an idiot, and now she's got me thinking I need a new float. Bloody girl's a menace.'

Molly patted his arm. 'Never mind, son. You'll get over it.'

He was about to protest when he caught the twinkle in her eye and burst out laughing. 'Fair go, Ma, but you've got to admit she's a handful.'

'Too right she is, but she can afford to be.' Molly eyed the grazing horses. 'Nice-looking animals though,' she said. 'Concentrate on them instead of letting her get under your skin. After all, Joe, it's what her dad's paying you for.'

The next six days went surprisingly well, despite his misgivings. With so many horses in the yard, he'd bent the rules and allowed the girl to help out. Eliza was up and ready to work as the sun rose, her clothes practical, her face bare of make-up to reveal freckles across her nose. She never once mentioned the scars on Joe's face or stared at them as she'd done before, and she proved to be an excellent horsewoman when she joined him and Bob for the morning and evening ride-outs.

Joe got used to her following him around the yard as she asked endless questions, and he was impressed by the intelligent way she discussed his training programme for her young horses. He discovered that despite her often brusque manner she could be quite charming when she made the effort, and as the days had gone on, she'd even managed to bewitch Bob into running errands for her.

Yet it was with a relieved sigh that Joe waved her off on the *Rotomahana* early that Friday morning, and he hoped it would be a long time before she returned.

As he collected the post from the harbourmaster and hooked up his battered old float to the truck, he had to smile. Eliza Frobisher was a pain in the rear end, and spoilt rotten, but she and her father knew good horseflesh when they saw it. Moonbeam was a natural over the sticks, her character as sturdy as her muscled hindquarters, and he was looking forward to seeing how she did in the next point-to-point.

Starstruck had a rare quality. His heart was as big as his personality and he'd fulfilled the promise of speed and enthusiasm for competing during the ride-outs each day. If luck held and things went to plan, Galway House might have a Melbourne Cup winner in the Arab – and that was worth putting up with a dozen Eliza Frobishers.

He sat in the utility and sifted through the mail. There were the usual catalogues and programmes from the various racing committees, a couple of letters for his mother and three cheques from the owners down in Hobart. He had set them aside and was about to leave when the harbourmaster tapped on the window.

'Sorry, Joe. This came too. I hope it's not bad news.'

He eyed the brown envelope – the symbol of bad news throughout the war – the dreaded telegram no one wanted to receive – and tore it open.

Ownership confirmed. Arriving Tasmania 14th October *Rotomahana*. Please meet. Pearson.

'You all right, mate?'

Joe stared at the ruddy-faced retired sea captain and shook his head. 'Not really,' he said. 'I've just got rid of one bossy female, now it looks as if I'm about to get another.'

'I should be so lucky, mate,' he said with a broad grin. 'Bossy or not, I could do with some female company.'

Joe laughed. 'Tell you what, mate – if this one turns out as tricky as the last, I'll drop her off at your place and let you deal with her.'

His thoughts raced as he began the long journey home. Miss Pearson obviously had money, probably talked as if she had a plum in her mouth, and was no doubt a spinster of a certain age who brooked no argument. He thought about the middle-aged Pommy women who'd come to visit the Allied wounded at the Sussex hospital where he'd recuperated. They were definitely a breed apart – redoubtable, and rigidly trussed in sensible suits and shoes. They had meant well, and were very kind with their gifts of home-made jam, cakes and knitted socks, but he'd had to struggle through a minefield of strangled vowels to understand a word they said. He suspected Miss Pearson would prove to be from the same mould, and if so, he was in for a rough few weeks.

The Port of London

'I hope I've remembered everything,' said Dolly, as she slipped the lightweight coat from her shoulders.

Excitement fluttered in Lulu's stomach, and it seemed she'd been smiling ever since she'd got out of bed this morning. 'Including the kitchen sink, I shouldn't wonder,' she replied. 'You've brought enough clothes to last a year.'

She thought of her single trunk and suitcase, then glanced at the taxi behind them. Dolly's two trunks were strapped to the roof, her suitcases piled inside, which meant Freddy and Bertie had had to hire a third cab and follow in convoy.

'One can't be sure of what one will need,' explained Dolly, lighting a cigarette and filling the taxi with smoke. 'I mean, darling, what on earth does one *wear* in Tasmania?'

Lulu opened the window so she could breathe. 'Country clothes, I would guess,' she said thoughtfully. 'It's been so long since I was there, and I never really noticed.' She eyed her friend's scarlet dress and cloche hat, the fine calf gloves and shoes and the slender legs encased in silk stockings. She might not remember much, but she had a sneaking suspicion Dolly would be overdressed for Tasmania.

She ran her fingers over her own new dress and admired the way the silky blue fabric fell over her knees. The matching coat she'd folded on the seat beside her was draped from the shoulders so that it swung when she walked, and her high-heeled shoes looked very smart with their T-bar straps. There was a new-found sense of freedom in Lulu that was quite heady and, as the taxi drew to a halt in front of a vast shed that had 'Departures' written on it, she grinned at Dolly. 'Are you as excited as me?'

Dolly took her hand and squeezed it. 'Of *course*, darling. This is going to be an absolute *hoot*, and I can hardly *wait* to get on board.'

'Have you seen or heard from you know who?'

Dolly grimaced. 'I bumped into him in Harrods. Quite *ghastly*, because I was with Freddy.'

'What happened?'

'Thankfully Freddy didn't spill the beans about Australia, and we were all *frightfully* polite to one another and I managed not to shudder every time he stared at me.' She smoked her cigarette and frowned. 'I'm just so relieved I'm leaving. I don't know how much longer I could have managed to avoid him. Hopefully, by the time we get back he'll have forgotten all about me.'

'Let's hope so,' agreed Lulu as the taxi came to a halt. As they clambered out, she was transfixed by the scene before her.

The dockyards stretched in every direction and were teaming with life. Great ships were being unloaded by what appeared to be hundreds of stevedores, their shouts mingling with the raucous screech of gulls and the rattle and tramp of horses, wagons and trolleys moving over the cobbles. Sailors were busy swabbing decks and tidying ropes, or leaning idly on railings as they smoked and conversed with their counterparts on nearby vessels. Little boats scuttled busily between the ships as they delivered their cargoes and ferried passengers, and enormous cranes rose against the smoke-laden sky as they deposited tons of coal into the ships' holds.

'Come on, darling, the men will organise the luggage and pay the taxis while we find where to book in. Give me your passport.'

Lulu dragged her attention from the bustling scene, handed Dolly her passport and followed her into the cavernous departure shed. She didn't quite know what to expect, but it wasn't this endless queue that seemed to meander back and forth like a shuffling serpent towards a line of tables.

'This way,' said Dolly, confidently striding towards the end of the shed where a solitary table was manned by a young man in uniform whites. The placard on his table read 'First Class Passengers.'

'We aren't travelling first class,' hissed Lulu, tugging on her arm.

Dolly grinned and waved the tickets. 'I thought we deserved a treat.' She must have seen Lulu's stricken expression, for she hurried on. 'It's on me, darling, don't fret.'

'But I can't . . .'

'Done and dusted,' said Dolly, handing over the tickets and passports to the young officer with a coquettish smile.

'Dolly,' she muttered crossly, 'you can't do this. I'm not a poor relation. If I'd wanted to travel first class I'm perfectly capable of paying for myself.'

'Don't be stuffy, darling. Think of it as an early Christmas present.'

Lulu simmered. That was typical of Dolly, generous to a fault, but totally unaware of how demeaning that almost careless generosity could be. She would find a way of paying her for those tickets.

'There you are,' said Bertie. 'It's like searching for a needle in a haystack in here.' His glanced at the placard and frowned. 'I didn't know you were going first class.'

'Neither did I,' replied Lulu drily.

'I decided we couldn't *possibly* travel steerage,' Dolly interrupted. 'Too ghastly for words. Where's Freddy?'

'Here I am, old thing.' Freddy pushed through the scrum. 'I thought you'd gone without saying goodbye.'

'Darling Freddy, as if I would.' Dolly kissed his cheek and gently tugged his moustache. 'Silly boy.'

Bertie gave a grunt that could have been interpreted as either irritation or embarrassment and steered them through the melee and on to the quayside. 'You'll have to take one of the ferries to the *Ormonde*,' he said. 'She's over there.'

Lulu looked across the water at the ship that would be their home for the next six weeks. She was quite impressive, with twin funnels and high masts fore and aft, but as she studied her elegant lines, Lulu suffered a sudden attack of doubt. Her decision to leave had hurt so many people, and Clarice had obviously not forgiven her, for there was no sign of her on the quay.

Dolly seemed to sense her thoughts and tucked her hand around her arm. 'Probably best to say goodbye here,' she murmured. 'I don't know about you, but I hate protracted partings. One always seems to run out of things to *say*.'

'I rather think I might come with you,' piped up Freddy. 'I'm sure I could get a berth, even at this late stage.'

Dolly was clearly horrified at this suggestion. 'I'm sorry, Freddy,' she spluttered, 'but you simply can't just drop everything now you've been promoted at the bank. We'll be back before you know it.'

Bertie put a brotherly arm around the dejected Freddy's shoulders. 'Freddy knows full well it would be madness to chuck it all in, and he'll be kept far too busy in the boardroom to be off on a sea cruise.'

Freddy looked to Dolly for guidance, but it was clear he was torn. 'Are you sure you don't want me to come with you?'

Dolly gave him a hug. 'Go and play with your family's money, dear boy, and don't worry about either of us. When I get back I expect to find you looking frightfully successful.'

Lulu shook Bertie's hand as Dolly said a passionate farewell to Freddy.

Bertie's smile didn't quite warm his dark eyes. '*Bon voyage*, Lulu. Don't stay away too long – and remember, I'm expecting great things from you. Don't disappoint me.'

Lulu and Dolly were helped to clamber down into a ferry which was stacked high with luggage. It wasn't an easy thing to do in high heels, and Dolly's hat was almost whipped away by the wind that blasted across the water. Laughing and joking, they found seats and turned to wave at the men on the quayside.

As they waited for the little boat to chug away from the dock, Lulu searched the crowds for the one face she really wanted to see – but of course there was no sign of Clarice, and she had to accept her great-aunt had no intention of wishing her God speed.

Clarice had tried to resist coming, but after a restless night had given in to the need. Now she sat in the back of a taxi, watching the two girls as they struggled with their silly shoes to clamber into the ferry. Lorelei looked happy enough, but she noticed how she continually searched the quay as if looking for someone, and wondered if she'd known she would be there to see her safely on her way.

What a coward she was, she thought – how weak not to get out of this taxi and let the girl know she was forgiven – loved –

missed already. But there were others to see her off who weren't afraid to show their affection. She probably wouldn't be missed.

Clarice stiffened her resolve and smiled as Lorelei laughed at something Dolly said. She looked so beautiful with her lovely hair tossed by the wind, and her blue eyes would be enhanced by the colour of her dress and shining with excitement.

The ropes were unwound from the capstans and coiled neatly on the ferry roof and, the little boat set off for the far shore with a series of defiant hoots from her stubby funnel.

The girls were waving to their friends on the quay, and for a moment Clarice lost sight of them as the men blocked her view. They moved further down the dock and Clarice leant forward, straining to keep Lorelei in view as she was carried towards the SS *Ormonde*.

All too soon the ferry was lost from sight as it rounded the *Ormonde*, and she slumped back and closed her eyes. 'Farewell, my darling girl,' she whispered. 'And God speed.'

'You all right, lady?'

She nodded at the Cockney driver and imperiously waved away his concern. 'You can take me back to the hotel now,' she said. 'I've seen enough.'

The past months had been most interesting as he'd followed Lulu Pearson around London and back down to Sussex. The newspaper cuttings of her successful exhibition and the inquest of her friend Maurice had been carefully cut out and delivered to the office, along with details of her visit to her aunt's solicitor and her reservation on the *Ormonde*. All he had to do now was write his final report and his job was done.

He stood on the quay long after the taxi had borne Clarice away, and watched as the *Ormonde* weighed anchor, his thoughts troubled. The brief to watch Lulu and send annual reports to a firm of London solicitors had never been fully explained, and until now that hadn't bothered him. He'd been grateful for the generous fees, had seen no reason to question his instructions and had fulfilled them to the letter. Now he was having doubts.

Things had moved swiftly after that first letter from Tasmania, and his years of experience as a private detective had taught him enough about human nature to know that something was amiss. Someone was manipulating Lulu Pearson – and it worried him that he had no idea who that was, or why they were doing it.

Lulu and Dolly had explored their cabin, exclaiming over the pretty bed coverings, the comfortable furniture, the neatly designed storage spaces and the huge bunches of flowers their friends had sent. Now they were bundled in their coats against the stiletto-sharp wind that knifed along the Thames as the sun sank low, sipping the champagne Lulu had ordered from the steward.

The deck was getting crowded as the time for departure drew near, and the excitement was tangible. Lulu leant on the railing as the sailors far below drew up the stairways that ran down the side of the ship, and hauled in ropes. She and Dolly had had to take off their shoes to negotiate those steps, which turned out to be quite a lark, for most of the other women had made the same mistake of wearing high heels. By the time they had reached the deck, they had laddered their stockings but made several friends.

She looked over to the docks and down the river to the open sea and the horizon beyond. 'Pinch me, Dolly. So I'll know it's real.'

Dolly laughed and gently tweaked her cheek.

The blast from the two funnels made them jump, and as the SS *Ormonde* slowly drew away from her moorings, Lulu raised her glass in silent salute to Clarice with a promise that she would return. Then she turned to Dolly, her smile wide and excited. 'Here's to friendship, to a smooth crossing . . .

'And Australia,' Dolly shouted. They clinked glasses and drank the last of the champagne as the Port of London slipped further and further behind them.

5

As August gave way to September, Clarice found that the nights were filled with a darkness that seemed to crowd and smother her. The soft groans and creaks of the old family home had always been a comfort, but they no longer brought companionship with their familiar complaints – merely a reminder she was alone but for Vera Cornish slumbering in her attic bedroom.

She lay, wide-eyed and sleepless, listening to the rattle of the water pipes, the whistle of the night air down the chimney and the sighs of the timber. It was as if the house was breathing – as if it too was unable be still. She had never believed in ghosts so was unafraid of the dark and, until now, had always appreciated her own company. Yet, as she waited for dawn's soft glow to chase the shadows into the corners, she was haunted by memories. They had come every night since Lorelei's departure. Worrying and persistent, demanding to be relived, they brought old sorrows and shame to torment her.

She closed her eyes and gave into them at last, for Lorelei would soon be landing in Australia, and that was where it had all begun.

Sydney, Australia, December 1886

Clarice had spent the past eleven months trying to avoid Lionel, but in such a small community it had proved almost impossible.

His manner towards her had been solicitous and gently teasing, his kindness that of an older brother, but she'd found herself drawn to him like a moth to flame, and she'd been thankful when he'd had to leave Sydney for several weeks on military business.

She prayed nightly for the strength to banish this terrible love she still possessed for her sister's husband – and steeled herself to remain aloof and coolly polite whenever he was near. As the months passed, it seemed her act was successful, for no one guessed at the turmoil beneath her calm exterior.

Her relationship with her sister had always been tenuous, the five-year age gap and the distance between them over the past years making them strangers. But to Clarice's delight their reunion had brought a closer understanding that she hoped would blossom into deeper friendship – and it was this bright hope she used as a shield against her wayward emotions.

Government House stood in several acres of formal gardens and overlooked Farm Cove. There was a veranda running along the eastern wall of the house, and an impressive portico had been added to the front. Clarice stood with Eunice in the shade of a tree, taking advantage of the cooling breeze that came in from the sea and channelled its way through the coves and inlets of the enormous harbour. They had come to attend the governor's birthday celebrations, and although the house was large, it had become stifling with so many people gathered in the reception rooms. 'I must say,' she said, as she eyed the impressive building, 'it is very ornate.'

Eunice glanced at it with disapproval. 'It's over-castellated, crenellated and turreted, and utterly pompous. A complete mare's nest if I ever saw one.'

Clarice smiled and dabbed the perspiration from her face. Eunice had never been afraid to speak her mind, and she had to admit, the house seemed unsure of its style and looked quite incongruous in this exotic setting. But the gardens were magnificent, with banks of brilliant flowers, lush ferns, delicate eucalyptus and soaring pines, and she never tired of visiting them. Even the birds added colour, painted as they were from a rainbow palette, and although the harsh cries of the wading ibis and the voracious gulls jarred on the ears, they couldn't completely drown the melodic notes of the songbirds.

Clarice blinked into the sun, reminded again of how very far she was from home. She reached for her sister's hand, thankful they had each other again.

Eunice returned the pressure on her fingers, perhaps understanding her thoughts and silently acknowledging the close bond they were forging.

Clarice eyed her sister, whose dark hair and eyes were enhanced by the lilac tea gown and the purple silk hat that fluttered with ribbons. She looked much younger than her years and as cool, composed and beautiful as always, and Clarice felt a pang of envy for, unlike her sister, she was suffering from the debilitating heat.

Eunice seemed aware of her discomfort. 'I see you continue to ignore my advice on appropriate clothing,' she said drily. 'You're quite red in the face, Clarry – which is most unbecoming.'

Clarice took a firmer grip of her parasol. 'It's the heat that bothers me, not my clothing,' she muttered defiantly.

Eunice raised an eyebrow. 'You wouldn't feel the heat if you didn't truss yourself up like a chicken,' she retorted.

'It isn't proper to go out in public half-dressed.' Clarice turned away and pretended to watch a swarm of seagulls squabbling above a fishing boat tacking across the harbour. It seemed she couldn't please anyone, and she was too hot and uncomfortable to have yet another argument about her attire.

'In that case, every woman in Australia is improperly dressed,' Eunice said crossly, 'but at least they aren't red in the face and fighting to survive heatstroke.' She seemed to relent and her expression softened. 'I always saw you as strong-minded and sensible, Clarry. Why do you let Algernon bully you so?'

'He doesn't bully me.'

'He tells you what to wear, who to talk to and what parties and receptions to attend,' Eunice reminded her, 'and I suspect he even takes charge of the books and newspapers you read.' She reached for Clarice's hand to show her words were kindly meant. 'I know Algernon can't be easy to live with – he's too like Papa – but you must stand up for yourself, Clarice.'

Clarice felt the awful shame of knowing how weak she must appear and how easily she'd yielded to Algernon's rules regardless of the distress and discomfort they caused her. 'You don't understand,' she said softly, dipping her chin so the hat brim shadowed her face.

'I think I do.' Eunice's brown eyes regarded her with compassion. 'You feel you have let him down by not giving him children – which is ridiculous. His first wife didn't give him any either, so it's probably his fault, not yours.'

Clarice could feel the blush rise at such intimate talk and was about to protest when Eunice rushed on.

'He's a man set in his old-fashioned ways and is finding it hard to come to terms with how we do things here. I think he feels insecure – a fish out of water, if you like – and although he maintains his air of authority in public, he is certain only of his control over his household and you. It's why he refuses to listen to advice and continues to force you to his will.'

Clarice stared at her sister, aware of the insight and common sense she had dared voice. The same thoughts had run through her own mind many a time, so why had she not heeded them before today? 'You're right,' she admitted, 'but it will not be easy to go against his wishes. I must find the right moment.'

'Don't leave it too long, Clarry, or this heat will kill you.' Eunice glanced at the approaching Algernon and snapped open her parasol. 'We will continue this discussion another time,' she said grimly.

Clarice pasted on a welcoming smile for her husband, but the fear of defying him was already making her heart thud.

It was three days after that conversation, and Clarice had dismissed her maid, not wanting her to see the agony of indecision she was going through as she stood in her bedroom and tried to gather her courage. She had taken all morning to prepare for this luncheon, and the bedroom was littered with clothes, shoes and hats.

Yet the pale blue muslin skirt felt so light with only a single petticoat beneath it, and although the matching jacket was lined and close-fitting, it hid only a thin chemise and was soft and cool against her skin. She moved about the room, revelling in the freedom of being able to breathe without the corset, and the way the muslin whispered against her bare legs. It was daring and exciting to be so liberated – but at the same time she felt naked and vulnerable.

Her glance fell on the petticoats she'd slung over a chair, to the abandoned stockings and corsets she'd left on the floor. Could she really do this? Did she have the courage to face Algernon and defy him so publicly?

'I have to,' she breathed. 'The heat is worse than ever, and I shall die if I don't.' She squared her shoulders and confronted the pier glass she'd been avoiding all morning.

Her blue eyes looked back at her with a trepidation that turned to amazement as she took in her reflection and realised she looked the same as always, despite having discarded two-thirds of her wardrobe.

Her fair hair was swept back from her face and pinned into a knot of curls on top of her head, the little straw hat placed at a jaunty angle to shield her from the sun. The neat, high-necked jacket emphasised her narrow waist just as it had when she'd worn a corset beneath it, and the bias-cut skirt still moulded to her hips before gathering at the back in a tumble of frills to reveal the lacy hem of her single petticoat. She giggled in delight. Eunice was right. She felt so cool and free – and not even Algernon could guess why.

She dabbed perfume on her wrists and neck with almost reckless abandon, and fixed the pearl studs in her ears before gathering up the frilled parasol with a flourish of bravado. Taking a deep breath, she opened the bedroom door and stepped purposefully into the passage. The distant sounds of the servants in the kitchen drifted up to her, but thankfully there was no sign of her husband. Clarice hurried down the stairs, out of the front door and down the steps to the cinder path that edged the lawn.

Mindful of her posture, and with her heart thudding, she opened the parasol and began to walk towards the arbour where they would have luncheon. The gardeners were raking the newly cut lawn, and one of the maids had emerged from the kitchen to pick herbs to garnish the fish. This would be the first test, and she steeled herself against their stares and sniggers, poised to race back to the house and dress properly.

The gardeners touched their hats in acknowledgement and, with barely a glance, carried on raking the lawn. The housemaid dipped a curtsy before continuing to cut the parsley. Clarice realised she'd been holding her breath, and as she reached the arbour, she sank gratefully into a cane chair and tried to relax. The real test was yet to come.

Eunice arrived moments later in a whisper of muslin and lace. 'You look a picture sitting there among the flowers,' she said as they embraced. She gave Clarice's waist a squeeze. 'And so free at last,' she murmured, with an approving smile.

Clarice drew back in alarm. 'You can tell?'

'Don't worry, Clarry,' she replied hastily. 'Only an embrace would give you away – and as we are not attending a ball you're quite safe.'

Clarice giggled. 'Oh, Eunice, you are a caution.' She took her hand. 'Thanks for coming early. You must have known how much I needed my big sister at my side today.'

'You can thank Gwendoline for our early arrival,' she replied drily. 'She's been pestering her father all morning because she wanted to visit your stables, and was in a positive fury because I was taking so long to get ready. I understand Algy's bought a new horse?'

Clarice's pulse jumped. She hadn't realised Lionel was back from Melbourne. Hastily gathering her wits, she nodded. 'He assures me it is of the highest breeding, and Mr Reilly seems certain it will do well at the races, but at sixteen hands and only partly broken, Sabre will be too wild for Gwendoline to ride.'

'Unfortunately my daughter will not agree – and one word of caution from me would have her more determined than ever. Let us hope Lionel can dissuade her, for he is the only one she listens to for advice.'

Clarice heard the bitter note in her sister's voice and eyed her sharply. 'Is Gwendoline proving difficult?'

Eunice bit her lip. 'Gwen has always been difficult,' she said flatly. 'She's too much like her father, and between the pair of them I am run ragged.'

'I didn't realise . . .'

Eunice shrugged and twirled her parasol. 'We have both married men who are dedicated to their careers and masculine pleasures. I learnt long ago to accept that and make the best of things.' Her expression became wistful. 'I had hoped my only child would favour me more, but it seems she's as wilful and self-ish as Lionel when it comes to getting her own way.'

Clarice saw the hurt in her sister's eyes and felt ashamed.

'You've listened to my woes, and yet I didn't even notice how unhappy you are.'

Eunice blinked against the sun. 'All women seem to share an aptitude for hiding their feelings behind a mask of manners and social etiquette. It is only when we are alone or with those closest to us that we dare admit to the truth.' She turned to Clarice, her dark eyes brimming. 'I have so longed for Gwen to love me – but it seems I have failed as a mother, and I no longer like or even understand my own child.'

'Oh, Eunice,' Clarice sighed.

'It's my own fault,' she admitted, dabbing her eyes with a handkerchief. 'I was so delighted Lionel was bewitched by his daughter that I let him spoil her. The child worships him, is blind to his faults and regards me almost as an interloper. She tolerates my presence only when he is away, but her temper tantrums leave me trembling.'

'A good smack on the bottom might cure her,' said Clarice drily.

Eunice gave a watery smile. 'Don't think I haven't resorted to that – but it only leads to days of sulking, and now she's almost thirteen, she's far too old to be smacked.'

Clarice didn't agree, but kept silent. 'Perhaps Lionel should discipline her,' she suggested gently.

'She's all smiles when he's around, so he never sees her at her worst. He refuses to believe his darling daughter can do any wrong, despite what I say,' she finished bitterly.

'It's a pity she didn't go back to London for her education,' muttered Clarice. 'That would have taught her discipline, if nothing else.'

'Lionel refused to send her away.' Eunice sat down in the shade of the arbour and took a glass of chilled lemonade. 'God,' she sighed, 'I hate this place. I wish I could go home.'

'Me too. But we are stuck here until our husbands have to leave, so we must make the best of it.' She raised her glass of lemonade and took a sip. 'At least you married for love, Eunice,' she said wistfully, 'and that must be of some comfort to you.'

Eunice drank from the crystal glass, her expression unreadable. 'I suppose it must,' she replied.

Clarice was about to question her when Lionel appeared at the end of the garden with Gwendoline clinging to his arm. He was as dashing and handsome as ever, making Clarice's pulse quicken, but because of Eunice's revelations, her gaze was drawn from him to the girl at his side. She was dressed in pink and white muslin with a fetching straw hat perched on her dark curls. She was tall and slender, and even from a distance, it was clear she was destined to be beautiful.

As Clarice watched them approach, she realised they were totally absorbed in one another, Lionel laughing at what she was saying, Gwendoline looking up at him in adoration. She experienced a pang of jealousy. No wonder Eunice felt so shut out in their company.

'Good afternoon, Aunt Clarice,' said Gwendoline, her brown curls bobbing as she curtsied. 'I've just been to visit Sabre, and Daddy says I may ride him if you give permission.' She fluttered her eyelashes, her brown eyes wide with appeal. 'Please say yes, Aunt Clarice – you know how much your approval means to me.'

Clarice noticed how the girl ignored Eunice's greeting, and was not inclined to be swayed by her overeagerness and flattery. 'You must ask Uncle Algernon for permission,' she said coolly. 'Sabre is his horse.'

The girl shrugged, continued to ignore Eunice and looked up at Lionel with a pout. 'You'll ask him, won't you, Daddy?'

'Of course, my sweet.' Lionel grinned and kissed the air above Clarice's fingers, his eyes full of laughter. 'It seems I cannot deny my daughter anything,' he said, 'even though Sabre is probably far too much to handle for such a delicate little girl.'

Clarice bit down on the sharp retort. Gwendoline might be slender, but that slight frame hid a core of steel honed from many hours on horseback. As for being a little girl . . . There was a spark of womanly wile in her eyes that was quite shocking for one not quite thirteen, and Clarice could see trouble looming. She raised an eyebrow at his preposterous statement and was saved from commenting by the arrival of Algernon with the last of their guests.

She felt strangely calm as his indifferent gaze swept over her and he introduced the finance minister and his wife. Eunice's confidences and Gwendoline's wiles had given her something far more important to worry about than the lack of corsets and petticoats.

Clarice gave up on sleep and threw the bedclothes aside. She slid her feet into her slippers and drew on the fleecy dressing gown over her nightdress. It was not quite dawn, she realised, as she drew back the curtains, but the scent of honeysuckle drifted up to her through the open window and she breathed it in with less pleasure than usual.

That day, so long ago and on the other side of the world, had been the start of her defiance of Algernon. She had never worn a corset or gloves again, except at evening receptions and balls, and had taken to reading every book and newspaper she could find – hiding them from Algernon in a bedroom drawer.

With Eunice beside her, she had attended concerts, tea parties and afternoon soirees where poets read their work or the guests were entertained by musicians. They had been small rebellions really, but they had taken a great deal of courage for one who'd been raised by a father who demanded strict adherence to his rule.

Clarice gave a wry smile. Those challenges to Algernon's control had seemed so daring back then, but the young people of today would see them as trifling, for no modern woman would put up with such male dominance. And yet she didn't envy them the independence they championed, for although it had given some of them the vote and the freedom to pursue their own careers, she suspected that this bright new world was far harder to fathom than the old one – and that the breaking down of social barriers and tradition left many women vulnerable to an uncertain future.

She pulled the dressing gown closer and shivered despite the mild dawn. Until that moment all those years ago she had never been mistress of her own destiny – there had always been a master to pave the way. She had learnt at great cost that freedom was a heady thing – that taken too lightly it could corrupt; and although none of them suspected it on that summer's day in Sydney, the dark clouds of that corruption were already gathering.

Tasmania

The September day had begun well. Tasmania's Spreyton Park racetrack was bustling with noise and colour and the owners from Hobart had seen their three-year-old filly win the open handicap and were richly rewarded for their long journey when their colt came in a surprising third in the top-class Plate Handicap.

Joe left them to their celebrations and headed for the stables, where Bob was preparing to ride Starstruck in the Maiden Plate. It would be the colt's first outing in Tasmania, and, as Bob was still an apprentice, could claim six pounds in weight.

'He's looking good,' Joe murmured, 'but he's got fair competition this afternoon, so don't give him his head too soon.' He glanced across at the handsome gelding being led from a nearby stall, and nodded a greeting to his weasel-faced trainer. 'If Holt's here, he expects to win,' he muttered, 'so keep your wits about you and watch out for his jockey. He's likely to cause mischief.'

Bob, resplendent in green, white and orange silks, gathered up the reins and tried to appear as relaxed as the other jockeys, but Joe could see he was sweating as much as the colt. 'Just do your best, mate,' he said, 'Starstruck will do the rest.'

'She ain't come then?' Bob glanced swiftly at the crowd in the enclosure, clearly disappointed at not seeing Eliza.

Joe shook his head. 'This is small beer compared to what they expect from Starstruck,' he said, 'but if he wins this, Eliza and her dad will probably come to the meeting down in Hobart.'

Bob visibly relaxed and nudged the colt into a walk. 'Catch ya later,' he said, as he headed for the starting line on the far side of the course.

Joe dug his hands in his pockets and studied the colt as Bob eased him into a gentle canter. Starstruck was moving well and had a real chance today if Bob didn't get overexcited and forget everything he knew.

'Hello, Joe.'

He turned, pulse racing at the sound of her voice. 'Penny,' he managed, 'what are you doing here?'

'I'm with Dad and Alec. We've got a filly in the next race.'

Joe noted how the sun sparked gold in her hair and eyelashes, and how her eyes seemed a deeper hazel than he remembered. He tugged his hat, glad she couldn't see the other side of his face. 'How are you?' he asked tentatively.

'Good,' she replied, 'and you? How are you coping at Galway House?'

Joe tore his gaze away and pretended to study the racetrack. Seeing her after so long wasn't as easy as he'd thought it would be. 'We've got ten horses now, with another due to arrive at the end of the month. I've had to take on two more jackaroos, and a girl to help Ma with the cooking. I seem to spend a lot of time trying to persuade the better jockeys to ride for us.'

'You shouldn't have to try too hard after today,' she murmured. 'Looks like you've got some good runners.'

'I've been lucky so far.' He glanced at her and looked away. The awkward silence lengthened between them.

'I hear you've got Lorelei Pearson's colt in training. Dad and I were surprised you wanted to do business with that family.'

Joe frowned as he looked down at her. 'How do you know Miss Pearson? She lives in England, and as far as I know, has no connection with Tasmania.'

'I've never met the woman, but she certainly has connections here – I know her mother all too well.' Her lips curled in distaste.

'Her mother lives here?'

'Unfortunately. Gwendoline Cole has a smallholding out near Poatina.'

He couldn't fail to notice the contempt in her voice and tried to put his whirling thoughts in order. 'Who is this woman, and what has she done to earn your scorn?'

Her eyes widened. 'Good God, Joe, you've lived in Tasmania all your life – don't you know anything?'

He could see the runners and riders preparing to gather at the starting line and became impatient. He didn't have time for Penny's games. 'I don't listen to gossip,' he said tersely. 'I have better things to do.'

'It's not gossip, Joe. It's hard facts, and if I had a spare week I'd list them.' She glanced over his shoulder. 'Talk of the devil,' she hissed, 'that's her, over there.'

His curiosity got the better of him and he followed her gaze to the woman standing by the railings. She was younger than he'd expected, but brassy, with glossy brown hair and a slim figure swathed in a fur coat. There was a man at her side and there was little doubt she was flirting with him, looking at him with wide eyes as he lit her cigarette, holding his hand to steady the flame, and laughing up into his face. If that was Miss Pearson's mother, then he'd made a serious error of judgement as to her age. 'Are you sure?'

Penny's gaze raked the other woman. 'No doubt about it,' she said sourly. 'All fur coat and probably no underwear, if her reputation's anything to go by. I wonder who the poor sap is she's latched on to now.' She turned back to Joe, her expression grim. 'Probably someone's husband – that's her usual target. If the daughter's anything like the mother, I'd run a mile if I was you, Joe. Gwendoline Cole is a cheat and a liar, and likes nothing better than causing trouble.'

Joe's earlier high spirits plunged as he remembered the strangeness surrounding Ocean Child's ownership and how he'd come to the yard through the mysterious Mr Carmichael. If Penny's judgement was true, then his initial suspicions were confirmed. Someone was out to make trouble. 'You seem very certain, Penny. Perhaps you should explain.'

'My sister had the misfortune to come up against her on the showjumping circuit. Gwen was in second place to Julia going into the final jump-off. She cost Julia the championships by accusing her of stealing a gold bracelet. She hadn't, of course, but the bracelet was found among Julia's tack and there was no way to disprove it.'

She tossed back her shoulder-length hair and dug her hands into the pockets of her coat. 'My sister hasn't competed since. Mud sticks, and in a small place like this there are always those who like to believe the worst.'

Joe glanced back at Gwendoline Cole. She had linked arms with her companion and they were both slightly unsteady as they weaved their way to the beer tent. It was clear it wasn't their first visit, and although Joe wasn't a prude, he didn't like to see any woman the worse for drink. 'I'm sorry about Julia,' he murmured, 'but I have no reason to believe Miss Pearson is anything like her mother.'

'I'm not saying she is,' she replied, 'but I've given you fair warning, Joe. Watch your back.'

'You make it all sound very dramatic,' he said with a lightness he didn't feel. 'Surely no one can be painted quite so black?'

'Hmph. You obviously have no idea just how devious she can be.' She cocked her head and looked up at him. 'Ask your mother, if you don't believe me.'

'Ma?' He stared at her in amazement. 'What on earth has she got to do with Gwendoline Cole?'

Penny shrugged. 'I don't really know,' she confessed, 'it was just something Dad said once, but it was about the past and I wasn't really listening. You know how he goes on.' She glanced at her watch. 'I must go. Alec will be waiting for me.'

Joe caught sight of the diamond on her finger. 'Do I take it congratulations are in order?' His voice was rough with emotion, all thoughts of Miss Pearson and her mother erased by the knowledge he had finally and irrevocably lost her.

Penny blushed and refused to meet his gaze. 'Alec and I are getting married in December,' she said softly. She put a placatory hand on his arm. 'I'm sorry, Joe.'

He swallowed, but his mouth was dry and it was painful. Alec Freeman had come home from France unscathed, and was making his name as a champion jockey. Joe and he had once shared a school desk, and he'd lost his collection of cigarette cards to him in a silly bet, but he'd never expected to lose his girl to him. 'Congratulations,' he managed. 'Alec's a bonzer bloke. I hope you'll be very happy.'

Her smile said it all as she turned to leave, and Joe felt the same deep sadness he'd suffered two years before, and wondered if he would ever get over her.

Starstruck came home a nose behind Holt's flashy gelding, and seemed very pleased with his achievement. No one could silence an exuberant Bob, who insisted upon recounting every detail of the race to whoever might listen. It was only when Joe threatened to lock him in the dunny and leave him there that he shut up.

The celebrations went on long after the last race and it was dark by the time the jackaroos had got the horses loaded into the two floats. They drove back in convoy, for in the likely event that the second truck broke down, all hands would be needed to get it going again.

Molly came to greet them as they entered the yard. She waved away the clouds of exhaust fumes and pulled a face. 'It's time you spent some money and got decent transport,' she said crossly. 'It's not as if you can't afford it.'

'I agree,' Joe said as he climbed out of the utility and stretched. 'That old boneshaker's about had it.'

'So has that float.' She sniffed. 'It looks ridiculous beside Eliza's.'

It certainly did, and Joe had already begun making enquiries about purchasing a new one. The reputation of the yard was paramount – it wasn't good business to turn up at the racetracks with dubious transport. He helped unload the horses, looked over the vehicles for any damage done by the drive and left Bob to regale the stable hands once again with the detailed account of the race he'd almost won as they settled them in for the night.

He wandered along the line of boxes as he did every evening, checking the horses and making a fuss of them by giving them an apple or a carrot. Ocean Child tossed his head in anticipation, and Joe patted his nose as the apple was snaffled from his hand. The colt would have his third race in four weeks' time, and it seemed the youngster had never been in better shape. What Miss Pearson would think of him was anyone's guess – but having talked to Penny today, and seen her mother, he dreaded her arrival.

Satisfied that all was well in the yard, he headed for the house. Molly was busy in the kitchen, and the smell of roast pork and potatoes made his mouth water. He hadn't eaten much all day and realised he was ravenous. 'When's tea?'

'In about half an hour,' she said, as she basted the joint. 'The boys will have finished in the yard by then, and no doubt sobered up as well.' She lifted lids on saucepans, tugged damp tendrils of hair from her hot face and finally sat down. 'I'll be glad when Dianne starts work tomorrow – it's all getting a bit much with so many to feed.'

Dianne lived on a neighbouring cattle station. The youngest daughter of six, she'd left school a few months before with little qualification for anything. 'She's a good kid, but not very bright,' muttered Joe. 'Are you sure she won't be more of a hindrance?'

Molly shrugged. 'She's another pair of hands. I'll soon sort her out.' She mopped her face. 'I listened to the races on the radio. Looks like Bob could turn out good, given the chance.'

'Yeah, I reckon, as long as he doesn't talk himself to death first. He's hardly stopped for breath since he dismounted.' He opened a bottle of beer for each of them. Despite the chill of the winter night, it was hot in the kitchen, and the beer slipped down nicely. 'I saw Penny today,' he said into the companionable silence.

Molly eyed him sharply across the scrubbed pine table. 'Oh yeah? How's she going?'

'She's good. Engaged to Alec Freeman.'

'That didn't take her long,' she snapped, fists clenched on the table.

He smiled and covered her hands with his own. 'Fair go, Ma. It's been almost two years, and Alec's a good bloke.'

Molly remained silent, but her thoughts were clear in her expression – she would never have made a poker player.

Joe sipped his beer and wondered how best to broach the subject of Gwendoline Cole and her relationship with Miss Pearson. 'She told me something interesting,' he began.

'Really?' Her tone was flat, her expression incurious.

'It seems our Miss Pearson has a relative here.'

Molly's interest was piqued, for she prided herself on knowing everyone within a hundred mile-radius. 'I don't recall any Pearsons,' she said thoughtfully,.'They can't be local.' She frowned as she sifted through her mental library of acquaintances. 'They must come from the south,' she said dismissively.

'Actually her mother lives just outside Poatina, and her name isn't Pearson – it's Cole. Gwendoline Cole.'

Molly froze, the drink held almost to her lips, her eyes wide with shock. She blinked and carefully placed the glass down on the table. 'Good God,' she breathed. 'I never thought I'd hear that name spoken in this house again.'

'So you do know her then? Penny said you would.'

'What can she possibly know? She wasn't even born when . . .'

Joe frowned. His mother's lips had formed a thin line, and her eyes, usually so full of laughter, were arctic. 'When what, Ma?'

'Never mind.' She shoved back her chair and folded her arms as she stared, unseeing, at the over-boiling saucepans. 'But it all suddenly makes sense,' she murmured almost to herself. 'Pearson, Bartholomew and Cole. Of course.'

'Who's Bartholomew?'

'It was that woman's maiden name before she married Ernie Cole.' Molly got to her feet, opened the range door and proceeded to prod the pork with rather more vigour than was warranted before turning her attention to the saucepans. 'Poor Ernie put up with her sluttish carrying-on far longer than anyone expected, and we all silently cheered when he drummed up the courage to leave her.'

'Where did the name Pearson come from then?'

'The baby was illegitimate; she was adopted.' Molly's expression was grim. 'I don't care how much money Miss Pearson has, or how good her colt is, I will *not* have that *bitch's* daughter in my house.'

Joe took a step back, stunned by her uncharacteristic vehemence.

'In fact,' she said, her bosom rising with ire, 'I'd rather not see her at all. She should catch the next boat home to England and leave decent people in peace.'

'But if she was adopted, she's probably very different to her mother,' Joe said with quiet reason. 'Don't you think you're being a bit harsh, judging her before she's even arrived?'

'Bad blood will out,' snapped Molly. 'Adopted or not, she's a part of Gwen Cole and I want nothing to do with her.'

Joe was becoming exasperated. 'She's arriving soon,' he said flatly. 'What am I supposed to do? Bar her from the yard?'

'You can do what you bloody like,' Molly snarled. 'Just keep her away from me!'

Joe was about to remonstrate with her when he heard the two-way radio burst into life in the hall. He stood in a quandary, unwilling to leave his mother in such a state, but anxious not to miss the call. At this time of night it was probably important.

'Well, *go* on. *Answer* the bloody thing,' Molly yelled, flicking a tea towel at him, 'and leave me to get on with this *flaming* tea.'

He eyed her warily and backed away. He had never seen his mother in such a temper, and it was quite extraordinary to behold. It was clear feelings ran deep where Gwen Cole was concerned, and Penny was not the only one to hate her – but he couldn't begin to guess the reason for his mother's reaction.

Beneath the clamour of the two-way radio's static, he could hear Molly crashing pans and plates and wondered how much of the crockery would survive the evening. Frowning, he snatched up the receiver. 'Galway House.'

'Joe Reilly?' The voice was deep, with an unmistakable Queensland twang.

'Yes. Who is this?'

'Carmichael. I was wondering if you've heard from Miss Pearson since you sent the documents to London?'

Joe gripped the receiver. It was definitely an evening for surprises, for this was the first time he'd actually spoken to the man. 'Indeed I have,' he said. 'She's confirmed ownership, and is due to arrive in Tasmania on the fourteenth of October.'

There was a long silence at the other end and Joe wondered if he'd been cut off. The line was unreliable at the best of times, the local exchange in the habit of ending calls mid-sentence when they considered people to have talked long enough. He listened to the static. 'Hello . . . ? Mr Carmichael?'

There was the faint sound of someone clearing their throat. 'That date's confirmed, is it?'

'She sent a telegram.'

'You're certain she hasn't changed her plans?'

There was a burst of static, but Joe could have sworn he'd caught an edge of wariness in the man's voice. 'Not to my knowledge,' he said curtly. 'I would have told you earlier, but you're a difficult man to contact.'

'I move around a lot. Is there anything else you need to tell me?'

Joe could still hear his mother crashing about in the kitchen and decided that while he had the elusive Carmichael on the phone, rather than discuss Ocean Child he would find out just how much he knew about Miss Pearson. 'Mr Carmichael, do you know a woman called Gwendoline Cole?'

There was another long silence from Carmichael. 'I'll contact you again, Mr Reilly. Please assure Miss Pearson that I have only *her* interests at heart.'

'But it would be better if I could call you,' said Joe. 'Will you give me a number where I can reach . . . ?' He stared at the angry buzz coming from the receiver.

'Your caller's hung up, Joe,' said Doreen, who ran the local exchange and was suspected of listening in to every call. 'Do you want to try him again?'

'Yes, Doreen, if you wouldn't mind.'

'No worries.'

There were a series of clicks and buzzes and lots of static before Doreen came back to him. 'He rang from a hotel lobby in Brisbane, Joe. The manager has no record of a Carmichael staying there, so I reckon he must have just been passing through.'

Joe wasn't surprised – Carmichael seemed determined to remain a mystery. 'Thanks, Doreen. Goodnight.'

'Goodnight, Joe, and say hello to your ma for me, will you? I'll catch up with her at the picnic races on Saturday.'

Joe disconnected the call and stood for a moment, hands in pockets, staring into space. His thoughts were in a whirl as he tried to make sense of what he'd learnt today. It was as if he'd been presented with a Pandora's box, and although he'd only been permitted a glimpse of what it contained, he was no nearer solving the conundrum. But it was clear that Carmichael had orchestrated everything, and that somehow Gwendoline Cole and her daughter were at the centre of it.

He grabbed his hat and left the house, letting the screen door crash behind him as he ran down the steps. There were too many questions and not enough answers, and as he strode across the paddocks trying to wrestle with it all, he came to the unhappy conclusion that Miss Pearson must hold the key.

He stopped walking and dug his hands in his pockets as he looked up at the night sky. The Milky Way glittered above him, a splash of a million stars against inky black. He shivered. If Miss Pearson held the key, then her arrival would open that Pandora's box. He suspected they would all be affected by the demons she freed.

6

England was having an Indian summer, and as Clarice picked blooms for the house she could feel perspiration beading her brow. Feeling slightly giddy from the heat, she picked up the trug – a small wooden basket made only in Sussex and used for carrying flowers and small gardening implements – and carried it into the shade of the magnolia tree. The blossom had long gone, but the leaves and spreading boughs provided shelter from the sun and she sank gratefully on to the garden bench.

Dabbing her face with a handkerchief, she gazed at the garden with pleasure. The gardeners had done well this summer. The hedges had been trimmed, lawns cut, beds weeded and the pond cleared. There was still work to be done on the tennis court, but as it hadn't been used since Lorelei's departure, it didn't really matter.

With just the right combination of rain and sun, the flower beds had been a riot of colour and the sweet-scented stocks had flourished. The scent seemed to fill the garden, but they couldn't overwhelm the unsettling perfume of the late roses. She eyed the perfect blood-red blooms which would never grace the inside of the house and tentatively breathed in their fragrance in the forlorn hope that time and distance had diluted the powerful memories it invoked. They had once been her favourite flower, but events in Australia had erased that pleasure, and as she sat there in the shade of the ancient magnolia tree, the scents and images of the past returned full force.

'I do not have time for frippery,' declared Algernon, his gaze fixed on the sheaf of papers before him.

Clarice stood in the doorway to his book-lined study and tamped down on her rising frustration. 'But it is Christmas Day,' she said. 'Surely your work can wait.'

He took off the spectacles and slung them on the desk with an impatient sigh. His gaze was cool as he regarded her. 'The governor has entrusted me to deal with a particularly thorny problem that must be resolved before the governing council sits again in the New Year.'

'Surely not even the governor would expect you to forgo Christmas luncheon with the family?'

'They are your family, not mine, thank God.' He picked up his glasses and began to polish them. 'My reputation and career are more important than frivolity,' he snapped. 'Both hang on the outcome of the work I'm doing, and if I'm to attain recognition for my services to Her Majesty before I retire, then my energies must be conserved wholly for my duties.'

Clarice returned his icy glare. It seemed her small rebellions against him had given her the ability to see him as he truly was – and she had little affection or respect for what she'd discovered. Algernon's ambition to be awarded a knighthood on his retirement twelve months hence had become a force that had driven a chasm between them – and where once there had been a sort of companionship, now there was only mutual disinterest. 'Then I shall attend on my own,' she said.

'Do as you like,' he muttered, as he perched the spectacles on his nose. 'Shut the door on your way out and tell the servants I am not to be disturbed.'

Clarice glared at him, but he didn't see, for he was already immersed in his papers. A sliver of her once passionate nature rose anew and made her want to scream at him, to beat him with her fists until he took notice of her – but she'd been married to him for too long and she no longer had the will, or the energy, to confront his indifference. She closed the door with a soft click and left him to the oppressive silence of a loveless house.

The short carriage ride took her through the almost deserted streets of Sydney town and into the northern suburbs, where the sea breeze lowered the temperature and offered respite. Eunice's new, two-storey home was perched on a hill that swept down to rocky cliffs and a small sandy bay. It was perfectly placed to take advantage of the cooling winds, and its many windows offered breathtaking vistas of the coastline. Shaded by trees, and surrounded with lush lawns and burgeoning flower beds, it offered a haven after the dour atmosphere she'd left behind.

As the carriage drew to a halt before the graceful wrap-around veranda, the front door opened and a maid came to take charge of the many packages she'd brought. Lionel followed her down the steps. 'You look especially lovely this morning,' he murmured as he handed Clarice down. 'Happy Christmas.'

She dipped a curtsy and avoided his gaze. 'Thank you, Lionel, and the best of the season's greetings to you too.' She had become inured to his flirtatious compliments and treated them lightly, but it was disconcerting that her pulse raced whenever his blue eyes looked into hers. 'You can let go of my hand now,' she prompted coolly.

He laughed and, instead of releasing her hand, tucked it into the crook of his arm. 'I see your husband has decided to remain at his desk, so I shall take advantage of his absence and make it my delightful duty to see that you have a splendid Christmas day.' He leant closer as they reached the entrance hall. 'There is a special gift for you in the drawing room,' he murmured, 'but you will have to be patient and wait until after luncheon to open it.'

Clarice felt a tingle of pleasure at his nearness and was warmed by his smile, but those pleasurable feelings couldn't quite banish the unhappiness of her situation. Algernon had always disliked the jollity surrounding Christmas and refused to countenance the giving and receiving of gifts. She'd had to hide the presents for Eunice and her family until this morning, and knew he would question the receipts when he came to do the monthly accounts.

Lionel drew to a halt and looked down at her, his finger gently raising her chin until she looked back at him. 'Why such a sad face, Clarry?'

She found she was mesmerised by his eyes and hastily stepped back. 'I'm not at all sad,' she protested.

The doubt was clear in his expression, but thankfully he didn't press her, and instead pointed to the chandelier above them. 'Do you know what that is?'

She eyed the plant hanging there. It had long, thick green leaves and starburst flowers of yellow and orange. 'I've seen it growing on trees,' she replied, 'so it's probably some sort of para-sitic weed.' She smiled at his astonishment. 'Algernon lent me a book on Australian botany to improve my education.'

'How very admirable of him,' he said drily. He took a step closer. 'It's mistletoe,' he said, 'and the cost of walking beneath it is a kiss.'

'Don't be silly,' she said, nervously backing away.

'I'm not being silly at all,' he replied as he advanced, 'and one has to keep the traditions going, even in the colonies.' The inten-sity in his eyes was suddenly vanquished by a boyish grin. 'It's only a bit of fun, Clarry, and what harm can there be in one little kiss?'

Clarice had a suspicion he wouldn't behave in such a manner if Algernon or Eunice were in sight. She swiftly glanced about the hall. They were alone, the sounds of the party drifting in through the doors to the garden. Looking back at him she saw his teasing smile and couldn't resist. 'One kiss, Lionel, and on the cheek. No cheating.'

'No cheating,' he promised as he bent towards her, his moustache twitching with his mischievous grin.

Clarice rose on the balls of her feet and rather unsteadily prepared to plant a hasty peck on the sweet-scented tanned flesh. She must have lost her balance, or he must have moved, for instead of his cheek beneath her lips, she felt his mouth – soft and warm, as delicate as a butterfly, it nevertheless scorched through her and stirred fires she thought long extinguished.

Almost swooning with desire, and fighting for breath, she had to force herself to push him away. 'Lionel,' she gasped, 'how dare you break your promise?'

He grinned without a shred of regret. 'I had my fingers crossed,' he said, 'so the promise didn't count.'

She decided attack was the best form of defence and plastered on her most stern expression. 'You really are the limit, Lionel. I don't know how my poor sister puts up with you.' Gathering the tatters of her pride, she marched towards the back of the house in search of the other guests. But her heart was pounding and she could still feel the touch of his lips. Lionel couldn't possibly know what a dangerous game he was playing, for his kiss had awakened something in her that must be suppressed vigorously before it could destroy her and everything she held dear.

'Of course you must attend. Get dressed immediately and stop making a fuss.'

Clarice bunched her fists. It was New Year's Eve, and she'd tried everything to avoid the party – to avoid Lionel – but it appeared Algernon was for once determined to escort her. 'I have a headache,' she said.

'Then take a powder.' He was eyeing his reflection in the mirror and straightening his bow tie.

'The powders don't work. They make me feel sick.'

He spun around and glared at her. 'Get *dressed*!' he roared. 'The governor expects us to attend, and I will *not* have you disgrace me!'

Clarice flinched but held her ground. 'There is no need to shout,' she said coldly. 'I'm sure half of Sydney does not wish to hear your temper.'

His glare remained, but his voice was lower now, and trembling with rage. 'Do as I say, woman, and be quick about it.'

Clarice knew she had no choice and left the dressing room. With angry tears almost blinding her, she marched down the corridor and slammed the bedroom door behind her with such force it made the glass rattle in the windows.

The maid leapt from the chair and nervously held out the pale yellow gown Algernon had bought her especially for the ball.

'I'll wear the red,' said Clarice.

'But the master . . .'

'The red, Freda.'

The little maid heard the determination in her voice and reluctantly pulled the gown from the cedar trunk. It was deepest rose-red silk, draped into a soft bustle held in place by a cluster of silken flowers, and with a daring décolletage that showed off her slender shoulders and still-pert bosom.

Clarice stepped into the petticoat, instructed Freda to keep the corset as loose as possible, and lifted her arms so the red silk could slide down her body. She stood impatiently as the maid fastened the tiny buttons that ran down the back of the dress, then sat before the mirror as the girl did her hair.

The effect of her temper was quite remarkable, for there was heightened colour in her cheeks and her eyes sparkled – for the first time in her life she felt beautiful. Freda had piled her fair hair into a posy of curls and pinned it in place with Algernon's mother's ruby tiara. More rubies glittered in her ears and at her throat, highlighting her pale skin, and the blush of defiance on her cheeks. Dabbing perfume on her neck and wrists, she nodded with approval.

'He's going to be ever so cross,' said Freda with a sniff.

'Good.' Clarice snatched up the gossamer shawl Lionel had given her for Christmas, glanced once more at her reflection and swept out of the room.

Algernon was pacing the hall, watch in hand, expression grim. He looked up as she approached and his face darkened. 'I thought I told you to wear the yellow.'

Clarice lifted her chin. 'I prefer red.'

'It's the colour of harlots,' he snapped.

Algernon had recently discovered religion, but she knew it was only another weapon in his armoury to attain his knighthood and refused to be cowed. 'It's the colour of roses,' she retorted, 'and as we are already late, there isn't time to discuss it.'

His brows lowered as he regarded her – then, without a word, he headed for the waiting carriage.

Clarice kept her head high and followed him. If he was determined she should attend the ball, then she was just as determined to enjoy it.

Government House, the same night

Clarice had been dancing all evening, for although Algernon had all but ignored her once he'd become immersed in tedious dialogue with another diplomat, left to her own devices she'd discovered she was in great demand.

Hot and breathless, she took another glass from the passing steward and drank thirstily. The room was a swirl of colour from the jewel-bright gowns and the scarlet uniforms, and as the orchestra continued to play enthusiastically, and the noise rose to even greater pitch, she began to feel the effects of heat, noise and rather too many glasses of champagne.

She glanced around the room. Algernon was still occupied, Eunice was dancing with Lionel, and Gwendoline, who in Clarice's opinion was far too young to even be here, was flirting outrageously with a group of young military officers. It seemed she was forgotten, but she shuddered at the thought of sitting with the dowagers and maiden aunts who were gossiping in the corner. Midnight was an hour away – it was the perfect time to get some fresh air and clear her head.

Clarice fetched her wrap and wound an unsteady path through the gathering that filled the reception rooms and spilled out into the gardens, and as she stepped through the French windows on to the veranda, she had to grasp the railing. It felt as if the veranda moved beneath her feet, and as she stood there and tried to stop her head from swimming, she gazed blearily at the garden. It looked lovely, with lanterns strung from the trees and comfortable chairs arranged to catch the refreshing breeze that came over the water, but she did wish she hadn't drunk quite so much champagne – she felt very odd.

She carefully descended the steps, acknowledging greetings and declining invitations to join the various groups who had made themselves comfortable on the lawns. She needed to be alone – to clear her head and stop the world spinning.

Unaware that a curious Gwendoline had followed her, Clarice headed for the rose garden.

It was a haven of tranquillity after the raucous bustle of the party. Lit only by the sickle moon, the deserted paths and arbours drew her in. The night air was soft and heavily perfumed, and as she walked along the deserted paths she breathed a sigh of contentment. The garden reminded her of Wealden House, of her mother's roses – the scents of home.

She came to a patch of lawn at the centre of the garden and sank down in a rather ungainly way that set off a fit of giggles. If Algernon could see her now he would be apoplectic – but she didn't care. It was good to be alone, to not worry about appearance and manners and all the other nonsense he considered so important – to just be herself.

Still giggling, and heedless of damage to her dress, she lay back on the manicured grass as if she was a child again and looked up. The stars were so bright and clear, the moon so serene, it was as if she might pluck them from the sky. She watched in wonder as a shooting star pierced the dark firmament, and tried to count the stars that swept above her in the great splash of the Milky Way.

As she lay there in the perfumed garden, her eyelids grew heavy and the sounds of the party faded further into the distance until all that was left was sweet silence.

Her dream was erotic and very real, for she could feel his lips on her neck, tracing fire at her throat and down to her breasts. His breath was warm on her skin as his teasing mouth found her nipple and she arched her back in supplication and need.

Fingers traced the line of her calf and up to the softness of her thigh. It was as if her limbs had become liquid, and she opened up to him, offering the heat and want that had built to an almost unbearable yearning. His fingers softly caressed and probed, increasing her desire, and as the tidal-wave of pleasure swept over her, she gasped at its force and was left trembling.

'That's a good girl,' he murmured. 'Now it's my turn.'

Her eyes snapped open. It wasn't a dream, and the euphoria swiftly died. Lionel's hand smothered her cry of protest, and his weight pinned her to the grass.

'Come on, Clarry,' he urged, 'you know you want to.'

She shook her head and wriggled beneath him in an attempt to throw him off as she clawed at his face.

He dodged her nails, swiftly stuffed a wad of the gossamer wrap into her mouth and captured her wrists with his strong hand. 'Stop fighting me, Clarry,' he hissed, his face twisted with lust. 'It's what you've wanted from the moment you arrived – and you will enjoy it, I promise.'

'No, please, no,' she begged through the wrap, her eyes pleading with him, her body rigid.

He was impervious to her pleas, lost in his own need as he forced her legs apart with his knees and entered her.

Clarice gasped and almost choked on the wrap. Despite her abhorrence for what was happening, her body reacted with traitorous fervour. She was still aroused and desirous – and as he plunged into her she felt her muscles clench, drawing him further in as another wave of lust threatened. She tried to fight it, but it was too strong, too demanding, and she found she was drowning in a vortex from which there was no escape.

She was left gasping for breath as he took the material from her mouth and rolled away. Every inch of her felt as if it was on fire. Her limbs trembled and her heart pounded. She had never experienced such pleasure, but as she felt the cool night air on her splayed thighs and naked breasts she shuddered with disgust. She was guilty of the worst betrayal.

Lionel was swiftly buttoning his trousers. 'We'd better get back before we're missed. It's almost midnight.'

Clarice adjusted her clothing and leapt to her feet, distressed and angry with them both – shocked by how little time had passed since she'd left the ballroom. 'How *dare* you?' she hiccupped through her tears.

His smile was unrepentant as he looked down at her. 'You've been in love with me for years,' he replied, 'and I thought it was time you learnt how a real man makes love to a woman.'

Her face burned with humiliation and her anger was stoked by it. 'Algernon is more of a real man than you'll ever be,' she hissed. 'At least he doesn't have to resort to *rape*.'

He threw back his head and laughed. 'That wasn't rape, Clarry. You enjoyed it too much.'

The sound of her hand hitting his face resounded in the quiet of the garden.

His expression hardened as he caught her wrist. 'Rape is an ugly word, Clarice, and I would advise you not to use it. You are as guilty as me regarding what happened tonight, and it is to remain our secret.' His eyes bored into her. 'Think of your sister – and the scandal it would cause. Algernon would never get his knighthood once it's revealed how his wife likes to couple out in the open.'

'You wouldn't *dare*,' she breathed. 'It would ruin your reputation just as much, and devastate Eunice.'

'Eunice is well acquainted with my little diversions,' he said blithely, 'but of course she wouldn't countenance you being one of them.' He released her wrist, his expression suddenly crafty. 'Rumour and gossip spread like wildfire here, and a single hint that the lovely Mrs Pearson is a trollop would be enough. The scandal wouldn't touch me.'

Clarice regarded him with loathing. How could she ever have loved him? How could she have spent so many wasted years yearning for a man with so few scruples? She hated Lionel for his arrogance and indifference to the pain he caused in his pursuit of self-gratification, but most of all she hated herself for her weakness and stupidity, her blindness to his true character and the ease with which he'd seduced her.

'It's probably best if we return separately,' he said, running his fingers through his hair and smoothing his moustache. 'I'll go first. You will need to tidy your hair and dress before you show yourself.' He spun on his heel, and was gone.

She stood in the pool of moonlight that shone on the trampled grass and tried to control her emotions. The night breeze had cooled, and she felt its chill, but she remained there, an alabaster statue but for the tears rolling down her face. The sky was still starlit, the moon still sailed overhead – but all she could smell was him – and the cloying scent of roses.

Clarice realised she was crying and swiftly composed herself. There had been too many tears shed for what had happened, and Lionel was not worthy of them. She adjusted the old straw hat she always wore when in the garden and coldly regarded the roses. The events of that night remained with her as sharply as ever – the shame still as strong.

She had not returned to the ballroom, but left a message for Algernon that she was unwell and leaving for home. She had maintained a stiff composure on the short drive and during the few moments it had taken to assure Freda she didn't need help to undress. But on gaining the sanctuary of her bedroom, and with the door firmly locked behind her, she'd torn off the dress and ripped it to shreds. She never wore red again.

Clarice glanced down at her hands. They were the hands of an old, tired woman. Knotted with veins and the onset of arthritis, they marked the passage of time more clearly than anything. In a way she was glad, for with age had come wisdom – but it had been hard-won, and the sacrifices it demanded still echoed today.

That night long ago should have been the end, for neither she nor Lionel spoke of it, and thankfully there was no child as a result. But neither of them could have known the terrible fate that awaited them – for Gwendoline had witnessed it all, and had waited until the optimum moment to reveal what she'd seen, thereby causing a rift that had ultimately damaged them all.

7

The log cabin was set among the trees in the valley, out of sight of the homestead and stables but within yards of the river. Joe's father had built it as a hideaway where he could tinker at leisure with old bits of machinery, cook over a campfire, drink too much beer or just doze in the shade waiting for the fish to bite. Since his death, it had been used as a repository for junk and left to moulder.

His mother had accepted that every Aussie man needed his shed and had come to enjoy the peace of having a tidy house to herself for a while. What she would think of Joe's plans for the cabin's future use was rather less certain.

Joe cleaned his hands on a rag and eyed the single room with satisfaction. He and the stable hands had spent every spare minute down here making it habitable again, and repairing the old copper boiler out the back. Now the roof was mended, the floor sanded and varnished and the shutters and screens replaced. The ancient range had been rubbed down and re-blacked, the flue cleaned out and the woodpile restocked. He'd fixed up a new dunny out the back, bought a tin bath, replaced the bed and brought fresh linen from the house, and even found a comfortable chair to put on the veranda. All he had to do now was convince his mother it was the perfect accommodation for Miss Pearson.

'So this is where you've been hiding. I suppose this means you'll be sloping off like your dad used to.'

Joe stuffed the rag in his pocket and turned to face her. 'It's not for me,' he said firmly, 'but for Miss Pearson.'

Molly folded her arms. 'Then you've wasted your time, because I've booked her in with the Gearings.'

'She's not going there, Ma.' He refused to be intimidated by her glare. 'The Gearings live too far away, she won't have any transport and this place is perfect.'

Molly's cheeks flushed with anger. 'She can borrow the ute. I don't want her on my property.'

Jack sighed in frustration. 'She's an owner, Ma. You can't keep avoiding her.'

Molly remained resolute, her plump little body almost vibrating with hostility. 'Too right I can,' she retorted. 'I don't mind accommodating the other owners up at the house – but even this shack is too close to home, and I won't have her here.'

'It's not really up to you, Ma,' he said gently. 'Dad left Galway House to me, remember? I can accommodate who I want.'

Molly bit her lip. 'Even if it means making me face someone I've spent most of my life avoiding?' There was a suspicion of tears in her eyes. 'Don't make me do that, Joe. Please.'

'Oh, Ma,' he sighed, 'I wish you'd tell me what the hell this is all about.'

'It's better to remain in ignorance,' she murmured. 'It's old history, and doesn't concern you.'

'It does when it affects my business. As for it being old history . . . if I had a penny for every time the subject of Gwen Cole has come up over the past months I'd be a rich man. It seems everyone knows her daughter's coming – and speculation on your reaction to her is rife.'

'Doreen's been listening in again,' muttered Molly. Her expression softened at last. 'I'm sorry, Joe. I know you think I'm being unreasonable, but I simply cannot risk coming face to face with that Cole woman.'

'She's unlikely to come out here for a family reunion,' he said flatly. 'I understand from all the gossip she's not exactly the doting mother.'

'You've got that right,' she snapped. 'The only thing that woman loves is herself – and making mischief.' She bit her lip. 'But I wouldn't mind betting she'll turn up to have a look at her. It has been sixteen years, and she's bound to be curious.'

Joe felt a pang of distress at the loathing in his mother's eyes. 'What did she do to make you hate her so, Ma?'

Molly took a deep breath. 'She tried to ruin your father.' She met his gaze defiantly. 'That is all I have to say on the subject, Joe, so don't push it.'

He knew his mother well enough not to probe further. He stuffed his hands in his pockets. 'Fair enough,' he said, 'but I still think you shouldn't judge the daughter before she gets here.'

Molly stood in silence as she regarded the cabin. 'It's getting late,' she muttered, 'and Tim is due any minute.'

Joe looked at his watch, frustrated by his mother's refusal to discuss anything fully and the short time left to him to persuade her otherwise. Tim Lennox was coming to check the cut on one of the horse's legs, the owners were expecting him to call after his visit and there was a mountain of paperwork to get through before the big race at the end of the month.

He watched as Molly opened the cabin door and surveyed the interior. The gossips were already having a field day, and as Friday approached it was reaching fever pitch. It was an impossible situation, worsened by his mother's obstinacy.

He was suddenly struck with an idea. 'You know, Ma,' he said carefully, 'you're letting Gwen Cole get the better of you.'

She whirled to face him. 'How exactly?'

'By refusing to accommodate her daughter, you'll prove to Gwen you still harbour the hurt she inflicted on you. And I don't think that's what you want, is it?'

Molly held his gaze as she digested this. After a prolonged silence she gave a sigh that seemed to release all the fight in her. 'No, it isn't,' she admitted. She eyed the cabin and dug her hands into her apron pockets. 'I suppose it's far enough away,' she said grudgingly.

'So Miss Pearson can stay?'

Molly nodded with obvious reluctance and without another word headed back to the house.

'I thought it was supposed to be sunny and dry in Australia,' grumbled Dolly, as they sought shelter beneath the Melbourne hotel's dripping awning.

Lulu stared miserably at the gloomy skies and the rivulets of water rushing along the gutters. It had been raining since they'd landed three days ago – not the introduction to Australia for Dolly that she'd hoped for. 'It's still only October and the start of spring,' she reasoned, 'but I'm disappointed you haven't seen Melbourne at its best. When Clarice brought me here before we caught the ship to England, it was summer, and absolutely glorious with blossom.'

They stood waiting for the taxi, their newly purchased umbrellas unfurled ready for the mad dash into the rain-soaked street. 'At least we managed to do some shopping,' said Dolly. 'Those lovely department stores in Bourke Street were utter *bliss* – and so many of them too. Quite like New York, and *most* unexpected.'

Lulu dredged up a smile. Dolly never stayed glum for long, but the endless quest for pleasure was beginning to wear her down. The weeks at sea had proved claustrophobic at times; Dolly's energy and enthusiasm for the shipboard parties, the dances and cocktails making Lulu yearn for some peace and quiet and an early night or two. She had taken to slipping away during the day with a book or her sketching materials, leaving Dolly to her flirtations, hoping the time spent apart might ease the tensions that had begun to show between them.

'Actually,' said Dolly, as she looked at the elegant Victorian buildings in the tree-lined the street, 'it's all very English, isn't it? Not at all what I imagined.'

Lulu's smile was genuine, her tone teasing. 'I bet you thought it would be flat, dry and dusty red, with kangaroos hopping about and drovers herding mobs of sheep and cattle into town?'

Dolly grinned. 'Something like that.'

Lulu laughed. 'I suspect the mobs are delivered to the markets by train now, and no self-respecting kangaroo would be seen within miles of all this traffic. But out there –' she pointed north – 'are thousands of miles of bush – and that's where you'll find them.'

'It's a pity we have so little time here,' said Dolly, her critical gaze following a fashionably dressed woman who was hurrying past. 'I would have loved to explore the bush.'

'No, you wouldn't,' teased Lulu, 'there aren't any shops, and you couldn't wear those shoes for a start.'

Dolly eyed the red leather high heels and chuckled. 'Maybe you're right.'

They fell into companionable silence, and Lulu breathed a sigh of contentment, for although the weather had been abysmal, and Dolly's behaviour less than demure, nothing could alter the fact that she was in Australia again. Melbourne had been a hazy childhood memory stirred back to life by the tan waters of the Yarra River, the rattling trams and the pale yellow sandstone and red brick of Flinders Street Station.

She and Dolly had made the most of the short time they had in Melbourne, and had visited the old jail where the notorious Ned Kelly had been hanged, seen a show at the baroque Princess Theatre, shopped in the Royal Arcade and taken a boat ride along the Yarra past acres of parkland and formal gardens. And yet, through it all, Lulu could not repress the excitement that bubbled inside her from the moment she woke each morning.

She had mentally ticked off each day until at last there were only hours to go before they sailed for Tasmania.

She looked out at the rain with a flutter of excitement. 'This time tomorrow I will be home,' she murmured.

'Let's hope it isn't raining there as well,' said Dolly with a grimace. 'I shall have webbed feet soon.'

Lulu decided it was not a good idea to comment on Tasmania's weather, for although her childhood memories were of sunshine – as are everyone's – she could also recall days of heavy rain and the freezing-cold mornings huddled over a fire as she dressed for school. Clarice had commented once that the island's single saving grace was that the climate was similar to England's and therefore unreliable. It was her only praise – and a dubious one at that.

'I say,' hissed Dolly, giving her a nudge, 'I've just seen my first cowboy.'

Lulu followed her gaze. He was ambling towards them, boots splashing in the puddles, rain dripping off his broad-brimmed hat. He had a saddle over one shoulder and a dog at his heels, and seemed cheerfully oblivious to the downpour.

'G'day, ladies,' he drawled, touching his hat, his very blue eyes taking them in as he passed.

Dolly clutched her arm. 'Now I know I'm in Australia,' she breathed, 'and if all the men in Tasmania look like that, then I'm going to love it.'

'Good grief,' breathed Lulu, as they arrived at Melbourne's Port Philip and gained the single deck of the *Rotomahana*. 'I swear it's the same ship Clarice and I were on sixteen years ago.'

'Certainly looks ancient enough, but she's rather grand, don't you think?'

Lulu took in the single funnel and the high masts that stood at bow and stern. The *Rotomahana* was the most elegant of ships despite her age, and certainly different to any other vessel in the port, and as if to prove her unique personality, she even had a bowsprit and figurehead. To the romantic Lulu it was like stepping back in time to the days of the ocean-going galleons that carried pirates, explorers and pioneers.

Their cabin proved to be small, but as comfortably furnished as the one on the *Ormonde*. Lulu pulled a warm sweater over her shirt and slacks, slipped on a soft pair of flat boots and gathered up her sketchbook and pencil. She had already filled two pads with drawings of the interesting places and people they had seen during the long journey south; now she wanted to capture the bustle and energy of the port.

'Are you coming up on deck?' she asked, tying her hair back with a scarf.

Dolly was repairing her make-up. 'I'll stay here in the warm, fix my face and get on with writing some letters.' She smiled at Lulu, who was clearly impatient to leave. 'Go on. You've been on tenterhooks all day, and it's your homecoming, not mine. I'll see you at dinner.'

Unable to mask her excitement, or her relief, Lulu hurried outside. It had finally stopped raining, and she leant on the railings to watch the stream of passengers climb the gangways as cars, cargo and livestock were loaded into the hold. The noise of the docks and the screaming gulls seemed to bring everything into sharp focus, and she opened her sketchbook.

Her pencil flew across the page, each line swiftly catching the movement on the quay and the great warehouses that loomed over the scene. It wasn't as exotic as Port Said, Singapore or Ceylon, but held a magic of its own – for this was the final leg of her long journey home.

Her pencil stilled as the ramps were drawn away with a clatter and the sailors untied the ropes. With a deep blast from her funnel, the *Rotomahana*'s engines rumbled into a roar.

Lulu's gaze was drawn to a man on the quay. He was standing apart from the bustle, his very stillness marking him out as he looked up at the ship. Lulu frowned, wondering where she'd seen him before. Then, as their eyes fleetingly met, she realised that although he didn't carry a saddle and there was no dog at his heels, he was Dolly's cowboy. 'How extraordinary,' she breathed.

He tipped his hat brim and turned away, pushing through the crowd until he was lost among a hundred others who looked the same.

Lulu came to the conclusion she was being fanciful, and swiftly forgot him as the ship laboriously drew away from the quay. The stretch of water widened as the great iron-clad steamer ploughed southward, and Lulu's pulse quickened. She loved being at sea, with the scent of salt in the air, the ever-changing colours of the water and the flotilla of gulls that hovered overhead whenever they approached land.

It was a love easily rekindled after the years of living in the heartland of Sussex where seaside visits were rare, for the solace she had found as a child in the sound of waves lapping at the shore and in the warmth of sand beneath her feet had remained with her. And soon, soon, she would see that beach again, feel the sand, smell the pine trees and wattle and dip her toes in the chill waters of the Bass Strait.

She closed her eyes against the prick of tears. The image of that beach was so clear; she prayed it hadn't changed.

The jostle of people around her made her feel rather foolish, and she opened her eyes and looked up. A break in the clouds revealed a patch of blue and the promise of sun. It was an omen, she decided. An omen that her homecoming would be all she had hoped and dreamed for.

'I'll be out when you get back,' said Molly. 'There's food in the meat safe. She can eat down at the cabin.'

'Why not up here with us?'

'I've agreed to her staying,' she replied tersely, 'but I won't have her in my home. If she needs anything, Dianne can run it down.'

Joe eyed the girl, who was pretending not to listen to this exchange as she did the washing-up. Dianne, fourteen, small, skinny, and with a lazy eye and a nose for gossip, would no doubt relay everything she heard to her gossip-hungry family. 'Miss Pearson probably won't stay long anyway,' he said evenly.

Molly shrugged and attacked the freshly laundered sheet with the flat-iron. 'Shouldn't you be on your way?' she muttered.

He looked at his watch and snatched up his hat. 'What time are you planning on getting back?'

'Late,' she replied, slamming the iron on to the range's hot-plate and picking up another. 'Dianne's in charge of tea. So you won't starve.'

Joe turned away so she wouldn't see the laughter in his eyes and hurried out to the utility. His mother was a tough nut to crack – but he could see she was beginning to struggle with her natural curiosity, and suspected it wouldn't be long before she sneaked a peek at their visitor.

As he drove along the narrow dirt tracks, his thoughts went round and round. His mother had obviously been badly hurt by the Cole woman, but as she refused to expand on why and how, he could only surmise the obvious. His dad must have had an affair with her – but had that been before or after he'd married Molly?

He grimaced as the truck jolted over the uneven ground. Gossip was rife, the long memories, harboured grudges and over-active imaginations fuelled by Doreen's eavesdropping at the exchange. That was the trouble with Tasmanians – if they didn't know the whole story, they made up the rest – and it was amazing how close to the truth they often came. His island home might be the same size as Switzerland, but the population was small and close-knit – a prime breeding ground for minding other people's business.

The track ended and the wheels hummed on the tarmac as he increased the speed. He was as guilty as the rest when it came to speculating on Miss Pearson, for although her imminent arrival had brought forth an avalanche of grievances against Gwen, it seemed no one was prepared to talk about her daughter – and that intrigued him.

'Probably because they know nothing about her,' he muttered, as he entered the outskirts of Launceston and headed for the port. 'No doubt that will change the minute they clap eyes on her.'

He parked the truck in its usual place beside the harbourmaster's cottage and turned off the engine. There was no sign of the *Rotomahana*, so he climbed down and wandered towards the shore to stretch his legs. It was a perfect spring day, with a bright sun, clear skies and crisp wind. If the weather stayed like this for the rest of the month, and there weren't any overnight frosts, then the going at Hobart would be perfect for Ocean Child.

His smile was wry as he gazed out at the sparkling water and bobbing plovers. At least the weather was welcoming, but he hoped Miss Pearson was thick-skinned enough to cope with the curiosity and hostility she was about to encounter.

There had been little sleep for either of them as the *Rotomahana* dipped and rolled through the rough seas of the Bass Strait. Lulu's wakefulness hadn't been caused by the turbulent passage or by Dolly's seasickness, but by the excitement of knowing that each dip and roll carried her closer to shore.

Dolly hadn't fared at all well, but when she eventually fell into an exhausted sleep, Lulu quickly dressed and went outside. The fresh air hit her and she breathed in great gulps of it to dispel the fetid aroma of the cabin. It was still early and she was the only passenger on deck, but the sun was already up, promising blue skies and a beautiful day. It was fitting weather for a home-coming.

She crammed her hair under a soft woollen beret, pulled her coat collar to her chin to ward off the chill wind and considered waking Dolly. The fresh air would do her good after being so sick, and the seas were running more smoothly. Yet it was a fleeting thought, and she wondered if she was being selfish by leaving Dolly to sleep so she could experience her first glimpse of Tasmania in solitary contentment.

Selfish or not, Lulu remained where she was. She didn't want to share this moment, for there on the horizon was the distinctive smudge of land she hadn't seen for sixteen years. Her heart thudded and she gripped the railing, the tears making it almost impossible to see as the *Rotomahana* ploughed southward and the smudge grew clearer.

Seabirds came to greet her with swirling white wings and mournful cries that drifted on the wind as stretches of yellow sand were revealed. Lulu drank in the sight of tiny coves and inlets sheltered by soaring bluffs of dark rock and wooded hills. She breathed in the scents of wattle, eucalyptus and pine, and watched the drift of woodsmoke coming from the chimneys of the white wooden houses that were perched on hillsides among the trees. Her gaze devoured the huddle of small towns, the piers and wharves where the fishing fleets bobbed at anchor and the vast timber-yards that smelled so sweetly of freshly cut wood. It was all so wonderfully, miraculously familiar, and she could hardly believe it was real.

But it was – it was – and her breath was a sob as the love she'd dared not express until now swelled and broke through the resistance of many years. She was home.

*

Joe watched as the ship dropped anchor and was tied up. The *Rotomahana* was due to be retired from service in a few weeks' time, and he realised he would miss her, for she was one of a kind. His gaze trawled the quay, noting many familiar faces among the farmers, shopkeepers and stockmen who were waiting there. The twice-weekly crossing from the mainland was a lifeline for the island, and a swifter, larger boat would bring greater trade in livestock and visitors.

He was feeling unaccountably nervous, and wished he was elsewhere as he leant against the bonnet of the ute and surveyed the bustling quay. He was about to refocus on the *Rotomahana*, when he caught sight of the one face he didn't expect to see. His spirits plunged. His mother had been right. Gwen Cole hadn't been able to resist taking a look at her daughter.

She was sitting behind the steering wheel of a utility parked off to one side of the quay, the smoke from her cigarette drifting out of the open window, her attention fixed on the boat. Her expression gave nothing away, and Joe wondered how she felt about her daughter's imminent arrival. Would there be a tearful reunion – or a slanging match? Or would she simply stay put and just watch? He hoped it was the latter, for he was ill-equipped to deal with catfights and tears.

He watched her light another cigarette from the butt of the first and blow smoke, her fingers rapping a tattoo on the steering wheel. It was obvious she was on edge, but was it nerves that made her restless – or something more deep-rooted?

Looking away, he realised too late that he was not the only one aware of her presence. There were muttering huddles of onlookers casting sly glances and knowing smirks across the quay. The atmosphere was electric and uncomfortable, but Gwen seemed unaware of it as she continued her scrutiny of the ship.

'G'day, mate. Looking forward to the fireworks then?' The farmer was a neighbour, his wife one of the biggest gossips in town.

Strewth, that was all he needed. 'Let's hope there aren't any,' he grumbled.

'I reckon they'll come sooner rather than later, knowing Gwen,' the farmer muttered with a knowing wink. 'The missus will be fair hopping out of her skin that she's missed this.'

Joe hoped profoundly that there wouldn't be anything to miss, and turned his attention to the alighting passengers. If he could work out which one was Miss Pearson, he might be able to whisk her away and avoid an embarrassing scene.

'I say, *do* be careful with that. Those cases are *frightfully* expensive, you know.'

The cut-glass accent was unmistakable and Joe eyed the young woman as she berated the hapless porter for dropping a piece of her luggage. He had to admit she was attractive, but she reminded him too much of Eliza, and his low spirits sank further.

'Flamin' hell,' he groaned. 'Here we go again.' He pushed away from the truck, and hurried towards her, uncomfortably aware he was the focus of attention of everyone on the quay. 'Miss Pearson?'

Hand on hip, and clearly angry, she spun to face him. 'You must be Reilly,' she snapped. '*Do* something about this chap, will you? He doesn't seem to realise how valuable those cases are, and I simply couldn't *bear* it if anything got damaged.'

Stung by her manner, he took in the wide brown eyes, flawless skin and petulant mouth. 'The name's Joe,' he said quietly, 'and I am *not* your servant.'

She stared back at him, clearly shocked by his plain speaking.

'Close your mouth, Dolly – you'll catch flies.'

Joe turned at the sound of this voice, and was robbed of speech. She was the most beautiful woman he'd ever seen, with cornflower eyes and the most glorious hair drifting about her face in swirls of spun copper and gold.

She smiled up at him as she held out her hand. 'Lorelei Pearson, but you must call me Lulu. This is my friend Dolly Carteret. Please excuse her – she isn't in the best of humour after the rough crossing. I'm guessing you're Joe Reilly?'

He realised he was staring at her like some dumb idiot in full sight of everyone on the quay and pulled himself together. 'G'day,' he managed.

'G'day, Joe.' Her blue eyes twinkled. 'If I could have my hand back . . . ?'

He dropped it like a hot coal. 'Sorry,' he muttered, red with embarrassment and flustered by their presence. He hadn't expected her to bring a friend, and the logistical problems this presented simply added to his worries. 'I'll sort out the luggage for you, and then we can get going.' He picked up two of the cases and shot a glance at Gwen Cole, who thankfully had remained in her ute. The need to escape those prying eyes was paramount, and he couldn't stack the bags on the wooden trolley fast enough.

Joe Reilly was much younger than Lulu had expected, and obviously shy – probably due to the terrible scars on his face – but his handshake had been firm, and there was honesty in his dark brown eyes she found reassuring. But she did wonder why he seemed to be in such a hurry to get their luggage stowed away.

'Such a *shame* about his face,' said Dolly. 'Reilly must have been terribly handsome once.'

'Shut up, Dolly, he'll hear you. And don't call him Reilly. Things are far less formal here and he'll take it as an insult.'

'Well, excuse *me*,' muttered Dolly petulantly. 'I didn't realise the men around here were so *sensitive*.'

'They aren't,' Lulu said on a sigh. 'They just have different ways, that's all.' She patted Dolly's arm. 'Don't worry, you'll soon get the hang of it.'

'I doubt it.' Dolly sniffed. 'How is one expected to simply *know* these things when they all look as if they've come straight off the farm?' She waved an imperious hand towards the people on the quay.

'Dolly,' Lulu snapped, 'keep your voice down, for goodness sake!' She steered her out of earshot of the clearly curious crowd. 'The class system doesn't work the same over here,' she said flatly, 'and if you make remarks like that you'll cause offence.'

Dolly's eyes widened. 'I only . . .'

Lulu took her hand, regretting her spike of temper. 'I know it's hard, but you'll soon catch on if you just keep quiet and watch how it's done,' she advised kindly. 'I had to learn the same lesson when I went to England, and if I can do it, so can you.'

'I'll try,' Dolly said reluctantly, 'but it all seems *frightfully* disorganised.' She went off to count her pieces of luggage and confirm it was all there, and undamaged.

Lulu took the opportunity to study Joe as he began to load the flatbed of the truck. The scars were cruel, but she had seen worse, and they didn't really detract from his dark brown eyes, straight nose and strong chin. His long legs were encased in moleskin trousers, the check shirt open just enough to give a glimpse of a muscled chest. Flat leather boots and the ubiquitous broad-brimmed hat completed the outfit. He was about thirty, she guessed, with the wiry strength and tanned skin of a man used to physical labour in all weathers.

As if aware of her scrutiny, he turned his head and their eyes met. His gaze was steady, almost challenging, before he dipped his chin and continued loading Dolly's luggage.

Dolly giggled and nudged her arm. 'I rather think he's taken a bit of a shine to you, Lulu, and I have to say he's a *vast* improvement on the chaps in London.'

'Don't be ridiculous,' Lulu snapped, stung that Dolly should have voiced her own thoughts. 'For goodness sake, Dolly, does every man we meet have to be ogled?' She didn't wait for an answer and headed for the utility. He was certainly handsome, and very masculine – a far cry from the chinless wonders of London's elite – but she would never admit it, especially not to Dolly.

Joe was holding the utility door open, clearly impatient to leave, but as they approached he seemed distracted, his gaze constantly flitting towards the far side of the quay.

Lulu glanced over her shoulder, curious as to what had caught his eye.

The utility truck seemed to come from nowhere. It roared towards her at great speed, the tyres screeching against the tarmac.

'Look out!'

Lulu dodged out of the way moments before the utility swerved violently off course, the tyres kicking up a hail of dust and gravel as the truck fish-tailed and fought for purchase, the metal bumper coming within inches of Lulu's legs.

She cowered in the lee of a sturdy cattle truck, blinded by the dust, heart racing, too terrified to even scream as with a final squeal of rubber the utility shot out of the dockyard and, with an angry blast from the horn, was gone.

'Strewth,' muttered Joe, as he raced to her side. 'Are you all right? Did she catch you? Are you hurt?'

Lulu blinked away her tears and looked up at him through the slowly disintegrating cloud of dust. 'I . . . I . . .'

'What is it? Where are you hurt?' His powerful arm encircled her waist with unexpected gentleness.

'I'm fine,' she managed. 'It didn't touch me, but the dust . . . it's making it hard for me to breathe.' She reached for her handbag, which she'd dropped in her panic, and quickly found her pills.

A mutter went through the crowd of onlookers as she rather shakily sat on the truck's running board.

'Show's over,' Joe shouted. 'Stand back and give her some air.'

She heard Dolly's imperious voice before she saw her, and Lulu could see the policeman she was dragging behind her as she shoved her way through the crowd. 'I don't want a fuss,' she said urgently to Joe. 'Just get me out of here.'

'But she deliberately tried to run you over,' he protested. 'Your friend's right. The police have to get involved.'

Lulu stared at him, the chill of foreboding prickling her skin. 'You saw who it was?'

He nodded and looked at the crowd, who obviously had no intention of leaving. 'We all did, isn't that right?'

There was a murmur of assent, and one or two voices were raised in condemnation. 'It's time that mad woman was locked up,' shouted one. 'Yeah, too right. She's a bloody menace,' shouted another.

Lulu was only vaguely aware of Dolly and the policeman standing beside her as she stared in horror at Joe. 'It was her, wasn't it? Gwen?'

Clearly embarrassed, he nodded.

The policeman opened his notebook and licked his pencil. 'I'll need a statement from everyone who witnessed this,' he boomed, enjoying his moment. He turned to Lorelei. 'If you're feeling well enough, miss, I'll begin with you.'

Lulu backed away. 'I won't be pressing charges,' she muttered.

'You can't mean that!' Dolly took her hand. 'She tried to kill you, Lulu. We all saw it.'

Another mutter of affirmation ran through the crowd as it edged nearer.

Lulu shook her head, her thoughts clearing as her breathing eased. 'Clarice said she was dangerous, but I didn't think she meant in that way. Maybe she was just trying to scare me,' she said, shaking the dust from her hair, 'and I must say, she succeeded. But there's no real harm done.'

'We should never have come,' said Dolly. 'Who's to say she won't try something again?'

'Forewarned is forearmed,' insisted Lulu, with rather more aplomb than she felt. 'If she tries again, I'll be ready for her.' She turned to Joe, who was frowning in consternation. 'I'm tougher than I look, Joe, but I'd appreciate it if you could get us away from this audience.'

'Come on then. I'll take you home.'

Lulu shuffled along the worn leather seat so Dolly could join her. The effect of the morning's events began to take their toll, and although her pills should have calmed her racing heart, it still beat erratically and she felt shaky and chilled. Leaning back against the cracked leather, she closed her eyes and willed her pulse to steady as Joe cranked up the starting motor, climbed in and slammed the door.

The utility smelled of horses, hay and manure, with an overriding aroma of damp dog. It reminded her of the old Labrador and the livery stables she'd left behind, and was strangely comforting. She opened her eyes, saw Dolly's nose wrinkle in distaste and prayed she would say nothing. There had been enough conflict for one day.

'Are you sure you don't need to see a doctor before we leave?'

She looked into his concerned eyes and smiled. 'Let's just get home.'

'Right then,' he said, 'if you're sure.' At her nod, he drove away from the quay.

Wedged between Dolly and Joe, Lulu became all too aware of the muscular thigh that flexed and tightened against her leg every time his foot pressed the clutch. She watched in fascination as muscle and sinew flexed beneath the tanned flesh of his arm as he turned the wheel and changed gear. It was only the interest of a sculptress, of course, but the sight was quite disturbing nevertheless. Joe seemed uncomfortable with the situation as well, she noticed with a modicum of amusement, for he kept trying to avoid contact. But it was a tight squeeze and there was nowhere to go.

'Is it terribly far? Only it smells as if something has died in here, and I'm feeling a little nauseous after that *ghastly* confrontation.' Dolly vigorously wound down the window.

'It'll take about three-quarters of an hour,' he replied, his expression unreadable. 'Sorry about the state of the ute. I meant to clean it out, but I've been busy.'

Dolly sniffed and was about to reply when Lulu nudged her in the ribs and glared her into silence. 'Have you always been a trainer, Joe?' she asked, trying desperately to lighten the mood.

'Yeah.'

'I suppose you didn't have much choice really, what with it being a family business.'

'Not really.'

'My great-aunt remembers your grandfather. Her husband used to have his horses trained by him.'

'I know.'

Joe Reilly might be handsome, but he certainly lacked the art of conversation. Lulu tried to engage him again. 'I suppose you've kept all the records?'

He nodded tersely, then seemed to remember his manners. 'We kept everything from the day Grandpa opened the yard.' His gaze flitted over her before returning to the road ahead. 'Your uncle had some good horses – but I don't reckon any of them could touch Ocean Child.'

'What's he like?' she asked eagerly. 'I can't wait to see him.'

He frowned. 'He's a little ripper,' he said, 'but you should know that. You bought him.'

Lulu shook her head. 'All the paperwork seems to confirm that, but I swear I had nothing to do with buying him.'

'But Carmichael definitely said he'd bought the colt on your instructions.'

'Then he's lying,' she said firmly, 'because I'd never heard of Carmichael before you wrote me that letter.'

Joe took the bend a little too sharply and she was thrust against him. He muttered an apology and shifted down a gear to tackle the rough country road at a slower pace. 'So Carmichael bought the Child and just gave him to you out of the blue?'

'He definitely bought the colt – the documents prove it – but was it his gift – or from someone who wants to remain anonymous?' She looked at him thoughtfully. 'Have you ever met Mr Carmichael?'

'No,' he muttered. 'The man's as difficult to pin down as fog.'

'I thought he might be,' said Lulu, 'which is why I'm here. We have a mystery on our hands, Joe, and I reckon that between us we can solve it.'

'Let's hope you're right,' Joe mumbled with little conviction. He drove the utility through the open five-bar gate and into the yard where they were greeted by the two collies. 'Welcome to Galway House,' he said, and switched off the engine.

Lulu assessed the homestead as he helped her down from the truck. It was a graceful brick house, probably built at the end of the last century, and shaded by mature trees. Verandas smothered in honeysuckle and roses gave access to both floors. Comfortable chairs beckoned from their depths, and there was smoke drifting from the chimney. It looked homely and welcoming, and the prospect of a soft bed and cool shade was enticing.

As she made a fuss of the collies she realised they were being watched. The stable hands were lounging about the yard, wide-eyed with curiosity, and she caught a glimpse of a girl's face at one of the back windows.

'That's Dianne in there. She helps out,' said Joe. 'And don't mind the men,' he added with a slow smile. 'They might look rough, but they're harmless.'

Lulu's grin and Dolly's wave were rewarded with shy smiles

and tipped hat brims before the stable hands seemed to melt away in the deep shadows of the yard, Lulu turned her attention to the horses that poked their heads out of the many stalls. 'Which one's Ocean Child?'

'He's over there in the spelling paddock.' He eyed Dolly's shoes. 'You might want to change them,' he said sagely. 'The cobbles could turn your ankle.'

'How *sweet* of you, but I've walked the length and breadth of Bond Street and Mayfair in high heels and these ankles are *not* for turning.'

Joe raised a wry eyebrow as she tottered off, and Lulu bit down on a smile. Joe would learn soon enough that no one could separate Dolly from her favourite shoes.

She joined her at the railings. The grass was high and lush, the paddock shaded by trees and verdant hills. Bellbirds were chiming, and a kookaburra chortled into raucous laughter. The scene was quintessentially Tasmanian – all she had hoped for and more – and Lulu fell deeply in love with it.

Ocean Child lifted his head from the grass and regarded them for a moment before deigning to approach. His coat gleamed copper in the morning sunlight, the beautifully forming muscles working smoothly beneath the flesh. There was a neat diamond blaze on his forehead, and his tail swished at the worrisome flies.

'Oh, Dolly,' she sighed, the tears brimming, 'he's so lovely.' She held out her hand and smiled as the velvet nose foraged in her palm.

'He's looking for an apple,' said Joe, 'but it's too early in the day. Perhaps later.'

Lulu ran her hand down the slender neck and tangled her fingers in the mane. 'He's going to be magnificent when he's fully matured. I can already see how well he's muscling up.' She swept back her hair and glanced over her shoulder at Joe. 'Is he a sprinter or a steeplechaser?'

'He's got a fair speed on him, but he likes the challenge of the sticks. He's done well in the few races he's entered, and it'll be interesting to see how he gets on at the end of the month.'

Her eyes widened in delight. 'He's racing this month?'

Joe nodded and began to explain about the class of the race and the course where it was being held when Dolly interrupted. 'This is all *frightfully* interesting, darlings, but I need to have a bath and lie down. I'm absolutely shattered.' She turned towards the homestead. 'I take it we're staying there?'

Joe cleared his throat, his face reddening. 'We thought you'd prefer to be away from the yard,' he said, his gaze firmly fixed on a distant point. 'You won't get so many flies, or be disturbed by the jackaroos mucking out at first light.' He fell silent, clearly uncomfortable. 'Your accommodation is a little more basic than the homestead, but you'll find everything you need.'

'Basic?' Dolly's eyes narrowed with suspicion. 'How basic?'

'Perhaps basic was the wrong word,' he said hastily. 'It's more of a log cabin, really.' His gaze slid to his boots. 'You might find it a little cramped though. We weren't expecting two of you,' he finished lamely.

'It sounds intriguing,' said Lulu, shooting Dolly a look of warning to keep quiet.

Dolly plastered on a brittle smile. 'I will reserve judgement until I've seen it,' she said ominously. 'Where is it exactly?'

'Down there in the bush.' He pointed towards the heavily timbered valley.

The smile faltered. 'There won't be bears or tigers or anything *dangerous* down there, will there?'

Joe shook his head, his solemnity marred by the amusement in his eyes. 'Just the occasional roo or wallaby. You might hear the Tassy devils shrieking during the night, but although they sound murderous, they won't come anywhere near you. You'll be quite safe,' he assured her.

Dolly frowned and Joe hurried to describe the fierce little creatures that were native to the island.

'What about snakes?' Lulu had vivid memories of snakes hiding in the woodpile and in the ivy that surrounded the back door of her childhood home.

'It's too cold for the snakes yet, but I've checked the place out for nests just in case. It's all clear.' Joe ushered them back into the utility, cranked the engine and, with the dogs riding pillion on the flatbed, set off across the paddock.

Lulu could see the pulse beating in his jaw and wondered what was bothering him. He'd said 'we' several times, and she had to conclude he was probably married, although there had been no mention of a wife and family. Perhaps they'd had a row – or were newly-weds. Either would explain why she and Dolly were being accommodated well away from the homestead.

She stopped worrying about Joe's domestic arrangements and enjoyed the scenery. This really was the most beautiful place, with sheltering hills, rolling paddocks and a swiftly moving river running along the deep valley. No wonder Joe had followed the family tradition and stayed here.

The utility ground to a halt and the silence was broken only by the tick of the cooling engine as she and Dolly regarded their accommodation.

'That,' said Dolly, 'is not a log cabin. It's a . . . a . . . shack, a shed . . . a hovel!'

'It's not a hovel,' he retorted.

'You sleep in it then.'

'It's certainly more basic than I expected,' said Lulu. She eyed Joe thoughtfully. 'I think it would be best if we stay in the homestead until you can find us a hotel.'

'There isn't a hotel for miles,' he spluttered, 'and my mother—'

'Your mother isn't being exiled to a shack in the woods,' snapped Dolly. 'I hardly think—'

'Dolly.' Lulu's stern tone interrupted her in full flow. 'Mrs Reilly apparently doesn't want her house filled with strangers, and it seems we have little choice.'

'What happened to the famous Australian hospitality you've been banging on about?' Dolly folded her arms and glared. 'This is hardly proving the most welcoming place, is it? First you get almost run down, and then we're expected to live in a shed. What next – a spell on the chain gang along with all the other undesirables?'

'Now you're just being silly,' snapped Lulu.

'If you'd take a minute to have a look inside, you'll find it's very comfortable,' said Joe hastily. 'Why don't you give it a go?'

Lulu heard the almost desperate plea in his voice and relented. His mother must be a complete dragon to force their guests down here. She turned to Dolly. 'I know you're not used to such basic conditions, but . . .'

'You're right. I'm not.' Dolly looked mutinous.

'Come on, Dolly.' Lulu touched her hand. 'At least have a look at the place before you condemn it.'

Dolly took a deep breath and lit a cigarette. 'All right,' she said flatly, 'but one glimpse of a spider or snake and I'm out of here.'

Joe led the way through the freshly mown grass, past the woodpile and on to the veranda, where the easy chair waited rather forlornly. He swung the door open and stepped back, his expression unreadable. 'I can get another bed, and whatever else you might need,' he said quietly.

Lulu decided to reserve judgement as she stepped into the gloom with Dolly clutching her arm. The single room smelled sweetly of freshly planed timber and was surprisingly spacious. It was spotlessly clean, with an iron bedstead made up with crisp linens, chintz curtains at the single window and a scrubbed pine table set conveniently by the unlit range. She noted the pots and pans hanging from the hooks above it, the kettle sitting on the cover of the hotplate and the cutlery and china stacked on a shelf nearby. Her spirits plummeted. She and Dolly were clearly expected to fend for themselves – they had indeed been exiled.

Dolly tenuously examined the rafters and every corner for spiders and snakes. She glanced at the pot-bellied stove with little interest, and patted the bed to test its comfort. She ran her hands over the linen and eyed the curtains, which had definitely seen better days. 'It will do for tonight, I suppose,' she said reluctantly.

Lulu linked arms with her. 'I think we might have to stay a little longer than that,' she said softly. 'Come on, Dolly, it's not so bad.'

'I'm not used to this sort of thing,' she hissed. 'Can't you make him change his mind?'

Lulu shot a glance at Joe, who was standing in the doorway as if determined to bar them from leaving. 'I don't think I can, Dolly,' she murmured. 'We'll just have to put up with it until we can find somewhere better.'

Joe cleared his throat. 'If that's settled, then I'll get your bags.'

'Just a minute,' commanded Dolly. 'Where's the bathroom?'

Lulu's spirits sank further. She had hoped that particular subject would not come up until after they had unpacked and settled in. She glanced at Joe, who shuffled his feet and looked more embarrassed than ever. 'There's probably a boiler outside to heat the water so we can fill that tub,' she explained, pointing to the vast tin bath that hung by the range. 'The other facilities will also be outside.'

Dolly's eyes widened in horror. 'You mean we have to go outside to . . . to . . . ?'

Lulu nodded and murmured in her ear, hoping Joe couldn't hear what she was saying.

Dolly sank on to the bed, her eyes sparking with fury. 'That just about puts the tin lid on it,' she snapped.

Lulu burst out laughing. 'Oh, Dolly,' she spluttered, 'you should see your face.'

'This isn't remotely funny,' Dolly shouted. 'I hate camping – could never see the point – and yet here I am forced to sleep in a shed and pee in a pot.' Her scarlet lips thinned as Lulu continued to chuckle. 'Lulu Pearson, you're stacking up a lifetime of favours, and if I survive this – which I doubt – you will be made to repay every last one.'

8

Clarice gazed through the streaming window at the October rain lashing the garden. The Indian summer had broken, and now the flowers were bedraggled, buckled beneath the weight of the downpour, their petals trampled like forgotten confetti. The distant hills were veiled in clouds and the gloomy day made her feel depressed.

She sighed and looked at the letters scattered on the table. They had arrived that morning, and she'd eagerly read them, hungry for Lorelei's news. She had described so well the places she'd seen on her journey, and had even enclosed sketches so that Clarice could share her experiences. It seemed that Lorelei had decided to remain in contact despite their terrible falling out, and Clarice was delighted, for she deeply regretted the way they had parted, and wanted only to repair the damage. There had been nothing from Australia – it was too soon – and she hoped that Lorelei's rose-tinted memories of her homeland would not be shattered by the reality.

Clarice sank into the chair by the window. It had been raining that day in Sydney, she remembered – that awful day when her world was torn apart and she lost everything that mattered.

Sydney, October 1888

Clarice had lived in fear for the first weeks of the New Year, but as time passed and there was no sign of the dreaded pregnancy, she breathed more easily. And yet she had changed. Gone was the defiance she'd so manfully struggled to attain – gone the spark of passion she'd held on to so tightly – and in their place was a haughty reserve that she wrapped around herself like a suit of armour.

She had never been good at falsehoods, and knew she didn't have the skills to withstand Algernon's probing questions, but it seemed he suspected nothing of the events of that fateful night and hadn't noticed the shift in her demeanour. In fact he appeared oblivious to everything but his work, and for that she was grateful.

Clarice avoided all but the most important social events and had become the dutiful wife. Taking charge of the servants, seeing that Algernon ate regular meals, and entertaining his tedious guests with cool grace, she'd discovered sanctuary in her metamorphosis, and welcomed it.

The hardest part was trying to avoid Eunice. It would have been impossible to face her in the first weeks – to have to sit in her company knowing the terrible secret she harboured. But as time went on, and Eunice began to question her withdrawal from society and her reluctance to visit, she'd realised she had to continue her relationship with her sister as if nothing had happened. It hadn't been easy – especially when Lionel seemed to make a point of being at home when she called.

But there were rumours that Lionel had found another distraction in the form of the young wife of a senior diplomat – and whether or not that was the reason, he began to spend more time away. Eunice never spoke of it, or confided in her sister about her husband's unfaithfulness, so Clarice was saved from having to discuss his nefarious ways. And yet she knew her sister was suffering – that she, Clarice, had become a part of that suffering – and she wished there was something she could do to ease it. But of course there wasn't, and Clarice's guilt bore down every time they were together.

The winter had been mild, but as October dawned, it brought heavy rain and a chill wind. Lionel was away, reportedly on military business in Brisbane, and Eunice had invited her for luncheon.

The delicious meal had been marred by Gwen's recalcitrant mood, but when it was over Clarice went to sit in her favourite chair so she could look at the spectacular view from the drawing-room window while she drank coffee. She drew the wrap over her shoulders as she watched the roiling sea crash to shore. It was still cold, despite the roaring fire in the hearth, for there was an easterly wind that bent the trees and blew horizontal rain past the windows.

'I'd like you to look at these and give me some advice,' said Eunice, as she picked up a catalogue.

'You don't need *her* advice,' said Gwen rudely. 'I know which dress I want.'

'It isn't appropriate, dear,' sighed Eunice. 'You're far too young for such a sophisticated style.'

'I'll be fifteen,' she snapped, 'and I will *not* turn up at my birthday party looking like this.' She flounced back in her chair and folded her arms.

Clarice regarded her coolly, unimpressed with her behaviour. Gwen's long brown hair was tied back with two white bows of ribbon, and her dress was blue with a sailor collar and deep cuffs. It fell to mid-calf, revealing thick black stockings and frilled white petticoats, and was the customary attire of every girl who had yet to make their debut.

'I never suggested you should,' said Eunice drily. 'I have chosen a perfectly good gown for you to wear on the night, which is stylish, but appropriately simple for your age. You will look lovely.'

'I'll look ridiculous,' she muttered. 'All my friends have been permitted to choose their gowns, so why can't I?'

'The décolletage is far too daring, and the style overly sophisticated for one so young. It will give entirely the wrong impression.' She looked to Clarice for support, clearly at the end of her tether with this ongoing argument.

Clarice eyed the truculent Gwen and realised she had to be handled diplomatically if there was not to be a tantrum. 'Why don't you show me the pattern?' she suggested. 'Perhaps we could find a way of adapting it that will satisfy you both.'

'It doesn't *need* adapting,' the girl said crossly. She grabbed the catalogue from her mother, riffled through the pages and slammed it back on the low table between them, making the coffee cups rattle in their saucers. 'There it is. See? It's perfect.'

Clarice looked at the photograph and shared her sister's misgivings. The catalogue was from a Paris fashion house, and proclaimed their designs to be the epitome of the current rage sweeping Europe – '*La Belle Epoque*'. The dress was cut low, the model's bosom pushed up by her corsetry and emphasised with a frilled bodice. The sleeves were fluted and highly decorated with more lace and ribbon, and the skirt swept from the tiny waist over a small padded bustle and into a layered train that was a lacy, beribboned waterfall. It was the most beautiful dress she had ever seen, and Clarice could understand why Gwen desired it – but it had been designed for a woman, not a child.

'I'm sorry, Gwen, but I agree with your mother,' she said quietly.

Gwen snatched the catalogue from her hands, her eyes glinting dangerously. 'I might have known you'd side with *her*,' she hissed.

'We both know what is appropriate, Gwen, dear,' soothed Eunice, 'and please don't be rude to your aunt. She's only trying to help.'

'Then she should mind her own business,' Gwen muttered. She returned to the chair and flicked through the pages. 'You're both too old to understand anything about today's fashions.' She met her mother's gaze belligerently. 'Those awful dresses you wear went out with the ark.'

'Gwen, behave, or I will cancel the party.'

Her laughter was scornful. 'Daddy promised me a party, and you wouldn't dare cancel it behind his back.'

'Your father left me in charge of the arrangements,' retorted Eunice. 'He will support my decision to cancel once he knows why.'

Gwen's eyes narrowed. 'He'd never do that, and you know it. Daddy made me a promise, and he would never break it.'

'Your father makes many promises,' murmured Eunice. 'He rarely keeps them.'

'He tells you what you want to hear to keep you quiet,' retorted Gwen. 'He's never lied to me or let me down – and never will.'

Clarice saw the blush in Eunice's cheeks and the capitulation in the slant of her shoulders. The girl obviously had as little respect for her mother as Lionel – and Eunice knew it. Her palm itched to slap that spiteful face as she silently urged her sister to stand up to her for once – to stop giving in to Lionel's undermining indulgences that had turned their daughter into a spoilt brat.

But Eunice had no fight left in her and remained silent.

Gwen's expression was crafty. 'He's already seen the dress and approves, and has promised to send me the material from Brisbane.' She tossed the catalogue on to the low table and leant back in her chair, the gleam of mocking humour still in her eyes as she twisted the white hair ribbon through her fingers. 'You might as well save your breath for something more worthwhile than empty threats.'

'Don't talk to your mother like that,' snapped Clarice.

'I'll talk to her any way I like,' she drawled, her fingers still twirling the ribbon.

'If you regard yourself sophisticated enough to wear such clothing, then you should address your manners,' replied Clarice, her spine rigid with contempt.

Gwen eyed her coldly. 'Since when did you take on the role of etiquette advisor?'

'I do not claim to be an expert,' said Clarice, 'but I have learnt that the way one deports oneself is vital. Society shuns those who do not conform, and it would be a pity to become alienated before you've even left the nursery.'

'I left the nursery long ago, and have no intention of being shunned by society. I'm perfectly aware of how to behave in public.'

'Then have the grace to mind your manners when you are at home,' Clarice said with a glare. 'There is no excuse for rudeness, and it is deeply unattractive.'

'I hardly think you're the right person to hand out advice. You're not exactly the social doyenne of Sydney, are you?' Her critical gaze travelled from Clarice's neat boots to the plain velvet hat. 'More the dull little housewife with aspirations of grandeur. You and that creep Algernon are perfectly suited to one another.'

'That's enough!' gasped Eunice. 'Go to your room.'

'Hmph. I don't think so.' Gwen stopped playing with the ribbon, picked up a book and flicked through the pages.

Eunice rose from her seat, grabbed the catalogue from the table and threw it into the blazing hearth. 'There,' she breathed, as she sat down again, 'it's gone. And so is your party.'

Incandescent with rage, Gwen flew out of her seat and upended the table. The scalding coffee pot landed in Eunice's lap, and she leapt from her seat with a cry of distress and pain.

Then Gwen raised her arm as if to strike Eunice, and Clarice made a grab for it. 'Stop it,' she barked. 'Stop this now.'

'Don't you touch me,' she snarled, wresting from her grasp and giving her a shove.

Clarice reacted without thinking and shoved her back.

'You bitch!' the girl spat, as she stumbled over the fallen coffee pot and sat down with a bump on the carpet. 'How dare you!'

'Pull yourself together, Gwendoline.' Eunice was holding up the folds of her sodden skirt in an attempt to keep it from touching her legs. She reached out a placating hand as Gwen scrambled to her feet. 'You're overwrought, dear, and will make yourself ill.'

She slapped it away. 'Leave me alone, you milk-sop sow,' she hissed.

Eunice paled. 'What did you say?'

'I called you a milk-sop sow! What's the matter, Mother? Have you lost your hearing?'

Eunice's hands were trembling. 'There's nothing wrong with my hearing, but I'm shocked you should use such disgusting language.'

'Why? Daddy uses it all the time.'

Eunice shook her head and took a step back, her eyes wide with horror. 'He doesn't,' she breathed.

'Oh yes, he does. I've heard him. But of course you choose to ignore it, just like you ignore everything else he does. He works so hard, and tries to please you, but your whining and pathetic nagging makes his life a misery. No wonder he has to have his mistresses.'

Eunice sank to the couch, her face ashen, the soaked skirt forgotten. 'How did you . . . ? You couldn't possibly . . .'

Clarice rushed to Eunice and put an arm around her trembling shoulders, trying to comfort her. She looked up at Gwen, who was obviously still intent on provoking a fight. 'I think you've said more than enough,' she said firmly, 'and if this is an example of your maturity, then I pity you.'

'I don't want your pity, you whey-faced trollop,' she said with deadly calm.

Clarice froze – trapped by the predatory gleam in the girl's eyes.

'Please, Gwen, stop,' sobbed Eunice.

'Why? Because I've made you cry? Tears don't work on Daddy, and they don't work on me. No wonder he prefers to spend time away – you've driven him out with your snivelling, forced him to seek comfort elsewhere.'

'I didn't drive him away,' Eunice whimpered. 'I was just not enough for him.' She lifted her tear-stained face in appeal. 'I love your father, Gwen, and thought that if I could make him see how much he's hurt me over the years, he'd stop his philandering and come back to me.' She put her face in her hands and sobbed. 'But he never did.'

There was no compassion in Gwen's face as she looked down at her mother – merely contempt. 'You stupid woman – of course he didn't. Why come home to a feeble fool who does nothing but weep and wail and behave like a doormat? Daddy's a handsome man, and women adore him. It isn't his fault they force themselves on him.'

Eunice had no answer, and Clarice felt chilled as Gwen's angry gaze swept over her before returning to Eunice.

'It's your fault Daddy spends so much time away. All you think about is yourself and what you need – you never give a thought to what I want. Well, I need him with me, and I want him to stay at home.'

'He's in the military,' sobbed Eunice. 'His work demands his absence.' She grasped Clarice's hand and leant on her shoulder. 'Please make her stop, Clarry. I can't take any more.'

Gwen watched them both with malevolence. 'You must think you're very lucky to have such a loving, *loyal* sister to depend on.'

Clarice found she couldn't breathe. Where was this going? Surely Gwen didn't know about that night in the rose garden? She was just a child – how could she?

Eunice clutched Clarice's hand. 'What do you mean?' she whispered.

Gwen wet her lips. 'Your precious sister knows what I mean.' Her gaze settled on Clarice. 'Why don't you explain? After all, you're one of the reasons Daddy has been away so much this year.'

Clarice released her hand from Eunice's grip. Her heart was pounding and her mouth was dry, but the steely reserve that she'd honed over the past months came to her rescue. 'Your spite will destroy your mother, and this has gone far enough,' she said icily. 'Stop now, Gwen, before you say something you will live to regret.'

Eunice was clearly confused as she turned to her sister. 'What are you both talking about, Clarry? Have you and Lionel had a falling-out? I don't understand.'

Clarice couldn't speak as her gaze met Gwen's.

'They haven't fallen out – far from it,' said Gwen triumphantly. 'Clarice is in love with Daddy, and has been pursuing him ever since she arrived here.'

'That's not true.' Clarice's voice rang out in the ensuing silence.

'Of course it isn't,' said Eunice without hesitation. 'I always knew she admired him, but it was just girlish hero worship.'

'Oh, it was far more than that, wasn't it, Clarice? You pursued Daddy relentlessly until he didn't know which way to turn.'

'I did not.'

'Of course she didn't,' said Eunice firmly. 'My sister would never betray me in such a way – and neither would your father.'

'Really? Then how do you explain what I saw in the rose garden at Government House on New Year's Eve?' Her malicious pleasure was clear as she paused for effect. 'You finally got what you wanted, didn't you, Clarice? I saw you and Daddy doing those disgusting things, and you were so wrapped up in each other you wouldn't have noticed if half of Sydney had been watching.'

Clarice felt as if she'd been turned to stone as she gazed into those triumphant brown eyes. And yet this was no child, despite the immature body and girlish ribbons – for she was already a consummate mischief-maker with a venomous tongue well versed in spite.

Eunice was unsteady on her feet as she rose from the chair. Her face was ashen as she faced her daughter. 'This can't be true,' she whispered. 'Please, Gwen, tell me you're lying.'

'You've only got to look at her face to know I'm telling the truth.'

Eunice turned to regard Clarice, the disbelief and bewilderment slowly dawning into wide-eyed horror.

'It wasn't how it looked,' Clarice stammered, as she got to her feet. 'I'd had too much champagne and went out to clear my head. I fell asleep, and he took advantage of me.'

Eunice's lip curled in disgust. 'You don't really expect me to believe that, do you?'

'But it's the truth,' she protested. 'I am not in love with Lionel, and we have not been conducting an affair. I never pursued him, Eunice. You have to believe me.'

'I'll never believe anything you say again,' she snapped.

'But, Eunice, she's got it all wrong. I didn't—'

'Did you have sex with my husband?' Her face was ugly with loathing, the eyes like flint.

Clarice stared at her in dumb dismay – how could she deny it? She gasped as Eunice struck her. Her head snapped back and she could taste blood on her lips.

Eunice gathered up the wrap and reticule from the chair and thrust them at her. 'Get out of my house, you lying, treacherous *trollop*. I never want to see you again.'

'But, Eunice, it wasn't my fault. I never encouraged him.' She glanced at the smirking Gwen, who was clearly enjoying the outcome of her meddling. 'Can't you see she's just making trouble? Please, Eunice, you've got to listen to my side of this and believe that I never wanted it to happen.'

'If you don't go, I shall call a manservant to throw you out.'

Clarice clutched her possessions to her chest. Her sister's coldness struck a chill in her heart. The family ties had been irrevocably broken by Gwen's vicious tongue and she could see no way of repairing them. With her tears mingling with the blood from her cut lip, she stumbled out of the house and into the rain.

Clarice blinked and returned to the present. The rain had stopped, but the skies still lowered and the light was fading from the room. She sat there in the twilight and stared into the flickering flames of the fire.

Gwen had got her revenge that day, but at a terrible cost to all involved. Lionel returned to Sydney and Eunice had little choice but to take him back. His downfall finally came a year later in a series of revelations that rocked Sydney society. He was first caught in flagrante with another man's wife, then the army discovered he'd 'borrowed' money from their funds and couldn't pay it back. The first scandal was swiftly covered up, but when he was cashiered and charged with theft, the wave of gossip could not be silenced.

Algernon's rage had been terrible to see, and she'd feared his heart would not stand the strain. He became convinced his knighthood was in jeopardy, and that his career was teetering on the edge of extinction because of the link between the families. He'd blamed her, of course, and she'd had little chance to defend herself against his ranting. But the effect of his rages paled in the light of her concern for Eunice, and although every one of her letters had been returned unopened, she continued to write to beg her forgiveness and offer love and support.

Clarice held her hands out to the flames, but their heat was not enough to take away the chill of those memories. Lionel had managed to secure a lowly office post in Brisbane – it would have been impossible for the family to return to England, for news of his disgrace would only follow them – but Eunice had not accompanied her husband. She had finally accepted the marriage was intolerable and had taken Gwen to Hobart in Tasmania. Clarice could only surmise that she had escaped to the island to find anonymity away from the claustrophobic atmosphere in Sydney.

Tasmania was sparsely populated in those days, but even so, the gossip had been rife and had soon travelled across the Bass Strait to the mainland, where Clarice had been disturbed and distressed by it.

Gwen's hatred for her mother had been stoked by the continued and hurtful silence from Lionel and her unseemly behaviour had become all too public. Eunice had shut herself away in a small house overlooking the River Derwent, and was rarely seen. But news of her frailty had Clarice at her wits' end, and she'd written daily. There had been no reply.

News of Lionel had drifted down from Brisbane to Sydney, and Clarice had not been surprised to learn that he was living openly with the daughter of an ex-convict, and had begun to gain the reputation of a reckless drunk who liked to race his horse and buggy at the country fairs. It hadn't been long before he'd been dismissed from his office post.

Algernon had been forced to retire two years later than planned, but before he was due to leave Australia he'd been awarded his knighthood. Yet he was never to fully enjoy the honour, for the tensions of the previous two years had taken their toll, and within weeks he was dead.

Clarice closed her eyes and returned to that spring of 1891. She had never loved Algernon, but his death had come as a terrible shock, and his funeral was an ordeal. She had returned to the silent, shrouded house and sat among the packing cases and dust sheets, contemplating her future. They had planned to return to England to her family home in Sussex, but the animosity between her and Eunice had not been resolved, and she'd been torn between her desire to leave Australia and her need to gain Eunice's forgiveness. With Algernon dead, she'd had important decisions to make.

The answer to what she should do next had come from Brisbane in the late summer of that year. Lionel had been killed shortly after Algernon's funeral. He'd been racing his horse and buggy whilst inebriated and the buggy had overturned. Clarice had again written to Eunice. She couldn't leave now – Eunice would need her help to get them all back to England.

But there was no reply, and as the rumours of Gwen's escalating wildness filtered through to Clarice over the following year, she began to fret for her sister's well-being. It was said the nineteen-year-old Gwen was too much like her father – that she had his appetites, and seemed determined to destroy herself and her mother in her grief at Lionel's passing.

Clarice rose slowly from the chair and took the silver-framed photograph off the piano. The sepia image was grainy and faded by the years, but as she looked at her sister's smiling face, she felt the prick of tears.

She had waited in Sydney a further two years in the hope her sister would write, and had reached the sad conclusion that Eunice would never forgive her. The arrangements had been made to sell the house and return to England, and she was doing the last of her packing when the letter she had so longed for was delivered.

Eunice's note had been brief and stilted – more of a summons than an attempt at reconciliation. But Clarice had thanked God for the chance to make amends and had swiftly changed her plans and booked passage to Tasmania.

Clarice set the photograph back on the piano and sighed. She'd had no idea then of the trouble and heartache she would experience over the coming years – for fate had yet to deal its final, devastating blow.

9

Dolly slammed the bucket down and stamped her foot. 'I *refuse* to carry any more water in. Look at my hands, Lulu – *and* I've broken a nail,' she wailed.

'If you want a bath, then you'll have to keep on carting water,' Lulu replied, out of breath after the many treks from the outside boiler.

'I will *not* live like this,' Dolly stormed.

'It will only be for a couple of days at the most,' Lulu cajoled. 'Come on, Dolly, try to see the funny side.'

The green eyes narrowed. '*You* might be used to such privations, but I'm *not*.'

Lulu's voice was dangerously calm. 'What do you mean by that?'

'You were born here, and no doubt consider living like this normal. Whereas I am used to the finer things and—'

'There's no call for you to be nasty,' she retorted. 'We're both in this, and I'm finding it just as hard, so stop behaving like a spoilt brat and look on the bright side. They could have put us in a tent.' She snatched up her sketchbook and a sweater as well as an apple from a bowl. 'I'm going for a walk. Hopefully by the time I get back you'll be in a more pleasant frame of mind.'

Dolly scowled and turned away, stubbing her toe on the iron bedstead Joe had brought down for her. With a howl of rage she grabbed the nearest thing, which happened to be the bucket, and threw it as hard as she could against the wall.

Lulu closed the door and left her to it. The stresses and strains of the long journey and the events that had marred her homecoming were beginning to tell on both of them. It was clear they couldn't put up with such conditions for long – not if their friendship was to survive.

She went down the steps and stood in the sunshine as she pondered which way to go for her walk. She needed the exercise after that sea-crossing, and a respite from Dolly's constant fault-finding, and as she didn't fancy getting lost in the bush on her first day, she set off along the riverbank, and headed back to the stables. Having the real Ocean Child to sketch was simply too tempting.

It was peaceful among the trees, with only birdsong and the chatter of the river for company. Her boots trampled pine needles and eucalyptus leaves, snapping twigs and brushing against ferns which evoked the more pleasant memories of childhood. She had been raised to the sounds of the kookaburras and bellbirds, and to the scents of wattle, pine and horses, and here, in this quiet corner of Joe's property, she could almost believe she'd returned.

The little house by the sea had been gloomy inside, she remembered, and cool even on the hottest of days. Almost surrounded by outbuildings and stables, it had sat squarely on a generous acreage which consisted of bush and paddocks. Tiny streams that had travelled from the distant mountains to reach the nearby shores of the Bass Strait laced the paddocks and kept them watered, and in the nights the hiss and crash of the sea beyond the bush acted as a lullaby.

Lulu breathed in the evocative aromas of warmed earth and freshly cut grass as she paused for a moment and looked around her. There had been no hills surrounding that childhood home, just blue smudges far into the distance – but here they reared up from the valley in undulating waves, their peaks shimmering in the afternoon heat. It was utterly beguiling to stand in this majestic place, to feel a part of it all even though she had never been here before.

With a sigh of pleasure, she gazed from the hills to the racing river. Was it heading for the sea to the very beach where she'd found sanctuary all those years ago? She loosely tied the sweater around her waist and continued walking, her thoughts leading her unwillingly into darker memories. With two bedrooms, a kitchen and sitting room, the house had been too small to escape the tensions within it, and she shivered as she recalled the scenes she'd witnessed there.

With a determined shake of her head, she dismissed them. This was not the time or the place to remember such unhappiness – to dwell on Gwen's simmering hatred. It was a time to rejoice in her homecoming – and yet she couldn't quite dismiss the suspicion that the mysterious gift of the colt was somehow linked to those darker days.

As she left the shelter of the bush she began to wish she'd worn a hat. The sun was quite strong, the extraordinary light so clear it almost dazzled her as she tramped purposefully across the clearing. But the long, upward slope had her heart thudding and the perspiration running down her back, and she had to stop to regain her breath. Sinking into the grass, she fanned her face with her sketchbook and regarded the view.

She was almost at the top, where a broad, flat stretch of land encompassed the homestead and stable-yard. Beyond the yard, and next to the home paddock, were a schooling ring and another paddock laid out with a series of jumps. No doubt that was where Ocean Child did most of his training. She leant back on her elbows and closed her eyes, revelling in the warmth of the sun on her face as a soft breeze ruffled her hair.

As her heartbeat slowed her restlessness returned. She was wasting time. Clutching her sketchbook, she slowly gained the hilltop and set off for the spelling paddock. There was no one around, so she clambered over the railings and headed for the stand of trees in the middle of the field.

Ocean Child was cropping the long grass on the far side of the paddock and looked at her inquisitively as she settled her back against a tree and opened her sketchbook. She smiled as she studied him. He was older and larger than her sculpture in England, his muscles more pronounced, but the sense of harnessed power was the same, as was the intelligence in his eyes. Her pencil poised over the clean page, the need to capture him irresistible.

Ocean Child approached slowly, his nose lifting to sniff the air at this unusual intrusion on his solitude.

Lulu kept an eye on him as her pencil flew over the page, delineating the prick of his ears, the carriage of his head and the curiosity in his eyes. She giggled in delight as the patrician nose explored her face. His whiskers were tickling, his grassy breath stirring her hair. 'Hello, boy,' she murmured. 'Do you like what you see? Are we to be friends?'

Ocean Child nudged the sketchbook and tried to take a bite out of it.

Lulu hid it behind her back and reached for the apple she'd put in her pocket. 'Don't you dare tell anyone about this,' she warned softly, 'or we'll both be in trouble.'

The colt snaffled the apple from her palm and chewed it with drooling alacrity before searching her trouser pocket for another.

'Get off.' She laughed, giving him a gentle push. 'There aren't any more.'

Ocean Child shook his head and snorted as if in disgust, then turned and resumed his grass-cropping.

Lulu watched him with interest. She had been around horses all her life, and although she'd never owned one before, she knew good breeding when she saw it. There was no doubt about it, she surmised, her gift was generous.

The colt continued to ignore her, his withers twitching as the worrisome flies buzzed and settled. Lulu retrieved her sketch pad and tried to capture his stance, the bend of his neck as he ripped at the grass and the silken ripple of his chestnut coat as it flexed over the beautifully formed muscles.

Her pencil stilled as Ocean Child raised his head, snorted and trotted towards the fence. Joe was coming through the gate, and he didn't look at all pleased to see Lulu. She closed the sketchbook with a sigh and got to her feet.

'You shouldn't be in here,' he drawled before she could say anything. 'I don't allow owners in the paddocks.'

His back was to the light, his features in shadow. Lulu shielded her eyes from the sun's glare and looked up at him. 'Perhaps you should give me a list of your rules. There seem to be a lot of them.'

He rammed his hands into his pockets and dipped his chin so she couldn't see his expression. 'There aren't that many,' he muttered, 'but this is a racing yard, and I can't have owners wandering about the place. It upsets the horses.'

'Ocean Child doesn't look the least upset,' she countered.

Joe glanced across at the colt, which had wandered off to doze in the shade. 'Maybe not,' he admitted, 'but it's a rule I won't have broken.'

'Oh dear.' She sighed. 'Are you really going to be so tiresome? I was only getting acquainted with him, you know.'

'Give in to one owner and I'll have all the rest getting in the flaming way,' he said defensively. 'If you want to get to know him, then do it on the other side of the fence, or in the yard.'

'Yes, sir.' She gave a mock salute.

He had the grace to grin shamefacedly as he scuffed the grass with the toe of his boot. 'Fair go, Lulu. A racing yard is not the place for inexperienced owners – it can be dangerous when a thoroughbred gets it into its head to throw a tantrum.'

'I know,' she said calmly, 'I've seen some nasty accidents in my time.'

He frowned. 'You're used to horses?'

'I've been around them since I could walk,' she replied, unwilling to go into further detail.

He glanced at her thoughtfully as they walked back to the gate. 'I suppose you must have,' he murmured. 'With your mother's showjumping and your uncle's horse racing.'

She turned to him as he fastened the gate, her spirits plunging. 'So, you know my mother then?'

Joe shrugged and refused to meet her gaze. 'Only by sight.'

He was clearly reluctant to discuss Gwen, which wasn't really surprising considering what had happened that morning. 'But this is a small island and everyone knows each other. Your paths must have crossed at some point.'

He was looking distinctly uncomfortable again. 'Never met her, but I've heard about her reputation for causing trouble,' he drawled.

Lulu digested this, accepting that after the incident with the truck there would be no longed-for reconciliation – and that Gwen's lack of popularity was only to be expected. Her thoughts made the natural progression and she decided to question him more closely. 'Is it usual for you to accommodate your owners down in the valley?'

'We don't have that many owners,' he said, refusing to look at her. 'I'm only just starting to get the business back on its feet.'

'But this has been a racing yard for years,' she persisted. 'Surely in your father and grandfather's day the yard would have been full.' She glanced across at the sprawling homestead. 'The house appears quite large for just you and your mother,' she said pointedly.

He reddened and scuffed the dirt. 'I don't have a wife and kids, if that's what you're suggesting,' he muttered, 'but Ma doesn't like having strangers in the house,' he muttered.

He refused to look at her, but she was determined to make him tell her the truth. 'Is it all strangers she doesn't like – or just Gwen Cole's daughter she has an objection to?'

He glanced uneasily at her from beneath the brim of his hat. 'She never really said,' he hedged.

'So,' she breathed, 'Gwen's poison is as potent as ever.' Tears pricked and she angrily blinked them away. 'I am not my mother, Joe,' she said on a trembling breath, 'and it's unfair to condemn me before I have had a chance to prove myself.'

Joe saw the tears glisten on her eyelashes and felt a pang of remorse. He'd hoped to avoid this conversation, but it had somehow sneaked up on him, and now he didn't know what to do. He hated lying – hated being put in this position. He touched her shoulder in sympathy. 'I'm sorry,' he said. 'Please don't think I had anything to do with all this.'

She shrugged his hand away. 'This is your yard,' she said with contempt. 'I'm sure you don't let your mother make *all* the rules.'

'Not usually,' he admitted shamefacedly, 'but you don't know Ma.' He glanced at her, realised she was unimpressed with this excuse and ploughed on. 'I did my best to persuade her she was being unreasonable,' he muttered, 'but when Ma gets an idea in her head, an earthquake wouldn't flamin' shift it.'

Lulu folded her arms, her expression unsympathetic.

Joe gave a deep sigh. 'There was nowhere within twenty miles for you to stay, and without transport you would have been stuck. It was my idea you settled in Dad's hideaway down by the river.'

'And she didn't object to that?'

He gave an uneasy smile. 'Let's just say she came to see it made sense.'

Her lovely blue eyes regarded him through unshed tears and tugged at his heart. 'Why did it make sense, Joe?'

There was no escape from that steady gaze. 'There's been a lot of gossip and speculation surrounding your arrival,' he said softly, 'especially about how you and Ma would get on – and what Gwen would make of it.'

She must have seen his reluctance to carry on, for she touched his arm and gave him a watery smile. 'I'm sorry you've been put in this invidious position, Joe, but you might as well tell me, because I won't stop asking until I know it all.'

He'd been afraid of that, but he soldiered on. 'Ma has a certain amount of stubborn pride,' he explained reluctantly. 'She realised that by refusing to accommodate you she was giving in to Gwen and proving the gossips right.'

'In what way?'

Joe took a deep breath. 'Ma and Gwen had a serious bust-up years ago. I have no idea what it was about,' he added hastily, 'but it was bad enough for Ma to harbour a lot of ill-will against Gwen.'

'But I'm not Gwen,' she said flatly. 'What has all this to do with me?'

Joe took a deep breath. 'She's afraid Gwen will show up here looking for you.'

Her laugh was bitter. 'Gwen's already done her best to get rid of me. I doubt she'll come all the way up from Poatina to try again, so your mother needn't worry on that score,' she retorted.

Joe shifted his feet. The hurt in her eyes belied her brave words, and was that fear trembling in her voice – or anger? He'd been shocked by Gwen's actions today, and the effects were obviously still troubling Lulu. How awful to know that her mother hated her so much she was prepared to do her harm. He wanted so badly to take her hand, to comfort and reassure her that she'd be safe at Galway House – but he didn't know how she might react, so he kept his hands firmly in his pockets.

It was as if she'd read his thoughts. 'Please don't feel sorry for me,' she said softly. 'Gwen and I loathe each other, and that will never change.'

He watched her compose herself, and saw how hard she was finding it. His admiration for this young woman soared, and he wished with all his heart that his mother could be here to see how strong she was – and how unlike Gwen.

She looked up at him and smiled. 'Changing the subject completely, does the homestead have a proper bathroom?'

He frowned, wondering where this was heading. 'It does,' he said hesitantly.

'Do you think your mother would agree to Dolly using it so she can soak in a proper tub? She's really not used to privations, and there have already been ructions.'

'It might be a bit awkward—'

'No, it won't,' she interrupted. 'I have no intention of stepping foot in your mother's house until she delivers a personal invitation, and I'm quite happy to bathe in a tin tub. I'm asking for Dolly.'

'I'll have a word with Ma when she gets back. I'm sure it will be fine . . .' he trailed off, feeling horribly embarrassed.

'Good, that's settled then.' She smiled up at him and turned away. 'I'd better go and tell Dolly the good news.' She paused in mid-stride and faced him again. 'Is there any chance of some transport? There are people and places I need to visit.'

'You can borrow one of the utes. They might look wrecks, but they're fairly reliable.'

She nodded her thanks and he watched her stride across the clearing and along the top of the hill. It wasn't long before she descended into the valley and was lost to sight. He was deep in thought as he headed for the yard, for his mother had to be made to realise that this hurtful and embarrassing situation must be brought to an immediate end.

Lulu knew he was watching her and kept her head high, her pace steady. But her heart was pounding and the tears were almost blinding her as she reached the dusty track and began the descent into the valley. On gaining the valley floor, the first sob escaped and, as she sank into the grass on the riverbank, the tears rolled freely.

The pain was one she'd thought banished long ago, and its return was more profound than ever. It was the pain of knowing her mother would never love her, that no matter how much she wished it, nothing had changed between them – and that the stigma of her birth could never be erased while prejudice was stoked by whispering tittle-tattle. Would it never be silenced? Would she ever be permitted to prove her own merit, or had she been condemned by Gwen's reputation – judged guilty of the same immorality and spite, and sentenced to a lifetime of being an outsider? Joe's mother obviously thought so, and the sheer unfairness of it all brought fresh tears.

She had struggled for years to undo the damage her mother had inflicted – had fought to walk her own path and prove she was worth something, that she could achieve recognition for her talents regardless of her background. And she had done just that when she'd escaped to England – for Clarice had loved and protected her, helped her to find the pride and belief in herself she'd so sorely lacked as a child. But she hadn't listened to Clarice's warnings, and here she was again – in Tasmania – her mother's reputation and hatred already casting poisonous clouds from which there seemed no escape.

Lulu's tears slowly died away, but far from draining her, they had somehow strengthened her resolve. As she blew her nose and looked around her, she realised time had moved on, and that the sun was on the point of sinking behind the hills. She got to her feet and took a deep breath. Dolly must never know how upset she was, for she would demand they leave – and that was not what she wanted. Mrs Reilly would no doubt love to see the back of her, but running away was not the answer.

She stuffed the handkerchief in her pocket and headed for the cabin, her determination lengthening her stride. Mrs Reilly would soon discover that despite gossip and perceived character flaws, Lulu Pearson was made of stern stuff, and that the years in England under Clarice's guardianship had imbued her with a spirit that would fight injustice to the end.

Joe had been kept busy for the rest of the afternoon and was just grooming the horses after their evening ride-out when he heard his mother's utility pull up in front of the homestead.

'Finish up here,' he said to Bob, throwing him the curry comb, 'and when you've done that, see to Ocean Child. It's going to be cold tonight, and he needs bringing in – and don't let him stuff himself with oats. You're far too lenient with him.'

Bob eyed him warily, and Joe realised he'd been sharp with the boy, but his endless questions about their visitors had set his frayed nerves on edge. He ruffled the boy's hair and smiled. 'You did good today, mate,' he said. 'Don't mind me.'

Bob's grin showed his relief. 'Reckon there's too many sheilas about the place for a bloke to keep his mind on things,' he replied.

'Too flamin' right,' Joe muttered as he headed for the house.

The dogs greeted him with fawning adoration and he distractedly made a fuss of them before leading them through the screen door and into the kitchen.

Molly was unpacking her shopping basket and restocking the pantry shelves. There was no sign of Dianne. 'You're early,' she said, as she emerged from the walk-in larder and gathered up two tins of IXL jam. 'Something up?'

'You could say that,' he growled.

Molly put down the jam and folded her arms. 'What's happened? It's not one of the horses, is it?'

Joe shook his head. 'It's you, Ma.'

'Me?' Her eyes widened. 'But what could I have done to upset you? I've been out all day.'

'Too right you have,' he said sourly. 'You made yourself scarce, and left me to deal with the flaming mess you left behind.'

Her face reddened, but she lifted her chin in defiance. 'I don't know what you mean.'

'You know very well what I'm talking about, so don't play the innocent.' He kept his voice low, but his frustration was at boiling point. 'Do you know what kind of day I've had?' He didn't wait for a reply and hurried on. 'I went to meet the boat, and there was Gwen Cole, as bold as brass in her ute.'

Molly paled and sank into a chair.

'Everyone saw her, and it was like walking on eggshells knowing they were watching me, waiting to get their first glimpse of the woman I was meeting, and relishing a showdown between them.'

'How was I to know Gwen would turn up? It was hardly my fault.' Her hands fluttered in her lap. 'As for the audience – it was only to be expected after all the gossip.'

'I suppose it was,' he admitted, 'but Gwen didn't help by trying to mow Lulu down with her ute.'

The eyes widened as she gasped. 'She didn't!'

'She got damned close to it,' he said. 'Luckily Lulu wasn't hurt – but it shook her up no end.'

Her worried expression turned to scorn. 'So it's Lulu now, is it? I might have known it wouldn't take her long to wind you around her little finger.' She paused. 'Like mother, like daughter,' she muttered.

He swallowed the sharp retort, knowing it wouldn't help. 'She's a nice lady – and I use that word purposely, because that's exactly what she is – a lady. Her friend is a bit too like Eliza, but she seems pleasant enough when she isn't putting on airs and graces.'

Molly's eyes narrowed. 'There are two of them?'

'Yes, and they're stuck down there in the valley with no proper washing facilities and no transport. How the hell can I let Dolly use our bathroom and deny it to Lulu? She already has a fair idea of what's going on, and it won't be long before they demand to be rehoused.'

'I see.' Molly studied her hands, which were knotted in her lap. She raised her head and regarded him hopefully. 'They can still go to the Gearings.'

'No, they can't,' he snapped. 'They have a right to be here. Damn it, Ma, can't you see what an impossible position you've put me in?' He took a series of deep breaths in an effort to remain calm. 'Lulu and Dolly are sophisticated, intelligent young women. We have insulted and humiliated them by putting them down there, and I will *not* let it continue.'

'What exactly does that mean?' Her whole posture was confrontational.

'They will move in here,' he said firmly, 'and be treated with respect and good old-fashioned Tasmanian hospitality, just like all our other owners.'

'I won't have it.'

'It's not up to you.'

'Then I'll move in with Doreen,' she said defiantly.

His bark of laughter rang out. 'Doreen would love that – she'd spread that tasty morsel the length and breadth of Tasmania in less than ten minutes.' He sat opposite her, his voice low and conciliatory. 'There's been enough gossip already, Ma. Don't make it worse.'

Her gaze dropped to her hands, now clasped on the table. 'There won't be room for all of us,' she said quietly, 'Eliza's due to arrive soon.'

'I'll clear out all the junk from the smallest bedroom. She can sleep in there.'

'She's used to the big room. She won't like it.'

'Then she'll have to go down to Dad's shed.'

'You can't put her . . .' She bit her lip, realising she'd fallen into his trap.

'Exactly my point,' he replied. 'If it's not good enough for Eliza, it's certainly not good enough for anyone else.'

Molly remained silent as the clock ticked, the dogs snored beneath the table and Dianne slipped into the room almost unnoticed. Molly finally looked back at him, her demeanour defeated. 'What do you make of her, Joe?'

He thought for a moment, not wanting to say the wrong thing now it looked as if he had his mother onside. 'She's tall and thin and speaks with a real Pommy accent. I'd guess she's been well educated, and by the look of her clothes, she isn't poor. She knows about horses though, and has already made friends with the Child.'

Her gaze was discerning. 'You like her, don't you?'

He nodded. 'She's a dinkum sheila and no mistake, and I reckon you'll find she's nothing like Gwen.'

'She's still her daughter,' she said with a flash of defiance, 'and blood will out, mark my words.'

Joe sighed and took her hands. 'At least give her a go, Ma.'

Molly's prolonged silence had him on edge before she squeezed his fingers and pulled away. 'I'll get Dianne to make up the spare room while you go and fetch them,' she said flatly.

Dolly was in a much calmer frame of mind. She'd had her meagre bath, changed into warmer clothes and poured a glass of champagne. But her expression was concerned as she leant over the bed. 'You don't look at all well, Lulu darling. Have you taken your pills?'

'Yes,' Lulu muttered. Despite the tablets, her heart was still beating like a battering ram against her ribs. 'I've overdone it, that's all,' she managed. She lay back on the pillows, the cool, damp cloth on her forehead going some way towards easing a pounding headache.

Dolly finished lighting the kerosene lamps, blew out the match and flicked her fringe out of her eyes. The bed dipped as she sat on the edge. 'I'm so sorry I lost my temper. It wasn't fair after everything that's happened today. And I bet you walked back to the farm to look at the colt, didn't you?'

Lulu nodded and winced as the pain shot behind her eyes and into the back of her neck. The long uphill walk, the confrontations, tears and heat had drained her and she felt as weak as a kitten.

'You've probably got heatstroke. I'd better go up to the house and get them to ring for a doctor.'

'No.' Lulu grabbed her hand. 'I'll be fine if you just leave me to rest.'

'I'm not leaving you anywhere,' Dolly muttered. She crossed the wooden floor, her high heels rapping on the bare boards. 'I've got some aspirin,' she said. 'We'll see how you are in an hour's time, and if there's no improvement I *am* calling a doctor.'

'Please don't fuss,' Lulu whispered, having dutifully swallowed the pills. 'I'll be fine.'

'You'd be even better if you weren't in this hovel,' hissed Dolly. 'Now night has fallen, it's positively freezing.' She shivered and rubbed her arms. 'God only knows what's lurking out there.' She pulled the blanket to Lulu's chin and patted her cheek. 'I'll let the aspirin do its work. Now, go to sleep. I'm here if you need me.'

Lulu closed her eyes as Dolly kicked off her shoes and climbed, fully dressed, into her own bed. Her heart was already slowing to a more even rhythm, and she was feeling sleepy.

Joe switched off the engine and regarded the flickering lanterns in the cabin window. He had rehearsed what he was going to say, and as he approached the veranda he went over it again. He raised his hand to knock just as Dolly opened the door.

'Have you brought our supper?' Dolly stood before him, bundled in at least three layers of clothing.

Joe took off his hat. 'Tea will be about another hour,' he said, his prepared speech in ruins at her interruption.

Dolly raised an eyebrow and closed the door softly behind her. 'So why have you come?'

He pulled the tatters of his announcement together and blurted out, 'I've come to collect you and Lulu and take you up to the house. If you bring enough things to see you through tonight, I'll fetch the rest of your stuff tomorrow.'

Dolly folded her arms and leant on the doorpost, a hint of wry amusement in the curl of her lips. 'So we've finally passed muster with your mama, have we?'

'It's not like that,' he muttered, mangling his hat. 'We just decided it would be too cold and isolated down here for you.'

'We wouldn't want to sully her privacy,' drawled Dolly.

'Fair go, Miss Carteret, Ma was only doing what she thought best. She's not like that, really she's not.'

'I can't say I shan't be relieved to get out of this hovel,' she replied, 'and the thought of a warm bed and a hot water bottle is absolute bliss. But Lulu and I are going nowhere tonight. She just isn't well enough.'

Joe was alarmed. 'What's the matter with her?'

'She walked too far in the heat,' Dolly explained, as she drew a pack of cigarettes from her pocket. 'It's her heart, you know,' she said, eyeing him over the flare of the lighter.

'Her heart?' This was getting worse and worse, and he was mortified to think that her accommodation and the exchange they'd had that afternoon could have had anything to do with it.

Dolly snapped the lighter shut and put it in her pocket. 'Lulu was born with a heart defect. She spent a lot of her childhood in hospital, and although it has improved somewhat as she's got older, she'll probably be on medication for the rest of her life. Today's events haven't exactly helped.'

Joe glanced towards the window, but it was impossible to see anything past the flickering kerosene lantern. 'I'll fetch the doctor.'

'She's already refused to see him.' Dolly took his arm and led him down the steps. 'She's asleep,' she explained, 'and I don't want to disturb her.'

'But she should see the doctor,' he insisted. 'What if she gets worse during the night?'

Dolly eyed him thoughtfully as she leant against the utility and smoked her cigarette. 'Perhaps it wasn't *awfully* wise to put us down here in the first place,' she mused. 'Did you and Lulu talk about that this afternoon?'

'It was mentioned,' he said stiffly.

'I thought as much.' She dropped the half-smoked cigarette and mashed it into the ground with her shoe. 'I've known Lulu since we were at boarding school, and although she's very good at masking her feelings, I always know when she's been upset. She might not have shown it, but she took this –' she waved an imperious hand towards the shack – 'as a personal insult because of who she is.'

Joe was held by the accusing glare. 'She made me aware of that,' he admitted guiltily.

Dolly regarded him in silence. 'I'm glad you're suitably chastened,' she said coolly. 'Lulu can be stubborn, and her pride has been knocked, so it will probably take some persuading to get her to move into the house

She pulled her many cardigans more closely around her narrow chest and climbed the step to the veranda. Turning at the door, she smiled. 'Don't bother about supper. Lulu won't want to eat, and I've got a bottle of champagne and a box of chocolates to keep me company.'

Joe was left standing in the darkness, staring at the closed door.

He slammed through the screen door and into the chaotic kitchen. Molly's hair was sticking out in damp coils from her sweaty face as she hurried from stove to table to linen cupboard. The dogs were getting under her feet as they joined in the chase, and Dianne added to the confusion by hovering in the way as condensation from the boiling saucepans ran down the windows.

Molly had an armful of sheets and pillowcases and didn't see him as she rushed towards the spare bedroom. They collided in the doorway.

'Whoa there, Ma,' he said, rescuing the tumbling linen. 'There's no rush.'

'They're not coming?' She wiped her hot face on a tea towel, her expression hopeful.

'Tomorrow,' he said, and went on to explain.

Molly dumped the linen into Dianne's arms, ordered her up to the spare room and sat down hard in the nearest chair. 'I remember now,' she said. 'The baby was born early and not expected to live.' Her expression hardened as her thoughts returned to the past. 'It was said Gwen hoped she would die. She didn't want a baby, let alone one that was damaged – it would make it harder to get it adopted, and therefore interrupt her social life.'

She gave a sigh and fingered her hair off her face. 'Gwen never even went back to the hospital to check on her. But that little mite was far stronger than anyone bargained for and she survived.'

'And Gwen's aunt adopted her?'

Molly shook her head. 'Not at the beginning – she wasn't around then. Gwen's mother refused to have the poor little thing farmed out to strangers and took over her care, but she never formally adopted her.' She rose wearily and began to lay the table. 'I wish I'd remembered all this before,' she sighed.

Joe rescued the saucepans that were in danger of boiling dry. He shared his mother's regret, and hoped this would be the end of any hostility. And yet he had a nagging sense that having the two of them in the same house wouldn't be all sweetness and light. Tomorrow could prove very awkward.

'You've got a visitor, Mum.' Vera Cornish stood in the doorway, stolid and stoic in headscarf, wrap-around florid pinafore, lisle stockings and sensible shoes. Her expression was disapproving as always.

Clarice put down her newspaper. 'I am not your mother, Vera. Please address me as either Lady Pearson, or Madam.'

'Yes, Mum. Shall I show 'im in then?'

It was obvious Vera would have no truck with changing a lifetime of bad habits, so it was pointless to argue further. 'Who is this visitor?'

Vera squinted at the calling card. 'Major Bertram Hopkins,' she recited.

It told Clarice nothing at all, and as Vera seemed in a hurry to escape the drawing room, she had better take a look at this mysterious visitor. 'Show him in,' she commanded. 'and don't bother about tea unless I ring for it. He probably won't be staying.'

Vera stomped out into the hall, and Clarice waited.

'Lady Pearson . . . ?' The dapper man in the tweed suit appeared in the doorway rather uncertainly. Vera had obviously stranded him in the hallway.

'Major Hopkins, do come in.'

She weighed him up as he made his way across the worn Turkish rug. He was tall, his figure robust, the moustache rather fine. There was a twinkle in his eye she found attractive, and when he smiled he showed a healthy set of teeth. His suit was of good-quality cloth and cut, and he carried a bowler hat, briefcase and tightly furled umbrella which Vera should have relieved him of.

'Delighted to meet you, Lady Pearson,' he said as he shook her hand.

Clarice dipped her chin in acknowledgement and silently indicated where he should sit. He seemed respectable enough, and knew his manners, and she waited for him to settle. 'What can I do for you, Major?'

He cleared his throat. 'It is a rather delicate matter, Lady Pearson, and I hope you will forgive me for intruding upon you like this.'

Clarice sighed. 'If you have come to sell me something, then I'm afraid you will be disappointed. There are far too many returned servicemen eking out a living by selling door to door, and I prefer to make my contributions directly to the appropriate charities.'

'I retired from the army many years ago, and have been gainfully employed ever since,' he replied. 'It is this employment which brings me here today.'

'And what is it you do?'

'I work for companies and private individuals in matters that require discretion and tact.' He smoothed his moustache and said proudly, 'In short, Lady Pearson, I am a private investigator.'

Clarice raised her eyebrows. 'Goodness me!' she said. 'I never expected to have a real Sherlock Holmes in my drawing room.'

He smiled. 'I don't profess to have his skills, Lady Pearson, and real life is far more complex than anything penned by Arthur Conan Doyle.'

Clarice was impressed despite her reservations and rang the bell to summon Vera. 'I'm most interested to hear the reason for your visit, Major Hopkins.'

He was reaching into his briefcase when Vera stuck her head around the door. 'You want tea, Mum?' At Clarice's nod she slammed the door, her heavy tread echoing down the hall and into the kitchen.

Clarice fluttered her hands, disconcerted by Vera's behaviour and the major's look of astonishment. 'My housekeeper is not yet conversant with the etiquette of the drawing room,' she said hurriedly, 'but it's so hard to get servants these days . . .' She trailed off, aware that she was twittering like a demented hen.

'It is a problem faced by many in these difficult times,' he murmured as he pulled a sheaf of papers from the battered leather briefcase. He placed the papers on the seat next to him and folded his hands on his knees. 'As I said, Lady Pearson, it is a delicate matter.'

'It had better wait,' she said hastily, as Vera crashed through the door with the trolley and steered it towards them.

They sat in silence as she clattered the cups and saucers and laid out a plate of sandwiches and a chocolate cake on to the low table between them. 'Is that all, Mum? Only I've got a bird in the oven, and it ain't 'appy.'

Clarice caught the major's eye and bit her lip. 'Thank you, Vera. You may go,' she said unsteadily. She lifted the heavy silver teapot, found her hand was shaking and put it down again. 'Oh dear,' she said with a nervous laugh, 'she is quite a card, isn't she?'

His eyes twinkled as he nodded and took over the teapot. 'I think Vera is missing her vocation. She should go on the stage.'

They settled down to drink their tea. 'You were saying . . . ?' she prompted minutes later.

'In my capacity as a private investigator, I am often asked to follow people and record where they go and who they meet and so on.' He took a deep breath. 'Sixteen years ago I was employed to make an annual visit to Sussex and report on the progress of Miss Lorelei Pearson.'

Clarice's teacup rattled against the saucer and she put it down. A chill ran up her spine as she stared at him. 'You have been watching Lorelei? For sixteen years?' she breathed. 'But why? Who ordered this?'

189

'My orders came from a firm of London solicitors. Here is their card.'

She eyed the heavily embossed business card and was none the wiser. 'What have they to do with Lorelei?' she demanded.

'It is probably best if I go back to when I first started my annual trips down here.' He swallowed nervously, no doubt quailing in the beam of Clarice's glare. He picked up the sheaf of papers. 'These are copies of all the reports I made over the years. They are innocuous, as you will see when you read them – merely dealing with her health, her schooling, her welfare, her hobbies and talents.'

Clarice took the papers and set them aside. She was too stunned and angry to read anything now. 'Go on,' she said ominously.

'There were photographs as well, but I didn't keep copies.' He hurried on, clearly discomforted by Clarice's lowering silence. 'I made my last visit here in February. My employers had informed me that she would soon be receiving a letter and I was to keep watch and see if she replied to it.' He eased his collar with a finger. 'Her reply was duly posted, and the second letter arrived several weeks later along with the proof of ownership for Ocean Child.'

'How do you know all this?'

'I have contacts at the post office, Your Ladyship.'

'Go on,' she said imperiously.

'It wasn't hard to keep track of her after that second letter arrived, and my last assignment was to see her off at the Port of London.' He cleared his throat. 'I had come to grow quite fond of Lorelei over the years, and looked forward to my annual trips. I was delighted she appeared so well after her ill health as a child – she's turned into a very beautiful and talented young woman.'

'You're nothing but a voyeur.' Clarice rose in fury.

He shot to his feet, the briefcase sliding to the floor and

spilling yet more papers and files. 'No, no, Lady Pearson, I assure you – it was nothing like that.'

'I think you'd better leave,' she said with dangerous calm.

'Please hear me out; it's important. I think Lorelei has been drawn into something that might harm her.'

Clarice sank back into the chair as the strength drained from her legs, the colour from her face. 'What do you mean?' she whispered.

'Someone is playing a devious game with your ward, Lady Pearson.' He gathered up the spilled files. 'I have many contacts all over London, and I managed to get hold of these.'

Clarice watched, stunned by the turn of events and chilled with fear as he sorted through his documents and selected a thick file.

'These are the communications between a firm of solicitors in Brisbane and the London office that employed me. They begin sixteen years ago and continue until Lorelei set sail for Australia.'

Clarice eyed the folder, the dread growing.

He selected a much slimmer folder. 'These are letters purporting to come from the same source, and are signed with the same name.' He offered them to her. 'They appeared to be genuine, but I had my doubts. I had a friend who is an expert in such things take a look at them. He confirmed they are very well-executed forgeries.'

Clarice struggled to keep her wits about her. She drank the last of her tea and tried to gather her thoughts. 'The first set of letters from Brisbane,' she rasped through a tight throat, 'what do they contain?'

'Instructions to the London solicitors to hire a private investigator and send regular reports on Lorelei Pearson. Mr Carmichael was most insistent that—'

'Mr Carmichael? The same Mr Carmichael who appears to have bought my ward a colt?'

He nodded.

'And the second set?'

'Also purporting to be from Mr Carmichael, but they are much more recent – and as I said before they . . .'

'I heard you the first time,' she snapped impatiently. 'What did these letters contain?'

'They carried instructions regarding the letters from Tasmania, Lady Pearson. Whoever sent those instructions seemed to know the contents of the letters from Joe Reilly, and insisted she should be followed even more closely once they had arrived.'

Clarice tried to assimilate what she'd heard, but her brain simply refused to comply.

Major Hopkins sank back as if exhausted. 'Telegrams were sent back and forth once I'd discovered she was leaving for Australia, and I have copies of them here.' His smile was wry. 'Solicitors keep a copy of everything, so it wasn't difficult to get hold of them.'

'And exactly how did you manage that?'

He reddened. 'I have contacts who have certain . . . useful skills,' he murmured.

She understood and eyed him sternly. 'I see. And what did these telegrams say?'

'The man purporting to be Carmichael wanted to know the date of her sailing, the name of the ship, ports of call and if she was travelling alone.'

'Thank God she isn't,' Clarice breathed.

'Have you heard from her since she left?'

She nodded. 'She arrived safely, was having fun and seemed very happy.' Clarice fell silent, recalling the letters and postcards she'd almost learnt by heart. Lorelei was clearly enjoying her adventure, and had given no hint of anything amiss.

She looked back at the major, her thoughts troubled. 'Lorelei has always been very protective of me – as have I of her. So I doubt she would write anything in her letters that might cause me to worry.'

'Do you have any inkling as to who the original Carmichael could be?'

Clarice hesitated, unwilling to voice her suspicions. 'None at all,' she said.

The sharp eyes seemed to bore into her. 'That's a shame, Lady Pearson, because if we could discover who he is, then we might have a chance of understanding why someone else should use his name and interfere with his earlier instructions.'

She realised the major was far more astute than she'd first credited, and because he seemed as concerned as she over Lorelei's safety, she decided to be honest with him. 'Any suspicions I may harbour will be of no help,' she said quietly, 'for I have no name, and no face to put to them.'

10

Lulu realised she had surprised Dolly by agreeing, without argument, to move up to the homestead. There were lots of reasons behind it, but the main one was the chance to show the Reilly woman she could be gracious in accepting her invitation and the tacit apology that went with it.

She was sitting on the veranda drinking her second cup of morning tea and listening to the beautiful dawn chorus as the birds flitted through the trees and swooped over the babbling river to drink. The early sunlight sparked diamonds on the water, but had yet to warm the shadows beneath the surrounding trees, which was why Lulu was warmly dressed. Evidence of the night frost remained in the grass, but she hadn't noticed its chill, for Dolly had, at some point, almost buried her in blankets.

Dolly appeared in the doorway, nursing a cup of evil-looking Camp Coffee. Too much champagne and chocolate, combined with a bad night's sleep, had left her looking frazzled. She squinted into the sun. 'What's making that heavenly sound?'

'It's the butcherbirds and magpies,' murmured Lulu. 'Glorious, isn't it?

They listened in awe to the rich, melodious piping that was interspersed with the musical 'Kar-week, week-kar,' of the currawongs, and the chortling of a nearby kookaburra.

'Rather puts our English songbirds in the shade, doesn't it?' Dolly stretched and yawned. 'I have to say, that was the most *ghastly* night, but the dawn chorus certainly makes up for it.'

Lulu was about to reply when the sound of engines muffled the birdsong. The two utilities bounced up the track towards them, the dogs in the flatbeds running back and forth, tails wagging, tongues lolling.

'G'day.' Joe climbed down with a wary smile and slammed the door. 'I hope you're feeling better, Lulu?'

'A good night's sleep always does the trick,' she said lightly.

His gaze lingered for a moment as if in doubt. 'I've brought Bob along to help with your luggage. Are you ready?'

She smiled and glanced at the dumbstruck Bob, who was looking at Dolly with undisguised adoration. 'We just need to clean the place up a bit,' she said, as she got to her feet.

'No worries,' said Joe. 'I'll come down later and sort it all out.' He nudged Bob. 'I think you've seen enough, mate. How about a hand with the stuff?'

Bob reddened and followed Joe into the cabin. The dogs continued their mad dash from side to side, clearly eager to jump down and give chase to any small creature lurking in the bush, but Joe told them firmly to stay put, and they sat panting. Within minutes, everything was neatly stacked and tied down in the back of Bob's ute.

'Isn't it dangerous to have them running around when you're on the move?' asked Lulu as she carried her overnight bag down the steps.

'Nah, they've been doing that since they were pups. They only have to fall off once to know not to do it again.' He grinned and opened the door. 'Hop in. Ma's got breakfast on the go, and it would be a shame to let it get cold.'

Lulu joined Dolly on the front seat and clutched her bag to her chest as Joe set the utility into a jolting dash across the rough track and up the steep hill. The dogs barked and whined and adjusted their stance like sailors on a rough sea, clearly enjoying this unexpected jaunt – but she could see Dolly was not nearly so happy.

'Are you all right?' she asked quietly, beneath the roar of the engine.

'I will be when I reach terra firma,' said Dolly grimly. 'Promise me, Lulu, don't let me eat so much chocolate again.'

Lulu grinned. Chocolate came a very close second to high heels in Dolly's list of passions, and this latest plea was one she'd heard before. Experience had taught her to ignore it.

As the utility gained the crest of the hill and thundered towards the homestead, Lulu felt a squirm of unease at the thought of meeting Joe's mother. She glanced across at him, saw the tic in his jaw and realised he was just as tense. It would have been most interesting, she thought, to have been a fly on the wall during what must have been a fraught scene the night before.

She had no more time to contemplate it, for they had arrived. Joe switched off the engine, the dogs leapt down and the front door was opening.

Lulu followed Dolly out of the utility, dusted herself down and regarded the woman waiting in the doorway. Short and plump, with greying, unruly dark hair and a weathered face, Mrs Reilly appeared to be the quintessential farmer's wife. Whether she could be trusted or not remained to be seen.

Lulu took a deep breath and strode towards her. 'Good morning, Mrs Reilly,' she said coolly, shaking the work-roughened hand. 'Lulu Pearson, and this is my friend, Dolly Carteret.'

There was a glint of humour behind the curiosity in the dark eyes, but the smile was tentative. 'Welcome to Galway House,' she murmured.

'Thank you,' replied Lulu.

'I'll leave the bags and things until after breakfast,' said Joe, breaking into the awkward silence. 'Go on in. Ma'll show you your rooms and where you can freshen up before you eat.'

Lulu was grateful for his intervention, for Mrs Reilly's disconcerting gaze had remained on her for too long. They followed her into the square hall and climbed the uncarpeted stairs. The long corridor ran the breadth of the house, and it was clear there were at least four bedrooms, which proved that lack of space wasn't an issue.

Molly opened one of the doors and they stepped into a large, sunny room that had double doors leading out on to the veranda. There were two comfortable-looking beds, a dressing table and stool, and a rug on the wooden floorboards. The chintz curtains matched the counterpanes, and from the window she could see across the paddocks to the valley. Compared to the shed in the valley it was a palace.

'How nice,' said Dolly with a large pinch of sarcasm. 'A comfortable bed at last.'

Molly's lips formed a thin line as she folded her arms. 'It's the best we can do in the circumstances,' she said gruffly. She shot a glance at Lulu, reddened when their eyes met, and turned away. 'Breakfast in ten minutes,' she said. 'The bathroom's next door.'

The bathroom turned out to be a narrow space between two other bedrooms. The enamel tub stood on clawed feet beneath the window, the brass taps polished to a gleam. The lavatory had to be flushed by pulling the long chain that hung from a wall-mounted cistern and the floor was covered in livid green linoleum. Towels had been draped from hooks close to the tiny basin above which hung a fly-spotted mirror.

Lulu washed her hands and stared at her reflection. Yesterday's sun had gilded her skin, bringing out the freckles across her nose and making her eyes appear bluer than usual, but the headache and palpitations she'd suffered the night before had left dark shadows her freckles couldn't hide. Her hair was a tangle of coils and curls, and quite impossible to brush, so she gave up the attempt and followed the mouth-watering aroma of frying bacon down the stairs and into the kitchen.

*

'That was a delicious breakfast, Mrs Reilly. I'm just sorry I couldn't do it justice.' Lulu nudged the plate of half-eaten food away and cradled the thick china mug of hot tea.

'Are you still feeling crook?' Molly frowned, her concern clear.

Lulu saw no reason to let her off the hook with platitudes. 'I still have a bit of a headache,' she said evenly, 'but it will pass.'

Dolly put her knife and fork together with a clatter and leant back in contentment. 'That was lovely, Mrs Reilly.' She sighed. 'I didn't realise how hungry I was.'

'Glad you liked it,' Molly said grudgingly. She eyed them both over her mug of tea. 'Everyone round here calls me Molly, by the way,' she added.

'Really?' said Lulu. 'Is that short for something?'

Molly's gaze wavered under Lulu's steady scrutiny. 'Margaret,' she replied.

'Such a sensible name,' Dolly said with a brittle smile. 'Dolores sounds as if I should be behind the bar in some dangerously seedy nightclub.' She shivered with relish. 'Mummy and Pa must have had a brainstorm when they named me after my great-grandmother. She was Argentinean, you know, married to a gaucho – *frightfully* romantic of course. They had a ranch just outside Buenos Aires.'

The eyebrow twitched and a smile lurked in the corners of Molly's mouth, but she made no comment.

'Mummy has often spoken of their wonderful hospitality, for although they lived on the pampas, their guests were housed in the most marvellous little houses, with every luxury.' Dolly's light tone was tinged with cattiness. 'Perhaps you should consider doing something with your shed? The position is ideal, but the accommodation leaves a lot to be desired.'

Molly reddened again, Dianne's eyes widened and Joe shifted in his chair. Lulu glanced at Dolly, who was holding Molly's gaze as if daring her to reply. The tension was electric.

'How very nice for your great-grandmother,' said Molly, her gaze unflinching, her voice dangerously calm. 'Perhaps you should consider visiting Argentina instead? I'm sure I could arrange the tickets.'

'I have no doubt of it,' retorted Dolly, 'but this is Lulu's homecoming, and although her welcome hasn't exactly been warm, she intends to stay.'

'I was sorry to hear what happened on the quay,' said Molly, her gaze settling on Lulu with an intensity that was unnerving. 'It must be difficult to have a mother like that.'

'I've learnt to live with it,' Lulu replied. 'We aren't in contact any more.' The atmosphere was poisonous, and unable to stand it any longer, she pushed back her chair. 'I'd like to come with you on the ride-outs each day,' she said to Joe. 'Do you have a quiet horse I could ride?'

The relief in Joe's face was clear as he turned to her. 'There's Sadie, my old mare. She'll appreciate the exercise.'

She smiled and nodded her thanks. 'There are things I want to do today, so perhaps tomorrow?'

'What about you, Dolly? Do you ride?'

'Since I could walk,' she replied, 'and I'd appreciate a horse that would give me a challenge.'

Joe's mouth twitched. 'Oh, I think I can find you something to give you a memorable experience.'

Lulu realised that Molly was watching her again with that same unnerving combination of curiosity and thoughtfulness. She touched her chin. 'Do I have something on my face?'

'No,' muttered Molly, looking away hastily. She cocked her head at the open-mouthed and clearly fascinated Dianne. 'Come on, we've got work to do.'

Lulu noticed how her hostess's hands shook as she gathered up the plates, dropping some of the cutlery on the floor. Molly Reilly was as affected as everyone else by the tension in the kitchen.

There was little doubt she regretted her invitation to the house, and Lulu was beginning to feel rather sorry for her. Dolly could be acerbic at times, and although she was only getting back at Molly to defend Lulu, Lulu wished she would ease off.

She turned to Joe again. 'Could we borrow a ute today?'

At his nod, Lulu thanked him and, with a meaningful look at Dolly, left the kitchen.

Dolly followed her into the bedroom and firmly shut the door. 'What is it with that woman?' she whispered. 'She couldn't take her eyes off you. I wonder why.'

Lulu gathered up the thick cardigan and woollen beret from the chair. 'Probably looking for similarities to my delightful mother,' she said flatly. 'Come on, Dolly, let's get out of here.'

Joe was tying the dogs to a post by their kennels when they met him outside. 'If I don't do this, you'll have unwanted passengers,' he said with a shy smile. He picked up the crank handle and eyed the two women doubtfully. 'You might find it a bit of a struggle to use this.'

Lulu smiled reassuringly and took the handle from him. 'I drove buses in London during the war,' she explained. 'I think I can manage to crank-start a ute.' She slotted the handle into the shaft and gave it a sharp turn. The engine roared into life and she swept back her hair in triumph – she didn't know what she'd have done if it had proved beyond her.

'No worries,' he murmured, the laughter dancing in his dark eyes. 'You're obviously tougher than you look.'

Lulu threw the handle on to the seat and climbed up to join Dolly. 'Thanks for the loan, Joe. See you later.'

'Where are you going?' He tipped back his hat, unaware that his scars were cruelly lit by the sun.

'To the beach.' She turned the wheel, pressed her foot on the accelerator and headed for the gate.

*

Joe scratched his head and grinned. Despite the willowy figure and delicate features, she was a tough little thing and no mistake. He rammed on his hat, realised Bob had done a disappearing act, and tackled the first of the cases. The more he saw of Lulu Pearson, the more he liked her, but he wished wholeheartedly that she didn't feel so uneasy in his home. The atmosphere at breakfast could have been cut with a knife.

As he went back and forth with their luggage, he mulled over his impressions of both young women. Dolly was quite a character, with a sharp wit and a readiness to fight fire with fire. His mother had already discovered she'd met her match in Dolly. As for Lulu – she was simply perfect in every way.

He dumped the last trunk in the middle of the bedroom and glanced at his watch. It was already past seven, daylight was wasting, and he'd spent far too much time mooning over the gorgeous Lulu Pearson – who was so far out of his league that he might as well try to fly to the moon. He stomped out of the bedroom, furious that he was acting as daft as the lovesick Bob.

'Are we really going to the beach?' asked Dolly, as they bounced and rattled along the hardened ruts of the dirt track.

'If I can find it,' muttered Lulu, who was concentrating on avoiding any pothole that might snap the axle. 'I wish I'd thought to buy a map, but I didn't expect to be out in the middle of nowhere. I don't recognise anything.'

'Don't you think it's rather cold for the seaside? I know the English can be stoic, huddled against the wind, eating sandy sandwiches and pretending to enjoy themselves, but I'm not like that.'

'Neither am I,' Lulu replied, 'but this is a very special beach, and it's been too long since I've seen it to worry about the weather.'

'Now I understand,' said Dolly, who'd heard all about this beach years ago. She fell silent, clinging to the door handle as the utility tackled a particularly rough piece of track. 'Look,' she exclaimed moments later, 'a signpost.'

The engine idled as Lulu tried to make out the words on the four weathered wooden arrows. 'It's this way,' she said, 'and closer than I thought.' She put her foot down and the ute rattled and complained over the final stretch of track until they reached the smoother tarmac.

They had travelled about thirty miles by the time they reached the outskirts of the seaside town. It hadn't changed much, and as they followed the winding coastal road, Lulu's emotions welled. There was the timber-yard and the train tracks, and the road that went from the river up to where she'd attended school. She decided to leave the school for another time – she was in a hurry.

Yet she paused to look at the low, undulating hills of the eastern shore of the Mersey River. There had once been a boat to take her over there, she remembered. It was a funny wooden boat, with a red-faced jolly captain who sang shanties as he rowed his passengers across. The fare had been a half-penny – a quarter of her pocket money – but the cost had never deterred her, even though Clarice would have been horrified if she'd ever discovered this minor weekly adventure.

'Oh, do look at that. How sweet.'

Lulu laughed in delight as she saw the doughty little ferry chug towards the landing steps. The master at the wheel was probably the original captain's grandson, and the ferry was a vast improvement on the original. 'I'm so glad it's still running,' she said, and explained why, before driving on.

With the river on her right, and the town to her left, Lulu followed the familiar narrow lane that had been metalled since she'd last seen it, through the tunnel of ancient pines and out again into the sun. The house she'd always admired was still on the corner, gleaming white, the latticed verandas now smothered in a dormant climbing rose, the garden as manicured as ever beneath a vast monkey-puzzle tree.

Her heart began to thud in anticipation as she followed the long bend in the road. The grassy area between lane and shore was still there, but the thick shrubs blocked her view of the sea. She leant forward, gripping the steering wheel as the bend flattened out and she saw the sports field – the paddocks, and playground – and finally – the beach.

She steered the utility on to the grass and turned off the engine. 'Oh, Dolly,' she breathed through threatening tears. 'I'm home – I'm really home.' Without waiting for a response, she opened the door and climbed down.

The wind whipped at her hair, the salt spray stinging her face. She could hear the lonely cries of the plovers and gulls, and smell salt and pine in the air. The tide was coming in, the waves racing up the dark yellow crescent of sand. Like a sleepwalker, she moved towards it.

Her gaze combed the beach, past the tiny kiosk where Clarice had bought ice cream and chocolate bars during the long, hot summers, to the dangerous glossy rocks of the ironstone bluff. The sea was crashing against it, the spume tossed high, to be blown away by the wind that bent the pine trees growing on its headland. She could hear the boom as the tide rushed into the blowhole on the far side, and with it came an outpouring of the yearning she had contained for too long.

Her tears were of joy and relief that nothing had changed – that nature in all its majestic glory had not failed her – for she had held the image of this beach in her heart like a precious, secret jewel, and now she could look upon it openly and rejoice.

She sat on the grassy bank with her back to the swings she had played on as a child and took off her boots and socks. Her toes dug tentatively into the soft sand, finding it chill, but, oh, so memorable. This had been her real playground, making castles in the sand – her first, tentative sculptures – as she dreamed her dreams, the grittiness clinging to her knitted swimsuit and wet skin as she'd let her imagination take her into a private world.

Lulu wriggled her toes and smiled, then walked towards the sea and the hard-packed wet sand where the plovers tiptoed along the water's edge. Looking behind her she could see her footprints, and she watched as they filled with water and slowly disappeared. It was as if she was newly born in a world yet to be discovered, and her solitude made it the rarest of gifts.

The sea was even icier than she recalled, and she shivered as it swirled around her ankles and sucked at her feet. Chilled to the bone, she reluctantly headed back to the grass, her smile wry. It seemed age had brought an awareness of the cold that hadn't appeared to touch her as a child, for she'd swum in that sea throughout the spring and autumn. She dried her feet with her socks, rammed on the boots and dragged the knitted beret over her ears. The bluff beckoned and she was impatient to be on the move again.

She tramped along the sand, glanced across at the track that would take her past the little house where she'd been raised and knew she was not yet ready to go and look at it. Instead she began the steep climb that would take her into the heart of the pine forest.

Its familiar gloom surrounded her as she slowed to catch her breath, and her boots stirred the pine needles, bringing their sharp scent to remind her of the times she'd been well enough to play here. Looking about her, she could almost hear the childish laughter as she and her friends had raced down the hill, swung from the trees or clambered over the rocks, daring one another to go nearer and nearer the blowhole. She closed her eyes, those echoes from the past fading in the sough of the wind through the trees. It was like a beautiful lullaby faintly remembered.

She opened her eyes and slowly went on up the steep hill. The golden wattle was past its best, but in the darkness of the forest the citrus rain of their yellow flowers still shone like beacons, their scent delicate and evocative. She walked quietly on, almost afraid to disturb the profound contentment of being alone in nature's cathedral.

Reaching the crest of the headland, she stood in the shelter of the forest boundary and looked beyond the lighthouse to the Bass Strait. The water mirrored the grey, angry sky and, as it rushed into the natural gully that divided the headland, it exploded through the blowhole. Lulu sat on the pine needles, her back against a sturdy tree, and drank in the vista before her, contented in her solitary worship.

Time lost meaning as she sat there, but she gradually became aware that the skies had darkened, and now rain threatened. She looked at her watch, and realised in horror that she'd been gone for over two hours. Dolly would be frantic. Leaping to her feet, she turned her back on the view, and began the steep descent through the deserted forest and back to the beach.

Dolly was pacing up and down the track, clearly furious. 'Where the *hell* have you been?' she shouted. 'I lost sight of you and . . . and . . .' She burst into tears and threw her arms around Lulu, clinging to her like a limpet. 'I thought you'd had an accident or something, and there was no one about – absolutely no one.'

'I'm so sorry. I lost track of the time.' Lulu dug a handkerchief out of her pocket and handed it over. 'I've been selfish,' she murmured, 'and you're freezing. Let's go into town and find a nice cup of tea.'

Dolly blew her nose. 'Next time you decide to take off, I'm coming with you,' she declared. She climbed into the ute and slammed the door so hard it rocked the chassis.

Lulu bit her lip, fully aware of how badly she'd scared her best friend. She fetched the crank handle and had just slotted it into the shaft when a movement at the far end of the beach caught her eye.

She peered through the gathering gloom and frowned as a man emerged from the forest and stood by the rocks. She had not been alone on the bluff after all.

Major Hopkins had stayed for supper, and they had exhausted every avenue in the quest to solve the mystery of Mr Carmichael and the person who'd forged his name. It was clear that whoever sent the initial instructions to the London solicitors had a different agenda to the forger. It was also clear that the gift had been an enticement to get Lorelei back to Tasmania. But why?

The major had proved to be an astute, deep-thinking man, but neither of them could come up with any answers, and Clarice had finally sent him back to London on the last train. They would keep each other informed if anything came to light, but she doubted it would, and she had spent the rest of the night fretting, sleep eluding her as she tossed and turned and tried to make sense of it all.

Clarice lay in the darkness staring at the ceiling, her thoughts drawn repeatedly to the same unpleasant but compelling conclusion. She punched the pillows and turned on to her side, refusing to let that insidious thought take hold. It was impossible, ridiculous – the rambling of a distressed and weary old woman. And yet, if by some extraordinary chance it was true, she had no possible way of intervening and bringing this twisted charade to an end – and that frightened her.

Dawn was not far away when Clarice gave up on sleep and dragged herself out of bed. She was utterly exhausted, and although she'd always prided herself on being sprightly for her age, she felt every one of her seventy years. Shoving her feet into slippers and pulling the dressing gown tightly around her, she slowly went downstairs to the kitchen. A cup of tea would soothe her, and hopefully chase away the night's demons.

'Hello, old girl,' she murmured fondly to the Labrador curled up in the basket. 'I'm glad to see someone's having a good rest.'

She filled the kettle and placed it on the hotplate. Hunting out a cup and two saucers, she put them on the table and rattled the biscuit tin. She and Bess liked a biscuit with their tea, and this had become an early morning ritual.

Keeping her mind firmly off her worries, she made the tea and poured some into a saucer. Adding milk, she placed it on the floor. 'Bess? You can't still be asleep. Come on, old thing, tea's up.'

She frowned as she realised there was none of the usual scuffling and snuffling, or the stretching of old limbs. 'Bess?'

Her heart began to thud and her mouth dried as she knelt and placed a trembling hand on the soft head. 'Bess, wake up, darling. I've made our tea.'

But the faithful old dog could no longer hear her.

Clarice sank to the floor and rested her cheek on the still, silent body of the companion she'd brought home as a puppy sixteen years ago. It was as if her world was falling apart, tumbling and whirling out of control as one by one the solid structures she had always depended upon were taken away.

The tears came with a great sob that encompassed all the sorrows she harboured. Then they tore through her, the well of despair finally breached.

Tasmania, January 1895

Clarice had fretted over the weeks it took to put her affairs in order. She had sold the house and most of the furniture, as well as Algernon's vast library of books; everything else was packed ready to be shipped to Tasmania. She didn't know what to expect when she arrived there, but concluded it would politic to rent a small house close to Eunice rather than move in with her and Gwen. The atmosphere was bound to be fraught initially, and putting some distance between them might ease it. She arranged through an agent in Sydney to find a suitable property within walking distance of Eunice's home.

Clarice finally booked a passage on the SS *Norkoowa*. She'd always prided herself on being a good sailor, but the Bass Straits had defeated her, and she arrived on the northern shores of Tasmania in a state of near collapse. Feeling decidedly unsteady, she'd been found a chair by one of the men, who placed it in the shade so she could orchestrate the loading of her crates on to a dray.

The men were almost finished when she saw her sister arrive in a carriage. Leaving instructions where to deliver the crates, she rose from the chair and nervously watched her approach. But as Eunice drew nearer, the nerves were replaced with concern, for she was far too thin, her complexion waxy and her steps halting. Gone was the pretty woman with dark hair and dancing eyes, and in her place was a frail greying matron who walked with the aid of a stick.

'Thank you for coming,' Eunice said stiffly. There was no kiss of welcome, and her dark eyes took in Clarice's neat skirt, mutton-sleeve blouse and jaunty straw hat with apparent indifference. 'You seem to have weathered the passing years better than I,' she murmured.

'I would have come sooner if you had replied to my letters,' she said gently. 'Why didn't you tell me you were ill?'

'Is it that obvious?' She gave a wry smile as she glanced at the walking stick. 'I suppose it is.' She regarded Clarice and gave a sigh. 'I was sorry to hear about Algernon, and started to write to you many times, but I found I just didn't have the heart for it.'

'So what has happened to make you change your mind?'

'I will tell you when we get home. Come, the carriage is wait-ing, and as he charges for every half hour, we are wasting money.'

It took a while to settle Eunice comfortably against the many cushions, and Clarice's concern grew. But Eunice made it clear she didn't want to discuss anything until they arrived at her house, and maintained a brooding silence.

Clarice sat beside her in the carriage and looked around with interest. It was just over forty years since the last convict had been transported to this island that had once been called Van Diemen's Land. The notoriety of those convict days had been well documented, and the privations and terrible punishments inflicted on those men at Port Arthur had been the moving force behind the abolition of transportation. Yet here in the north there was little sign of the island's iniquitous history, for all seemed tranquil and verdant in the summer sun.

They were travelling through a tunnel of vast pine trees on a narrow track that ran parallel to the river. As they emerged into the sunlight and followed the long bend, they were greeted by the sparkle of water and a sandy beach which was sheltered at one end by a headland of dark rocks and more pine trees.

The carriage rattled along almost to the end of the beach before the track took them inland. The horse turned off shortly after and came to a halt in front of a tiny wooden cottage. It had once been painted white, but the elements had made it shabby, and the single chimney and corrugated iron roof had been fre-quently repaired. Set back from the main track, it was surrounded by paddocks and outbuildings and overshadowed by trees. Chick-ens pecked in the grass, horses and sheep grazed nearby, and there was a goat tethered to a post near the front door. Clarice was dumbfounded.

'It might not look much,' said Eunice defensively, 'but it's cheap to run and convenient.' She paid the driver and opened the front door.

Clarice was still wrestling with this conundrum as she

followed her sister into the gloom of a narrow hall that had two doors leading off it and into an even darker kitchen that spanned the width of the house at the back. She stood in silence as Eunice set about making a pot of tea. This room was obviously used as a cooking and living space, for it was cluttered with furniture. The back door was heavily screened and looked out on wooden outbuildings whose purpose she could only guess at. It was a far cry from the beautiful house in Coogee Bay, and Clarice couldn't begin to understand why her sister was living in such poverty.

'I've had another bed put in my room, so I hope you don't mind sharing?'

'I wish you hadn't gone to so much trouble,' murmured Clarice, as she sat on one of the uncomfortable kitchen chairs and pulled off her gloves. 'I've rented a small house nearby. The agent assures me it's within walking distance, so I can visit every day if you wish.'

Eunice placed the cups and saucers on the table next to the teapot and sat down. 'That was thoughtful of you,' she replied, her expression unreadable. 'There isn't really enough room for all of us here, and I know you're used to having more space.'

'My dear,' Clarice began, 'why do you choose to live like this when—'

'I have my reasons,' she said flatly. 'Please don't pry.'

'But there's no need . . .'

'If you're going to question me, then you'd better leave.'

Stung by her sister's tone, Clarice fell silent. 'Have you seen a doctor?' she said when the silence became unbearable.

'Of course. But it was a waste of time.' Eunice sipped her tea. 'He can't do much,' she said with weary acceptance. 'It seems I have some sort of creeping paralysis that has no cure.' There was no self-pity in her gaze as she faced Clarice. 'I have good days and bad, but at least I'm not bedridden – yet.'

'Oh, my dear,' she sighed, finally understanding why Eunice had asked her to come. 'I wish you'd told me sooner, then perhaps I could have sent out a Sydney doctor to look at you.'

'Why waste money when there's no point?'

'There must be specialists in England. Why don't I book passage? We could reopen the family home in Sussex, and—'

'No,' Eunice said sharply.

'Why ever not?'

Eunice held her gaze for a length of silence and then sighed. 'There are a lot of reasons, Clarice. Suffice to say I have responsibilities here that I cannot abandon.'

Clarice frowned and was about to question her further when a cheerful voice came from the hallway.

'Cooee, only me.' A woman came into the kitchen, bringing the scent of the outdoors with her. Her clothes were neat, but her hair was coming loose from its pins in dark drifts about her cheerful, pretty face. She had a fair-haired baby of about a year old on her hip, who stared solemnly at Eunice before shyly burying her face in the woman's shoulder.

'This is Primrose,' said Eunice, her face lighting up, 'but she prefers we call her Primmy.'

'Nice to meet you, I'm sure.' Primmy bobbed a curtsy.

Eunice held out her arms, took the baby on to her lap and kissed the golden curls before handing her a biscuit.

'I can't stay, Mrs Bartholomew. My old man's due home and he and the kids will be wanting their tea. Is there anything you need before I go?'

'Thank you, no. I'll see you at the same time tomorrow.'

Primmy nodded and hurried down the hall, banging the front door behind her.

Clarice rose in alarm. 'She's in such a hurry she's forgotten her baby.'

'It isn't her baby,' said Eunice, her fingers gently stroking through the pale yellow curls. 'Lorelei is my granddaughter.'

Clarice sat down with a bump, noted Eunice's defiant gaze and tried hard to disguise her shock. 'Gwen is married?'

Eunice kissed the baby's neck, making her giggle. 'No,' she said.

Clarice was reeling from the thunderbolt Eunice had delivered, and she had to battle to maintain an air of calm. Logically she knew she shouldn't be so dumbstruck, for the gossip surrounding Gwen's behaviour had been rife – the consequences obvious if one thought about it – but she simply couldn't digest the appalling shame Gwen had brought to her family. She regarded the child and shivered. 'Why hasn't she been adopted?'

'Lorelei was born too soon, and her heart wasn't properly formed. Gwen wanted to give her away, but I couldn't let her go to strangers – she's far too precious.'

'But she's *illegitimate*,' Clarice hissed.

'She's a baby.' Eunice's level gaze never faltered. 'The time will come when she has to face up to things – for now I just want her to have the best start in life that I can possibly give her.'

'Is that why you moved up here from Hobart?' Clarice's voice was strained.

Eunice nodded. 'Gwen seemed to enjoy flaunting her condition and stirring up trouble, but I found it intolerable and thought we might escape the worst of it if we moved here.' She fell silent. 'We didn't of course,' she said flatly. 'The island is too small – but we had nowhere else to go.'

'You could have come to me,' said Clarice.

'That would not have been wise.' She gave a sad smile. 'Your expression gives you away, Clarice. You could never have countenanced such a thing.' She hitched the baby up her lap. 'There's been enough scandal attached to my family in Sydney without adding to your discomfort, and I'm simply not strong enough to bear more shame.'

Clarice was chastened. 'Then why didn't you go back to

England? You could have pretended Gwen was widowed – that would have explained everything.'

'I couldn't afford it – not then,' she stated baldly. 'Besides, too many people already know the truth. I had a letter only the other month from a so-called friend asking about Gwen and her baby. I tore it up.'

'Where is Gwen? Why isn't she looking after her child?'

Eunice handed Lorelei another biscuit. 'She will have nothing to do with her,' she said sadly. 'I have done my best to encourage her to love her baby, but she simply ignores her.' She kissed the soft cheek as the little girl laughed and smeared biscuit down her frock. There were tears in Eunice's eyes as she looked back at Clarice. 'I know it isn't easy to care for a sick child, but she grows stronger every day, and I simply don't understand how Gwen can be so uncaring.'

Clarice glanced about the room, noting the worn furniture, the scruffy paintwork and faded curtains. Doctor's bills must be making a huge hole in Eunice's pocket – it was the only explanation for the poor surroundings. 'The father should share the responsibility of raising the child,' she said. 'Where is he – and why hasn't he done the honourable thing by marrying Gwen?'

The narrow shoulders drooped. 'I have no idea. Gwen refuses to discuss him.'

Clarice stiffened her spine. 'Well, it's not good enough. He must be found, and made to face up to his responsibilities. What's his name?'

'That's none of your business.'

Gwen was standing in the doorway, and Clarice turned to face her. 'It is when my sister is left to raise your sick child,' she retorted. 'You and the father should be made accountable.'

Gwen strolled into the room, poured a cup of tea and flopped on to the couch. She was dressed for riding, and she'd brought the scent of the stables with her into the room. 'I never wanted it in the first place,' she said coolly, her disinterested gaze flitting past the baby. 'Mother decided to keep it, so it's up to her to provide for it.'

'She is still your child,' said Clarice with equal coolness, 'and you and the father have a duty to her welfare. Who is he?'

Gwen drained the cup and balanced it on the arm of the couch. 'As I said before, Clarice, it really is none of your business.'

'You are as rude and spiteful as ever, I see,' snapped Clarice.

Gwen's expression hardened. 'And you're still the nosy bitch who sleeps with other women's husbands and ruins lives,' she retorted.

She saw Eunice wince, but Clarice couldn't be hurt by words any more and refused to rise to the bait. 'If you'd had a shred of decency, you would have made the father marry you – or at least ensure he pays his share of the child's upkeep. It's obvious your mother can't cope.'

'Then she shouldn't have taken it on.' Gwen rose from the couch and dug her hands into the pockets of her riding skirt.

Clarice eyed the insolent girl who stood before her. Gwen would have been beautiful but for the scowl. 'If you give me his name, then I will arrange to meet him discreetly and have a solicitor draw up a contract so he pays his share of Lorelei's upkeep.'

Gwen snorted. 'I don't think so,' she scoffed.

Clarice spoke sharply. 'Is he married? Is that why he didn't marry you?'

She smirked and strolled towards the back door. Opening it, she turned and regarded the little tableau of mother, aunt and child. 'That is something you will never know,' she said slyly, 'because I will never reveal his name.' She took a breath, clearly enjoying the drama of the moment. 'In fact, I will take his name to my grave just to spite all of you for ruining my life.' With that, she shoved through the screen door and let it slam behind her.

The silence was heavy in the cluttered kitchen. Clarice's anger was at boiling point, but as she saw the hurt and shame in her sister's face it dissolved. 'Oh, Eunice,' she breathed, 'thank God you asked me to come.'

'I didn't want to,' she replied, her cheek resting on the baby's head.

'You still haven't forgiven me,' she said flatly.

Eunice's brown eyes stared at her from across the table. 'I realised long ago what sort of man I'd married,' she said, 'but I refused to acknowledge it. What happened between you was shocking, and although it has taken a long time, I have come to terms with that.'

'I didn't encourage him, Eunice.'

Her gaze was steady. 'Not deliberately, I know. But Lionel could never resist a pretty, besotted young woman – and you *did* think you were in love with him, didn't you?'

Clarice dipped her chin. 'Yes,' she admitted. 'What a fool I was. I'm so sorry, Eunice. Can you ever truly forgive me?'

'There is nothing to forgive. Not any more.' She reached across the table for Clarice's hand. 'It was my pride that stopped me from writing, and as the years went on it became harder to find the right words to say. But when Lorelei came along and my health deteriorated, I knew I had to see you again before it was too late.'

Clarice moved around the table to Eunice and gently embraced her. 'Oh, my dear, dear sister,' she sighed. 'We will see this through, you and I, and I promise I will never hurt you again.'

Eunice's smile faltered as tears threatened. 'Would you like to hold Lorelei?'

Clarice hesitantly picked up the little girl and perched her on her hip. She had little experience of small children and in truth she was terrified of dropping her, but as she looked at the child she found she was being solemnly regarded by cornflower-blue

215

eyes. Her heart melted as a star-like hand reached up to touch her face, and as they gazed at one another, Clarice was overwhelmed with the most powerful love she'd ever experienced.

Clarice had dried her tears and covered Bess with a blanket. Vera would soon come bustling down, and she could ask the gardener to bury Bess beneath the magnolia. It had been Bess's favourite spot during the warm summer days, and she would be at peace there.

She sat in the silence, her thoughts returning to that other kitchen in Tasmania. The depth of her love for Lorelei had come as a surprise to her, but it had never faltered. As for Gwen – she had kept her silence, and to this day Clarice had no idea of the identity of Lorelei's father.

Joe appraised Ocean Child and decided he was putting on weight. 'Enough pasture for you, mate. Time you went indoors and stuck to a diet.'

He led the colt out of the spelling paddock and into the yard where Bob was grooming Moonbeam. 'Racing fodder from now on for this young 'un, Bob, or he'll be lumbering down the Hobart racetrack like an overstuffed wombat.'

'Righto.' Bob made a last sweep of the cloth over Moonbeam's glossy hindquarters and grinned with pride. 'Reckon I could get first prize for the best-turned-out filly, Joe? Eliza would like that, wouldn't she?'

Joe smiled. 'I thought you'd given your heart to Dolly now,' he teased.

Bob blushed. 'Fair go,' he grumbled. 'A bloke's gotta keep his options open, ain't 'e?'

Joe shook his head at the fickleness of Bob's passions and headed for his office. There was time before tea to finish the accounts, write out the order for the feed merchant and make sure everything was in place for the race meeting. He was deeply immersed in paperwork when his mother interrupted.

'I've brought you a cup of tea,' she said, plonking it down on his desk.

'Thanks,' he muttered, his finger marking the place on the account sheet. He looked up at her and grinned. 'You don't usually bring me tea. You must be after something.'

Molly sat down and began to tidy up the papers on his desk.

'Don't do that,' he said hastily. 'I can never find anything when you tidy up, so leave it, Ma, please.' He eyed her affectionately as she slumped back in the chair and folded her arms. 'What's up?'

'I've been thinking,' she said, and fell silent.

Joe gave up on the accounts and stretched out his long legs. 'And?' he prompted.

'Lorelei doesn't look at all like Gwen, does she?'

'From the little I've seen of Gwen, I would say not,' he replied, wondering where this was going.

'That's what I thought.' Molly sighed and picked at the corner of her apron. 'But she does remind me of someone, and I've been wracking my brains to think who.'

He smiled and dug his hands in his pockets. 'And did you come to any conclusions?'

'Mmmm.' Molly's gaze clouded over as she gave it more thought. 'It was a long time ago, and we were just kids, but . . .' Her gaze cleared as she focused on him, her usually sunny expression solemn. 'I've never told you why I loathe that woman so much, have I?'

He shifted in his chair. 'Are we talking about Gwen, or Lulu?'

'Gwen of course,' she said crossly. 'Do keep up, Joe.'

'I can only guess you and she fell out over dad,' he replied uneasily.

She eyed him sharply and clucked her tongue in annoyance. 'It was nothing like that,' she snapped. 'Your father was the most honourable, faithful husband, and wouldn't have given Gwen Bartholomew the time of day.'

She leant back in the chair, her hands deep in the apron pockets. 'But that didn't stop her pointing the finger at him when she had that baby. She turned up here, as bold as brass, demanding money – saying she would sully his name and ruin his business if he didn't cough up. She gave him a week to think about it.' She blinked back angry tears. 'We were rich then, the yard home to some of the best racehorses in the country.'

Joe remained silent, trying to imagine his quiet, gentle father facing that vindictive harpy. No wonder his mother hated her.

'I'd been away visiting a sick friend – and your grandfather was down in Hobart with a couple of horses, which was probably why Gwen chose that precise moment to pounce. Luckily your father was an honest man, and when I got back he told me everything.' She took a deep breath. 'Gwen had a reputation for liking the men and had made it clear she was after your dad, even though he was married and we had you. She hadn't been best pleased when he'd given her short shrift and warned her off, so to get her revenge she tried to blackmail him into paying for her kid.'

Joe gave a long, low whistle. 'Surely Dad didn't fall for that.'

Molly's laugh was bitter. 'He was in a terrible state about it at first, because he thought he couldn't prove anything. It would be his word against hers, and in the process his name would be blackened, the business destroyed.'

She returned to shredding the hem of her apron. 'Gwen's name had been linked to a dozen men, and any one of them could have been the father, but I knew my Patrick was not one of them. I got out the record books and went back to the months in which that child could have been conceived. She'd arrived early, so I had to do some very careful calculations.'

Her face brightened. 'Your dad was in Melbourne for most of

August that year and then he went straight on to Sydney for another month to look at a couple of promising fillies. He didn't get back here until just before Christmas, so he could prove he wasn't Lorelei's father.'

'I bet that went down like a ton of bricks with Gwen,' Joe murmured.

'Your dad, grandad and I faced her together, and she didn't like it – but she couldn't dispute the truth. Patrick warned her that if she spread any malicious rumours about him or his family, he would go to the police. We heard nothing more.'

'I suspect that wasn't the last of it though. If she couldn't get money out of Dad, she'd have gone elsewhere.'

'I agree,' said Molly thoughtfully, 'because although she's kept tight-lipped about the identity of the father, and no one has owned up, I think she knew all along who it was.'

'Then why didn't she just go straight to him and demand he support her and the baby?'

'Because he didn't have any money back then, and she thought Patrick was a better bet financially.'

Joe eyed her sharply. 'What are you trying to say, Ma?'

'I think I know who Lulu's father is.'

11

Lulu had been in Tasmania for two weeks, and although Molly's attitude seemed to have softened towards her, there was still tension between her and Dolly. Lulu She stood silently in the doorway watching Molly stuff the chickens. The gawky Dianna had gone home, Dolly was having a bath and the men were busy outside. It was the perfect time to try to make peace.

'Can I help with anything?'

Molly finished trussing the two chickens, dumped them in a roasting tin and wiped her hands on her apron. 'Thanks, but I'm done here.' She placed the birds in the oven and slammed the door.

'It must be hard work feeding so many,' said Lulu, 'I admire your stamina.'

Molly shot her a wary glance. 'Thanks,' she muttered, 'but I'm used to it.'

'I suppose you must be.' Lulu sat down at the table. 'Do you think I could have a cup of tea, Molly? I'm very dry after the evening ride-out.'

Molly lifted the kettle on to the hob and busied herself with cups, tea and sugar. The silence was uneasy, and Lulu bent to pat one of the dogs which had sneaked into the kitchen and was sitting with its head on her lap. 'I do like dogs, don't you? They never let you down or judge you.'

Molly placed two mugs of tea on the table and sat down. 'A

house isn't a home without a couple of dogs about,' she said, still wary. 'Do you have one back in England?'

Lulu nodded. 'Her name's Bess. My aunt Clarice gave her to me when she was just a puppy, but she's old now.' She sipped the tea. 'Molly, I realise we got off to a bad start, and although you were clearly unhappy to have me here, you've been a marvellous hostess. I do hope we can put our differences aside and become friends.'

Molly's lips twitched. 'I have no quarrel with you,' she murmured, 'but your friend has a sharp tongue, and I will not be spoken to like that in my own home.'

'Dolly's very protective of me,' she replied evenly. 'We've been friends for years, and although she can be tricky at times, she has a good heart.'

'I can see that.' Molly's gaze was steady and penetrating. 'I don't mind admitting I didn't want you here – but now you are, I realise I got you all wrong. You're not a bit like Gwen, are you?'

'I hope not,' replied Lulu with feeling. 'But then I haven't had anything to do with her for years.'

Molly grinned and flicked away a stray curl that dangled over her eyes. 'I reckon you and me will get along just fine,' she said. 'With so many men about, we women should stick together. I get bored sometimes with all their talk of horses and races and feed and two-up – it's been fun listening to you two talk about feminine things.' She sighed and tugged at the vast cotton apron that covered her old trousers and shirt. 'I can't remember the last time I wore a dress or a fancy hat.'

Lulu saw the wistfulness in her expression and her heart melted. Life had been tough for Molly Reilly. 'You'll get the chance when we go to Hobart for the race meeting,' she said, 'and Dolly has enough spare hats to supply Harrods – I'm sure she'll lend you one.'

'That's kind of you, dear, but I don't go to the races. Someone has to stay here and keep an eye on the men and horses.' Her smile was soft. 'No worries, love, the thought was appreciated.'

The sound of out-of-tune singing floated down the stairs, and they shared a grin. 'Why don't you give the Child his bedtime apple while Dolly has her bath?'

'As long as you don't need help here.'

Molly handed her an apple and gave her a gentle nudge towards the doorway. 'You're only young once,' she said. 'Get out of here.'

Lulu went upstairs and grabbed a cardigan. Dolly would be occupied for at least an hour, and now things had been settled with Molly, she was looking forward to spending some quiet time with Ocean Child.

She sat on the cane chair beside the front door and pulled on her boots as she admired the view she had come to love. The sun was almost down, the wind had dropped and the birds were returning to their night roosts with a clatter of wings and a cacophony of calls. She breathed in the perfume of honeysuckle and the sweetness rising from warm earth dampened by rain. This really was the most beautiful corner of the world, she concluded, as she gazed at the majestic trees and the great sweep of sky.

Tucking the apple in her pocket, she strolled over to the stables, the dogs at her heels. Bob and the other stable hands were deeply involved in a game of two-up behind their living quarters. It appeared to be a nightly ritual, and she stood and watched them for a while.

The pennies were placed on a piece of flat wood, then spun high. The anticipation mounted as every eye watched their progress to the ground. Shouts of glee and disappointment split the quietness of the evening, but the horses seemed quite inured to this and didn't bat an eye. Bob was clearly having a lucky run, for he held out a handful of coins and winked at her before immersing himself in the next throw.

Lulu left them to it and wandered into the yard to greet the horses who poked out their heads to watch her. She had always loved the smell and vigour of a clean stable-yard and was delighted by the inquisitiveness of the horses, who seemed so pleased to see her. She knew them all by name now, having ridden out each morning on Joe's gentle old mare to watch them being exercised on the gallops.

'Hello, boy,' she murmured to Ocean Child. She stroked his neck and nose, and fondled his ears in the way he adored. He was drooling with pleasure and resting his chin on her shoulder as her strong fingers worked their magic.

'I'm glad to see you two are getting on so well.'

Lulu turned and smiled at Joe, who was leaning against the corner of the stable, watching her. 'He's just a big soft lump really,' she replied, 'but I do wish he didn't dribble quite so much – my shirt's soaked.'

He grinned. 'I reckon that's got something to do with the apple in your pocket,' he drawled, 'but I'd appreciate it if you didn't give it to him. He's supposed to be on a diet.'

Lulu's eyes widened. 'Why? He looks in peak condition.'

Joe shoved away from the wall and ambled over, his boot heels ringing on the cobbles. 'He is, and I aim to keep him that way. No more pasture and treats until after the big race.' He looked down at her. 'He's the same as any human athlete,' he explained, 'and has to be fully prepared.'

'Sorry, boy,' she murmured to the colt. She patted his neck and stepped back, looking up at Joe as she plucked at the sodden shirt. 'Has the rain affected the going, do you think?'

He shook his head. 'He likes it a bit soft, and as long as there isn't anything too heavy coming down in Hobart over the next few days, he should be right.'

'I understand another owner is arriving tomorrow. Are her horses running?'

'Moonbeam's racing in the filly's maiden plate.' He glanced down at her, his smile wry. 'You'll like Eliza. She's a younger version of Dolly, but without the Pommy accent.'

'Oh dear.' Lulu laughed. 'Poor Joe, surrounded by bossy women. No wonder you spend most of your time with horses.'

'They certainly give me less bother,' he admitted drily. 'You know where you are with a horse – whereas women . . .'

'Are an entirely different species,' she finished. She glanced at him and wondered if he'd been unlucky in love – whether the scars had made him reclusive and shy, and she had to conclude they probably had – that they were the reason he rarely left Galway House. It was a terrible shame, for he was a quiet, gentle man with an attractive way about him that she had been drawn to during the past two weeks.

Her gaze travelled from the open collar that exposed a triangle of tanned flesh, to the slim hips, strong arms and capable hands. He was more than attractive, she realised, and quickly looked away.

She pulled her rambling thoughts together and dug her hands in her pockets, only to find the forgotten apple. With a questioning look to Joe, she fed it to one of the other horses and hoped Ocean Child wasn't watching.

Joe noticed how the dying sun sparked gold, bronze and copper in her hair, and the way she seemed so at ease in the stable-yard. He'd been watching her for some time before he spoke to her, and he realised he finally felt comfortable with her. The fact that he'd left his hat in the office was testament to that, and it came as a pleasant surprise to discover she appeared to accept who he was, even liked what she saw and wasn't repulsed.

He caught her eye and felt the heat rush through him as he

wondered if she had read his thoughts. He cleared his throat and looked at his boots. 'Any plans for tomorrow?'

'I'd like to come up to the gallops as usual. It's exciting watching Dolly giving you all a run for your money.'

'Yeah, she's quite a girl,' Joe agreed. 'I never suspected she could ride like that – and over the sticks too. If she wasn't a sheila, I'd give her a job tomorrow as a jockey.'

Lulu grinned. 'She's been hunting and competing in point-to-point since she could sit in a saddle. I envy her actually, because if I tried to ride like that I'd end up in bed for weeks.'

'Dolly said you have a problem with your heart.'

She shrugged. 'It's more of an inconvenience than a problem. I've learnt to live with it.' She seemed reluctant to discuss her health for she swiftly changed the subject. 'I've had a couple of messages come through from girls I went to school with, and thought I'd visit them and the old school tomorrow. After that I'll take another walk around town. I didn't get to see much of it the first time.'

'I bet you'll find it hasn't changed much,' he said. 'Nothing does down here.'

She nodded and scuffed her boots on the cobbles. 'Could we walk for a while?' she asked hesitantly. 'Only there are some things I'd like to mull over with you.'

He whistled, and the dogs came bounding out of the barn where they'd been hunting rats. They galloped ahead as he and Lulu strolled out of the yard and across the paddocks. He had no idea what she wanted to discuss, but he was wary. His mother had got a bee in her bonnet about Lulu's father, but had refused to enlighten him until she could prove who he was. How the hell she would do that was anyone's guess, but it was a topic he certainly didn't want to go over with Lulu.

He walked beside her, shortening his stride to match hers, enjoying the faint flowery perfume that drifted from her and the occasional brush of her arm against his. The only sound between them was the swish of grass against their boots and the steady beat of his heart.

'We never did talk about Mr Carmichael,' she said, breaking the companionable silence after they had been walking for some minutes. 'Have you come to any conclusions?'

They had reached the far paddock fence, and he leant against it and squinted into the low sun, watching the dogs haring about down by the river. 'He's a mystery man,' he replied. 'Does all his business by mail, two-way radio or telephone, and never leaves a contact number or address.'

'That's an unusual way to do business, don't you think?'

'I agree, and it seems he's set on helping me revive the yard – though why is yet another mystery.' He saw her frown, so went on to explain. 'No one seems to have heard of him before he sent Ocean Child here, but once that was done, he advised Eliza's dad to bring his horses, and three others have come indirectly through him as well.' He glanced down at her. 'Having said that, I know as much about him now as I did before – which is precisely nothing.'

He saw her bite her lip, a delightful little frown creasing her brow as she digested this. 'Ocean Child came from an auction. Did you try to find out who sold him initially?'

Joe gazed out across the darkening valley, where the dogs were giving chase to a rabbit. 'When you first denied ownership, I did some digging. The Child was one of a mob of brumbies sent to the sales by a cooperative of squatters in Queensland.'

'What are brumbies?'

He was surprised she didn't know, considering her background, but then she'd been a long time in England. 'They're wild horses,' he explained. He settled his back more comfortably against the railings. 'With so many men away during the war, a lot of horses escaped from the outback properties and mixed with the wild ones. There were thoroughbreds, hacks, ponies and stock horses all running free, causing havoc with crops and pastures. When the outlanders came back, they decided to round them up, keep the best for themselves and sell the rest. I reckon a few thoroughbreds were mixed in with that particular mob, because the Child is definitely from good stock.'

'Then I'm surprised no one noticed and kept him.'

Joe shrugged. 'Stockmen want tough little ponies, not thoroughbred colts that could prove headstrong and difficult to break.'

'Mr Carmichael obviously saw his potential,' she said thoughtfully.

'Yeah, whoever he is, he knows his horses,' Joe agreed.

'It's a shame we don't have a list of those squatters,' she said. 'One of them might give us a clue as to Carmichael's identity.'

'The list is in my office, but the names meant nothing to me, so I doubt they'll be much help.'

'I'm probably clutching at straws, but Carmichael didn't surface until he bought Ocean Child – and the Child is linked to the squatters. It's coincidental, but it is a link of sorts and might provide a clue.'

He nodded thoughtfully. 'You could be right. Come on, let's find the list and see what we can make of it.' He whistled up the dogs, who raced towards them, tongues lolling, tails like flags.

'Watch out, you're about to get another soaking,' he warned. But it was too late. The dogs shook themselves vigorously, showering both of them with muddy water.

'It looks like this shirt is fated,' laughed Lulu. 'Never mind, the dogs have clearly had a wonderful time, and the shirt will wash.'

Joe's heart melted at the sound of her laughter and the way she didn't seem to mind getting splattered by two filthy dogs. She was a rare woman, for most would have been furious.

They hurried back to the office, and as Joe stepped inside, he saw it with fresh eyes and realised it really was a tip. He shut the dogs outside, went straight to the shelf where he'd left the list, and sifted through the collection of letters and receipts. Unable to find it, he frowned and went through everything more slowly. 'It was definitely here,' he muttered.

'It could be anywhere,' she replied, her glance taking in the general clutter.

'No,' he murmured, returning the pile of papers to the shelf. 'It might look a mess, but I know where everything is, and I made a point of putting that list close to hand.' He avoided her gaze as he made another fruitless trawl through the paperwork on his desk. She must think him completely incompetent.

'Could someone have moved it?'

He was about to shake his head when he remembered seeing his mother come into the office as he'd left for the evening ride-out. 'Ma's probably been tidying up again,' he muttered. 'I do wish she wouldn't.'

Lulu grinned as she took in the mess. 'If this is tidy, I hate to think what it was like before,' she teased.

He felt the heat rise into his neck and face. 'I reckon you could be right,' he admitted. 'It is a bit of a dog's breakfast.' He was saved from further searching by the clatter of the dinner bell. 'Tea's up,' he muttered. 'I'll come back after and give this whole place a once-over. The list is bound to turn up sooner or later.'

The talk around the table was all about horses and the coming race meeting in Hobart. Bob and the other stable hands were eager to return to their game of two-up and so quickly shovelled down the food and clattered back outside. Lulu and Dolly had gone to their room straight after the meal, and Joe could hear the occasional ripple of laughter floating down the stairs.

Pleasantly sated with roast chook, veggies and his mother's special onion gravy, he stirred sugar into his tea. He would go back to the office soon, but for now he was content to sit in the

warmth of the kitchen and flick through the latest farming catalogue as Molly cleared the dishes. There were some useful-looking
trucks for sale as well as a couple of horse floats, and he was
trying to work out what he could afford when Molly interrupted
his calculations.

'You'll have to get one of the boys to cut more firewood,' she
said, as she plumped down into the chair beside him and poured
a second cup of tea. 'Dolly's baths use up all the hot water and,
with so many women in the house, that boiler will be working
overtime once Eliza arrives.'

'I'll get Bob to do it first thing,' he muttered, giving up on the
catalogue. 'Did Eliza contact you?'

'She got through on the two-way this afternoon. She's making
her own way here, so you won't have to go all the way to Launceston tomorrow to pick her up. She's got a surprise for you,
evidently, but I dread to think what it is.' Molly smiled and
sipped her tea. 'Lord knows how I'll cope with her *and* Dolly.'

He noted the liveliness in her expression. 'You'll cope, Ma. In
fact I think you're looking forward to it.'

She put down her cup and rested her chin in her hand. 'Reckon
I am too,' she admitted. 'It's good to have a house full of young
people again.'

'So you don't regret having them here?'

She shook her head. 'They're good company, and Lulu's a nice
girl. Quiet and well-mannered, charming and likeable – she's a
credit to Lady Pearson.'

Joe spluttered on his tea. 'Her aunt's titled?'

'Yeah. Her husband was a diplomat or something in Sydney.
He was knighted only just before he died.' She cocked her head as
she studied him. 'I sense you've come to like Lulu too.'

He could feel himself redden. 'She's all right,' he replied, his
gaze fixed to the cover of the catalogue.

Molly laughed. 'I reckon you think she's more than just all

229

right.' She put a hand on his arm, her expression suddenly more serious. 'Be careful, Joe. I've seen the way you look at her, and a girl like that will only break your heart.'

He looked down at her careworn hand on his tanned arm and sadly acknowledged she was right. The fact that she'd been raised by a titled lady and had no doubt had the best of everything put her even further out of his league.

He cleared his throat and changed the subject. 'Did you tidy up my office this evening?'

'I tried,' she said flatly, 'but it's beyond me.'

'I can't find the list of squatters who sold Ocean Child. You didn't see it did you?'

'I might have cleared it up with all the other rubbish,' she said nonchalantly. 'You really ought to get a proper filing system going, Joe. That place is a worse than a mare's nest.'

Joe saw how she kept her gaze averted. 'Did you see the list?' he persisted.

She shrugged. 'I don't recall it.' She pushed back the chair. 'I'll leave the washing-up for Dianne tomorrow,' she said through a vast yawn. 'Can't do much without hot water.' She dropped a kiss on his head. 'G'night, Joe. Sleep well.'

Joe sat there long after she'd hurried from the room. His thoughts were whirling as he went over the events and conversations of the past two weeks. He finally came to the conclusion that he wouldn't find that list, no matter how hard he looked. For reasons he couldn't begin to fathom – his mother had taken it.

Lulu and Dolly had come to enjoy the ride-outs each morning, and although Lulu was forced to take things easy and watch from the sidelines, Joe's pleasant company was a bonus. There was a camaraderie among the jackaroos as they competed against Dolly, and a sense of contentment in seeing the pride and hope in Joe's face as he watched. Lulu had never felt so at home, and as the days had gone on she'd become ever more deeply attached to Galway House and the quiet, shy man who lived there.

She and Dolly had washed and changed after the morning's exercise and were now on their way to Lulu's old school, where she was welcomed enthusiastically by those who remembered her and spent a happy hour touring the classrooms and having coffee with the headmistress. Then Lulu bought some flowers and went and placed them lovingly on her grandmother's grave. The memory of her was hazy, but she knew the old lady had cared for and protected her, and she was pleased to see that the tiny cemetery was beautifully looked after.

Having left the cemetery, Lulu visited the three young women who had sat next to her in class, had been her closest childhood friends and were still living locally. It was clear from the offset that their lives had followed very different paths, and there was a touch of resentment in their eyes as they regarded her expensive clothes, but the awkwardness faded as they realised Lulu had not forgotten them, and hadn't really changed. The years and the differences fell away as they exchanged memories of teachers and pranks, and they had left with promises to meet again soon.

The town itself had hardly changed, and as they strolled along the boardwalk they had been greeted by people who remembered Lulu as a little girl. The walk that should have taken only minutes took over an hour – prolonged further when Lulu spotted the doll-maker's shop.

She had dragged Dolly inside to be greeted by the familiar heady scent of wood shavings, glue and tobacco, and the warm welcome of the old man who sat behind his work-bench lovingly mending a doll as he smoked his pipe. She had spent many hours as a child in here with Primmy, watching him, listening to his stories, following his gnarled hands as they lovingly smoothed and repaired broken toys. It was as if time had stood still, and Lulu had been entranced.

Now they were strolling along the beach. The sea was still too cold for paddling, so they kept to the powdery sand by the grass as they headed for the rocks. Gulls hovered above them riding the wind like children's kites as plovers darted back and forth in the ripples, searching for food.

As they reached the end of the beach, Lulu came to a halt. The wind was at her back, whipping her hair into her face, and chilling the warmth of the welcome she'd received earlier. 'I don't know if I can do this,' she said, looking up the narrow road that led inland.

'Then don't,' insisted Dolly. 'Why put yourself through something that will ultimately be painful?'

Lulu silently acknowledged her friend's wisdom, but knew she would ignore it. The memories were too strong, the draw of the past impossible to resist. 'I must if I'm to put the ghosts to rest,' she breathed.

Dolly took her hand. 'Then let's get it over with.' She squeezed her fingers. 'You're not a little girl any more, Lulu. You don't have to be afraid of shadows.'

Lulu's smile was tentative as she took the first step on the road that led to the house in the bush. Her heart was pounding, her mouth dry, and as they reached the turn-off she had to steal herself to look up the track.

It was much smaller than she remembered – like a doll's house in the woods. Someone had recently painted the weatherboard white and the fly-screens blue. The chimney and roof had been replaced, and a lawn had been cut on either side of the cinder path that led to the front door.

Her gaze travelled fearfully beyond the house to the outbuildings. The old stables were still there, as were the barn and sheds, and although some of the bush had been cleared to extend the paddocks, the trees cast long, menacing shadows that seemed to beckon.

Lulu shivered and became the child again – the recurring nightmare all too real.

Small, defenceless and barely five years old, she could now recognise the all-too familiar figure who had crept through that bedroom door clutching the smothering feather pillow – could hear her voice as she lied to Clarice about her intentions.

But there were other images – other sounds that carried long-buried terrors she'd tried so hard to forget. She could hear the creaking branches tap on the tin roof of the shed and the moan of the wind. She was alone. Locked in the dark with no understanding of why she was being punished. There was no point in screaming, for no one would come – no point in crying, for her tears would simply prolong the sentence.

She saw herself curled in a corner, face buried against her knees to stifle her sobs. Surrounded by the rustling skitter of spiders and insects, she listened to the flight of buzzing flies and tried to pierce the darkness in search of hibernating snakes. The terror was acid in her throat, cold in the drenching sweat. She curled tighter, trying desperately to become invisible.

And then – after what felt like a lifetime – came the most terrifying sound of all: the rasp of the bolt being shot back.

She cringed from the figure standing there and cowered into the corner – waiting for the strike, the tugging fingers in her hair, the kick of a boot. 'Don't hurt me, Mamma,' she sobbed. 'Please don't hurt me.'

Cruel fingers grasped her hair, making her cry out as she was yanked to her feet. 'I told you never to call me that,' snarled Gwen.

Her head rang from the vicious slap that made her struggling heart stutter. 'I'm s-sorry,' she whimpered. But the punishment was not over, and she froze with fear – unable to cry out, to sob or even think as Gwen grabbed her and carried her across the deserted yard to the barn.

'Think you're so sweet, don't you? Grandma and Auntie's favourite little girl, with her big blue eyes and yellow curls? Their little pet lambkin?' Her grip was remorseless in her hair as she reached up to the hook on the barn wall and took down the shears. 'Let's see how this particular lambkin looks when she's been shorn.'

'Lulu! Lulu, what is it? You've gone very pale.'

She emerged from those terrible memories, strengthened by the knowledge she could overcome them. 'She cut off my hair,' she said flatly. 'She cut and cut and cut – and didn't care when the shears caught my scalp and my ear.'

There were no tears in her eyes when she looked at her friend, for there had been too many spilt over the years, and they solved nothing. 'I was only just nine, but I can remember the smell of those rusty shears, and the way they rasped and sliced over my head. I was so terrified she was going to kill me I could hardly breathe.'

Dolly wordlessly pulled her into a tight embrace and Lulu could feel her gentle fingers running through her hair and over her scalp, like a healing balm. She rested her head on the comforting shoulder. 'Clarice had to cut my hair whilst I was asleep as a child. Silly, I know, but I simply can't stand the sound of the snip, snip, snip.'

'But why do such a thing to a child? It's barbaric.'

Lulu felt chilled at the memory of the sly pinches and slaps, and the hurtful words that had shattered her fragile confidence during her childhood. They had made her life a misery, but the hacking off of her hair had almost destroyed her. 'She was jealous.'

'Of a defenceless child?'

234

Lulu felt no emotion as she turned her back on the house. 'I didn't understand it then, but the passing years have given me an insight into why Gwen acted as she did.' She took a deep breath. 'She didn't want me, but because Grandma Eunice insisted upon keeping me, she was forced to face me every day. I was a reminder of her shame – proof that my father – whoever he was – didn't care enough to marry her. And, of course, a barrier to any decent marriage she might have made. To make matters worse, she thought I'd usurped her place in her mother's affections.'

'What a gold-plated bitch!' spat Dolly. She gave Lulu a hug. 'I'm amazed Clarice and your grandmother let her get away with it.'

'It only happened when they were out of the house.' Lulu tucked her hands in her jacket pockets as she looked up the road. 'Grandma wasn't well and spent a lot of time in hospital. Clarice would leave me behind when she went visiting; she didn't approve of small girls in hospital unless they were patients – and I'd had my fair share of that. She never knew what really happened, because Gwen always had some viable explanation for the bruises, and I was too terrified to say anything against her.'

'How did she explain the haircut?'

'She never really did.' Lulu's expression was grim. 'It happened the day before Grandma died, and as Gwen had done one of her disappearing tricks, and Clarice was wracked with grief, the subject never really came up.'

'I'd be amazed if Clarice didn't face her with it.'

'They had a terrible set-to a couple of days after Grandma's funeral, and it was only then that Clarice mentioned it. I was in the room with them, but they didn't know, and I only understood half of what they were saying. But it turned out to be the last day I saw Gwen.'

'No wonder you escaped to the beach when you could. It sounds like the house from hell.'

Lulu smiled and linked arms with her friend. 'But I escaped, Dolly, and that's all that matters. Clarice and I didn't part on good terms, which I know she regrets as much I do, and that's why I keep writing to her. She has loved me unreservedly ever since I was a baby and given me a life I never would have had if I'd stayed here.' She laughed. 'Funny, isn't it? I've had to come to the other side of the world to fully appreciate my blessings.'

Dolly squeezed her arm and looked at her watch. 'We'd better go soon. Molly wants us back in time to meet Eliza.'

Lulu was aware that her emotional journey back to the house had left her exhausted. Yet, as she looked up the track, she felt a lightening of her spirits. Memories could be powerful, bringing back forgotten hurts and fears, but the years had diluted them, and when she'd been called upon to do so, she had managed to face them – and thereby banish them.

'I'd like to see if Primmy is still around,' she said. 'She was like a mother to me, and I can't leave without visiting her.'

They walked up the narrow track and came to a halt outside a row of small peg-boarded bungalows. 'She might not still live here,' said Lulu as she opened the gate in the white picket fence. 'But someone might know what's become of her.'

The door was flung open seconds after Lulu knocked. 'I knew you'd come to see me sooner or later.' Primmy stood before them, plump and smiling, her grey hair plaited in a coil around her head. She opened her arms and Lulu stepped into the familiar warm embrace.

'Oh, Primmy,' she sighed. 'It's been so long.'

'Come on in and I'll make us a cuppa. We've got a lot to catch up on.' Her laughing eyes settled on Dolly. 'Who's this?'

Lulu made the introductions and they were led into a tiny neat room that served as sitting room and kitchen. Primmy fussed about making tea, chattering like a parakeet all the while, scarcely pausing for breath. She had three grown children, two grandchildren and a great-grandchild expected at any minute. Her life was busy, her husband had retired from his job at the post office and all in all she was very content.

'But what about you?' she said finally. 'I always worried about you, you know – with that mother of yours.'

Lulu gave her a potted version of her life since leaving Tasmania, and finished by giving a dramatic, almost comic description of how Gwen had tried to run her over at the docks.

Primmy sniffed. 'She's not changed much, I know, but I suppose one ought to feel sorry for her, considering.'

Lulu set aside the teacup. 'Considering what?'

Primmy settled back into her comfortable armchair and folded her arms. 'I suppose you were too young to know all about her father, and I doubt your aunt would have said anything. Proud old lady, and not one to rake over family scandals.'

Lulu glanced at Dolly before encouraging Primmy to continue.

'It was all a long time ago, but I remember the gossip as if it were yesterday,' Primmy began. 'Your grandpapa, General Bartholomew, liked the ladies by all accounts, and wasn't too bothered that his wife knew about his affairs. But he had one too many and got caught by the lady's husband.' Her eyes gleamed with relish as she licked her lips. 'That wouldn't have been so bad, but then he was caught helping himself to military funds and was cashiered.'

Shocked though she was by these revelations, Lulu still found them fascinating. 'Clarice certainly never told me any of this. Go on, Primmy.'

'Well,' she sat forward in her eagerness, 'I heard tell he went to Brisbane and got involved with some tarty piece up there. He took to drink and buggy racing, both of which killed him in the end.' She shook her head. 'It was a terrible scandal,' she said, 'and it was thought at the time to be the cause of Sir Algernon's fatal heart attack – but of course we'll never know for sure.'

Lulu leant forward in her chair. 'But Grandma Eunice had left him long before that to come to Tasmania?'

Primmy nodded. 'That was the start of all the trouble with Gwen. She adored that no-good wastrel, hated her mother for leaving him and was heartbroken when he simply ignored her.' She leant her elbows on her knees and sighed. 'He never wrote to her, you know. The poor girl was devastated when she heard he'd been killed.'

'None of that can excuse the way she was,' said Lulu flatly.

'I agree, and I'm sorry if all this talk has upset you.'

Lulu felt remarkably calm. 'I don't suppose you know anything about my father?'

'Sorry, my dear, but that was one subject Gwen kept to herself. None of us knew – but of course there was enormous speculation at the time because there were so many candidates.' She patted Lulu's knee. 'Sorry, my dear, that was a little harsh, but then it's all old history. And look at you – a fine, beautiful young lady with the world at your feet. I always knew you'd turn out right in spite of Gwen.'

Lulu and Dolly said their goodbyes half an hour later and, with promises to visit again, returned to the utility.

'Good heavens,' breathed Dolly. 'No wonder Clarice tried to stop you from coming here. The scandal back then must have been horrendous.'

'But it didn't really concern her, did it? It was her sister's husband and Gwen who caused all the trouble.'

'Mud sticks, as we both know, and things were different in those days. Clarice was probably just as ashamed as her sister over what was a family scandal.'

Lulu wasn't totally convinced, but as she had nothing sensible to add to the debate, she kept silent.

As they drove away, neither of them noticed the man who emerged from behind the shuttered kiosk to watch their departure. He stood in the shadows long after they had gone, and when he finally turned away it was with the slow steps of a person deep in thought.

It seemed to be a day of contemplation for Clarice – a day when the past haunted her and the future beckoned with icy fingers. She sat on the hard wooden pew and tried to ignore the erratic beat of her heart as she gazed at the shafts of sunlight coming through the stained-glass windows. They fell on the white altar cloth in a rainbow of colour and burnished the gold crucifix and candlesticks to an almost dazzling intensity.

Her gaze drifted from the chancel to the dark wooden pulpit, then on to the memorial wall plaques and engraved marble slabs on the floor that marked the final resting places of local gentry. She had been christened in the stone font with its ornately carved cover, and would be buried in the graveyard alongside her parents – it seemed her life had turned full circle.

The church had been built by the Saxons, and between these tranquil, silent walls she hoped to find the solace that in the past had eluded her. She closed her eyes and breathed in the perfume of candlewax, damp stone, flowers and incense, her thoughts drifting.

Going to church had always been a duty – expected of her from the day she'd been born and carried out with reluctance. She had never quite seen the point of it all when God was so evident in the beauty of nature, and therefore had never found the same comfort as Algernon in the rituals and faintly ridiculous posturing of the sanctimonious clergy. But today was different, and as she sat there she could almost feel the tranquillity seep into her bones, bringing with it an assurance of an afterlife.

She must have dozed off, for when she opened her eyes again she realised with a start that the sunbeams had moved and were now highlighting the ancient paintings of the fourteen Stations of the Cross. Gathering up her handbag and gloves, she rose stiffly from the uncomfortable pew and made her slow way down the aisle she had once trodden as a bride. Where had she gone, that young woman who'd been so full of hope for the future? How swiftly time had flown, and what a mark those passing years had left behind.

Clarice grew impatient with her thoughts as she stepped into the sunlight. Death would come soon enough – there was no point in dwelling on such maudlin meanderings.

The grass in the churchyard had been freshly scythed and the scent of it filled the air as she walked down the cinder path and through the shadows of overhanging yews. Most of the headstones in the older part of the cemetery were so weathered they were illegible, and the iron railings of the table-tombs had disintegrated with rust. The sight of so many blank-eyed angels and lichen-stained cherubs depressed her, and without sparing a glance for the family plot, she pushed through the lychgate and into the lane.

It was unseasonably hot again, and as she approached the side gate that led into her garden she began to regret her short outing. Her heart was beating far too rapidly, her head was buzzing and her swollen ankles ached. Staggering across the lawn, she collapsed on to the bench beneath the magnolia tree and mopped her face.

She would have liked a cup of tea, but as Vera Cornish was nowhere in sight, and she didn't have the energy to go looking for her, she gave up on the idea. Too many restless nights and too many memories had taken their toll, and she couldn't help but smile at the irony of having been told by Dr Williams that her blood pressure was far too high. She had used that ruse to try and keep Lorelei in England, now it seemed she was paying the price for being dishonest.

Regarding the freshly dug earth and neat wooden cross that

marked Bess's final resting place, her thoughts turned to the tiny cemetery in Tasmania, and another death. It had been stiflingly hot that day too, she remembered.

It was February 1903, and Clarice had long since given up the lease on the cottage to move in with Eunice so she could help with the bewitching Lorelei. Her sister's failing health meant she was almost bedridden, but even on her worst days she insisted upon spending time with the child, and it was clear they both benefited from these short visits. A close bond had formed between them, and Clarice was thankful that Lorelei brought Eunice so much joy – for it was this delight in the little girl that kept her interested in life.

Despite her love for Lorelei, Clarice had soon discovered it wasn't easy sharing a house with Gwen, who treated it like a hotel and showed little interest in her mother's health or her daughter's welfare. Her horses mattered to her more, and she was, thankfully, often away competing in the showjumping rings.

But these lengthy absences led to unsavoury affairs, and Clarice had had to swallow her disgust when brazenly presented with the latest conquest: usually an itinerant cowboy or stable hand. Gwen would never change, and while her sister, Eunice, was alive, Clarice would keep her opinions to herself and do the best she could to make sure Lorelei was raised decently.

Lorelei's ninth birthday had been celebrated the week before, with a small tea-party for her school friends. Her heart condition seemed to be improving, and Clarice put that down to a healthy diet, plenty of sunshine and careful exercise – but there were other more worrying things which had never been satisfactorily explained.

The child was too quiet, especially when Gwen was at home, often disappearing for hours to the beach, or hiding away in one of the stables. And then there were the bruises which Lorelei insisted were the results of falls or rough games. Clarice had not been convinced, for those bruises only appeared after she'd been left with her mother.

She had tried to get to the truth, but was met by a barrier of silence, and all she could do was keep a closer watch on Lorelei. This too had proved almost impossible when Eunice had been taken into hospital, and although Primmy had her own family to care for, she'd helped when she could. Gwen was often the only one around to leave her with.

Late one afternoon Clarice had returned to the house in the bush, weary from a long day of sitting by her sister's bed. Eunice was fading fast, and before she had fallen into an exhausted asleep she had asked to see Lorelei and Gwen. But as Clarice stepped into the kitchen, she could see no sign of either of them, just a note by the kettle informing her that Gwen had gone away for five days. She assumed Lorelei was in the yard, so set about making a cup of tea.

Her hand stilled as she heard the heart-rending sob. Finding the little girl hiding in a miserable curl under the table, Clarice had to coax her out. Lorelei emerged sobbing, shivering and fighting for breath.

Clarice stared in horror at the tufts of hair sticking out of the raw scalp, and felt rage gather at the dark bruising around her fragile wrists and the blood congealing on wounds obviously inflicted by a sharp blade. She took Lorelei into her arms and wept. She cried over the cruelty of a mother who could have done such a thing, shed hot tears for her sister who was already on her final journey and felt her heart break at the pain and suffering of the little girl she'd failed to protect. She should never have left her with Gwen.

It had taken a long time to soothe the child's breathing, bathe the wounds and try to repair the damage done to the beautiful hair. Eunice must not see her – it would be too distressing – so she took Lorelei to Primmy's house up the road. Primmy crooned and fussed over the child, finding her a pretty scarf to wear beneath the frilly bonnet, and Clarice had left reluctantly, but assured that Lorelei would be safe.

Eunice had never woken from her sleep, and slipped away as dawn lightened the sky. The years of heartache and shame had finally taken their toll.

Clarice made the funeral arrangements and returned to the house to care for the distraught Lorelei, mourn for her beloved sister and wait for Gwen.

The day of the funeral arrived and Gwen still had not returned. Clarice's sadness deepened when it became clear that Eunice had made few friends during her years in Tasmania, for the only mourners to attend the short service were her doctor, her solicitor and Primmy.

Lorelei had begged to come, and Clarice had compromised by letting her stay in the carriage with the driver at the church gate. It wasn't right for one so young to attend, and the child was still too traumatised by everything that had happened to be able to face such an ordeal.

The slam of the screen door two days later heralded Gwen's return, and Clarice, unaware that Lorelei was playing with her doll beneath the table, steeled herself for what was to come. 'Where have you been?' she asked coldly.

'None of your business.' Gwen helped herself to a cup of tea and began to make a sandwich.

'Leave that,' snapped Clarice, 'and sit down.'

Something in her tone must have registered, for Gwen plumped down on a kitchen chair and folded her arms like a petulant child.

'There's no easy way to say this, Gwen. Your mother is dead.'

A spark of something flitted in her eyes to be swiftly extinguished. 'It was only to be expected.' Gwen shrugged. 'When's the funeral?'

'Two days ago.'

Gwen digested this, her gaze never moving from Clarice. 'That was quick,' she muttered. 'I've only been away a week.'

'It has been ten days,' Clarice said sharply. 'She died the day you left, and I've had to deal with everything on my own.'

'Poor you.' There was flat insolence in her tone as she rose to resume making the sandwich. 'When's the will being read?'

'It was read yesterday.' Clarice folded her hands on the table, preparing herself for the storm that was about to erupt.

Gwen chewed on the sandwich, her eyes speculative. 'She couldn't have left much. We haven't exactly been living in luxury since she left Daddy. But she did have some good jewellery, and that's probably worth something.'

Clarice took a deep breath. 'Your mother left her jewellery to me,' she said. 'The pieces were part of my grandmother's collection, and will go to the next generation when I die. There were a couple of small bequests – to Primmy, and a charity for orphans.' She kept her gaze fixed on Gwen. 'This house and everything in it is yours, including the horses and farm stock, and she has provided a trust which will pay you a yearly income, but the bulk of her estate is to be kept in trust for Lorelei.'

Gwen was clearly shocked. 'What do you mean, "the bulk of her estate"? What estate? I thought we were poor and this house was rented.'

'Eunice didn't want you to know how much money there was because she knew you would either fritter it away or attract unsavoury fortune hunters. She bought this place with what was left after your father's debts had been settled from the sale of the house in Coogee.'

Gwen's eyes narrowed, and her voice was dangerously low. 'Just how much money did she have?'

Clarice opened the drawer in the kitchen table and pulled out the will. 'Read it for yourself. It's all quite clearly explained.'

Gwen snatched the will. It didn't take long to read, but by the time she'd reached the end she was ashen. 'She was rich all the time and never said a word,' she hissed. Her fingers clenched around the document. 'And she left everything to that . . . that . . . snivelling brat.' Colour flooded into the bleached face and the eyes sparked venom. 'What about me? I'm her daughter and by rights I should have it all.'

'She may have given birth to you, but you haven't been a daughter to Eunice for years.' Clarice felt extraordinarily calm as the storm raged in Gwen's face. 'As the will clearly states, the house will provide you with a home, and the income from the trust will support you quite comfortably.'

'It's a drop in the ocean compared to what that bitch has got.'

Clarice gritted her teeth. 'Lorelei has not had your advantages. The trust will provide her with a good education and help protect her from the shame of being illegitimate.'

'This is your doing,' she snarled. 'You made her change her will. She wasn't right in the head when she signed it, and I'll prove it. I'll sue you, the solicitor and that brat to get what's rightfully mine.' She stood over Clarice, fists clenched, chest rising and falling with every furious breath. 'That's *my* money, and I will *not* give it up without a fight.'

Clarice rose from the chair and faced her. 'Eunice wrote that will within months of Lorelei's birth. She was of sound mind, and even had her doctor confirm that she knew exactly what she was doing.' She kept her steady gaze on the young woman's face. 'She knew you would rail against the will – knew you would cause as much trouble as you could to deny Lorelei her inheritance – and took the appropriate steps to forestall you.'

Gwen's shoulders slumped, and tears of disappointment and frustration ran down her face as she sat down again. 'But where did she get all that money?' she whined. 'Daddy was declared bankrupt, and we lived like church mice.'

Clarice eyed Gwen without pity. 'Our mother had been widowed for some years and died around the time Lorelei was born. She was a wealthy woman, and her fortune was split between me and Eunice.'

'It's not fair.'

Clarice shrugged. 'Life rarely is. You'll just have to learn to put up with it.' She turned her back on Gwen and poured herself a cup of tea. 'But you'll have to live with it alone,' she added, 'because I'm taking Lorelei back to England.'

Gwen sniffed back the tears as she scraped the chair against the wooden floor and stood. 'You can't take her anywhere,' she snarled.

Clarice turned to face her. 'I think you'll find I can.'

'No, you can't. She's my daughter, not yours.'

'Don't insult me with that argument,' snapped Clarice. 'You haven't had a kind word or look for that poor mite since the day she was born. You're not a mother – you're a vindictive, spiteful harpy who uses a defenceless child as a punchbag – and don't you dare deny it – I've seen the bruises, and what you did to her hair.'

'She's lying.'

'She's never said a word against you,' hissed Clarice, 'and that's what really breaks my heart. She's terrified of you, but the poor little thing still loves you – still seeks your approval and wants to call you Mamma.'

Gwen gave a mocking snigger. 'Then she's even more stupid than I thought.' Her eyes became almost feral. 'But she's mine, and there's nothing you can do about it. She's staying here.'

Clarice was taken aback. She'd thought Gwen would be only too pleased to be rid of Lorelei – and yet she seemed determined to keep her. She eyed Gwen thoughtfully. It was not through love of her daughter, that was certain. 'If you think that by keeping Lorelei you will get your hands on that trust fund, then you're sorely mistaken,' she said coldly. 'The bank has charge of it, and is under firm instructions to keep it that way until Lorelei reaches adulthood.'

Gwen simmered, her hate-filled gaze never leaving Clarice as she sat down again.

Clarice went on. 'Our family has had enough dirty laundry washed in public, but I will go to court to fight for that child. And when I do, I shall list the catalogue of ill-treatment you've dished out to her. I will prove you're unfit to care for her, and that your morals are that of a streetwalker. There have been enough men over the past few years to make quite a considerable list – and I'm sure the married ones will not want their names dragged into this.'

'You wouldn't dare.'

'Try me.' Clarice held her ground, determined to win the battle by any means.

Gwen folded her arms, her expression thoughtful. The gleam of avarice lit in her eyes and she gave a sly smile. 'I'll agree – but it will cost you.'

'I thought it might. I'll make arrangements with the bank. You will receive one hundred pounds a year until Lorelei turns twenty-one.'

'It's not enough.'

'One hundred pounds a year or I go to the courts.'

The blue eyes were steady and speculative, and Clarice kept her nerve.

'All right,' said Gwen. 'When do I get the first payment?'

'When you have signed the legal papers awarding me her guardianship. I'll make an appointment with the solicitor for next Monday.'

Clarice's bags and boxes had been packed for almost a week and she and Lorelei left the house within hours of that unpleasant exchange. They moved into a small hotel until the papers were signed and sealed. Then they left for Melbourne.

Clarice then booked passage to England and eight months later they sailed to their new life. Gwen got her first payment, but Clarice finally had a daughter to cherish and call her own.

12

The October day had remained clear and sunny, but as the afternoon wore on and the shadows crept across the paddocks it grew chilly. Bob had finished putting Ocean Child and Moonbeam through their paces over the brush fences, and Joe was pleased with both of them. With a bit of luck and a fair wind, they could do very well in Hobart.

He was trying to rub the Child down after his exercise, but the colt was proving skittish. He was getting a little too full of himself and needed reminding he was not yet a champion. Joe tugged on the cheek-strap. 'Stand still, you bugger,' he growled. 'You're not going anywhere until I've got the sweat off you.'

The Child tossed his head and snorted as he danced on the cobbles and sideswiped Joe with his hindquarters.

'Do you want a hand?'

Joe glanced at Lulu and hastily skipped away from the clattering hooves. 'He's playing up rough,' he muttered, 'so mind your toes.'

Her hand closed over his on the cheek-strap, and the warmth of it seemed to go right to his boots. 'Hold tight then,' he said, grabbing the leading rein. 'If he breaks for it, we'll never catch him.'

Lulu crooned to the Child and massaged his ears. 'You're just being a naughty little boy, aren't you?' she murmured. 'Steady, there, steady.'

Joe watched dumbfounded as the colt stopped prancing and leant his chin on Lulu's shoulder, eyelids fluttering in ecstasy. 'Strewth!' he muttered in disgust. 'Now I've seen it all.'

She looked up at him with an impish grin. 'Like most males, he's a sucker for a woman's touch.'

There was no reply to that, but he could feel the heat flood through him as their gazes met and held. 'I'd better get him rubbed down and in his box,' he muttered.

'I'll help.' She took the cloth and began to rub it vigorously over the chestnut coat, talking all the while to the Child, keeping him sweet-tempered and calm.

Joe picked up the brush and curry comb and they worked together in a silence electrified by their closeness and the shared glances and smiles. All too soon they had finished, and Lulu led the Child into his box and left him to tear at his hay-net.

'You've certainly got a way with him,' Joe murmured, unable to take his gaze off her as she stood inches away.

'So have you.' Her eyes were the deepest blue, her face glowing, lips slightly parted and just asking to be kissed. He swayed towards her, mesmerised.

The moment was broken by a shout from the homestead. 'They're here, Joe. Come and look at this.'

'Bloody hell,' Joe sighed.

Lulu giggled and blushed. 'I suppose we'd better see what all the fuss is about.'

He nodded reluctantly, but his heart was hammering with hope and happiness. She had wanted him to kiss her.

He grabbed his hat, and they headed for the front of the homestead. He could hear laughter and cries of delight and wondered what the hell was going on. As they rounded the corner he came to a stunned halt.

'G'day, Joe. Look what I've brought you.' Eliza was smiling as she advanced on him in a flutter of lemon silk and tucked her hand through his arm. 'The floats are both yours, and one of the utes – but there's more, Joe. Lots more.'

He felt her tug on his arm, but he seemed to be glued to the ground. He stared at the cavalcade, hardly daring to believe it. The horse floats were the most modern and expensive ones he'd seen in the catalogues, and the ute was far sturdier than the old models he already had. 'You can't buy me things like that,' he protested.

'I knew you'd be difficult,' she said with a pout and a flutter of her eyelashes, 'but you see, it's important you have those floats – and the ute – because you're going to need them from now on.' She called out to the drivers: 'Show him what we've brought.'

There was a collective gasp of admiration as four thoroughbreds tripped daintily down the two ramps. The jackaroos swarmed, Dianne giggled and Molly stood with her hand over her mouth, eyes wide as if she couldn't believe what she was seeing.

'I have to say,' drawled Dolly, 'not even my father has such good bloodstock, and he rides with the Beaufort Hunt.'

'What do you think, Joe?' Eliza's eyes were shining as she clung to his arm. 'They aren't mine, and they're hardly a gift, but when I told my friend about you she insisted I bring them over for you to train.'

He eased from her grip and ran his hand over the muscled chests and hindquarters, looked into the intelligent eyes and checked their mouths, legs and hooves. 'Beauty,' he breathed.

Eliza clapped her hands with glee. 'I do so love giving people surprises.'

Joe's smile wavered. 'That's all very well, but now I'm going to have to find more stable hands to look after them.'

'I thought of that too,' she replied. 'Davy and Clem have looked after those four horses since they got back from Gallipoli, and they'd like to stay with them.' She leant closer, her musky perfume drifting up to him. 'They were both invalided home,' she whispered, 'but they're fit now and won't let you down.'

Joe eyed each man, liked what he saw, and shook their work-roughened hands. 'I pay standard wages, but you get tucker and board thrown in.' He grinned. 'Ma does the cooking, so you'll be right.'

Lulu realised she'd been forgotten in the whirlwind that was Eliza, and a stab of something approaching jealousy shot through her as the girl held on to his arm and smiled flirtatiously up at him. Dressed in a yellow silk dress and coat, with matching high heels, she looked as if she was ready to attend a palace garden party. Her make-up was flawless, if a little heavy-handed, and her bobbed hair was held in place with a sparkling butterfly pin.

Lulu looked away, only to discover that Molly had moved to stand beside her. There was a strange expression on her face that was soon explained by her muttered words. 'I have high hopes of those two,' she confided. 'Eliza's good for Joe, and they have a lot in common. It wouldn't do the yard any harm having her in the family either.' Her gaze was not unkind, but it was steady and full of meaning, the message quite clear.

'Then let us hope Joe sees things in the same light,' Lulu replied in the same confidential tone, resisting adding that Eliza might be a little rich for his blood. Not wanting to prolong the conversation and risk Molly reading her hurt, Lulu dug her hands into her trouser pockets and moved away as the cavalcade trooped into the yard.

The thoroughbreds were set loose in the paddock and the horseboxes stowed carefully under cover by the barn. The chatter and laughter swirled around as Lulu followed Joe and Eliza's progress about the yard.

She was very pretty, she silently admitted, but Lulu suspected she was barely eighteen, and there was something that didn't ring true about her. The girlish enthusiasm didn't match the sophisticated clothes and heavy make-up – neither did it quite mask the determined coquettishness in her eyes every time she looked at Joe. It was clear she was a favourite in the yard – and was basking in the attention – but Lulu, usually so loathe to judge too quickly, couldn't take to her at all.

'She's frightfully nice, isn't she?' Dolly carefully negotiated the cobbles in her high heels and leant against the stable wall.

'I wouldn't know,' replied Lulu. 'I haven't had the chance to talk to her yet.'

Dolly eyed her, frowned and dismissed the rather sharp retort. 'She reminds me of someone, but I can't think who.'

'Look in a mirror, Dolly – she could be your younger sister.'

'I suppose she could, and she certainly has my flair for colour and style. I like the pin in her hair.' She flicked her fringe out of her eyes, watched the melee surrounding Eliza and lit a cigarette. 'She's still frightfully young of course, but I've seen the way she looks at Joe. He's a lucky man. Not many girls come armed with gifts like that.'

Lulu shrugged as if it didn't matter and turned away to pet the Child.

'Oh dear. Have I put my foot in it?' Dolly put a hand on Lulu's shoulder. 'I'm sorry, darling, I didn't realise you fancied him for yourself.'

'Don't be silly,' she muttered, moving away. 'He's just training my horse, and I'm lucky he's so good at it. We have little in common but for Ocean Child.'

Dolly puffed on the cigarette. 'Mmm. Methinks she doth protest too much,' she murmured. There was a moment of silence. 'Do be careful, darling,' she said softly. 'You're only here such a short while, and it wouldn't be fair to upset the apple cart by leading him on.'

'I'm not leading anyone anywhere,' she snapped. 'Put a sock in it, Dolly. You're talking nonsense.' Despite her waspish reply, Lulu realised Dolly's advice was warranted, for she'd wanted Joe to kiss her – even though it would have been a terrible mistake.

Dolly opened her mouth to argue when a voice interrupted. 'G'day, you must be Lulu and Dolly. Good to meet you.'

'How do you do?' Lulu coolly shook the proffered hand. Closer inspection confirmed her suspicions; there was a hardness behind Eliza's smile that made Lulu mistrust her.

Eliza made little pretence of cutting Lulu as she turned to Dolly. 'Let's leave the blokes to it and go and have a cuppa. I want to hear all the gossip from England, what the fashions are like, and if you've actually met any of the royal family.' She linked arms with Dolly and drew her towards the homestead.

Lulu realised she'd been forgotten – that Dolly had fallen under Eliza's spell just like everyone else.

She looked away and found Joe was watching her. Their gazes met, and she dipped her chin, her thoughts troubled by the message in his dark eyes. The attraction between them had grown over the past two weeks, and today it had almost blossomed into something far more serious. Feelings like that were dangerous. She was not one for casual affairs, and knew instinctively that he felt the same. Her life was in England and his was here – probably with the artful, generous Eliza who had his mother's blessing. With aching honesty, she silently admitted she was jealous.

The trip to Hobart would take several days, and would have meant leaving the place to Molly and one jackaroo – thereby endangering the security of the valuable horses left behind, so Joe was grateful to Eliza for bringing in extra men.

He'd pondered on how to feed so many people around his mother's kitchen table, and had gone to take a look at the state of the old cookhouse. It had been built in his grandfather's time and had served the men who worked here for decades, but as the stables had declined, the cookhouse had fallen into disrepair. He had set the men to clearing it out while he repaired the benches and table and sorted out the water supply.

He stood in the doorway and smiled as the hands tucked into the heaped plates of food Dianne had brought from the house. The sound of voices rising again to the exposed beams of the great roof was one that evoked happy memories, and although there was still a lot to do, it served its purpose well enough for tonight.

Tired but exhilarated by the events of the day, he headed back to the homestead, kicked his filthy boots off and stood in his equally grubby socks on the veranda looking up at the stars. It was a clear night, which promised a frost but no rain – and as long as the ground didn't get too hard, he stood a chance of winning enough prize money in Hobart to pay Eliza back. Her generosity had stunned him, but he didn't feel easy accepting such expensive gifts, however well-meant. Eliza was young and impressionable, with a childish glee for giving presents. She enjoyed being the centre of attention, was probably in the throes of hero worship – although why was a mystery to him – and he wanted there to be no misunderstandings.

His thoughts turned to Lulu and the kiss they had almost shared. He closed his eyes, imagining his lips on that lovely mouth, his hands cupping her head, fingers buried in her glorious hair as she melted into his arms.

The rasping screech of a barn owl brought him to his senses. He watched with a wry smile as the ghostly bird flew across the blackness of the sky. Possessing the love of a woman like Lulu was as much of a fantasy as the Aboriginal belief that the white-faced owl was a magic being who bore messages from the spirit ancestors when something momentous was about to happen. She might have been willing to kiss him, but it was probably only curiosity on her part – or more likely a moment of madness she would instantly regret.

He gave a sigh, turned his back on the sky, pushed through the recently oiled screen door and padded down the hall. He could hear Dolly and Lulu moving about upstairs, no doubt packing for the early start tomorrow, but as he approached the kitchen he heard Eliza say something that made him pause.

'She's the spitting image, Molly. I swear, you could have knocked me down with a feather when I first saw her.'

'So, I was right,' breathed Molly. 'But what do I do now?'

'That's a tough one. You can't very well get on the two-way and come straight out with it.'

'Come out with what?' Joe stepped into the kitchen.

Molly grabbed a sheet of paper off the table and stuffed it into her apron pocket. 'Nothing.' Her face reddened and she wouldn't look at him.

'You're both looking very guilty over nothing,' he said quietly. 'And what's that you're trying to hide, Ma? It wouldn't be the list of owners I was looking for, would it?'

Eliza exchanged glances with Molly. 'You'd better come clean, Molly. Joe's not going to let it rest otherwise.'

Molly bit her lip, her expression worried. Then she sighed. 'Shut the door, Joe. I don't want Lulu to hear any of this.' She waited until he'd sat down before she pulled the paper out of her pocket and smoothed it on the table. 'If I tell you, then you have to promise to keep it to yourself.'

Joe frowned, unwilling to commit until he knew more. 'If this is to do with Lulu, then surely she has a right to know.'

Molly shook her head. 'It isn't as straightforward as that,' she said, her hands still uncreasing the crumpled paper. 'You see, I began to wonder if Ocean Child came from Lulu's father– it was the only explanation that made any sense.' She glanced at Eliza, who nodded encouragement. 'Finding the list and talking to Eliza has confirmed at least who her father is.'

Joe leant forward and took the list. 'Which one is he?'

Molly's finger came down on the fourth name. 'That's him. There's absolutely no doubt.'

The name was a common one and meant little. 'So what's your problem? Why not tell Lulu and help her contact him?'

'Because it's only a suspicion. I can't be certain he gave her the horse,' she protested. 'He might not know anything about her or care less – and the poor girl has gone through enough without getting hurt again. It's lucky I didn't tell her that I suspected Carmichael and her father were one and the same – because it turns out I was wrong.'

Joe frowned. 'How do you know? 'Molly carefully folded the list and returned it to her pocket. 'Carmichael got through on the two-way when you were in the yard, and I knew he couldn't possibly be Lulu's father.'

'How on earth can you be so certain?'

'Because the man I spoke to had a young voice, and he was calling from a roadhouse in Deloraine'

'Voices are deceptive on the two-way, what with all the static and Doreen's heavy breathing. You're jumping to conclusions, Ma.'

Molly shook her head. 'This man – Lulu's father – suffered a stroke about eighteen months ago. Eliza knows him well and she told me his speech has been impaired and when she last saw him he wasn't capable of travelling anywhere, certainly not all the way from outback Queensland to Deloraine.'

Joe mulled this over in the ensuing silence. 'What did Carmichael want when he called?'

'To know if Ocean Child was still running on Saturday.'

Joe took a deep breath and tried to dispel the worrying thoughts his mother had invoked. 'Then he must just be an agent employed by Lulu's father to keep an eye on the colt's progress. If he is, then it's likely he'll be in Hobart to watch the colt run.' His frown deepened as he tried to make sense of it all. 'But then that would mean her father had bought the colt for her as a gift, but that he's employing Carmichael to keep an eye on her too.'

'If he knew Lulu existed and wanted to make contact with her, then why didn't he just write to her?' Molly twisted her apron in her fingers. 'The man I knew all those years ago was the plain-speaking kind, and according to Eliza, he hasn't changed.'

Joe felt a chill of foreboding. 'Carmichael is at the centre of this, and until we know who he is, he's not to be trusted. From now on we must keep a close eye on Lulu until we track him down, but you are to say nothing to her.'

He saw a flash of something in Eliza's eyes that he couldn't identify but didn't like. 'I hope I can rely on both of you to keep this to yourselves?' he said evenly.

'If you say so,' said Molly, 'but it won't be easy.'

The man who called himself Carmichael had been travelling all day. He'd brought the utility over from the mainland, and it had proved to be a wise decision, for it allowed him to follow Lulu Pearson more closely and get a real sense of her. He'd watched her on the bluff and followed her to the house in the bush, and during the weeks she'd been in Tasmania he'd come to feel that what he was about to do was justified.

It was a long journey back to Hobart and the Elwick track, but he had plenty of time, and it wouldn't hurt to rest his injured knee a while. He took a detour out to Poatina to have a look at Gwen Cole's place. Not that he wanted to come face to face with her – it was the simple curiosity of being able to put flesh to the bones of the woman he knew only as a name on a piece of paper.

He parked under an overhanging tree and walked stiffly down the narrow dirt track to lean on a fence and watch as she tended the horses. The smallholding covered about sixty acres in a beautiful valley, with good paddocks for the fine-looking horses that grazed there. But the house and garden were unkempt and neglected, the dog kennels abandoned, the chicken coop held together with string and wire. It was obvious there was no man about – or if there was, he was a lazy bastard.

As he watched her through the foliage, he came to the conclusion that her one saving grace was her undeniable passion for her horses – but the sight of her left him cold, and he returned to the ute.

He'd left Poatina way behind him and having negotiated the rough track that followed the east bank of Great Lake and headed south, now he was almost at Bothwell. He would camp there overnight and get an early start in the morning.

He frowned as he drove through the gloom, his thoughts mulling over the plan he'd spent so long orchestrating. It had worked well so far – better than he'd dared hope. But there were always unforeseen pitfalls to negotiate – and he had a feeling Lorelei Pearson would not willingly cooperate. It was imperative he reached Hobart before her so he had everything in place, and all eventualities covered.

13

The convoy of new trucks and floats had been moving steadily southwards since before dawn, and despite her vow the previous night to put all feelings for him aside, Lulu was all too aware of Joe as he sat beside her.

Bob and another stable hand were sitting in the flatbed, backs to the rear window and surrounded by saddles, bags, tack and spare horse-shoes. Dolly had elected to accompany her new friend Eliza, who was driving the second utility, which was similarly loaded with men and luggage, and Ocean Child and Moonbeam were travelling in style alongside the Hobart-owned horses, Danny Boy and Friar's Lass, in the two floats. Joe had arranged for everyone to stay with the Hobart owners, where all four horses could be spelled after their journey so they would be fresh for their races on Saturday.

Lulu wound down the window and gazed in awe at the scenery. Her childhood was in the time before cars and trucks were commonplace, when travel for pleasure was rare and the horse was the only form of land transport – therefore she'd never gone further than the seaside town's borders before she'd left for the mainland and England, and knew nothing of what lay beyond them. This journey south was proving a revelation and she longed to be able to stop for a while, to get out her sketch-book– for the colours were soft and almost sensuous, the enormous sky quite breathtaking.

They had been driving through the vast valley for almost an hour, and still it went on. The seemingly endless chain of surrounding mountains was misty blue in the first light of this new day, and the peaceful pastures and tiny farmhouses they passed looked like images from a book. 'It reminds me of pictures of Scotland,' she murmured. 'All that's missing is the heather.'

'Who needs heather when we've got alpine heath, wax-flowers and rock-daisy bushes?' He glanced at her and smiled. 'If you come this way between November and February, you'll find the place covered in them.'

'What a shame I'll be back in England by then.' She looked away as she saw the disappointment in his eyes.

His silence was eloquent as he kept his gaze on the road. 'I thought you might stick around a bit longer than that,' he said finally. 'We've only just started the really busy part of the racing season, and I'm hoping to enter the Child in some important events on the mainland.'

'Our return passage is booked for the end of November,' she said regretfully.

'You could always change your ticket.'

Lulu shook her head. 'I have responsibilities in England,' she reminded him softly. 'Clarice is getting old, and although it may take time for us to be reconciled, it's important not to leave her alone for too long.' She lifted her hair from her neck and enjoyed the soft breeze coming through the window. 'Besides, I have my work to consider, and I can't let Bertie down after he's been so patient with me.'

'Bertie? Who's Bertie?'

His expression was grim, and she had to bite down on the smile. 'He's my benefactor and patron,' she said, and went on to explain. 'I have commissions on hold, so if I want my career to go anywhere, I need to be back in England.'

'So there isn't anyone special waiting for you then?'

'There was once, but he died in France.'

He touched his scars as if to remind himself of the price he'd paid for being one of the lucky ones who survived.

Lulu studied him thoughtfully, and her voice was gentle as she spoke. 'Do you want to tell me what happened – or is the subject still too painful?'

'I forget about the mess on my face most of the time,' he said with a rueful smile. 'It's only when I have to meet people that I'm made aware of it.' He eased his shoulders and shifted in the seat. 'It bothers some and fascinates others – but I've had to accept there is little I can do about it.'

She remained silent, waiting to see if he felt comfortable enough with her to talk. Time passed and she was about to change the subject, when he broke the silence.

'I survived Gallipoli with a minor leg wound and was taken to a hospital ship to recuperate. I thought France would be a picnic after the hell we'd all been through, but then we were sent to a place called Fromelles.'

Lulu frowned. 'I don't recall a battle there,' she said, 'and I followed the news most carefully.'

'I'm not surprised,' he said shortly. 'Haig and his generals changed the name at least three times to cover up their disgraceful failings as leaders of men. We should never have been there, but they wanted the ANZACs to provide a diversion by drawing enemy fire away from a bigger raid further south.'

His face was etched with anger as he stared at the road. 'Haig was too intent upon his southern raid to take any notice of the reports coming in of a huge enemy presence that had been dug in at Fromelles for several weeks. We were like lambs to the slaughter. The battle lasted less than a day, but when it was over we'd lost more men in those few hours than we had in the nine months at Gallipoli.'

Lulu didn't know what to say, for there could be no words to comfort such awful pain. She'd heard Maurice talk of the incompetence of the generals and their laissez-faire attitude that had sent thousands of barely trained boys from stinking, rat-infested trenches to face barbed wire and scything bullets. His experiences had lived with him long after he'd returned home, and she suspected it was the same for Joe. And yet Joe seemed to have come to terms with his war, unlike poor Maurice, whose memories had eventually proven more than he could tolerate.

She drew back from her thoughts as Joe resumed his story.

'Fromelles is as flat and featureless as a pancake. We were caught in no-man's-land, enemy fire coming at us from all directions. There was nowhere to hide. Our captain was a kid from Queensland. He was only in his twenties, but had enough courage for ten men. He believed in leading his platoon, not sitting in safety miles from the front line.'

Lulu watched the expressions flit across his face as he spoke and knew those hours would be forever burned in his memory. But she also knew he was finding some release in being able to talk about it.

'It was raining and we were trapped, half of us already dead, men screaming on the wire and in the stinking mud for help. Mortar fire was blowing us apart and making huge craters which quickly filled with water, and the machine-guns were cutting us down like ninepins. The captain and I were hit at about the same time. I grabbed him by the leg and we fell into one of the craters.'

He took a shuddering breath, and his knuckles whitened as he gripped the steering wheel. 'I knew half my face was gone, but strangely enough it didn't hurt – not then, anyway. But I also knew I had to get us out of there or we'd be blown to bits.'

He gave a wry smile. 'I've never been more scared in my life, I don't mind admitting it, but terror gave me the strength to haul him on my back and get us both to the field hospital behind our lines.'

'That was incredibly brave,' breathed Lulu.

He grimaced and shrugged. 'A thousand men would have done the same. There were many acts of bravery that day far greater than mine – but I was scared witless and acted almost without thinking.'

'Did the captain survive?'

'They told me he was already dead when I came sliding down into that trench and fainted at their feet.' He gave a deep sigh. 'It was the end of the war for both of us – but I got away lightly compared to that poor kid.'

'Poor Joe,' she murmured, her fingers lightly brushing his cheek.

He flinched and captured her hand, moving it from his face to her lap. 'Please don't do that. The last thing I need is your pity.'

She moved instinctively to plant a soft kiss on the warm scarred flesh. 'It's not pity, Joe,' she whispered against his cheek, 'but pride, thankfulness and love for what you did and who you are.' She drew back, realising that what she'd said had come from the heart and that it was too late to take it back. 'I'm sorry,' she said, 'I didn't mean to embarrass you.'

His smile was shy as he glanced across at her. 'I think you've embarrassed yourself,' he teased. 'As for me, I rather liked it.'

Lulu blushed and looked down. His tanned, calloused hand still swamped hers, their fingers intertwined on her lap, the warmth and strength running through her like fire. It would be so easy to love him – so easy to give in to the emotions he stirred in her. But love and compassion were powerfully deceptive and not easily distinguished from one another – and she didn't want to make the same mistake with Joe that she had with Maurice.

She squeezed Joe's fingers and gently placed his hand on the steering wheel. 'You'd better concentrate,' she said through a tight throat, 'or you'll have us in the ditch.'

*

Lulu had her first sight of Mount Wellington late in the afternoon. It dominated the skyline above Hobart, its dark, rocky slopes menacing beneath a thick cap of cloud.

Joe turned off from the main road and on to the Girrabong Road, which led them into the heart of the bush-land suburb of Merton. 'We're about halfway between Glenorchy and the Lenah Valley,' he said. 'Elwick racetrack's in Glenorchy – another Hobart suburb – and it will take just minutes to get there tomorrow.'

Built in the previous century, the grand old house was set in grounds that could have graced an English stately home. It had elegant verandas decorated with white wrought-iron lace that was almost smothered in wisteria and bougainvillea. Chimneys, turrets and towers poked out of the red-tiled roof, and the ochre bricks looked mellow in the sunlight. Orchards spread from one side of the house and nestled at the foot of the mountain, and from the acres of nearby bush came the screeches of galahs and the melodic ring of the bellbirds.

Joe led the convoy down a broad dirt track hedged with bright blue hydrangeas into an enormous stable-yard close to which was a series of white-fenced paddocks where mares grazed with their foals.

'It's stunning,' breathed Lulu, bewitched by the foals and the magnificent mountain backdrop.

'Yeah, they run a good place here. Dave and Julia breed some of the best thoroughbreds in Australia.' He drew the utility to a halt and waved as a middle-aged couple emerged from a nearby barn.

David and Julia White proved to be generous, welcoming hosts, and once the horses were sorted out and the men had worked out where they would bunk, Lulu and the others were taken back to the house and shown their rooms.

'I say,' breathed Dolly as she eyed their luxuriously appointed bedroom, 'it's just like home.' She knelt on the window seat and looked out over the orchard to the mountain. 'Super view as well, but I wonder how close we are to Hobart and the shops.'

Lulu grabbed her sketchbook. 'Probably too far to walk.' She laughed. 'I'm going out while there's still light. This is too good to resist, and I've been itching to draw all day.'

'Want me to come with you?'

Dolly didn't seem eager to leave the comfort of the bedroom, and Lulu wanted time alone, so she shook her head. 'Stay and wallow in a bath. I'll be back in time for dinner,' she said.

Lulu soon lost track of time as she sketched the dams and foals. She had taken particular care over one of the foals that was drinking from its mother, little tail swishing in delight, front legs spread, behind in the air as it suckled. It would make a wonderful sculpture. She concentrated on the contentment in the mare as she bent her neck to nuzzle the little creature. If she could capture it now, it would be invaluable for when she began to mould the clay.

Her pencil finally stilled and she eyed her work critically. Any more and it would be spoilt – and the light was so dim she couldn't really see well enough to carry on anyway.

'I reckon that's about perfect.'

She started at the sound of his voice and looked back at him with a quizzical smile. 'How long have you been watching me?'

'Long enough.' His gaze remained on her drawing. 'You really do know what you're doing, don't you?'

'I'm learning,' she said softly, and closed the sketchbook. 'When I get back to England I'll use these drawings to help me model the sculpture.' She looked at the scene before her and let her gaze drift to the blossom in the orchard, the dark hues of the purple-shadowed mountain and the profound green of the untamed bush. 'It's at times like this I wish I could capture all of it,' she sighed, 'but there isn't a canvas big enough.'

There was a sadness behind his smile that tugged at her heart. He held out his hand. 'If you stayed longer you might manage to do most of it.'

'You know I can't.' She looked into his eyes as he drew her to her feet. His touch and the nearness of him made her breathless, and as they stood there in the lengthening shadows it was as if the world encompassed only the two of them.

His large hand folded around her fingers and she felt more alive at this moment than she'd ever been. She looked up at him, willing him to kiss her.

His lips touched hers and she felt a jolt of desire and longing as she leant into him.

'I'm sorry,' he said, hastily moving away and dropping her hand. 'I shouldn't have done that.'

'I was rather enjoying it,' she breathed, the warmth and desire still coursing through her as she closed the gap between them.

His breath stirred her hair and eyelashes, his chest rising and falling as his heartbeat raced.

Lulu yearned to feel his strong arms around her, his fingers in her hair, his kiss on her mouth. She wanted to be crushed to him, to feel his heart beating against hers, to know his desire was as great as hers – and to rake her fingers down his back and feel the heat of skin against skin. She swayed towards him.

He took a step back, his strong hands holding her from him. 'We must not do this, Lulu,' he said, his voice rough with emotion.

'Why?' She felt suddenly stranded and shy.

'It wouldn't be right to start something we have no chance of taking further,' he said hoarsely. He glanced over her shoulder. 'And I don't think you'd appreciate having such an audience.'

She suddenly realised there was an interested line of stable hands lolling about in the nearby yard, and blushed furiously.

He took her hand and kissed the palm, his eyes as dark as molten chocolate. 'I think we should go in for dinner. The bell rang at least half an hour ago.'

Friday, Hobart

The northern suburb of Glenorchy was home to Elwick Race-course and Showground. It had views over the River Derwent to the Meehan Range in the east and the magnificent cloud-veiled Mount Wellington to the west.

It was early morning, the horses had been exercised and spelled, and Joe wanted to walk the course with Bob and Eliza before the race meeting the next day. The stable hands were hitching a ride in the back, for an outing to Elwick was a rare pleasure, and not to be missed.

As he drove through the gates past the busy showground and into the almost deserted parking area, he tried to put Lulu out of his mind. There was work to be done and he had to concentrate – but it was difficult knowing she was near, for the memory of their fleeting kiss still lingered and taunted him.

He climbed down from the ute as Eliza pulled up next to him. He waited until the three young women alighted, and couldn't help but feel a sense of pride in the place as they looked around. 'What do you think?'

Lulu's eyes shone. 'I think it's wonderful, and I particularly like the grandstand – it's very . . . grand.'

He laughed. 'That's Hobart's pride and joy, built towards the end of the last century when the course was first opened. There's been talk of pulling it down and building another, but I reckon the old place will still be standing a hundred years from now.'

She eyed the brick building with its ironwork veranda railings and curious tower that rounded off one end. 'The Victorians certainly knew how to build things to last, but their style is a little too fanciful for my taste.' She grinned. 'But it is great fun – no wonder Hobart is proud of it.'

'I need to talk to the clerk and check out a few things before we walk the course. Eliza wants to come with me to sort out stabling for Moonbeam, so you'll be on your own for a while. Will you be right until I get back?'

'Of course,' she replied, relieved Eliza would be occupied elsewhere – but unnerved by the fact she would be with Joe. 'Dolly and I are curious as to what's going on over there.' She pointed to a large area beyond the track which was fluttering with bunting.

'That's the showground,' Joe replied, as he squinted into the sun. 'There must be a gymkhana or something going on.' He frowned. 'Perhaps I should get one of the stable hands to go with you?'

'We don't need a babysitter,' retorted Lulu. 'It's hardly a trek to outer Mongolia.'

'I'd prefer you weren't left on your own,' he said firmly, and beckoned to one of the men lolling against the ute. 'Charlie here will escort you.' He tipped his hat and strode away with Eliza before they could reply.

'Well, really,' huffed Lulu.

'I reckon he just wants to make sure you ladies don't get lost,' drawled Charlie, a broad-shouldered man of middle years with the face of a boxer who'd had one too many fights. He lit a smoke, cupping his hands around the match.

'I hardly think we'll get lost between here and there,' muttered Dolly crossly.

Charlie eyed the high-heeled shoes, his grin exposing tombstone teeth. 'But you might need help with them fancy footwear,' he replied. 'Don't worry, Miss, I'll carry you over the muddy bits so you don't get stuck.'

Lulu smothered a giggle. 'Come on, Dolly. You never know, you might enjoy it.'

'I doubt it,' she muttered, as they linked arms and walked across the grass. 'He's more Lon Chaney than Douglas Fairbanks.'

Lulu giggled. 'Shh, he'll hear you.'

'I'm surprised he can hear anything through those cauliflower ears,' she giggled back.

They made their precarious way over the long grass and rutted pathways to the showground. As they drew nearer, they could hear the sound of a brass band and someone's distorted voice speaking through a loudhailer. Cars, buggies, horseboxes and trucks were parked on the far side of a large showjumping arena, next to which lay the dressage ring.

Lulu clutched Dolly's arm. 'My goodness,' she said, 'it's years since I attended one of these.' She looked around at the bustle surrounding the field where horses and riders were preparing for competition. 'Let's find a seat and watch for a while. I've always enjoyed the dressage.'

He'd found the ideal place to watch her, and as he stood in the shadow of the stands where she sat in the front row with her friend, he knew she wouldn't see him. He tugged the brim of his hat, dug his hands in his pockets and settled down to wait. It was mildly irritating that Joe Reilly had sent that bruiser to watch over her, and that she was never on her own, but the opportunity would surely come in the next two days. All he had to do was be patient.

While Dolly was deeply immersed in the programme for the day, Lulu enjoyed sitting in the sun beneath her Japanese parasol in quiet contemplation of the beautifully trained, sleek horses performing like dancers in the ring.

The pleasant scene brought back happy memories of her and

Clarice attending such events in the north after dearest Eunice had died. It was usually to watch Gwen compete in the show-jumping, but Lulu had preferred the noise, colour and bustle beyond the arenas. Now she could smell the sweetness of cotton candy and toffee apples drifting from the booths near the stands, hear the brass band playing, and see the farmers doing a roaring trade in what looked like home-brewed cider and beer. The scene was one that hadn't changed since she was a little girl – and she suspected it never would, for the Tasmanians were as passionate about a good day out as they were about their horses.

She looked back to the ever-present parade of people strolling along the path in front of the stand. The women wore fancy hats and pretty dresses, the men were in suits or the more practical moleskins and shirts, their broad-brimmed hats pulled low. It was such a shame that Molly hadn't come; she would have loved the chance to dress up – but Dianne wasn't competent enough to look after everything, and Molly had been reluctant to leave her in charge.

Her gaze trawled the ever-moving cavalcade – and froze – the scene around her fading until there was only Gwen. She was walking a horse along the path and hadn't yet seen her, but Lulu's heart was pounding and her mouth was dry. She had faced the demon memories – now she would have to face the demon-maker.

Gwen's pace faltered as she made eye contact. Her lips thinned and her gaze was openly hostile.

Lulu was trapped.

Gwen's eyes were cold and impersonal as they darted over her, and a sneer of contempt curled her scarlet lips as that arctic gaze returned to Lulu's face. Her footsteps slowed even further, as if she was fully aware of the effect she was having on Lulu and wanted to prolong it.

Lulu steeled herself to return that scrutiny, knowing that to flinch from it would bring Gwen twisted satisfaction. She took in the hair that had obviously been dyed, the overdone make-up and the clothes that were designed for a much younger woman. The bright sun highlighted the lines around her eyes and smirking mouth and emphasised the sagging jawline. Gwen wasn't yet fifty, but she had not aged well.

Gwen's smirk faded as Lulu continued to glare back at her, and her pace quickened as she reached the end of the stand and headed towards the gathering of horseboxes on the far side of the arena.

Lulu's heartbeat was surprisingly steady as she watched Gwen disappear into the crowd. She had realised in that fleeting moment that she had nothing to fear from that ageing, bitter woman, that she felt no pity for her obvious attempts to cheat the passing years – and certainly no love. Their brief and silent encounter had merely reinforced and acknowledged their mutual loathing.

He'd watched the silent exchange with curiosity and interest. It was clear there was no love lost between them, which had come as no surprise, but Gwen had thrown a challenge to Lorelei, and the younger woman had tossed it back with aplomb. If Gwen had been affected by that, he had no way of knowing, for her expression gave nothing away.

His gaze travelled back to Lorelei, who sat coolly in the stands as if nothing had happened. She might not be like her mother in any way, but she had certainly inherited the art of an enigmatic expression, he thought wryly.

Gwen's step had quickened, and he melted into the shadows as she passed. He couldn't take the risk of being seen, for she would know immediately who he was and he wasn't willing to be unmasked until he had done all he had planned.

*

'You're very quiet,' said Joe, as they left the racecourse and headed back to the house. 'Something on your mind?'

'I saw my mother today.'

Joe felt a pang of concern as he glanced across at her. 'That must have been a bit of a shock after what happened when you arrived.'

'It was at first,' she replied, 'because I wasn't prepared.'

'What did she say?'

'We didn't speak. The looks we exchanged said it all.'

He drove in silence for a while, his thoughts churning as he tried to think of something to say.

'Please don't be concerned on my account, Joe,' she said, as if reading his thoughts. 'I learnt an invaluable lesson today.'

'And what was that?'

Lulu leant back in the seat, elbow hitched out of the open window. 'That I have a great deal to thank Gwen for,' she said bluntly. She must have seen his look of astonishment, for she laughed. 'I'm grateful she didn't want me, for Clarice was the best mother anyone could have had. I'm also grateful that her scorn and refusal to acknowledge me made me determined to succeed in all I do. If my life hadn't begun in such a way, I would never have become the woman I am today.'

He gave a low whistle. 'That was quite a lesson.'

She smiled. 'Yes, it was, wasn't it? But all artists, be they writers, painters, poets or sculptors, have to have experienced some emotional turmoil – it's what gives them the edge – spurs them on to greater things. It is said that the only barrier to aspiration and imagination is the self. Success brings confidence and self-belief, which, in turn, breaks down those barriers and sets us free to fly.'

Joe saw the passion in her eyes and the heightened colour in her cheeks and his spirits sank. There was little doubt Lulu was an ambitious and talented artist who was already on the brink of great success. She belonged in a far bigger world than any he could offer. His heart ached at the thought, but he resolved to keep his burgeoning love for her a secret, so she could spread her wings and take that flight she so longed for.

14

'It will hardly be Ascot,' said Dolly. 'Are you sure this isn't too much?'

'Definitely not,' said Eliza, eyeing the scarlet dress and matching shoes with a degree of envy. 'I just wish I'd thought to bring something as glamorous.'

Dolly picked up the black felt hat and carefully placed it on her head before standing back to admire the effect. The silk roses on the side of the cloche matched the dress, falling in a tumble to caress her cheek.

'You look bonzer,' Eliza breathed, eyes shining with admiration.

'Thank you, darling. One hopes that's a compliment,' she said drily as she put on her black swing-coat with the white fox-fur collar.

'It certainly is,' said Eliza. 'Did that hat come from London?'

Lulu remained silent as she buttoned the straps on her shoes and tried to ignore the mutual admiration society on the far side of the room. Eliza had insisted upon coming to their room this morning, and Dolly seemed so wrapped up in the girl she'd barely had a word for Lulu since breakfast. It rankled, but she was determined not to let it show.

She stood and eyed her reflection in the pier glass. The turquoise silk-and-lace dress fell from her shoulders in a slender tube, the handkerchief-hem skirt swirling from below her hips to her calves. Her shoes were dark blue, as was the velvet band she had tied around her head and pinned with a turquoise silk rose and a jaunty feather. Her hair tumbled from this restraint in a waterfall of curls – and the flush in her cheeks enhanced the colour of her eyes.

'Very attractive,' said Eliza, 'but I'm surprised you don't cut your hair more fashionably. That length is so outdated.'

'I prefer it long,' Lulu retorted.

Eliza's glance was scathing before she turned back to Dolly. 'You look so gorgeous you're bound to be picked for the beauty pageant.'

'The what?' Dolly looked at her in horror.

Eliza giggled. 'You don't have to enter, even if you are invited,' she said, 'but I've been in several, and they're great fun.'

Lulu picked up her lipstick. She remembered the pageants, and the way she'd squirmed with embarrassment when Gwen paraded up and down and flirted outrageously with every man watching.

'We'd better go,' said Eliza reluctantly.

'In a minute.' Dolly was rooting about in the wardrobe. She finally managed to find what she was looking for and pulled it out with a smile of satisfaction. 'There you are, Eliza. It will look stunning with your colouring.'

Lulu watched dumbfounded as Eliza eyed the lovely dress Dolly had had made in Singapore. Dolly adored that dress and was usually possessive over her clothing – but it seemed she was happily handing it over.

Eliza wasted no time in shamelessly stripping to her underwear. The sheath of apricot silk whispered over her head and down her slender body, and she twirled delightedly before the mirror. Embroidered butterflies and flowers danced diagonally from shoulder to narrow hip, the hem floating just below her knee. It was a perfect fit.

Dolly nodded with satisfaction. 'Now for a hat. This one, I think. Oh, and the shoes. We look about the same size. Try these.'

Eliza wriggled into them. 'Perfect,' she said breathlessly.

Lulu sat on the bed as Dolly fussed with the simple straw hat that had a peach-coloured ribbon around the crown. As the girl twisted and turned before the mirror, Lulu realised with a pang that although she was only eighteen, she was woman enough to steal Joe's heart.

They were driven to the course in David's Model T Ford, which was his pride and joy, but it meant hanging on to their seats as he bowled down the road at a precarious thirty miles an hour.

The gymkhana was into its second day in the showground, but as they approached the racecourse it looked very different today. Bunting fluttered, flags flew from the poles fixed to the grandstand, a band played, cars, trucks and horseboxes were gathered in the parking area and a sense of excitement pervaded the milling, colourful crowd who flocked into the grandstand and along the white railings.

Lulu felt a thrill as more memories were brought to life by the colour, noise and exuberance of the crowd. But there was little time to take it all in, for their hosts were leading them past the grandstand to the fenced-off area for owners, trainers and jockeys.

She watched as horses stamped and snorted, jockeys swore and owners and trainers engaged in deep discussions over tactics. She took in the coloured silks of the jockeys, the gleam of prime horseflesh groomed especially for the day, and the fancy hats and dresses of the women. They needn't have feared being over-dressed, she thought wryly, as she watched a woman teeter past in high heels, dressed in bright yellow with a hat overly laden with citrus-green silk flowers to match her parasol.

The sun blazed down, making it quite oppressive in the stable area, and she eased her coat off and opened her own parasol. Made of thick paper, it was richly painted with birds of paradise which matched her dress. Dolly had a red one, and she'd lent her spare, which happened to be deep orange, to Eliza. Lulu's smile was amused. They must look like something from a Gilbert and Sullivan operetta.

Joe was deep in conversation with Eliza and David, no doubt discussing the up-coming races. He obviously couldn't have seen her, for he didn't look her way at all, and hadn't even said hello.

'This is all frightfully boring,' muttered Dolly, twirling her parasol. 'I saw a champagne tent as we came through. Let's go and have a drink.'

'It's a bit early,' replied Lulu. She glanced across at Joe, who was still engrossed with Eliza. 'But why not?' She turned her back on them and went to follow Dolly through the crowd.

'Hold up. Where are you going?'

'In search of champagne,' said Lulu, not breaking stride.

'Then take Charlie with you.'

'Whatever for?' She came to a halt.

'It's better if someone escorts you,' Joe blustered. 'There are some rough types at these meetings.'

Lulu's eyes narrowed as she regarded him thoughtfully. 'You seem very keen to safeguard us,' she said coolly, 'and we're most grateful. But Dolly and I have managed to cross from one side of the world to the other without coming to any harm. I hardly think Elwick Racecourse is more dangerous than Port Said.'

'But . . .'

'No, Joe,' she said firmly. 'We wish to enjoy our day, and not have your minder follow us about. Go back to your horses and we'll see you when you are less occupied.' She turned, hooked her arm in Dolly's and marched off.

'Well, that told him.' Dolly laughed. 'What has the poor man done to deserve such a dressing-down?'

She was puzzled by his attitude. He'd obviously known she was there all the time and had been deliberately ignoring her – until she left the yard – and then he hadn't even said hello, or complimented her on her outfit, before bossing her about. And as for insisting upon Charlie escorting them . . . 'Nothing,' she lied.

Dolly's knowing look said it all as they entered the champagne tent.

He climbed out of the utility and slammed the door. It had been a restless night, but he wasn't at all tired, for the excitement was mounting. He could see her and her friend sipping champagne and laughing with some of the other owners as they wandered towards the parade ring. She looked very lovely in that blue, her hair a shining mass of tawny browns and gold that caught the sun and emphasised her femininity.

He followed them to the ring where the runners and riders paraded before the first race. Ocean Child was not due to run for about an hour, so he had plenty of time to watch her. Leaning against the rail some few feet away, he had his first close look at the young woman he'd been following. It was a strangely familiar face, and as he watched the animation light up her eyes he wondered how she would feel if she knew she was being regarded with such interest and curiosity.

'There you are. You could have waited for me, Dolly, I adore champagne.'

He froze at the sound of her voice. Eliza Frobisher was an unexpected stumbling block to his plans. He ducked his head as he swiftly turned and walked away. All he needed now, he thought anxiously, was to bump into Gwen Cole.

Lulu had won place money on Eliza's Moonbeam as well as on Friar's Lass, and was celebrating with the owners in the champagne tent. She discreetly set aside the foaming glass, for she'd already had three and was beginning to feel light-headed. 'I must go and wish Bob luck,' she said. 'Ocean Child's running next and I've put all my winnings on him.'

They waved their betting slips to show they too had backed Lulu's colt, and she was smiling as she left the tent and headed for the yard. Her smile faltered as she saw Charlie emerge from the side of the tent and follow her. It seemed Joe had ignored her request to be left alone, and she wondered why he was so determined to have her chaperoned. Surely he didn't really think she was in any danger?

She brushed off the irritation as she caught sight of Ocean Child. He was wonderfully turned out, his coat gleaming, neck arched as if he knew he looked handsome. Bob, who wore the Galway House silks of the Irish tricolour, stood proudly beside the Child as Joe gave him last-minute instructions.

Lulu ran her hand down Ocean Child's neck, and he nudged her cheek and tried to nibble the feather in her headband. She stepped back. 'I don't think that's a very good idea,' she giggled, her fingers massaging his ears. 'You're not supposed to eat just before a race.'

'Don't do that thing with his ears,' said Joe sharply. 'He goes all unnecessary and he needs to stay alert for the next half-hour.'

Lulu stopped petting the horse and turned to Bob. 'You look very handsome,' she said. 'Best of luck, and have a good race.'

'Bob knows what to do,' said Joe rather tersely.

'I'm sure he does,' she replied coolly.

Joe gave Bob a leg-up. 'We have to go. Charlie will see you back to the stand.'

With a toss of her head, she marched back to the grandstand, all too aware of Charlie lumbering behind her. As she was about to turn the corner and climb the steps she came to a sudden halt and spun around. 'Why did Joe ask you to follow me?'

He looked shifty as he shrugged massive shoulders. 'The boss 'as 'is reasons. Not my place to ask what they are.'

'I think you know very well why,' she said crossly. 'Come on, Charlie, out with it.'

'I dunno really,' he said, avoiding her gaze. 'He just said not to let you wander off, and told me to keep an eye out.'

'For what?' The hairs on the back of her neck were prickling and she shot a wary glance over her shoulder – although she had no idea what she was looking for.

Charlie scuffed his boot against the cinder path. 'I reckon 'e's worried about that Carmichael bloke turning up.'

Lulu noticed he looked shiftier than ever. 'Carmichael poses no threat – why should Joe think otherwise?'

'He don't trust 'im.' His gaze flitted over her before returning to his boots. 'I'd appreciate it if you don't tell 'im,' he mumbled. 'He'd 'ave me guts for garters and I'd be out of a job.'

Lulu heaved a sigh. The poor man didn't deserve to lose his job. Joe was being over-protective, and Charlie was merely following orders. She smiled up at him. 'No worries, Charlie. Your secret's safe with me.'

'Good on ya, Miss. I knew you was a dinkum sheila the minute I saw yer.'

'That's nice,' she murmured, as she climbed the steps to join the others.

The twelve colts were milling about on the far side of the track. The eight brush hurdles were placed intermittently down the two-mile course, and to Lulu they looked rather daunting for such young horses. Her mouth dried and her heart began to pound as she borrowed David's binoculars and waited for the starter's flag to go down.

The colts were nudged and cajoled into a ragged line. The flag went down. They were off.

Lulu lost sight of Ocean Child and began to panic. Then she saw the flash of green, white and orange silks and relaxed. He was in the middle of the bunch and heading for the first hurdle.

They all went safely over and headed for the next – a particularly devious fence with a trench of water in front of it. Ocean Child flew over it, narrowly missing the horse next to him, who stumbled and almost fell. He was well placed and storming through the field.

Two fell at the next, and there was a refusal at the fourth. A loose horse ran right in front of the leaders as they approached the fifth and there was a collective gasp from the crowd as it brought down the favourite. There were six left in the race – and Ocean Child was steaming up on the inside to contend with the leaders.

The six colts thundered over the next two hurdles, but they were more spread out now, and as they prepared to fly over the final hurdle, Ocean Child stretched his neck and drew alongside Firefly, the leader. They landed together, and the crowd roared encouragement.

Ocean Child stumbled as Bob appeared to lose control and almost went over his head. Lulu gripped the binoculars and adjusted the sights. The jockey on Firefly was kicking out at Bob's stirrup, doing his best to unseat him.

The crowd were on their feet, their voices rising with excitement.

Ocean Child recovered from his stumble and Bob clung on low in the saddle, one foot free of the stirrup.

It was a cruel climb to the final straight and the finishing post, and some of the back-markers began to lag. Both leading horses looked to have plenty of running in them despite the antics of the men on their backs – and they passed the winning post at what looked like the same time.

As the horses drew to a halt Bob leapt down, hauled Firefly's jockey from his saddle and punched him. Firefly's rider retaliated and within seconds they were beating the hell out of each other.

The crowd roared encouragement and waved their programmes. The other jockeys milled about, uncertain as to what to do. Ocean Child and Firefly ambled off to the other side of the circuit and settled down to munch on the long grass beside the track.

Lulu gasped as Bob was punched to the ground and Firefly's jockey started kicking him. 'Why doesn't someone stop them?' she shouted above the roar of the crowd. 'Bob's going to get seriously hurt.'

'Joe's going in there to sort them out,' said David grimly.

Lulu saw Joe storm across the track and grasp both jockeys by the collar. He held each wriggling, kicking man at arm's length until the stewards came to haul them away. Joe's face was dark with rage as he confronted Firefly's trainer. The two men were almost nose to nose, fingers pointing in their heated exchange. The crowd was hushed and the raised voices could be heard all around the course.

The crowd was enthralled. This was why they came to the races.

'I'm going down to make sure Ocean Child's all right,' Lulu muttered, handing back the binoculars.

'Best stay well out of it, love,' David replied, 'and as you can see, the Child's come to no harm.'

Lulu glanced back at the track and sighed with relief when she saw her colt being led towards the stables. 'What will happen, David? Will he be disqualified?'

David shrugged. 'Probably, though it wasn't really Bob's fault. If the silly bugger hadn't lost his temper and hit the other jockey, then he'd have been guaranteed a win.' He sighed. 'As it is . . . that's up to the stewards.'

The chatter around them rose in volume as the speculation mounted and the fight was replayed and discussed with great relish.

Lulu saw Joe striding towards the stewards' office, his face grim. 'How long before we know?'

David shrugged. 'Could be a while. Tempers are frayed already, and no doubt there'll be another punch-up before nightfall.'

Lulu was shifting from one foot to the other in frustration, her gaze fixed on the closed door of the stewards' office. Bob and the other jockey appeared from the stable-yard, both sporting black eyes and bloody noses. It was clear they hadn't settled their differences, for they glared at one another and jostled their way through the door.

Dolly gripped Lulu's hand. 'I've never had so much excitement in my life,' she gasped. 'Nothing like this ever happens at Ascot. You Tasmanians certainly know how to put on a show.'

'I don't know about that,' replied Lulu, 'but I do wish they'd hurry up and make a decision one way or the other. The suspense is killing me.'

Joe finally emerged from the stewards' box. He looked more grim than ever as he hauled Bob out of sight towards the stables, and Lulu feared the boy was in for another battering.

The voice over the loudspeaker echoed around the hushed, expectant crowd. 'Firefly and Ocean Child have been disqualified. Both jockeys suspended for eight weeks. The winner is . . .'

Lulu didn't wait to hear the rest of the announcement. 'I must get down there to check Ocean Child and make sure Joe hasn't beaten Bob to a pulp.' She raced down the steps and pushed her way through the crowd towards the stables.

'You bloody idiot!' Joe's voice rang out from behind the stable door. 'You threw that bloody race the minute you hit that bastard. And although he deserved it, you cost that horse his first really important race.'

Lulu came to a halt in the yard. It seemed everyone had stopped what they were doing to listen in to Bob being torn off a strip.

'He was trying to knock me off,' Bob protested, 'and he got me with his whip on the blind side of the course. I'll have that bastard if he comes anywhere near me again.'

'You've been suspended, Bob, for eight bloody weeks. You won't be going near anyone – least of all a flaming racecourse. And what the hell am I supposed to do for a jockey in the meantime? Eh?'

'I'm sorry, Joe. I didn't think. I was that angry.'

'You want to thank your flaming stars I don't give you another black eye.'

Everyone started as the stable door was slammed back and Joe marched out. 'What the hell are you lot standing about for? There's bloody work to done. Get on with it.' His angry glare settled on Lulu. 'This is no place for you,' he growled. 'Go back to the stands.'

'I want to see Ocean Child and make sure he's all right.'

'He's fine,' he said curtly. 'Go away, Lulu.'

Lulu tried not to let his brusque rejection hurt, but after his fleeting kiss and the intimate moments in the yard and on the gallops at Galway House it did. She swallowed and turned away, sad but relieved she would be leaving at the end of the month. Joe had shown a very different side to himself today, and she wasn't at all sure she liked it – but that didn't stop her yearning for what might have been.

She began to push her way through the tightly packed crowd that encircled the winners' ring and betting stalls and spilled out past the tents. It was hard going – like walking against the tide.

The hand grasped her arm, pulling her to a halt. 'Commiserations, Miss Pearson. Ocean Child would have won that race but for your jockey losing his temper.'

'Thank you,' she said, without giving him a glance. 'You're very kind, but I must get back to my friends.' His grip tightened and Lulu felt a charge of alarm.

'I would appreciate it if you could give me a minute, Miss Pearson, only I have some important things to discuss with you.'

She looked at him then and gasped. It was Dolly's handsome cowboy from Melbourne. 'Who are you, and why are you following me?'

'That's what I need to talk to you about.'

'Then let go of me,' she demanded.

His grip lessened, but remained firm enough to keep her close, and her fear of him gathered strength. 'What do you want of me?'

'Just a few moments of your time.'

Lulu realised that as they'd been talking he'd manoeuvred her out of the crush to the isolated area behind the row of betting tents. 'Let me go,' she snapped, fear making her strong as she wrestled to free herself. 'I'll scream,' she warned.

'Please don't be afraid, Lorelei. I'm not going to hurt you,' he said softly.

'How do you know my name?' She was cold with fear and her gaze darted beyond him in desperate search of a familiar face among the crowd.

He released her but remained close enough to block any escape. 'I've known your name, and who you are, for almost two years,' he said. 'I'm sorry if I've frightened you, but I needed to get you alone so we could talk.'

She rubbed her arm and took a step back as she warily regarded him. He was about her age, with thick curly hair, dark blue eyes and a pleasant smile – but she didn't trust him an inch. 'You've got precisely sixty seconds to explain who the hell you are and why you've seen fit to manhandle me – and then I'm leaving. Touch me again, and I'll scream.'

He took off the bushman's hat. 'My name is Peter White,' he said, 'but you'd know me better as Carmichael.'

Joe had given Ocean Child a good rub-down and set him loose in the paddock. The colt had done well today, but Joe still simmered over Bob's lack of control which had cost him the race.

He leant against the railing, his anger ebbing. No doubt Lulu was furious with him, and he could hardly blame her. He'd been boorish and bad-tempered, and she hadn't deserved that. Regret flooded through him. She would no doubt keep her distance from now on, for he'd shown a side of himself that shamed him to the core. The outbursts were extremely rare, and as swiftly over as a summer storm – and usually he managed to quell them. Now Lulu would think he was an oaf, and quite rightly refuse to have any more to do with him.

He gave a sigh and pushed away from the railings. Perhaps it had all turned out for the best. She would be leaving at the end of November, and he knew deep down that once she was back in England she would forget all about him.

He was in the middle of discussing tactics with the jockey he'd had to hire at the last minute to ride Danny Boy, when Dolly interrupted.

'Have you seen Lulu? I can't find her anywhere.'

He felt a tingle of foreboding. 'I thought she was with you?'

'She said she was coming here.'

'She did.' He reddened. 'I sent her back to you.' The foreboding strengthened. 'Where did you see her last?'

'In the stands,' said Dolly and Eliza in unison.

'I told you to keep an eye on her, Eliza,' he snapped. 'Why the hell did you let her just wander off?'

'It wasn't my fault,' she retorted. 'If you were that bothered, you shouldn't have sent her back.'

'Stop it, the pair of you.' Dolly stamped her foot. 'Lulu's missing, and we've got to find her. I don't know why you've had her followed all day, but it's time you explained. It might give us a clue as to where she's gone.'

'Later,' he said grimly. 'Let's go back to the stands. She can't have gone far.'

Charlie lumbered into them as they were leaving. He was out of breath and sweating. 'She's gorn, Joe. I lost 'er in the crowd. But I thought I saw some bloke talking to 'er.'

'Where?'

'Over there. But I can't find 'er, and I've looked all over.'

'Come with us,' growled Joe, 'and when we get to the rails spread out. Holler if you spot her.'

Lulu's heart was pounding and the combination of shock, heat and champagne were taking their toll. She needed to sit down, but that would make her even more vulnerable. Battling to remain calm, and work out the quickest escape route should he grab her again, she faced him. 'Carmichael,' she said flatly. 'So, you show yourself at last.'

'I'm sorry if I've upset you,' he began.

'You've got a lot of explaining to do,' she said between sharp intakes of breath, 'so get on with it.'

His expression became concerned. 'Are you not well?'

'Well enough,' she said shortly. 'All I need from you is an explanation.'

He didn't seem convinced, but as she glared up at him he must have realised she would brook no further delay. 'I didn't choose the name Carmichael,' he began. 'It was already in use, and I just borrowed it.'

She shifted her feet, not trusting him, poised to run if he made a grab for her again. 'Why use another name at all? What skulduggery are you up to?'

'I know you must see what I've done as underhand, but I had very strong reasons for it.'

She remained silent, her gaze steady and cynical as he lit a cigarette.

'It was the name used on the instructions to the London solicitors,' he said quietly. 'They hired a private detective to watch you and report back.'

Her heart skipped a beat, and she gripped the parasol more tightly. 'Someone's been watching me? Who – and for how long?'

'I believe he is a retired major. He's been watching you from the day you arrived in England.'

'Did Clarice know about this?'

He shook his head. 'I doubt it. He was very discreet.'

She was confused, frightened and close to tears. 'I don't understand any of this,' she said breathlessly. 'Why should someone want me watched – and why hide their identity – an identity you've borrowed so you could play your twisted game with me?

'It might seem twisted to you, Lorelei, but it was the only way I could get you to Tasmania. Ocean Child was a gift of mystery – I knew you couldn't resist it.'

'Just who the hell are you?' she breathed.

His gaze was steady. 'I'm your half-brother.'

Joe rounded the tent and took in the scene with one swift glance. He strode over and grasped the man's collar, almost jerking him off his feet. 'Right, you mongrel, start talking or I'll punch your lights out.'

'No.' Lulu staggered as she reached out to stop him. 'Let him speak, Joe. This is Carmichael.' Her breath hitched and she swayed against him. 'He says . . . he says he's my brother.'

'Yeah, right – and I'm Father flaming Christmas.' His grip tightened on Peter's collar as he eyed the other man from boots to hat. 'You'd better not be messing her about, mate, or you'll have me to answer to,' he growled, 'and believe me, I'm just in the mood for a fight.'

'Please, Joe, there's been enough fighting for one day.'

His grip lessened as he looked down at Lulu. She was deathly pale and clearly distressed. He released Carmichael and gave him a shove. 'Move a muscle and you're dead,' he barked before turning to Lulu. 'Sit down,' he said softly as he pulled out a bale of hay from a nearby pile. 'Don't worry, I'm not leaving you alone with him, but I do have to let the others know I've found you.'

She opened her parasol, dug in her purse and swallowed a pill, but her eyes looked haunted and she was clearly struggling to breathe.

Joe gave a loud holler and waved his hat as he saw Dolly.

Dolly immediately raced to Lulu's side in concern as Eliza hovered in the background. Bob and Charlie stood beside Joe, fists clenched, ready for action.

'You'd better have your say,' Joe snapped at Carmichael. 'My patience won't last all day.'

Lulu's whole being was concentrated on Peter White as he explained who he was and why he'd accosted her. She felt easier now Joe was here, but was still wary. 'I was Gwen's only child,' she said as he fell silent. 'You can't be my brother.'

'We share the same father.'

Lulu noted his very blue eyes, saw the way his hair curled at his nape and over his forehead, and recognised something of herself in him – and yet the doubts remained. 'I don't believe you,' she replied.

'He's here in Hobart. If I took you to see him, would that convince you?'

Hope shot through her, to be quickly extinguished by fear. 'How could it?' she countered. 'I've never met him, and don't even know his name. He could be anyone.'

Peter eyed the other men, dragged over a second bale and sat down. 'I think I'd better start at the beginning,' he said. 'It's fairly complicated.'

Lulu clung to Dolly's hand. He seemed very sure of himself, but maybe he was just a consummate liar and conman – and yet she wanted so much to believe him. The cocktail of emotions was draining and she leant against Dolly's shoulder.

Peter stamped out his smoke, his boot-heel grinding it into the turf. 'My father – our father – had a stroke about eighteen months back, and I took over running our property in Queensland. I was going through his desk looking for an invoice when I opened a locked drawer and found a file.'

His gaze was direct and unwavering. 'It was a file full of letters addressed to a Mr Carmichael at a post-office box number in Brisbane. Dad rarely left the property, so must have arranged to have them sent on.'

'And these letters were from the London solicitors?'

'They dated back to the year you left Tasmania. There was a report on your progress and health every year, usually accompanied with photographs.' His smile was warm as he looked at her. 'It was obvious Dad regretted the circumstances of your birth, and cared enough to keep an eye on you.'

'Then why didn't he write to me instead of having me watched?'

'I suspect that had something to do with the bank statements which showed regular payments to your mother.'

Lulu went cold. This had too much ring of truth to it. 'Gwen was blackmailing him.' Her tone was flat.

'From the year you were born until my mother's death two years ago.' He sighed. 'After Mum died, Dad obviously decided Gwen could do what she liked – it didn't matter to him any more, because Mum could no longer be affected.'

Lulu recognised hurt in his eyes and relented. 'How did you feel when you discovered all this?'

'I was shocked at first,' he admitted. 'I thought my dad had always been faithful to Mum – even though they didn't have what you might call an easy relationship. But it seems he wasn't. My brother was four when you were born, maybe he and Mum had one of their rows and he strayed – I don't know.'

'Gwen's an awful liar,' said Lulu, her thoughts jumbled. 'How can any of us be sure I'm his daughter at all?'

Peter grinned. 'No doubt about it,' he said. 'You're the spitting image of Dad's sister, Sybilla. It was quite a shock when I saw you the first time, but the fact that she's an artist too sort of proves it.'

'Molly and I can vouch for that,' interrupted Eliza. 'We knew you had to be related.'

'You knew?' Lulu stared at Eliza, the anger rising. 'You knew all along who my father was and discussed it with Molly without saying a word to me? How *dare* you?'

Eliza's expression hardened. 'We didn't know what to do for the best,' she said defensively. 'Your father might not have wanted to see you – Carmichael was still a mystery – and we still had no idea who'd given you the colt.'

'Did you know about this, Dolly?'

'It's news to me,' she replied, giving Eliza a stony glare.

'What about you, Joe? Did Molly confide in you too?'

'Only three days ago, and I was more concerned about Carmichael's part in everything,' he said.

'So, even you kept this to yourself,' she said quietly, her chin dipping. It was all too much to take in, but as her thoughts whirled she came to realise they had been placed in an insidious position, unable to decide what to do for the best. Whether she could forgive them or not was another matter.

She turned back to Peter. 'You were talking about your parents,' she prompted.

Peter lit another cigarette and watched the smoke drift skywards. 'They loved each other, and could never spend long apart, even though they were always arguing.' He sighed. 'I was born a year after you, so whatever happened between them had obviously been patched up.'

The honesty in his eyes could not be denied, and at last she dared to believe he really was her brother. 'There are two of you?'

Peter's expression saddened. 'Andy was killed at Fromelles.'

Lulu heard Joe's gasp, saw the shock on his face and the slow recognition as he stared at Peter. 'Was Andy a captain in the Australian 14th Brigade at Fromelles? Was he carried under fire across no-man's-land by a certain Joe Reilly?'

Peter looked up at Joe. 'Yes,' he said gruffly. 'And if you're Joe Reilly then I know what you did for him. That's why I had to send you those horses, to repay you.'

Joe shifted his feet, clearly embarrassed. 'There was no need, mate,' he muttered, 'but I appreciate it.'

Peter looked away, his eyes glazed. 'Dad never got over Andy's death. He was the favourite elder son – the golden boy with a golden future,' he said, but with a marked absence of bitterness. 'He wasn't an unkind father, but he was blinkered when it came to Andy, and although I returned from France virtually unscathed, he couldn't accept that Andy would never come home. My mother and brother were dead, my father living in his own world – I had lost my family and never felt so alone, until I found that file.'

He looked almost shamefaced as he refused to meet Lulu's gaze. 'I discovered I had a sister – someone who might finally understand how isolated I felt – someone who was also exiled from their family. I had to find you – to bring you home.'

The tears welled and her heart went out to him, but she remained silent, unwilling to break the spell he had woven.

'With Dad so crook, it was impossible to leave the station and go to England to find you, so I got a licence as a bloodstock agent in the name of Carmichael. Ocean Child had come in with the brumbies, and I knew immediately he had great potential. Buying him at the auction, I put your name on the paperwork and sent him to Joe. Over the next few months I began to spread the word that Joe's yard was up and running again and persuaded people like the Frobishers to send over their horses.'

He glanced at Joe. 'It was the only practical way I could think of to repay your courage.'

'No worries, mate,' said Joe gruffly. 'Anyone would have done it. Andy was a bonzer bloke and a good cobber.'

Peter nodded before continuing. 'The gift of a yearling is an unusual one, but I knew from the detective's reports that you enjoyed riding, and had even sculpted a colt which you called Ocean Child – presumably named after you received Joe's letter.' He grinned as she nodded. 'I knew he would write to you about Ocean Child's progress, so all I had to do was copy my father's signature on the letters to the London solicitors and sit back and wait.' His blue eyes were teasing. 'It didn't take long, did it?'

She returned his smile. 'I was certainly intrigued,' she admitted, 'and of course it gave me the excuse to come home.' Her expression grew serious as she remembered poor Maurice, the fight with Bertie and the pain she'd caused Clarice. 'But my homecoming didn't please everyone,' she said sadly. 'Clarice even cut me out of her will.'

'Perhaps she was concerned you were heading for trouble,' he said. 'If the stories about the years she spent in Australia are true, then she probably didn't want you hearing them and thinking less of her.'

'I should say she didn't.'

They all turned at the sound of Gwen's voice to find her leaning on the arm of a red-faced man in a garish kipper tie and loud check suit. 'A family reunion. How cosy,' she sneered. Her gaze trawled over Peter with barely disguised contempt. 'You must be Frank's son – you look just like him.'

'You're not welcome, Gwen. Please leave.' Lulu brushed off Dolly's restraining hand and stood to face her.

'I'll go when I'm ready,' she said, grasping hold of her silent companion to steady herself. Her speech was slurred and it was clear she'd been drinking. 'Let me tell you about Clarice, and why she didn't want you here.'

'I think we should leave it there, Gwen,' muttered the man, eyes darting warily from Joe to Charlie and back to Peter.

'Not until I've had my say,' she snarled. Wrenching herself from his hold, she pushed past a shocked Eliza and staggered towards Lulu. 'Clarice had an affair with my father,' she said triumphantly. 'In fact, she was so desperate to get her claws into him, she had sex with him in the governor's rose garden.'

Lulu felt the colour flood her face. 'That's a spiteful lie,' she snapped. 'Clarice is a lady; she wouldn't do such a thing.'

Gwen gave a derisive snort. 'Oh, wouldn't she?' She smirked. 'She wasn't being very ladylike that night,' she drawled, 'far from it, with her chest exposed and her legs wrapped round my father's waist.'

'You're a liar,' spat Lulu.

Gwen's smile was vindictive. 'Am I? Why don't you ask Clarice? She won't be able to deny it.'

'I wouldn't demean her with such an insulting question.'

Gwen swept back her hair and sneered. 'The sainted Clarice was a tart and a home-wrecker who betrayed her sister and destroyed my family.' She inched nearer, her breath foul with alcohol and stale tobacco. 'Clarice stole everything from me – she even stole you.'

Lulu stood her ground. 'Thank God she did,' she retorted. 'You were the bitch from hell and I had a lucky escape.'

'Ooh, the little mouse squeaks.' She swayed as she regarded them all. 'How very brave you are when you're not on your own.'

Lulu was calmer than she had ever been as she looked into that loathsome face. 'Believe me, Gwen, you wouldn't like being alone with me,' she said. 'I'm not a little girl any more – not small and defenceless to be used as your punchbag. See these hands? They're strong from years of moulding clay, and could wring your scrawny neck as easily as that.' She snapped her fingers beneath Gwen's nose.

A shaft of fear lit Gwen's eyes and she took a step back. 'You'll pay for that,' she slurred, 'and more. I haven't forgotten how you stole my inheritance – and my mother.'

Lulu turned her back on Gwen and calmly sat down. 'You should leave while you can still walk,' she said coldly. 'The beer tent's over there.'

'Oh, I haven't finished yet,' she snarled. Shaking off her companion's warning hand, she swayed on her feet and turned her attention to Peter. 'Your dad owes me two years' money,' she barked.

'He owes you nothing.'

'Yes, he does,' she yelled, 'and if I don't get my money, I'll make sure everyone knows what kind of a bastard he really is.'

The man in the hideous check suit grasped her arm. 'You've said enough, Gwen. We're leaving.'

She swung a fist, narrowly missing his chin as she stumbled. 'I'm not finished yet,' she spat. 'I want my money.'

His puce face clashed with the suit and garish tie. 'It's time you sobered up,' he snarled, his grip tightening on her arm as he dragged her away.

'Strewth,' breathed Eliza. 'Is that *really* your *mother*?'

'Unfortunately,' replied Lulu coldly, 'but I don't boast about it.'

She pushed past the gloating Eliza and watched as Gwen's companion manhandled her towards the car park. Gwen was fighting him every inch of the way and yelling obscenities as he dragged her through the bemused and fascinated crowd. Their raised voices could be heard quite clearly and there was sniggering and laughter amongst bystanders as he shoved her into the ute, slammed the door and drove away at speed.

'I think we all deserve a glass of champagne after that,' announced Dolly, 'and I'm buying. I haven't had this much entertainment in one day for years.'

Eliza tucked her hand in Dolly's arm. 'That's a bonzer idea,' she replied, looking up at Joe. 'Are you coming too?'

He glanced at Lulu. 'I need to keep a clear head,' he muttered. 'There's still another race to run and owners to pacify.'

Eliza pouted prettily and fluttered her lashes. 'I'll save a glass for you,' she said, 'so don't be too long.'

'What about you, Lulu?' Dolly gently extracted Eliza's clutching fingers from her arm and reached out to her friend.

'Champagne and pills don't really go together,' she said with a grateful smile. 'You go on. Peter and I need to talk.'

Dolly nodded with understanding and herded Eliza away. When everyone had gone, even the reluctant Joe, Lulu turned to Peter. 'Let's walk down to the river,' she said. 'It might be cooler.'

They strolled down to the Derwent, found a bench beneath a tree and sat down. Lulu stared at the sparkling water and attempted to put all she'd learnt today into some kind of order. She was exhausted, but elated, confused and utterly beguiled by the thought of finally knowing her father.

'For most of my life I've tried to imagine what my father was like. When I was little he was a prince on a white horse –' she grinned at the thought – 'but as I grew older I became more realistic. I can't believe that at last I can find out about him. Tell me everything, Peter.'

'His name is Franklin John White – Frank to everyone. He was born not far from here fifty-six years ago, on a small cattle station at Collinsvale. The family wasn't rich then, merely making enough to scrape by. Dad's sister, Sybilla, married a Brisbane man and moved to the mainland. Mum and Dad took over the property when it got too much for his parents. Dad had always been ambitious, so when his parents retired to a seaside cabin down in Snug, he followed his sister to Queensland and ploughed all his money into a property at Augathella.'

'Where on earth is that?'

He smiled. 'It's a tiny settlement in what the Aborigines call the never-never.'

'That sounds very romantic.' She sighed.

He laughed. 'There's nothing romantic about three thousand head of cattle raising a cloud of dust as we move them from one failing waterhole to the next. You're on the back of a horse for days at a time, eaten up by flies and wilting from the heat. Droughts last for years, floods wash away barns and houses and leave the beasts stranded or drowned, swarms of locusts and mobs of roos eat everything in sight, and we have to watch the herd like hawks when the cows are birthing. Dingoes and eagles like nothing better than a tasty young calf. It's a tough life – especially for a woman – but I wouldn't change it for anything.'

Lulu saw the animation in his face, and knew he would never be happier than in the dusty brown land beyond civilisation. But his words had conjured up images of a lonely, precarious life. 'Your mother must have been an extraordinary woman,' she murmured.

'She was as tough and bloody-minded as Dad, and liked nothing better than joining the annual drove to the markets in Brisbane.' He sighed and leant back on the bench. 'I miss her,' he said with simple sadness.

'You said your – our – father had a stroke. How severe was it?'

'It's taken a while, but he's finally on the mend. The doctor told him to take it easy from now on, but he's always been a vigorous man and finds it frustrating to sit and do nothing.' He smiled. 'Would you like to meet him?'

Her pulse jumped. 'Of course,' she breathed.

'There's a very good clinic here that helps people who've suffered strokes. The treatment's very modern and involves physiotherapy and speech coaching, and he's so determined to get back in the saddle again he's a star pupil.' He chortled. 'I had the devil's own trouble persuading him to come back to Tassy, but I think he's glad he did,'

Lulu eyed him thoughtfully. 'Does he know you found that file and that I'm here in Hobart?'

Peter shook his head. 'I haven't told him anything yet. I wanted to make sure about you first. I had no idea how you would react to all this, and didn't want to get his hopes up in case you refused to see him.'

'I think you'd better prepare him,' she said quietly. 'Something like this could give him the most awful shock.' She had a sudden, terrible thought. 'What if he doesn't want to see me?'

'I hadn't thought of that.' He frowned as he stared at the river. 'But why wouldn't he? He's kept watch over you all your life – and that isn't the action of a man who doesn't care.'

She rose from the seat, opened the Japanese parasol and turned towards the racecourse. 'It has been quite a day,' she said, glancing up at him as they strolled back to the course. 'What made you choose such a lovely name for the colt?'

'That was easy,' he said, coming to a standstill. 'There were lots of photographs in that file. All the ones of you as a small child were taken on the beach up north. Dad had written, "My little water-baby," and your age, on the back of each one.'

Lulu felt the prick of tears. He must have loved her, and she'd never known. 'Talk to him tonight, Peter,' she said, her voice rough with emotion. 'I so desperately want to meet him.'

15

Joe's mind was so occupied with Lulu that he found it impossible to hold a sensible conversation with his owners whilst trying to keep an eye on her and Peter. He finally managed to escape and stood at the far edge of the grounds, his focus pinned on the two figures in the distance.

He studied the man walking at Lulu's side. Peter White was taller and broader than Andy had been, his gait hampered by a limp, but there was a definite likeness, and it was also apparent in Lulu. He dug his hands in his pockets and watched them approach, his thoughts churning.

There was little doubt Peter was Lulu's half-brother, and that he'd gone to extraordinary lengths to get her here. But, in spite of his generous help in re-establishing Galway House Racing Stables, Joe felt uneasy. He didn't like secrecy, certainly didn't appreciate being manipulated, and was worried that Lulu had been swept far too easily into something that might prove difficult to get out of.

He narrowed his eyes against the sun as they embraced and went their separate ways. Lulu was clearly animated as she caught sight of him and waved, and although he'd vowed to keep his feelings under control, he couldn't ignore the way his heart skipped a beat as she drew closer.

'Still keeping an eye on me, Joe?' She smiled up at him, her beautiful eyes shining with happiness.

'I just wanted to make sure you could find me in the crowd,' he drawled. 'We've got an early start in the morning, so it's best we leave soon.'

She bit her lip, suddenly hesitant. 'I'm sorry, Joe, but Dolly and I won't be going back with you tomorrow. Peter is booking us into a hotel, and we'll stay here until I've had the chance to talk to my father.'

Joe's concern deepened as she clutched his arm, her face animated and glowing. 'Oh, Joe, you have no idea what this means to me,' she breathed. 'I've waited so long to meet him. Don't you think it's wonderful that I finally have the chance?'

When he looked into her face, so alive with excitement and hope, he was loath to dampen her spirits, but he had to speak. 'I can understand how exciting it must be,' he said carefully, 'but don't you think things are moving too fast?'

She frowned. 'Peter spent almost two years planning this, and I've waited all my life. I hardly think—'

'You know nothing about him, Lulu – or about your father – and although it's tempting to rush into this, I really think you should . . .'

The light died in her eyes. 'Are you determined to ruin what has, up until now, been an extraordinary day?'

'Of course not,' he said quietly. 'I just don't want you getting hurt.'

'How could meeting my father hurt me?' Her expression had grown mutinous.

The truth was unpalatable, but he had to speak his mind. 'What if he refuses to see you?'

'He wouldn't do that,' she retorted.

'He's kept his distance all your life. There's no guarantee he'll want to actually meet you.' He reached out and took her hand, disconcerted to discover it was cold and trembling. 'Oh, Lulu,' he murmured, 'I'm sorry if I've spoilt things for you.'

There was a teardrop caught in her lashes, blinked away as she refused to look at him. 'You're right,' she murmured, 'of course you are.' She lifted her chin and gave a tremulous smile. 'Thanks for caring, Joe.'

He would always care – but she would never know how much, how difficult it was not to touch her lovely face and kiss her sweet mouth.

'Trust me to deal with this in my own way,' she said quietly. 'There have been too many years wasted already, and I need to discover who I am, and where I belong. If it all ends in tears, so be it, but I need to know.'

He understood then that nothing he could say would change her mind. 'I don't like leaving you,' he said, 'but I can see I have no choice. We'll be gone at first light tomorrow, but if you need me, get on the two-way and I'll come straight back.'

'You're a good man, Joe Reilly,' she murmured, slipping her hand into his.

Joe smiled down at her, yearning to pull her into his arms and hold her close. But he must be content with the friendship and trust she was giving him, and his heart ached in the knowledge that this was only the first of their goodbyes.

Clarice had not been feeling at all well lately, and although the doctor had prescribed tablets for her high blood pressure, her ankles were still swollen and she found she was as tired in the mornings as when she'd gone to bed.

She'd risen later than usual and was picking at her breakfast when Vera startled her by crashing into the dining-room.

'He's 'ere again, Mum,' she said, meaty arms folded beneath her bosom. 'Though what 'e's doing disturbin' decent folk at this time of the mornin' I don't know.'

Clarice glared. 'I do wish you'd knock before barging in,' she snapped. '*Who* is here?'

'That Major 'Opkins.' She sniffed.

'Well, show him in then, and bring a fresh pot of tea and another cup – and Vera, don't call me Mum.'

'No, Mum,' she muttered, turning on her heel and disappearing out of the door.

Clarice sighed as she heard Vera gruffly tell the major where to go. It really was too bad, she thought in despair. Oh, for the days when servants knew their place and how to conduct themselves.

'Good morning, Lady Pearson.' Major Hopkins stood uncertainly in the doorway. 'I'm sorry to disturb you so early.'

She greeted him and indicated he should sit on the other side of the table.

He settled in the chair and cleared his throat. 'My reason for calling at such an hour is that I have discovered something which I think you might find interesting.'

'I have asked Vera to make fresh tea. Perhaps it would be better to wait a moment.'

They exchanged small talk about the weather, his journey from London and their health until Vera had plonked the tea pot on the table alongside a fresh cup and saucer and slammed the door behind her. 'Oh dear,' said the major, his moustache tweaking, 'it seems I have disgruntled the sterling Vera.'

'It is in Vera's nature to be disgruntled,' Clarice replied as she poured tea, 'and I think she rather enjoys it. What is it you have to tell me?'

'I started to do some digging after we talked last –' he reached into his jacket pocket and pulled out an envelope – 'and I received this yesterday morning. It is a list of the farmers who sent Ocean Child to auction, and a short résumé of each man's history. I'm hoping that at least one of the names might mean something to you, and perhaps lead us to Carmichael.'

'I doubt it. I have not been in that unfortunate country for many years, and I certainly did not mix socially with farmers.'

His moustache tweaked again and Clarice eyed him suspiciously over her reading glasses before turning her attention to the list. The name leapt out at her, and after she'd scanned the brief biography she dropped the piece of paper on to the table. 'How extraordinary,' she murmured.

He sat forward eagerly. 'You have recognised someone?'

'Oh yes,' she murmured, 'and now it all suddenly makes sense.'

'Does he pose a danger to Lorelei?' he said sharply.

Clarice shook her head and smiled. 'On the contrary,' she replied. 'Frank White is Lorelei's father.' She sipped her tea, rather pleased with his startled reaction. 'Of course I didn't realise it at the time – none of us knew who her father was – but his name on that list explains everything.'

'I am at a loss, Lady Pearson.'

She barely heard him as she let the snippets of memory come together. They fitted perfectly. 'I met him once, a long time ago. He brought me a milk cow.' Clarice leant back in her chair, her visitor forgotten as she relived that encounter.

It was May 1896, and Eunice was having her usual afternoon rest. Gwen was away and Lorelei was busy with a colouring book and crayons on the rug Clarice had spread on the front lawn. It was a crisp autumnal day, so she'd wrapped up the two-year-old against the chill and was doing some needlepoint when she heard the sound of a horse coming up the lane. She put down her sewing, her curiosity piqued, for few people came this way.

It proved to be a man driving a wagon, behind which was tethered a plump, sleek cow. 'G'day. Are you Lady Pearson?' he called.

She beckoned him to come down the track, for she was not in the habit of conducting conversations in such an unladylike fashion. As he brought the wagon to a halt and clambered down, she was struck by how tall and handsome he was. It was a blessing Gwen was away, for he had the rough sort of good looks the girl admired, with dark blue eyes and the long curly hair and tanned skin of a gypsy. But she noted that he had a nice smile, and seemed to know his manners, for he took off his hat to greet her.

'Frank White,' he said with the lazy drawl of all Tasmanians. 'I've brought the cow you bought from my mate at the sales.' His gaze drifted to the little girl on the rug and back to the cow. 'Sal here's a good old girl,' he said. 'She'll give you plenty of milk for the little one.'

'That is why I have bought the beast,' she said, coolly. 'Lorelei is not very sturdy, and I thought fresh milk each day might put some flesh on her bones.'

'Too right it will,' he said, his gaze returning to the child, his smile wide. 'She's a little ripper, ain't she?'

Clarice couldn't resist hearing Lorelei praised, and beamed back at him. 'She's a darling child, Mr White, a little angel.'

Lorelei must have realised she was the centre of attention, for she got to her feet and toddled over. To Clarice's amazement, she didn't hide behind her skirts as she usually did, but grasped Mr White's sturdy leg and looked up at him with wide blue eyes.

Clarice's first instinct was to pick her up. She didn't know this man – he could be anybody. But then he squatted down to Lorelei's level, and they gazed at one another as if mesmerised. It was almost uncanny how their eyes were the same shade of blue, she thought distractedly, and it seemed they were completely absorbed in one another in a way that was quite extraordinary.

She watched in amazement as Mr White gently poked her tummy with his finger and made her giggle, then picked her up and swung her around. Quiet little Lorelei was shrieking with laughter, head flung back, legs kicking in delight.

'Please be careful,' she said fretfully. 'She has a heart condition and is very delicate.'

'I reckon she's stronger than you think, Missus,' he replied, setting Lorelei carefully back on her feet, his great hand swamping the tiny fingers that gripped so tightly. 'With a laugh like that, she'll take on the world and eat it up.'

Clarice gave him a hesitant smile. 'Do you have children, Mr White? You seem very at ease with Lorelei.'

He tugged his hat brim. 'I've got two sons,' he said gruffly. He gently extricated Lorelei's hold on his fingers and nudged her towards Clarice. His gaze followed the child as she held out her arms for Clarice to pick her up. Clearing his throat, he became businesslike and untied the cow. 'We'd better get Sal settled and I'll be on my way. It's a long trip back home to Hobart.'

'Lady Pearson? Lady Pearson, are you not well?'

Clarice returned to the present. 'I am quite well, thank you,' she replied with asperity. 'I was just remembering the one and only time I met Frank White. I'd bought a cow from the farmer's market, and he delivered it. He evidently came up from Hobart twice a year, which was quite a journey in those days, and was doing his farmer friend a favour.'

The major scanned the biographies. 'I should have seen the connection with Tasmania,' he said. 'I must be losing my touch.' He sat back in the chair and eyed her thoughtfully. 'Will you write and tell Lorelei about Mr White?'

'Most certainly,' she replied, 'but I have the feeling she already knows. If Frank White is still the man I remember, he won't waste time telling her himself.'

'I wonder why he's waited until now to make contact?' he muttered. 'And we still haven't solved the mystery of the forged instructions.'

'I suspect his tardiness had something to do with Lorelei's mother. But no doubt the mystery will be solved soon enough.' She smiled sweetly. 'More tea, Major?'

*

Lulu had spent a restless night, her dreams confused and disturbing, her waking moments filled with doubt. She had risen early and gone in search of Joe, but there was no sign of him, and she had to accept he'd already left for Galway House.

She had stood in the paddock and watched the mares with their foals, reluctant to return to the house and begin the day. Joe's advice had been wise – it had certainly made her stop and think – but although her emotions were in turmoil, she knew she had to meet her father, regardless of the consequences.

It was almost noon, and she and Dolly had said goodbye to their hosts on the hotel steps over three hours ago. The weather had changed overnight, and although it was sunny, there was a chill wind blowing in off the Tasman Sea.

'What do we do now?' Lulu dug her hands in her coat pocket and buried her nose in the collar to fend off the cold as they emerged from the quayside hotel. 'This waiting's unbearable. Half the day is gone, and I still haven't heard from Peter.'

'You'll drive yourself mad if you hang about here. Let's explore Sullivan's Cove and see if we can find somewhere to have lunch and perhaps do a spot of shopping.'

'I'm really not in the mood,' she grumbled, 'and Peter might ring while we're out. He'll think I've changed my mind.' The doubts had grown as Peter's silence continued. 'What if he doesn't call at all? What if . . . ?'

'Stop it.' Dolly put an arm around her shoulder. 'Come on, darling, don't fret so. If he calls while we're out, the hotel will take a message, and I expect this delay is only because it's taken a bit of time to own up to what he's done and deal with the consequences. It probably came as a shock to his father – I mean, it's not every day your son finds out you've had an affair, and then tries to present you with the daughter you've kept secret for twenty-six years.'

'I suppose so.' She sighed. She looked out across the cobbled square to the Edwardian customs houses, government buildings and warehouses in search of Peter, but there was still no sign of him, and the doubts increased. 'But what if Joe was right?' She turned back to Dolly, seeking reassurance and guidance. 'What if he refuses to see me, or forbids Peter to have any more to do with me – what then?'

'We'll cross that bridge when we come to it,' replied Dolly, 'but if you keep this up you'll make yourself ill.'

Lulu took a deep breath and tried to regain her composure. Dolly was right; she needed to keep her overactive imagination under control. 'Come on then,' she said determinedly, 'but I don't want to be away for too long.'

Peter had left the racecourse too late to see his father that night, and had planned to get to the clinic early so he could talk to him before the day's treatments began. But after a disturbed night he'd overslept, and had arrived at the clinic to discover his father was already having his physiotherapy.

As the morning dragged on, his frustration grew. Frank had refused to see him until he'd finished his game of dominoes, and then insisted Peter joined him and his new-found mates for a lengthy lunch in the dining hall. It seemed there would never be an opportunity to talk to the old man in private and, burning with impatience, Peter had left the dining hall to go and have a smoke in the garden.

He sat in the summer house and looked at his watch. Lorelei must be as on edge as he was – but he had nothing new to tell her, and he didn't want to raise her hopes by ringing the hotel only to disappoint her. He fidgeted in the cane chair and tried to concentrate on the newspaper, found it impossible and gave up.

'There you are. I've been looking for you everywhere.' Frank White leant heavily on the walking stick as he negotiated the stone steps that led down to the lawn and the summer house. 'Leave me,' he commanded, as Peter jumped from his chair to help, 'I'm not a cripple. I can manage a few steps.'

Duly chastened, but made extremely nervous by his father's cavalier attitude, Peter stood by ready to catch the silly old bugger if he fell. 'You'll end up breaking your flaming hip,' he warned.

Frank collapsed in a chair and hooked the walking stick over the arm. 'Tough as old boots, these hips,' he declared, with only a hint of the slur that had recently made his speech almost unintelligible. 'They'll see me right, no worries.'

The old man's irascibility had worsened since his stroke, and despite knowing it stemmed from frustration, Peter found it difficult to tolerate – especially today. His palms were sweating and his mouth was dry as he waited for his father to settle. He'd rehearsed what to say, but now the time had come, he couldn't find the words.

'What's on your mind, son?'

Peter looked into the eyes that had lost none of their colour and were still as keenly intelligent as ever. He licked his lips. 'Dad, I've done something you may not approve of, but I did it with the best of intentions.'

The thick white eyebrows drew together. 'The road to hell is paved with good intentions, boy,' he growled. 'Go on, spit it out.'

Peter took a deep breath and began to speak. He could see he had his father's full attention, but it was impossible to read his thoughts. He told him everything, and waited in an agony of silence for his father's reaction.

Frank sat in a shaft of pale sunlight, his head bowed, hands resting in his lap. They were the hands of someone who'd worked in the outdoors, who'd handled horses and cattle from the moment he was old enough to walk. This was his father, the man he respected and loved – the man whose secret was no longer his own. Peter watched him, suddenly afraid. The deeds had been done, the confession made – but had his actions merely made things worse between them?

'You had no business going through my things,' Frank said gruffly, 'but I suppose it doesn't matter any more.' He raised his head and looked at his son. 'It would have killed your mother if she'd known. That's why I kept paying.'

'I guessed as much.' Peter wanted to take his hand, but knew his father didn't approve of such shows of affection, so he leant back in the chair, his fingers knotted in his own lap, the knuckles white with tension.

'The stupid thing was I didn't even know if the kid *was* mine.' Frank gazed across the garden to the fine view of the city below. 'I learnt much later that I wasn't Gwen's first target,' he said, his expression grim. 'She'd tried to blackmail several others first – they were richer than me at the time, so I suppose she thought they'd be a better bet. Trouble was, I *had* slept with her – and I was ashamed, and terrified your mother would find out, so I paid up. Only a fool would cross Gwen, for she could make more trouble than a possum in a hen house.' Frank grimaced. 'But I didn't just take her word for it. I did my own bit of detective work.'

'How? You lived down here, and Clarice was up on the north coast.'

Frank tapped the side of his nose. 'A mate of mine mentioned that he had sold a cow to a Clarice Pearson, so I got myself up there and delivered it for him. The minute I saw that kid, I knew.' He fell silent, perhaps remembering that day. 'She was a little ripper,' he said, 'and so like my sister at that age.'

Peter tamped down his impatience as Frank once again fell silent. Time was ticking away, and Lorelei was waiting to hear from him.

'What you did for Joe was commendable,' Frank said finally, 'and I wish I'd read that letter from his commanding officer – then maybe I could have done something for him myself.' His gaze was filled with regret. 'But I couldn't bear to read it right through, didn't have the stomach for it. My son was dead. I didn't need to know how it had happened.'

'I can understand that,' Peter replied softly. 'I miss him too, Dad, and there's hardly a day goes by when I don't think about him.'

'His going like that left a terrible void in our lives,' Frank murmured.

'There have been times when I wished it was me who'd never come home, and that Andy had had my luck,' Peter confessed softly, 'because then you would have been spared the pain of losing your favourite son.'

The bright blue eyes regarded him with shocked disapproval. 'That's a wicked thing to say,' Frank snapped. 'What kind of man do you think I am to wish either of my sons dead – to favour one over the other? Your mother and me were blessed when you came home with just a bullet wound, and I've thanked God every day since you were spared.'

'Then why have you never shown it?'

Frank's expression was puzzled. 'I'm not one for sentimental nonsense,' he growled. 'You know that, son.'

Peter took a deep breath. 'Everything I do is overshadowed by Andy. Everything I am is compared to him and found wanting. I always knew he was your favourite, but that didn't bother me because I loved and admired him too. He was my big brother, the adventurous one, the boy who was forever getting into some scrape or another, and going that daring step further – the one who seemed to lead a charmed life. I was happy to tag along, to bask in his long shadow, but I needed your love and approval as well – and you've always seemed incapable of giving it.'

He dipped his head, almost ashamed to look in his father's face. 'I love and respect you, Dad, but I know I can never take Andy's place, and I wouldn't want to. I am my own man. My

311

family was lost to me once Mum and Andy were gone. I'd hoped you would finally see *me*, and realise I need you as much as Andy did, but you buried yourself in your own world.'

He rose from the chair and leant against the door frame, his back to his father, tears blinding him. 'When Andy came home from Brisbane in 1914 and told us he'd enlisted, I wanted to show you I was just as brave. But joining the RAAF meant I wasn't with Andy when he died – and that guilt will always live with me.' He gave a deep sigh. 'Finding out about Lorelei was a miracle. I had a sister who perhaps understood what it was like to be over-looked and cast aside – and I was determined to bring her home.'

'I never realised you felt that way.' Frank's sigh was weary. 'I didn't mean to shut you out, son – but losing your brother and then your mother . . .' He blinked and dug a handkerchief from his pocket. 'It was too much, and I couldn't see beyond my own pain.' He dabbed his eyes. 'I'm sorry, Peter.'

His father's sincerity was palpable, and Peter swallowed the lump in his throat. The old man had loved him, and still did – he just didn't know how to show it. He put a hand on his father's shoulder, shocked to feel the frailness of that once-strong body. 'There's no need to apologise, Dad,' he said softly, 'and now I've found Lorelei, perhaps you'll begin to enjoy life again and we can be a proper family.'

Frank stiffened, his gaze fixed to a far point of the garden. 'She's got her own life. She doesn't need me.'

'But she does, Dad, that's the whole point. Every child deserves to know who their father is and have the chance to get to know him. Gwen never told anyone about you, so Lorelei has lived for twenty-six years without having that chance. You can't deny her now, surely?'

There was a long silence, and Peter wondered if he was remem-bering that day so many years before when he'd seen Lorelei as a little girl – or was he remembering his affair with the woman who'd held him to ransom?

'Does Gwen know she's here?'

'Yes.'

The blue gaze was direct and penetrating. 'You've seen her?'

'At the races, yesterday. She was drunk and caused a scene. Even the seedy-looking bloke with her was clearly sick of her awful behaviour and hauled her away.'

Frank grimaced. 'Doesn't sound like she's changed much,' he muttered. 'I suppose she was demanding money?'

Peter nodded. 'I put her straight on that,' he replied. 'She won't bother us again.'

'I wouldn't bank on it. That bitch is like a terrier with a rat, and this bloody little island is no keeper of secrets – she'll find out where I am soon enough, you can bet on it.'

'Let's not talk about her,' said Peter, 'she's not important. Lorelei is waiting close by, anxious to see you. Can I bring her to visit?'

Frank turned his gaze once more to the view below him. 'Let me sleep on it. It's been a long day and all of this has come as a bit of a shock.'

Peter helped him to his feet and handed him the walking stick. 'Tomorrow, then?'

Frank came to a halt and looked back at him. 'I know everything about that girl,' he said gruffly, 'and Clarice has done a good job raising her. I'm just an old cattleman who's more at home on the back of a horse than in some fancy drawing room. We have nothing in common, Peter, so what is the point?'

Peter stared at him in disbelief. 'She's your daughter – that's the point.'

'Shared blood isn't enough – not after all this time.' He shuffled forward, clearly exhausted by everything that had happened. 'I kept an eye on her out of curiosity – nothing more. I never planned to meet her.'

Peter had a suspicion the old man felt far more for Lorelei

than he was letting on and that it was his stubborn pride that was holding him back. 'Aren't you just a bit curious to see what she's really like?'

Frank shrugged. 'A little,' he confessed, 'but who'd want an old bludger like me for a dad, eh? It's best left, son.'

'At least give her the chance to make up her own mind,' said Peter, with a note of asperity. 'She's waited all her life to meet you – don't let her down now. Please.'

The gaze was steady, the expression unyielding. 'It would have been kinder to leave her in England and in ignorance,' Frank rasped. 'You've raised her hopes, made promises you can't keep.' His voice subsided and his shoulders slumped. 'I don't know if I can face her after all this time and have her judge me.'

'If you let her down now you'll be hurting her far more than you ever have.' He grasped Frank's arm, willing him to change his mind. 'If you don't do this, you'll always regret it.'

The blue eyes were quizzical. 'This really matters to you, doesn't it?'

'Of course it does. She's my half-sister. I like her, and I want her to become part of this family.'

Frank nodded thoughtfully and began the short climb up the steps. When he'd gained the terrace, he stood for a moment, leaning heavily on his walking stick. 'You can bring her tomorrow about three.' The gimlet gaze held him. 'But don't tell her till the last minute, cos I might change my mind come morning.'

Lulu was exhausted, nerves shredded, thoughts haywire. The day had dragged on with no message from Peter, and she could only come to the conclusion that her father had not taken Peter's confession well. She was desperately trying to contain her disappointment as she sat in the hotel sitting room with Dolly, grateful her friend understood her need for calm and silence.

'You've got a visitor,' said Dolly quietly.

Lulu didn't wait for him to sit down before she bombarded

him with questions. 'What did he say? How did he take it? Can I see him tonight? Or is to be tomorrow?' His silence and solemn expression finally quelled her excitement and she slumped back into the couch. 'He doesn't want to meet me, does he?'

'I'm working on it, Lorelei,' he said, taking her hand, 'but he's an old man set in his ways, and this has all come as a bit of a shock.' His smile was wan. 'Give him time,' he coaxed. 'He'll come round, I'm sure.'

Lulu saw the uncertainty in his eyes, and understood he was trying to let her down gently. 'None of this could have been easy for you, and I do appreciate all you've done.' She blinked back the tears and steeled her resolve. 'It wasn't fair of either of us to expect so much from him. But at least we've found each other'

'Tomorrow is another day,' he said. 'You never know, he may change his mind.'

'He might.' Lulu capitulated to the flicker of hope that still lingered, and gave him a watery smile. 'I'll stay in Hobart until the end of the week, but if by then . . .' She gave a shrug. 'We'll see.'

Her bitter disappointment meant she couldn't sleep, and she eventually gave up and clambered on to the window seat to watch the moon sail beyond Mount Wellington. Her father was somewhere on the slopes of that mountain – was he too having a restless night – was he thinking of her, wondering, perhaps regretting his decision not to see her? She had to keep the hope alive that he would change his mind, for regardless of the outcome, she knew she couldn't leave Hobart without seeing him.

The next day

Peter was booked into a small commercial hotel down by the docks. He hadn't liked lying to Lorelei, but he'd had no choice and consequently had spent another restless night.

He was out of bed and dressed at dawn, and as it was far too early for breakfast, and his nerves were stretched to breaking-point, he took himself off for a brisk walk. His shattered knee ached, but at least it gave him something else to focus upon.

As the morning progressed he found he was on edge every time the telephone rang, and the receptionist began to look uncomfortable at his hovering presence.

The call came at two o'clock.

'I'm sorry, son,' said Frank down the crackling line, 'I can't see her. Tell her I wish her luck.'

The line was disconnected abruptly, and Peter was left staring at the buzzing receiver. He caught the eye of the girl behind the desk and hooked it back in place before storming out of the hotel. His anger was all-consuming and he felt like hitting something – anything – to release it. Thank God he hadn't told Lorelei about the appointment at three, and thank God he wasn't with his father at this minute, because he wouldn't be responsible for what he said or did.

'Old bastard,' he growled, slamming the utility's door so hard it rocked on its chassis. 'I thought you had balls, Dad, but where are they now, eh? Coward. Bloody coward.'

He simmered and glared out of the window as he smoked one cigarette after another and tried to plan what to do next. Lulu would have to be told, and he didn't relish that ordeal – but there was little point in her staying in Hobart, not now the old man's mind had been made up.

'Flaming hell!' He shoved open the door, slotted in the crank handle and gave it a vicious jerk. The engine roared into life and he climbed in, slammed the door and rammed it into gear. He had no idea what he would say to Lulu, and was definitely not looking forward to the rest of the day. He'd never imagined that the only real stumbling block to his plans would be his father, and he hoped Lulu was strong enough to accept the stubborn old fool's decision.

Lulu had held on to the glimmer of hope and dressed accordingly. The soft blue of her sweater enhanced the colour of her eyes, the tailored slacks were practical against Hobart's weather and the jaunty knitted beret gave her spirits a lift. She was ready to meet him if he changed his mind.

It was windy, with clouds scudding across a grey sky that threatened rain. The boats moored in the harbour swayed in the rising swell, their rigging making a tuneless clatter as gulls screamed overhead. Despite her determination to remain cheerful, the morning dragged as she and Dolly walked around the harbour and glanced in the shop windows lining the main street. They had an early lunch in a restaurant that specialised in crayfish and green-lipped mussels, but she found she had little appetite for the delicious food and left most of it on her plate.

'He's not going to change his mind, is he?' she asked, as Dolly checked the bill.

'Neither of us knows that,' said Dolly firmly. She paid the waitress and steered Lulu out of the restaurant and on to the cobbles. 'Give him time. He's an old man whose sins have caught up with him. I expect he's as shell-shocked as you over all this.'

Lulu pulled a face. 'Maybe. But I would have thought—'

'You've done too much thinking over the past couple of days. Come on, let's go back to the hotel and relax. You look done in.'

Lulu saw the utility race along the cobbles and screech to a halt outside their hotel, and her heart missed a beat. It was Peter.

'We need to talk,' he said, taking her arm and steering her up the steps into the lounge.

There was an aura of pent-up fury about Peter, and Lulu didn't question him until they'd reached a quiet corner of the lounge. 'What's happened? He hasn't taken a turn for the worse, has he?'

317

'Nothing that simple,' he muttered. He took her hand. 'I'm sorry, Lulu, I've really messed things up. I hope you can forgive me.'

'He doesn't want to see me, does he?'

He ran his fingers through his hair and refused to look at her. 'I really thought he might,' he said, 'but he telephoned me and made it clear he doesn't have the courage to face you.'

Lulu leant back in the chair, her gaze fixed on Peter. The poor man was obviously distraught – and she couldn't blame him – but her disappointment was stiletto sharp.

They sat in silence. The minutes ticked by – and Lulu's resolve hardened. 'I've waited too long for this,' she said finally, 'and I'm not leaving Hobart without seeing him.' She regarded Peter steadily. 'From what you've said, I gather he's not a man accustomed to shying from confrontation.'

'He meets things head-on. Always has done.'

'Until now,' said Lulu softly. 'He's probably ashamed he abandoned me, and maybe scared I'll judge him and find him wanting.' She took a deep breath. 'But I'm determined to see him. He has to realise he has nothing to fear from me.'

'He'll be furious,' Peter warned. 'Dad's used to having his own way.'

'He's my father. He'll get over it.'

'And if he doesn't?'

Lulu tamped down on the squirm of fear and gathered up her coat and handbag. 'We'll cross that bridge when we come to it,' she retorted with more composure than she felt. She looked down at Peter, who was still slumped in his chair. 'Will you take me, or do I have to call a taxi?'

Peter rose from the chair, clearly unhappy. 'I'd better take you,' he muttered, 'but you'll need to prepare yourself for what could turn out to be an ugly confrontation.'

'If he's that unpleasant I will leave, and that will be the end to it,' she said, lifting her chin in defiance.

'Do you want me to come?' Dolly was already gathering her things from the couch.

Lulu shook her head. 'I need to do this alone, Dolly.'

Dolly gave her hug and kissed her cheek. 'Best of luck, darling, and if the old blighter gives you any trouble, I'll soon sort him out.'

Lulu smiled her appreciation of Dolly's support and followed Peter to the utility. She was thankful for his silence as he drove out of Sullivan's Cove and up the winding, steep route towards the mountain, for her thoughts were whirling – the burst of defiance and courage ebbing with every mile.

The narrow road was lined with trees and shrubs that almost hid the tiny wooden houses that perched at the very foot of the great mountain. And as they climbed, she looked back and saw Hobart sprawling beneath them, and the glitter of the sea and river. But the peak was shrouded in grey swirling cloud. Perhaps it was an omen, she thought, and shivered.

Peter drove through the wide iron gates and drew to a halt on the gravelled driveway. He helped her down, his expression anxious. 'Are you sure you want to do this?'

'Absolutely.'

Peter smiled. 'I can see you're nervous, despite the brave face, but I admire you, Lulu, and I'm sure Dad will too. Just remember that his bark is far worse than his bite, and don't let him bully you.'

'I know how to handle bullies,' she muttered. 'Let's get on with it.'

He led her along a path lined with hydrangeas to the wide expanse of lawn. The house was perched on the hill, the mountain soaring behind it, Hobart spread below. There were green shutters at every window, and glass doors lead to a broad terrace where chairs and tables waited for more clement weather.

Her heart was hammering as Peter led her up the steps to the

319

terrace and into a large reception hall where men and women were sitting playing board games or chatting over a cup of tea. Her gaze flitted from face to face, waiting for a reaction – wondering which one was her father – almost dreading seeing him.

'He'll be in his room listening to the radio as it's too cold to go outside,' Peter murmured, as he led her down a long corridor and stopped in front of a closed door.

Lulu's legs threatened to buckle and she grabbed his arm. 'I don't know if I can do this,' she said in sudden panic.

'Then we'll leave.'

Lulu felt as if she was glued to the floor with indecision. She'd come so far, was only a few steps from the man she had wanted to meet all her life. She had to find the courage to see this through or she would regret it for ever. Looking up at Peter, she could see he was as nervous and unsure as she. 'Promise you won't leave me.'

Peter nodded.

She gathered her courage and opened the door.

Frank White was sitting in a high-backed chair by the window, his hat on the table beside him, his attention so avidly fixed to the radio show that he was unaware of his visitors.

Lulu stood in the doorway and regarded him with open curiosity, for this was the father she'd never known, the man whose face she'd never seen – not even in her dreams. He had a shock of curly silver hair that reached almost to his collar, and his leathery skin spoke of living and working in the sun, but the lines and crevasses of his face merely enhanced his rugged appearance. Frank White had once been a very handsome man.

She stepped into the room, her fear quashed, confidence soaring.

Frank turned from the radio, his bright blue eyes widening as they settled upon her. 'What are you doing here?' he rasped, fumbling for his walking stick. 'I told Peter you weren't to come.'

'I'll leave if you want me to,' she replied coolly, 'but it would be a shame if I did, because then we couldn't get to know one another.'

Frank struggled to his feet and switched off the radio. 'You've got a nerve, girlie, I'll say that for you,' he growled.

'It seemed silly not to meet when we are both in the same town,' she said, taking a step towards him, 'and I had to come to satisfy my own curiosity.'

Frank grinned and glanced at Peter. 'She's a real Pommy sheila, ain't she? Talks like someone on the BBC.'

'Clarice made me have elocution lessons. I hated every last one of them,' she said evenly.

His smile faltered as his gaze travelled from her head to her sensible boots. 'The last time we met, you were just a nipper,' he said gruffly, 'but my, oh my, how you've grown.'

Her pulse raced. 'We've met before?'

'A long, long time ago,' he said softly.

'So why didn't you want to see me again?'

He sank back into the chair and refused to meet her gaze. 'Lost me nerve, I reckon,' he admitted. 'This has all come as a bit of shock, and at my age, that's not too good.' He looked up at her then, his eyes twinkling with mischief. 'But there's nothing like a pretty face to cheer up an old cobber like me. Sit down, Lorelei,' he patted the chair next to him. 'I'm getting a crook in me neck looking up at you.'

She heard the slur in his speech, and as she sat down she noted the way his mouth drooped to one side and his hand trembled on the head of the walking stick. The stroke had obviously affected him, but his sense of humour and sharp mind had remained intact. 'You said we've met before, but I would have remembered if we had.'

'You were only two. A lovely, bright little thing you were.' His eyes swam with unshed tears. 'You grasped my leg and looked up

321

at me with those big eyes and I was lost.' He dabbed his eyes. 'Your tiny fingers held so tightly to mine it was as if you never wanted to let me go. Leaving you behind was the hardest thing I'd ever done.'

Lulu felt strangely unaffected by his distress. 'Then why did you?'

'I had a wife and two boys. I couldn't hurt them.'

She felt a rush of anger. 'But you didn't mind hurting me,' she said flatly. 'And you didn't think of your wife and son when you slept with my mother.'

'I was young, foolish and hot-blooded,' he snapped. 'I'd left home after a row with Peter's mother, and Gwen . . .' He gave a sigh, his anger depleted. 'She was hard to resist, and I've regretted my foolishness ever since,' he finished.

'Because of the hurt you've caused, or because of Gwen's demands for money?'

He glared at her from under bushy eyebrows. 'Both,' he rasped. 'It hasn't been easy.'

Her contemptuous grunt echoed between them. 'You should have tried it on my side of the fence,' she retorted. 'I had to grow up without a father – never knowing who you were, or why you abandoned me to Gwen's tender mercies.' She took a deep breath to quell the building rage. 'Can you imagine what it's like being branded illegitimate?'

His expression hardened, his glare settling on Peter. 'This is why I didn't want to see her,' he barked. 'I knew it was a mistake.'

'Mistakes seem to be your forte,' Lulu said evenly, 'but I've had to live with them all my life. They made me different to everyone else – not only because of my accent, and my stupid heart condition, but because of my family circumstances. I didn't have a father – I didn't even have a mother – and I was being raised by a woman old enough to be my grandmother. That's a tough thing to brazen out – especially in a private girls' school in England where snobbery is rife and ancestry is all-important.'

'You're angry,' he muttered, 'and I don't blame you.'

'Damn right I'm angry,' she retorted, sweeping off the beret and shaking out her hair.

'I'm sorry.'

'It's a bit late for apologies,' she snapped. The rage in her was shocking, and although this was not how she'd planned to conduct this meeting, it was as if that anger had been stored up over twenty-six years and would not be denied. 'The damage was done years ago when you slept with Gwen. It lives on in the tittle-tattle and prejudice here in Tasmania and will no doubt follow me to the grave.' She took a breath. 'No amount of apology will counter that.'

He raised his head, his blue eyes piercing in their directness. 'The circumstances surrounding your birth were shameful, I admit. And I am truly sorry for that. You were the innocent who had to pay a high price for what me and your mother did all those years ago. But I never forgot you, and tried my best to keep an eye out for you.'

'By having someone spy on me?'

He eyed her sharply. 'You have a sour tongue, Missy.'

'It comes with bitter memories.' She grabbed her beret and handbag. 'This was a mistake,' she said to Peter. 'Will you take me back to the hotel, please?

'I thought you were made of tougher stuff,' Frank barked as they reached the door. 'Gwen would have stayed and fought it out – not run away.'

'You know nothing about me,' she shot back. 'And don't you *ever* compare me to Gwen.'

'You'll be back,' he rasped.

'Don't count on it.'

She hurried out and ran down the stairs to the ute. Slamming the door, she waited for Peter, blinded by tears. She had invested so much hope in that meeting and she'd squandered it. The years of humiliation and resentment had been too pent-up, the emotions too strong.

Peter climbed in beside her. 'Do you really want to leave?' he asked quietly.

She nodded and blinked away the tears.

'I can understand how angry and hurt you must be,' he said, 'but reconciliation will take time – for both of you. Give him another chance, Lulu.'

She turned her head and looked through the window at the clinic. She'd been wrong to storm out like that, to show such lack of control, but the thought of going back in there today and apologising to him was too humiliating.

'I'll think about it,' she murmured.

Three days later, Lulu was waiting for Dolly to return from the hairdresser when Peter strode into the hotel lounge.

'He telephoned again this morning, asking to see you,' he said. 'I think he's genuinely sorry the meeting didn't go well and wants to clear the air.'

Lulu saw the silent plea in his eyes and realised she was being pig-headed and unfair. Peter had come every day, begging her to reconsider and relaying Frank's many telephone messages. It would be churlish to refuse to see him – a lost opportunity she knew she would always regret. She picked up her coat and bag. 'Let's go before I change my mind.'

Leaving a message for Dolly at reception, they drove away from the hotel and once again climbed the steep mountain road.

Lulu's heart was beating steadily, her emotions firmly under control as they took the last long bend and caught their first glimpse of the clinic through the trees.

The utility came from nowhere. It was heading straight for them on the wrong side of the road, and going much too fast.

'Hold on,' yelled Peter as he yanked on the steering wheel. The tyres screeched, and as he slammed on the brakes they skidded into the gravel at the side of the road, narrowly missing a large tree.

The other utility rocked on its chassis as it swerved back to the right side of the road and raced away.

'Bloody hell!' Peter gasped. 'That was close.' He turned to look at Lulu. 'Are you hurt? You've gone awfully pale.'

She shook her head distractedly. 'Did you see the driver?'

'I was too busy trying not to crash into the idiot.'

'It was Gwen.'

His face blanched beneath the tan. 'You don't think she . . . ?'

'We'd better get up there,' said Lulu. 'Frank could be in trouble.'

Peter engaged the gears and they shot out of the gravel and took the rest of the bend too fast. Hurtling through the ornate iron gates, they skidded to a halt at the bottom of the steps.

Lulu was out of the truck before the engine had died. Up the steps and along the hall she ran, the sound of Peter's heavier tread gaining on her. She thrust open the door to Frank's room and came to an abrupt halt.

Frank was in his chair, a middle-aged nurse leaning over him with a bag of ice pressed to his cheek. She turned and glared. 'Get out,' she snapped. 'Frank's had enough visitors for one day.'

Frank pushed away the ice. 'Stop making such a fuss woman,' he growled. 'This is my son and daughter, and I want to see them.'

'But . . .'

'But nothing. Get out and leave me be.'

She dumped the ice pack in his lap and left in a bustle of starched uniform, her face glowing with righteous indignation.

Lulu hurried across the room, Peter at her heels. She stared in horror at the livid marks on his cheek and the swelling above his eye. 'Did Gwen do that?'

Frank eyed them both shamefacedly. 'I didn't see it coming,' he confessed. 'One minute she was yelling at me, the next – *wham*.' He winced as he pressed the ice to his face. 'The bitch has a punch worthy of Jack Dempsey,' he muttered.

'What did she want?'

His blue eyes gleamed. 'Money. It's all she ever wants.' His pride returned and he lifted his chin. 'I told her to go to hell and threatened to call the cops.' He chuckled. 'The expression on her face was almost worth the black eye.'

'It must have shaken you up,' said Peter, inspecting the damage. 'I'll get the doctor to give you the once-over.'

'I might be getting on, but I'm not so decrepit I can't take a punch from a flaming woman.' Frank glared. 'Sit down, the pair of you, and stop making such a bloody fuss.'

Lulu sat in the chair she'd occupied before and eyed him warily. He was obviously used to getting his own way and got easily roused when thwarted. He couldn't be an easy man to live with.

'Don't look at me like that, Lorelei. I'm not about to eat you,' he growled. He regarded her in silence. 'I'm sorry we got off to a bad start the other day. Thanks for coming.'

'I'm sorry too,' she said evenly. 'When we saw Gwen driving so recklessly away from here I realised how important it was to put things right between us. I'm just thankful she did you no real harm.'

His smile was wry. 'Only to me pride, girl – only to me pride.' His blue eyes twinkled. 'I always knew you'd turn into a beauty,' he said gruffly.

Feeling ridiculously pleased, she reddened. 'I don't see how,' she replied. 'The last time you saw me I was only a baby.'

'I used to go to the beach to watch you when I went up north. You were there most days regardless of the weather.' He reached out and touched her hair. 'You were my secret little water baby, and Peter chose well when he named the colt.'

Lulu swallowed the lump in her throat. 'Why didn't you let me know you were there, and who you were? I so wanted to have a father.'

'You know why, and I admit it was cowardly.' He blinked and looked down at his hands. 'I had very little to offer, especially in those early years, and I knew Clarice loved you, and would give you the best of everything once you'd escaped Gwen's clutches and settled in England.'

He dropped the ice bag on the table and kept his gaze averted. 'I never planned for us to meet,' he said, his voice rough with emotion. 'It was enough for me to know you were thriving.' He looked at her then. 'It's only now I realise how wrong I was. Will you forgive me?'

Lulu felt the old hurts and resentments melt away as she took his hand. 'Of course,' she breathed.

'I thought I knew everything about you, but now you're here I realise I know nothing at all. Tell me about yourself, Lorelei.'

'My friends call me Lulu,' she replied, 'although Clarice refuses to do so.' She grinned. 'She thinks it's common to shorten names.'

His gaze was penetrating and steady. 'Am I to be your friend?'

'I hope so,' she said honestly, 'but it could take a while.'

It was a week later, and Joe could imagine her perched on a stool in the hotel telephone booth, the receiver pressed to her ear, her hair tumbling about her lovely face. 'As I haven't heard from you for a week, I was getting worried,' he said, pedalling hard on the two-way to keep up the charge from the generator. 'How's it going?'

'Gwen turned up at the nursing home and caused trouble, but they've tightened up security and she won't be able to get to him again.'

Joe felt a jolt of fear. 'You've got to be careful, Lulu,' he said urgently. 'She might come looking for you next.'

Her laughter came down the line. 'I'm quite safe,' she assured him. 'The hotel is locked at night, and I'm on the fourth floor.'

He wasn't convinced, but decided not to push it. There was no point in making her fearful. 'Mum's been telling me about Frank. She knew him when they were kids. How's it going with him?'

'He's not the easiest man, and it was tough at first, but we're slowly getting to know one another.' Her voice cut through the static so clearly it was as if she was in the next room, not at the other end of the island. 'He's not at all what I'd imagined,' she confided, 'and I can now understand why he and Peter don't get on. He's too fond of getting his own way, and has a tendency to bark at people.'

'But you don't regret getting in touch with him?'

'No, of course not. He's my father.' She paused, and for a moment he wondered if Doreen had cut them off. 'You'll never guess,' she continued, 'his sister is the well-known landscape artist Sybilla Henderson, and she's going to exhibit her work in London next year. How about that?'

He could hear the laughter in her voice and ached to see her. 'Can't say I've ever heard of her,' he drawled, 'but then I don't think I could name any artist.'

'I saw some of her work in the Melbourne gallery, and loved the bush paintings. You could almost smell the eucalyptus and felt you could rustle through the leaves on the bush floor. She's very talented.'

He smiled at that, for he loved her enthusiasm. 'So what do you and Frank talk about?'

'Everything,' she said simply. 'We have a lot to catch up on.'

'I'm glad it's turning out all right,' he said sincerely. 'When do you think you'll be coming back here?'

'I'm not sure. Frank's still recovering, and I want to spend as much time with him as I can.' She paused. 'How's Ocean Child?'

'He's fit and ready for his next race, but I think he's missing you.'

'I miss him too. Give his ears a good rub. That should cheer him up.' The static buzzed and clicked. 'How's Molly . . . and Eliza?'

'Ma's doing good now Dianne's taken on a lot of the heavy work. Eliza's gone back to the mainland, but she plans to come back soon, because her dad's bought a place out at Deloraine. How's Dolly doing down there?'

'She's good, but getting a little bored, I think. She's run out of shops.'

'Eliza said to send her love, and to remind Dolly she promised her a hat from Harrods.'

Lulu's voice became crisp, her tone businesslike. 'I have to go. Peter's waiting to take me up to the clinic. It was lovely to speak to you. I'll call back when I have more idea of my plans.'

'Goodbye, Lulu.' Joe stopped pedalling and sat for a moment, unwilling to let the memory of her voice escape.

His reverie was interrupted by Molly, who came bustling into the hall. 'What was all that about Gwen?' She listened as he told her and her frown deepened. 'I don't like the sound of that,' she muttered. 'The woman's dangerous. You don't think she'd come up here and do any damage, do you?'

'I shouldn't think so,' he assured her. 'She lives almost a hundred miles away, and she's more interested in getting her own back on Frank at the moment.'

'Mmm. I hope you're right. With so many valuable animals in the yard, we can't afford to be complacent.'

'If it makes you feel any easier, I'll check the place each night and tell Charlie and the others to keep an eye open for anyone lurking about.'

'I think that might be a very good idea,' she said.

*

329

They were sitting in the sunshine of an early-spring day, with the sound of many birds to accompany them. Lulu felt easier with Frank now they had spent so much time together, more able to confide in him. They were discussing Gwen.

'I'd hoped she would learn to love me, but when she tried to run me over on the quay that day, I finally had to accept she never will. The ensuing encounters merely confirmed it.'

'How do you feel about that?' The blue gaze was direct.

'Liberated,' she replied, and smiled as he raised a questioning eyebrow. 'The loathing is mutual, and I no longer fear her or want anything to do with her. I'm strong and capable enough to be myself – and I'm proud of who I am, and what I've become.'

'Ha!' He slapped his thigh and glanced at Peter. 'Spoken like a true White! Good on you, girl. That's the spirit.'

She laughed. 'I think it probably has more to do with being raised by Clarice,' she replied drily. 'She's a woman of strong principles and rarely minces her words.'

'You could be right,' he agreed with a chuckle. 'That woman has a glare that would stop the tide coming in.'

'We've talked about me long enough. I want to know more about you.'

'My life isn't very interesting,' he drawled.

'Tell me anyway.'

He pulled a face and reluctantly told her his life story. 'I'm almost sixty,' he said finally, 'and when I lost Andy and Caroline a part of me died too.' He looked at Peter, who'd remained silent throughout. 'I haven't been a good father, and I'm sorry I've let both of you down.'

'It's all right, Dad,' Peter responded gruffly.

'Of course it is,' said Lulu, 'and I'm grateful to both of you for letting me have this chance to make things right.'

Frank threw off the blanket that had been covering his knees.

'Do you know what?' he declared. 'I'm going to get out of this place and take you both home to Queensland.'

Lulu gasped. 'But I'm leaving for England in less than three weeks.'

'Cancel your booking,' he ordered. 'We've wasted too many years already, and I want to get to know you properly. The only place to do that is in the Outback, with just the cattle and the big blue above us for company. What d'you say?'

Lulu looked helplessly at Peter. 'I don't know. It's all a bit sudden, and I have responsibilities in England.'

'Dad, you can't make Lulu change her plans like that. And I don't think it's wise for you to travel so far again so soon,' muttered Peter.

'Rubbish,' Frank retorted, before turning back to Lulu. 'Come on, girl – where's your spirit of adventure?'

'It's alive and well,' she replied. 'That's why I'm here – but Peter's right. I can't just take off for Queensland. What about Clarice? She's expecting me home.'

He waved away her objection. 'She'll understand,' he said dismissively.

'I have work waiting for me, things I must do if my career isn't to come to a grinding halt. And then there's Dolly. I can't expect her to fall in with your plans.'

'Having met her a couple of times, I reckon she won't be able to resist,' he said with breathtaking implacability. 'Queensland is God's own country, and there isn't another place in the world like it. I take it she can ride?'

'Yes, but—'

'Then she'll fit right in.'

Lulu didn't appreciate being steamrollered in this fashion, but the idea of going to Queensland was enticing. 'As long as Dolly agrees, I suppose we could change our booking and stay for a couple of weeks,' she said cautiously, 'but Clarice isn't as strong as she thinks she is, and I don't want to leave her too long.'

'That's settled then,' he said, slapping his knee. 'Help me up, Peter. I need to sign out and shake the dust of this place off my boots.'

16

The next two days passed in a whirl of activity, and Lulu was still finding it hard to come to terms with being swept along by her father's enthusiasm. She had telephoned Joe to warn him they were driving up from Hobart and would need to be accommodated overnight on their way to catch the boat from the mainland. Dolly had been surprisingly eager to make the trip to Queensland, but Lulu continued to have second thoughts.

'I'm really not convinced it's the right thing to do,' she said, as they packed their bags on their final morning in Hobart. 'Clarice is expecting me home, and I don't like to disappoint her.'

'Frank certainly knows how to bully people into things,' agreed Dolly, 'but a few extra weeks won't really make much difference to Clarice, surely?'

Lulu heaved a sigh and sat on the bed. 'It's so frustrating not to be able to speak to her. It takes ages for letters to get through, and it's impossible to telephone from here.' She eyed the case. 'Bertie will not be pleased,' she muttered. 'I promised him faithfully I'd be back in December.'

Dolly sat beside her. 'If you're that worried, then we won't go,' she said. 'I'm sure I can change the tickets back again.'

'I'm torn,' Lulu admitted. 'I'd love to see Queensland, but I'm worried about letting Clarice and Bertie down. On the other hand, I don't want to disappoint my father. He's cheered up no end now he's got things to plan.' She looked at Dolly. 'What do you think I should do?'

'Still got that penny I gave you back in London?' At Lulu's nod, she grinned. 'Hand it over, and we'll see what happens.'

Lulu watched as she flicked the coin in the air. 'Heads for London, tails for Queensland,' she murmured.

'Tails it is.'

Lulu smiled as the relief flooded through her. 'Queensland here we come,' she said, 'but first I'm going to send Clarice and Bertie a telegram; then I'll write them each a long letter explaining everything in more detail.'

'Are you going to tell her what Gwen said?'

Lulu shook her head. 'I'm sure she's already guessed Gwen wouldn't keep that tasty morsel to herself – it was probably the reason she was so determined I shouldn't come here.' She let her thoughts meander. 'Who would have thought it?' she mused. 'Clarice and her sister's husband – I wonder if he's the reason she never married again?'

Dolly flopped back against the pillows. 'The older generation call us flappers and hold their hands up in horror – but actually they were just as bad. I suppose she never got over the shame of it, which is terribly sad. No wonder Gwen turned out the way she did.'

'Mmm. I almost feel sorry for her,' said Lulu.

'Who? Gwen?' Dolly snorted. 'I wouldn't give her an ounce of pity after the way she treated you.'

Lulu resumed her packing and finally locked the case. 'Hurry up, Dolly. I'm famished and they'll stop serving breakfast soon.'

'Peter's awfully nice, isn't he?' Dolly hovered by the bed, the contents of her case still spilling out on to the counterpane.

Lulu raised an eyebrow. 'Yes,' she replied, 'and I've seen the way you look at him. I hope you aren't—'

'Nothing like that,' she retorted with a flick of her hair. 'He's *very* handsome, I admit, but of course one couldn't *possibly* contemplate anything more than a mild flirtation when there is *absolutely* no future in it.'

Lulu turned her back on Dolly and stared out of the window, reluctant for her to see the sadness she knew must be in her eyes. The memories of Joe's face, his laughter and the deep drawling voice were poignant and sharp. They would meet for the last time tonight, and with so many people in the house it would be impossible to snatch any time alone with him. She dipped her chin and wrapped her arms around her waist.

Perhaps it was for the best. Dolly was wise not to get entangled so far from home – it could only lead to heartache.

'Will you come back to Tasmania?'

She withdrew reluctantly from her thoughts. 'I don't know,' she said truthfully, 'but I like to think I might one day.'

'To Tasmania – or to Joe?' With an impish smile, Dolly flicked the coin in the air.

Lulu glanced at her friend and smiled. 'That is a leading question, Dolly, and not to be determined by the toss of a coin.'

Galway House Racing Stables

Lulu and Dolly shared the driving. The second utility had proved necessary when it became obvious they couldn't all fit in with Peter. It had been borrowed from an old friend of Frank's, and Joe would drive it back down when he attended the December race meeting. They arrived at Galway House just as the sun dropped behind the hills.

Lights twinkled from the homestead windows, making it look warm and welcoming after the long drive. The dogs were barking, prancing back and forth, tails wagging furiously.

As Lulu switched off the engine and eased the crick in her back and neck, the door was flung open and light spilled out on to the drive. Joe ambled out and stood on the step, Dianne peeked around the doorway and Molly came bustling towards Peter's utility.

'As I live and breathe,' she shouted, 'Frank White! How you going, Frank? It's good to see you.'

Lulu clambered out of the utility and watched as Peter helped Frank down. She smiled as Molly swamped him in a hug.

'Look out, woman,' Frank grumbled. 'You'll have me off me bloody feet.'

'You haven't changed, you old bludger,' she said fondly as she released him. 'Still cantankerous, with no idea of how to treat a lady.'

'When I see a lady, I'll know how to treat her,' he drawled, the twinkle in his eye belying his words. He slipped his hand around her generous waist and gave her a squeeze. 'Still a cuddly bundle, Moll. I always liked that about you.'

She laughed and playfully slapped his hand. 'Don't touch what you can't afford, Frank White,' she warned him with a wagging finger. She turned to Peter. 'You're as handsome as your dad used to be,' she said, shaking his hand, 'but I hope you haven't inherited his flaming manners. Now get indoors, all of you. Tea's getting cold.'

'I could do with a cold beer,' Frank retorted, snatching the hated walking stick from Peter.

'The doctor said no beer until you've finished your course of pills.'

'Phwah!' He grimaced with disgust. 'If a man can't have a beer now and again, then life's not worth living,' he growled. 'Lead on, Moll – I can taste it already.'

Lulu's gaze drifted past them to the doorway and Joe. He was still nonchalant, standing with his hands in his pockets, an amused tilt to his mouth as he watched the reunion of Molly and Frank. It was as if her arrival meant nothing. She turned back to the utility to unhook the tarpaulin from the flatbed and retrieve their bags.

'I'll do that,' he murmured.

She turned and found he was standing very close. Looking up at him, she held his gaze, almost afraid to break the spell.

'Ocean Child will be pleased you're back,' he said. 'He's off his feed.'

He'd given nothing away, and she had no idea if he was pleased to see her, if he had missed her – or even thought much about her during her absence. She followed his example and remained businesslike. 'Then I'll go and see him now,' she said evenly. 'Thanks for helping with the bags.'

Walking away into the darkness of the stable-yard, she didn't look back; it would only add to the disappointment of his lack of welcome if he wasn't watching her. She hurried into the feed store and took a couple of apples from the bin.

Ocean Child's head leant out of his box. He gave a whicker of welcome and his soft nose nudged her face, his hay-breath stirring her hair.

'At least you're pleased to see me,' she murmured as she massaged his ears. 'Did you miss me, boy? Is that why you're off your feed?'

He snaffled one of the apples and chewed it with relish. The second apple disappeared the same way, and as her strong fingers worked their magic on his ears, his eyelids fluttered in ecstasy and he dribbled over her shoulder.

She rested her cheek on his, fighting the tears. She would probably never see him or Joe again after tonight – and they would both forget her.

Joe regretted not saying what was in his heart when she first returned. But he couldn't tell if she was pleased to see him, if she had missed him, or even thought of him – so he'd stuck to being the trainer of her colt and kept it impersonal. But to see her again, to hear her voice and her laughter in his home, warmed him and at the same time saddened him. This would be the last night and, as he watched her throughout the evening, he tried to burn the memory of her into his heart.

There was heightened colour in her face and her eyes had darkened to the deepest violet. She laughed easily, her hands moving expressively as she spoke. It was clear she was reborn since finding Frank and Peter, and although he knew they would take her from him in the morning, he had to grudgingly admit he liked them both.

He eyed his mother, a little embarrassed at the girlish blush to her cheek and the flirtatious way she reacted to Frank's teasing. They had been born within a few miles of each other, had attended the same school and country dances and shared many memories. He hadn't seen his mother this animated for years, and it crossed his mind that she and Frank might have had something going before she married his dad. He caught Peter's eye and realised he was wondering the same thing.

Joe leant back in his chair and let the chatter flow around him. Lulu was listening avidly to Frank regaling Molly with tall stories of his adventures on the cattle station. Dolly was pestering Peter with questions about the Outback, and Joe wondered wryly how she would fare so far from civilisation. Yet he suspected she was resourceful enough to find a way – and it was clear there was a spark of something between her and Peter which would help.

Feeling adrift and forgotten, he pushed back from the table and left the kitchen. Tugging on the thick waterproof against the night's chill, he wandered out to the yard to do the nightly rounds. His smile was wry as he tramped past the bunkhouse and checked the bolts on the feed store and tack room. Love was in the air, but not for him. Lulu had stirred his heart, making him want something he could never have. After tomorrow she wouldn't give him another thought.

All was quiet in the yard but for the scamper of a possum on the stable roof and the sleepy chirrup of a bird. He walked across the cobbles, checking each stall until he came to Ocean Child. 'It's just you and me now, mate,' he murmured, as he stroked the fine head. 'I reckon we'll soon be forgotten.'

'I'll never forget either of you.'

He turned at the sound of her voice, his heart hammering. The moonlight caught her hair, turning it into spun gold, and her lovely face was touched by the glow. 'You'll be having too good a time in Queensland to think about me and the Child,' he said.

'Do I detect a note of jealousy?' Her smile was teasing. 'You are silly, Joe. I won't be gone for ever – not now I have family here.'

He had to fight the urge to kiss her. 'So, you'll come back?' he asked tentatively.

She regarded him wistfully. 'One day,' she said, 'but it might not be for a long time. When I do, I promise to drop in for a visit and see how you're getting on.' She hesitated, stuffed her hands in her trouser pockets and looked at Ocean Child. 'You must keep me up to date with his progress,' she said, 'and I'll write and let you know how things are going for me.'

He studied her in the moonlight, hearing her words and understanding their underlying meaning. His spirits plummeted, leaving him feeling bereft. She was offering him friendship, not love, not the promise of a life together.

'I'll keep you posted on the Child,' he said almost formally, 'and I look forward to reading all your news. I hope Bertie won't be too cross about you extending your stay.'

'Bless you,' she said, brushing her soft hand fleetingly against his cheek. 'Don't worry about Bertie – I can handle him.'

Joe saw the tears glisten on her face and his resistance crumbled. He crushed her to him, burying his fingers in her hair, capturing her sweet lips and breathing in her scent. 'Oh, Lulu,' he groaned against her trembling mouth, 'I wish . . .'

'I know,' she murmured, her fingers tracing his face and the line of his lips before she pulled regretfully away. 'But it's just not meant to be.' Turning from him, she rubbed Ocean Child's ears and rested her damp cheek on his forehead. 'I shall miss both of you very much,' she said with a sob, before running off into the darkness.

Joe wanted to follow her – to tell her she was mistaken – that it *was* meant to be, and that he would follow her to the ends of the earth and love her for ever. But practicalities and reason were cold and swift, staying his feet and silencing him. Only fate would determine what happened next.

'It'll take about two hours to reach Warrego Station,' shouted Peter over his shoulder. 'Sit back and enjoy the ride.'

'What an *extraordinary* journey,' yelled Dolly, as the small plane raced along the dirt runway in Queensland and lifted off. 'I never expected to be up in one of these. Isn't it *utterly* thrilling?'

Lulu wasn't finding it thrilling at all. She closed her eyes, hunched down and gripped her seat. It was a very small plane, seemingly held together with string and sealing wax. She and Dolly were jammed in behind Peter in a seat meant for a solitary rear gunner. There was no roof and the noise from the engine was deafening.

As they soared miles above solid ground the wind made her eyes water, despite the goggles. Peter had flown throughout the war without crashing – the injury to his knee caused by a stray bullet during a dogfight – but no amount of reassurance could convince her that this redesigned fighter plane was a safe mode of transport.

Lulu groaned and huddled even further down. She must have been mad to agree to this. Why on earth didn't she go with Frank in the utility? The journey would certainly have taken longer, but it couldn't possibly be as terrifying.

Dolly nudged her and held out a silver brandy flask.

Lulu gasped as the brandy hit the back of her throat. She took another drink and handed back the flask with a weak smile of thanks. Closing her eyes again, she forced herself to think of anything other than where she was.

Leaving Galway House and Joe had been harder than she'd imagined. The last few words they'd exchanged still lingered, as did the warmth of his embrace and the passion of his kiss. She'd thought of him every day since, and often lay awake at night remembering the quiet moments they had shared around the stables and the electrifying emotion of that last moonlit night. Those memories were precious, but the regrets for what might have been were painful.

Huddled against the buffeting, freezing wind, she determinedly kept her thoughts on the past rather than the present. They had been travelling for days. Frank tired easily and it had been necessary to stay in Melbourne until he recovered from the sea-crossing. From there, they had driven across country to Sydney, where they'd loaded Peter's ute on to the train that would taken them north to Brisbane.

She had loved that part of the journey, for it gave her the chance to see so much of the majestic country and the dramatic eastern coastline. It had been fun to sleep on the train in the tiny, curtained-off compartments as they chugged through the night, and interesting to note how different the Australians were to the English when they travelled. Conversation was lively, food and drink happily shared, and their English accents brought forth stories of relatives and memories of 'home', even though most of them had never been to England.

They had stayed in a comfortable hotel in Brisbane so Frank could rest and wait for the drover who was bringing a mob of cows to the market. He arrived almost a week later, and was now driving Frank home in the utility. The clinic had forbidden him to fly for at least a year, and despite him railing against this advice, Peter had finally forced him to see reason.

The engine noise abated somewhat as they levelled out, and the combination of the continuous drone, the energy-sapping fear and two hefty slugs of brandy sent her to sleep.

'Oh, do look, Lulu. Kangaroos – and ostriches – and cows. Lots and lots of cows.'

Lulu stirred as Dolly's elbow dug in her ribs, and without thinking, she looked over the side. 'They're emus,' she said sleepily. 'Ostriches are African.'

Peter was flying much lower now, the wind was warm and she forgot her fear as she stared in awe at the scenery below them.

The land stretched from horizon to horizon in an amber swathe that encompassed craggy copper mountains, dusty brown valleys and scrub-grazing, where solitary men on horseback looked up and waved their hats before returning to their lonely vigil over the cattle. The glint of waterholes peeked from beneath stands of delicate gum trees, and the snake of a river meandered through towering canyons and acres of pale yellow grass. Mobs of cattle wandered through the scrub, kangaroos bounded with surprising swiftness as the shadow of the small plane chased them across the vast landscape and emus waggled their tail feathers as they lolloped away from the noise.

Far from desolate, this Outback land was teaming with life – and Lulu felt a tug of something akin to love as she realised it probably hadn't changed since man first walked upon it. She felt tears prick as she embraced it, for it was an ancient land – a land of dangerous beauty – her country.

'Hold tight,' shouted Peter some time later. 'We're coming in to land.'

Lulu gripped the seat and shut her eyes as they hurtled towards earth and landed with a thump. She fearfully opened one eye, but could see nothing as they raced along the ground, for they were at the centre of a whirlwind of red dust.

'Righto,' said Peter, when the dust had settled and he'd switched off the engine. 'Welcome to Warrego Station.'

Lulu and Dolly were stiff after sitting so long in the cold, cramped seat, and Peter had to lift them down. The heat hit them like a furnace blast, and they had to shield their eyes from the glare.

They had landed on a strip of earth that had been cleared through a vast field of tough yellow grass. Beyond the railing fence stood the homestead. Built of wood, with a tiled roof, it was positioned to avoid the sun. Sheltered on the east and west by stands of tall trees, its veranda looked cool and welcoming behind the fly-netting. In the clearing beside the house were barns and outbuildings and a series of corrals and animal pens. Several utilities and farm vehicles were drawn up near these pens, and Lulu could see men and horses moving about, stirring up the dust. A metal windmill creaked as it pumped water from the sluggish river, and there was a flock of white cockatoos screeching in the trees. And yet, despite those sounds, there was an awesome silence that seemed to fill her with peace.

'I hope you like it,' said Peter, as he came to stand beside her. 'It's pretty basic, but it is home.'

Lulu stood and drank it all in, her mind already working on the drawings she would do. The sky seemed so big; bleached of colour by the heat, it encompassed the Outback land like a great pale dome. 'Home,' she breathed. 'Yes, I like the sound of that.'

'It is quite *extraordinary*,' said Dolly, 'and *terribly* Australian.' She turned to Peter, her face alight with excitement. 'Will I get the chance to wrangle a steer or go on a round-up with real cowboys?'

He tipped back his hat and scratched his head as he grinned. 'This isn't America,' he chided softly, 'but I reckon we might make a jillaroo out of you before you leave, no worries.'

'At last. I never thought you'd get here.' The screen door opened and a vision in pink and orange chiffon stood on the veranda. 'What kept you, Peter, and how's Frank?'

'He's on his way,' Peter said, as he took off his flying helmet and shook out the dust. 'What are you doing here, Aunt Sybilla?'

'Brisbane is full of tourists,' she replied scornfully. 'It's impossible to work in peace.' Paint-spattered fingers flicked her hair out of her eyes, making her earrings swing and her many bracelets jangle. There was a paintbrush behind one ear and a smudge of vermilion on her cheek, and her feet were encased in gold bejewelled sandals. She finally acknowledged Lulu and Dolly, but her expression was unwelcoming.

Lulu knew she was staring, but couldn't help it. But for the age difference and the silver in her hair, it was like looking into a mirror of the future. 'I'm Lulu,' she breathed. 'It's such a pleasure to meet you, because I so admire—'

'I know who you are.' Frank's sister eyed her coldly. 'I suppose you'd better come in.'

'Strewth, Aunt Sybilla. Can't you even pretend to be polite for once?'

'Why should I?' she retorted. 'I speak as I find. That way everyone knows exactly where they stand.'

They had entered the house and were now standing awkwardly in the shadowy hall.

'Give her a fair go, Syb,' he said. 'She's one of us.'

Sybilla's nose became pinched and her eyes narrowed as she tossed back her mane of hair and looked at Lulu. 'That she might be, but she's Gwen's daughter. What's she after? A share in the station – or a pay-off?'

'I want nothing from you,' retorted Lulu, ashamed and trembling with rage at the woman's lack of charm. 'Peter instigated this reunion – not me. And I certainly don't want money or a share in this place. I am *not* Gwen, and if you can't keep a civil tongue in your head, I suggest you shut up.'

There was a shocked silence.

Sybilla's eyes flashed. 'I suppose I asked for that,' she said stiffly. 'But at least you know how to call a spade a shovel, and I suppose one should be grateful you aren't a whinging Pom, despite the accent.' She turned to Peter. 'I'll be in the studio for the rest of the day.' With a toss of her head she walked away, the garish chiffon floating around her, gold sandals clacking on the wooden floor.

'I'm sorry about that,' Peter said hastily, 'but Aunt Syb has always spoken her mind, and if I'd known she'd be here, I would have warned you. She'll be fine once she gets to know you better.'

'Let us hope so,' muttered Lulu, 'because if she carries on like that I won't be staying.'

Clarice was suffering from a cold, which had annoyingly gone to her chest. She was swathed in cardigans and a scarf as she sat in the drawing room by the fire, feeling rather sorry for herself on this bleak December day.

Lorelei's letters had been devoured so many times Clarice could almost recite them, but she opened the box she kept them in and settled down with a glass of sherry to enjoy them again.

Frank White had proved to be an irascible old man, easily frustrated by his impaired ability to ride with the mob of cattle, and quick to find fault if his orders weren't instantly obeyed. Lulu found him difficult to get on with, but as the weeks had passed, she'd learnt to accept he would never change, and they had begun to form a close friendship.

Peter was a hard-working, patient man of few words, who rarely left the cattle station now his father was incapacitated. He was still single – romance being hard to find when the population was spread over thousands of miles – but he and Dolly had taken a shine to one another and were getting along famously.

Lorelei had written reams on Dolly, for her friend had changed since their stay in Tasmania. She'd matured, grown quieter and more thoughtful as she'd become used to the routine of Joe's yard and witnessed the realities of Lorelei's past. On arriving at Warrego Station, she had enthusiastically thrown herself into the Outback life, the high heels and make-up abandoned for boots, shirt and riding breeches. She wore one of Peter's old bush hats, rode out with him to check the stock, helped with the branding – and didn't even complain that the bath water was a strange green colour and sometimes contained dead insects, leaves and even tiny frogs.

Clarice had laughed at that, and she smiled now as she read on. Frank's sister, Sybilla, had thawed somewhat when she discovered Lulu wouldn't take any nonsense from her, and was a gifted artist in her own right. And although she still spoke without thinking, and was as demanding and irascible as her brother Frank, and a hard taskmaster, she had insisted upon teaching Lorelei to paint in oils. They had ridden out at sunrise each day to paint waterholes, trees and mesas, and through their art, they had learnt to respect one another.

There were charcoal and pencil drawings enclosed with the letters, and Clarice looked at them again in admiration. Lorelei had captured the house, the corrals and pens, even the sense of the vastness of the Outback station, in those sketches, and Clarice felt she'd been there and could feel the heat and hear the great silence that had impressed the girl.

A protracted coughing fit was soothed with a sip of sherry, and she tucked the letters and pictures away, feeling quite exhausted. She'd been disappointed when Lorelei postponed her return until the New Year, but it was clear the girl was having the time of her life, so she shouldn't really be surprised. The letters and pictures kept her in touch with what she was doing, and she felt she was sharing her adventure. She remembered the debilitating heat and the dust and flies of a Sydney summer, and almost envied her as she listened to the wind blowing the rain against the windows.

She gathered up the precious box and slowly rose from the chair, her joints aching with the chill she could never seem to banish. As she turned to head for the bureau, her foot caught the edge of the ancient Turkish rug and she stumbled. Making a grab for her chair, she missed it and went flying into the small table beside it. The table tipped and the sherry bottle shattered into a thousand pieces as everything crashed to the floor.

Clarice went headlong into the grand piano, cracking her cheek against a sharp corner. Her leg twisted awkwardly beneath her, and as she fell to the floor her bony hip thudded against the unforgiving boards.

She lay there stunned and breathless, surrounded by splintered glass and Lulu's letters.

'What you done?' Vera rushed in and squatted beside her. 'It's all right, Mum, I'm 'ere. Does it 'urt anywhere?'

'My hip,' groaned Clarice. 'The pain is unbearable.'

'Don't move,' said Vera bossily. She hurried off to gather things from the couch and, with surprising gentleness, eased a cushion beneath her head and covered her with a blanket. 'I'm going to telephone the doctor,' she said. 'Don't you try and do anything while I'm gorn.'

Clarice battled with another coughing fit that intensified the agony in her hip. She closed her eyes. Her heart was pounding, she felt nauseous, and despite the roaring fire and the blanket, she was chilled to the bone.

'Right,' said Vera, as she came back, 'I've spoke to 'im and 'e's coming straight over.' She patted Clarice's hand. 'Don't worry, Mum – I'll clear up the sherry before 'e gets 'ere. Don't want 'im thinking you're tipsy, now do we?'

Clarice's protest was cut short as the pain seared through her hip and down to her toes. How could she have been so careless? What a stupid, stupid thing to do. Her eyelids fluttered as black swirls filled her head and she fell into blissful oblivion.

*

The prick of a needle in her arm roused her and she opened her eyes, confused by the bright light and the white walls.

'You are in the cottage hospital, Lady Pearson,' said Doctor Williams. 'We have managed to manipulate your dislocated hip back into place, but unfortunately there is also a fracture of the *acetabulum*.' He smiled reassuringly. 'It is the socket into which your thigh bone fits. It is only a hairline fracture and I foresee no reason why you should not make a full recovery once we've tackled your chest infection and high temperature.'

'How long will I have to be in here?' She was finding it hard to stay awake.

'You must have complete bed rest for at least eight weeks,' he replied. 'The anaesthetic will keep you sleepy for a while, and once it wears off, I will prescribe stronger pain relief.'

Clarice closed her eyes, and when she next opened them she found Vera sitting in the chair next to her bed with her knitting. She took in the sensible hat and overcoat and the dour expression and dredged up a wan smile. 'Thank you, Vera,' she whispered.

'No need to thank me, Mum,' she said gruffly, as she dumped her knitting in a bag. 'You fair scared the life out of me, lying there on the floor, I don't mind telling you.' She sniffed and eyed the private room with disdain. 'This place could do with a good clean, and no mistake.'

Clarice didn't have the energy to argue or even talk, so she let her ramble on. It felt as if something heavy was pressing on her chest, making her breathless, and she was very hot. Thankfully the tablets were working on the pain in her hip, but she did feel strange – as if she was drifting.

'D'you want me to send a telegram to Lulu?' asked Vera, 'only I think she should be told what's 'appened.'

'No. I forbid it,' rasped Clarice. She sank back into the pillows, the coughing fit leaving her exhausted.

Vera pulled a face. 'If you say so, Mum. But if you die, she won't 'alf be cross I didn't tell 'er.'

Clarice closed her eyes as sleep enticed her. Vera always looked on the dark side of things, and as she had no intentions of dying just yet, she certainly didn't want Lorelei bothered by her silly accident.

Warrego Station

The heat shimmered on the horizon in a watery mirage, its intensity making the earth hum. The sky was the clearest blue, with a solitary cloud poised over the nearby hills, and here, in the shade of the gum trees, Lulu could hear the sibilant hiss of numerous insects. It didn't feel strange at all that it would soon be Christmas, and she was looking forward to celebrating it in the sun for the first time in too many years.

She examined the drawing she had just finished, and set it aside. The tree had been an interesting subject, the bark peeling away like paper to reveal red gashes, the branches bent like arthritic hands to the blazing sky as if in supplication. 'It's too hot,' she sighed. 'My hands are so sweaty they're leaving marks on the paper. Even the pencil is melting.'

'Wonderful, isn't it?' sighed Dolly. 'Just think, it's probably below zero back in London.' She was stretched out on a blanket, hands behind her head, staring up into the canopy of trees. She was dressed, like Lulu, in boots, trousers and shirt, and her borrowed hat had been slung on to the blanket beside her. 'What I wouldn't do for our swimming pool at home. I'd sit in it up to my neck and stay there for weeks on end.'

'You'd get horribly wrinkled,' laughed Lulu, as she lay beside her and munched on a sandwich. They had brought a picnic with them, and the two horses were hobbled nearby. 'It's funny,' she said, 'but I almost miss the uncertainty of the English weather.'

'Me too,' murmured Dolly. 'But it does get very cold here at night, which sort of makes up for it.' She opened one eye and regarded Lulu. 'Don't tell me you're actually homesick for England?'

Lulu rolled on to her elbow, her head propped up by her hand. 'I am, in a way,' she admitted, 'but I miss Tasmania more.' She gazed at the view through the trees. 'This has been an incredible experience, and I wouldn't have missed it for the world.' She paused. 'But despite the way this place has inspired me and given me something to cherish, I know I don't belong here.'

Dolly sat up. 'But I thought—'

'I'm not saying I don't belong in Australia,' Lulu said hurriedly. 'I'm just saying I don't feel I fit in here – in the Outback.' She smiled and shrugged. 'I thought I would – after all, my family is here – but this is not my world, and I would soon feel imprisoned.'

Dolly's eyes widened. 'In all this space?'

Lulu laughed. 'It does sound silly, doesn't it? But the isolation is a kind of prison – there's little chance of escape – and with the men out all day, sometimes for weeks, a woman would get very lonely.'

'I suppose so, but if I lived here, I'd be out with the men. It's far more exciting and rewarding than housework.'

'Housework? You haven't done a stroke of housework since you were born,' she spluttered. She eyed her friend with interest. 'You've really taken to this life, haven't you?'

Dolly nodded, her expression contented and dreamy. 'I feel useful for the first time in my life,' she replied. 'It's satisfying to work hard all day and know your muscles are aching because you've actually achieved something.' She flopped back on to the blanket. 'Looking back, I can see how empty my life has been – and how pointless – rushing from one party to the next, keeping up with the latest fashions, and flirting with every man I meet just because it's expected of me.'

'You'll probably change your mind once you get back to London.'

'Actually,' she replied, 'I don't think I will. After experiencing all this, London will seem terribly false and overrated.'

'Do I detect romance between you and Peter?'

'We like each other and get along famously, but that's as far as it goes, and I've made certain he's aware of that.' She rolled on to her stomach and plucked at a loose thread in the blanket. 'I love it here,' she said simply, 'but like you, I don't belong. This amazing, ancient country is not for me. I'm too English, used to rain, misty mornings and gentle summers.' She leant her chin on her hands. 'I shall miss Australia, and Peter, but they will stay in my memory for the rest of my life.'

'You're being very profound,' Lulu teased.

Dolly sat up and hugged her knees. 'I suppose I am,' she admitted. 'But this trip has been a rite of passage for me. I feel I've grown up at last, and know what I want to do with the rest of my life.'

'Which is?' Lulu prompted, intrigued by this serious, mature Dolly.

'To let Freddy down gently and give him the chance to find a girl who will really love him.' She gave a sigh as she picked up her hat. 'Our families expected us to marry, and we sort of went along with it because it seemed the thing to do – but I don't honestly believe either of us was ever in love.'

'Oh, Dolly, I am sorry.'

Dolly shrugged. '*C'est la vie.* Better to sort things out now before it's too late, than spend the rest of our lives in misery.'

'What about the man threatening you with blackmail?'

'I suspect he's forgotten all about me by now,' she murmured, 'but if not, I shall simply call his bluff and deny everything once Freddy is out of the picture.'

'And your other ambitions for this new life?'

'We have a vast cattle herd on the estate, and I plan to get the farm manager to teach me everything he knows. Having worked here and listened to Peter, I can see I have a lot to learn, but I'm determined to make our herd one of the finest in England.'

Lulu looked at her in amazement. 'You plan to spend the rest of your life nursemaiding cows?'

'Yep.' She began to pack up the picnic basket. 'I'll also attend hunt balls, farmers' markets and stud farms – I might even travel up to Scotland and have a look at the Highland cattle.' Her green eyes sparkled. 'I can hardly wait to see the look on Pa's face when I tell him.'

'Will he agree to it, do you think?'

Dolly grinned. 'He won't have much choice. Pa always regretted not having a son to run the place, and now I'm going to prove to him that a daughter can do just as well, if not better.' She fastened the leather strap on the basket. 'What about you, Lulu? What are your plans for the future? Will you go back to Tasmania and give it a go, as they say here?'

'I miss Joe dreadfully,' she admitted, 'and really look forward to our chats on the two-way – once Frank has finished flirting so outrageously with Molly – but they're almost impersonal, and I really don't know how he feels about me. It could be years before I'm able to return, and by then my feelings will probably have changed and I'll be married to some stockbroker and have several children.'

'You'd hate being married to one of them – they're frightfully pompous.' Dolly shook out the rug and stuffed it into the saddlebag. 'I'm not surprised you keep any hint of romance out of your conversations on the two-way,' she said thoughtfully. 'There always seem to be a hundred people listening in – and two hundred more waiting for the gossip – everyone knows everyone's business. It must be impossible to keep secrets out here.'

'That's exactly my point about the isolation,' said Lulu, as she climbed into the saddle. 'It's about the only entertainment to be had.'

They rode in companionable silence back to the homestead. Lulu was pleasantly tired after the long ride, and was looking forward to a wash and a change of clothes. The dust clung to everything, her skin felt gritty and her hair was a tangled mess.

With the horses rubbed down and watered, they let them loose in the paddock and headed for the house. As they climbed the steps to the veranda, the screen door was opened by Sybilla, who was looking uncharacteristically flustered.

'We've had a message come over the two-way for you. They won't tell me what it's about, so you'll have to call them back.'

'If it's Joe, I'll call him once I've cleaned up.'

Sybilla's expression was solemn. 'It was Augathella police station.'

Lulu's heart was thudding as she followed Sybilla into the kitchen where the radio took up most of one corner. She sat before it and began to pedal so it fired up. Her hands shook as she picked up the handset. 'This is Warrego Station. Lulu Pearson here. I need to speak to the Augathella police.'

The static buzzed and crackled. 'Sergeant Roberts here, Miss Pearson. Is there someone with you?'

'Yes,' shouted Lulu through the static. 'What is it? What's happened?'

'I have a telegram here from a Vera Cornish in England.'

Lulu's pulse was racing and she went cold. 'What does it say?'

'Lady Pearson in hospital. Doctor concerned. Suggest get home quickly.'

'Dear God, what happened to her?'

'I dunno, Miss Pearson. It doesn't say anything more.'

Sybilla replaced the handset for her. 'Do you need one of your pills?' she asked quietly. At Lulu's nod she signalled to Dolly, who rushed off to their room. 'Just breathe as steadily as you can. She'll back in a minute.'

Lulu's thoughts were in a whirl as she waited for the pill to take effect. 'I have to go to her,' she gasped, 'but we're so far away and it will take weeks, and she could be dead by then.' The tears ran unheeded down her face and splashed on to her grubby shirt.

'Stop that,' Sybilla ordered gruffly. 'Tears won't get you to England, but Frank might.' She grasped Lulu's arm and helped her to her feet. 'Let's go and find him.'

He was in his office going through some paperwork, but he set it aside immediately and listened as Sybilla explained. 'Go and wash and change while I sort something out,' he said kindly. Seeing the fresh tears, he patted her arm. 'Try not to worry, love. That old girl is tougher than you think – she'll make it through.'

'I know, but all the same . . .'

'Go on,' he said, his brusque manner returning. 'Leave me to organise things.'

Lulu had bathed and changed into fresh clothes within minutes, but an agonising hour had passed before Frank came to find her and Dolly. 'Peter will fly you to Darwin,' he said. 'My mate has a big spread up there and he'll fly you to Java via Timor and then on to the northern tip of Sumatra. He's arranging passage for you on a cargo boat to Ceylon, and you'll pick up the SS *Clarion* in Columbo, which will take you to London.'

Lulu's heart had stopped racing, but her chest felt tight, her shoulders weighed down with worry. 'Thank you,' she said tremulously, reaching for his work-roughened hand. 'Thank you so much.'

He brushed off her thanks. 'Go and put on thicker clothes and pack a small bag. I'll send the rest of your stuff on to London.' He smiled. 'Don't fret. That old lady is as tough as an ox – she'll be right.'

He turned to Sybilla. 'Get that lazy cook to do some food they can take with them,' he ordered. 'It's a long journey.'

The next half hour passed in a blur as they hastily packed the bare essentials and swathed themselves in hats, gloves, scarves and thick coats.

Lulu kissed Frank and hugged him. 'Thanks,' she said again, 'and I promise I will stay in touch. I never want to lose you again.'

'Get outta here, girlie. You're wasting time,' he said, not quite able to disguise his emotions.

Sybilla gave her a pat on the shoulder. 'I don't do kissing,' she said brusquely, 'but I'll see you in London next year, and you can give me back my coat then. I hope all goes well with Clarice.'

They dashed into the night towards the sound of the plane's propellers gathering momentum. There was just time to wave a final goodbye before Peter boosted the engine's roar and the plane began to trundle down the airstrip, which had been marked by beacons lit in metal baskets down the length of the runway. As the plane began to gather speed, the dust made it impossible to see the homestead or the people they knew were watching from the veranda.

Lulu adjusted the goggles, shifted low in the seat and tucked her chin into the fur collar of Sybilla's coat, praying they would get to Sussex before it was too late.

17

Joe kicked off his boots and accompanied the dogs into the kitchen. Molly had hung paper chains everywhere in preparation for Christmas, and there was a little fir tree in the hall she had yet to decorate with the tinsel and silver balls they'd kept since his childhood.

He took a beer from the gas fridge and took a long, grateful slug. It had been a hot one today, and he reckoned he'd earned it. Leaning against the sink, he stared out of the window and wondered how Lulu was coping with the heat in Queensland. It would be far fiercer; drier than Tasmanian heat, with no respite from a sea breeze.

Taking the beer with him, he ambled down the passage towards the two-way. He hadn't spoken to her for a couple of days, and he missed the sound of her voice. There was also something he had to tell her – a surprise he had planned – and he hoped she would be pleased.

'If you're thinking of talking to Lulu, don't bother,' said Molly, bustling through the front door. 'I've just had a call from Frank. She's on her way to England.'

'But she isn't due to leave until the very end of January.'

'Clarice is in hospital. It doesn't look good.'

Joe's disappointment weighed heavily. 'I'd planned to surprise her in Melbourne before she sailed,' he said. 'The dates fitted right in, and I was hoping to take her to the Australia Day celebrations.'

Molly shrugged and moved past him on the way to the kitchen. 'Perhaps it's for the best,' she said, slipping her arms into the floral apron and tying it. Her gaze was direct, but not unkind. 'I know you felt something for her, Joe,' she said softly, 'but it wouldn't have worked – not when you live on opposite sides of the world.'

He knew she was right, but still couldn't accept it. Lulu was gone, and already the world seemed a much emptier place.

There was a January pea-souper fog hanging over London as they docked, and after a hasty goodbye to Dolly, Lulu clambered into a taxi and headed for Sussex. She was utterly exhausted and sick with worry, but nothing she could do would make the taxi go faster. It seemed that the last few miles of any journey were always the longest.

Four hours later she arrived at the cottage hospital. Clarice was in a deep sleep. Her face was ashen and drawn, and she looked unbearably small and frail in the great iron bed as she struggled to breathe. Lulu sank into the chair beside her, the despair and weariness making her weep. It had taken so long to get here, but was she too late? Would she ever have the chance to tell Clarice how much she loved her?

The doctor's expression was solemn as he came into the room. 'I'm glad you could make it in time,' he said.

'What happened? She's not going to die, is she?'

He regarded Clarice, refusing to meet Lulu's gaze as he told her about the fall. 'The scar on her face looks worse than it is and is healing nicely,' he said. 'The fracture has knitted, and she was making a good recovery until her chest infection worsened.' His expression grew even more solemn. 'Pneumonia has set in, I'm afraid, and her heart is struggling. She is very frail, so you must expect the worst.'

Lulu's tears blinded her. 'How long?' she whispered.

357

'A few days at most,' he replied softly. He eyed her travel-stained clothes, the bag at her feet and the bruising of weariness and anguish beneath her eyes. He'd been her doctor since her arrival in England as a child. 'She's heavily sedated at the moment. Why don't you go home and rest? I'll call if things change.'

Lulu shook her head. 'I'm going nowhere,' she said firmly.

'Do you have your own medication, Lulu? You don't look at all well yourself.'

'I'm fine.' She took the tiny frail hand that lay so still on the starched sheet, and held it to her cheek. 'Will I have a chance to talk to her?'

'She has drifted in and out of consciousness for the past two weeks, but her waking moments aren't very lucid. I wouldn't hope for too much, Lulu.'

The nurses and doctors came and went throughout the day and night. Lulu remained at the bedside, Clarice's hand gently held in her own as she softly told her about the adventure they'd had to get here. Lulu had no idea if she could hear her, but keeping up the monologue distilled the hushed silence in that hospital room.

Vera Cornish eased in through the door the next morning. 'I heard you was back,' she said in a stage whisper. 'I brought these – thought they might cheer her up.' She placed the daffodils on the bedside cupboard and looked down at Clarice. 'No change, I suppose?'

Lulu had snatched a few moments of sleep during the night and was feeling limp with fatigue – the sight of the wonderfully familiar Vera was too much and she clung to her, sobbing. 'She's dying, Vera. I should never have gone.'

Vera gave her a handkerchief and gently nudged her towards the door. 'Dry your eyes and go and have a wash,' she said gruffly. 'Madam won't want to see you in such a terrible state.' She scrabbled in her large shopping bag and pulled out several packets wrapped with greaseproof paper which she placed on the side. 'When you've tidied yourself up, you can eat. There's steak-and-kidney pie, still hot from the oven, a flask of tea and a slab of cake.' She looked with disapproval at Lulu's slenderness and clucked like a mother hen.

Lulu felt slightly better after her wash, but she discovered she had no appetite despite the heavenly aroma of Vera's cooking. She forced herself to eat enough to satisfy Vera, who fussed and bustled about for a while before she left with the promise to return later. Lulu sat quietly at Clarice's side and began to open the letters Vera had brought with her.

They were mostly for Clarice, wishing her a speedy recovery. There was nothing from Joe – it was too soon,.

'Lorelei?'

She dropped the letters and rushed to Clarice's side. 'Thank God, oh thank God,' she sobbed, as she took the birdlike hand and held it to her cheek.

'What are you doing here?' The voice was thin and bewildered.

'I've come home,' she said, as she tenderly brushed the silver hair from the pale forehead. 'I'm here, Little Mother, and I'll never leave you again.'

Clarice shifted her head on the pillow, her eyes bright with tears. 'Little Mother,' she sighed. 'How lovely.'

'I'm just so sorry I never said it before.' She leant on the bed, her face close to Clarice's. 'You're the only mother I ever had – the best mother in the world, and I love you so much.'

'I love you too,' Clarice murmured.

Lulu kept hold of her hand as she fell asleep again. Hope surged and ebbed as she watched her. Did she dare to believe Clarice would recover? 'You must get well again,' she whispered. 'I need you, Clarice.'

But Clarice didn't wake again for another three days.

*

Huddled over the radiator while the snow softly fell outside the window, Lulu was rereading an old letter of Joe's. The tone was a little stilted, but full of the day-to-day happenings at Galway House, the race meetings and the successes and failures of the horses in the yard. Bob was back in the saddle, and he and Ocean Child had won a couple of races and earned a handicap, so he was entering him for an important meeting in Melbourne in the New Year. Molly and Frank's daily chats over the two-way were causing gossip, and Eliza and her father had moved to a house out at Deloaine, which was only a few miles away. She'd become a bit of a fixture around the yard – which pleased Molly no end, but he was concerned the stable hands were becoming distracted.

Lulu tried to ignore the twist of jealousy. She had no right to feel like that. But his letter made her yearn to see him again.

Dolly's hastily scrawled note had come from the family country estate, where she was happily ensconced and already learning how to improve the bloodline of their stock. Her father had been shocked by her decision, but was coming around to the idea now he could see she wasn't doing it on a whim. The engagement to Freddy had been quietly shelved with no regrets on either side, there had been no communication from her blackmailer, and she was looking forward to the local hunt ball, which she would attend on the arm of a young man who bred Brahman bulls on a large nearby estate.

Bertie's letter was short and to the point. He was delighted she was back, sorry Clarice was unwell and interested to learn that Lulu was related to Sybilla Henderson. He ended his letter by asking when he could expect the finished commissions.

Lulu heard a rustle of bedclothes and rushed to Clarice's side. 'Hello, Little Mother,' she crooned as she kissed the pale forehead.

Clarice's grip on her fingers was weak. 'I'm glad . . . found him,' she managed through her ragged breathing. 'Frank's . . . good man.'

The short speech seemed to exhaust her and she fell silent, struggling to breathe, and clearly in pain.

'Shall I get the doctor? Do you need some more medication?'

Clarice closed her eyes and moved her head on the pillow. 'No,' she rasped. 'Did . . . see Gwen?'

Lulu bit her lip. 'Briefly,' she replied. 'We didn't have much to say to each other.'

The faded blue eyes were unwavering as the breath rattled in her chest. 'So,' gasped Clarice, 'she told you . . . me and . . . father?'

'She said something,' Lulu hedged, 'but she's always been such a liar, I didn't believe her.'

'It was true,' she panted. 'Thought . . . loved him . . . What happened . . . not my making.'

'You don't have to explain, Mother. Please don't tire yourself.'

The grip tightened on her fingers, her expression telling of her need to speak, to explain before it was too late. 'Took advantage . . . foolish young woman.' She lapsed into silence, her colour hectic, her chest rising and falling with the effort of breathing.

'He treated all of you badly in the end,' said Lulu. 'Primmy told me. I almost feel sorry for Gwen,' she admitted, 'because she adored him and he deserted her.' She leant closer. 'But it took me that long journey to understand why Gwen behaved as she did – and to realise how blessed I am in you, Mother. Thank you for rescuing me and loving me.'

A solitary tear ran down the parchment skin to fall on the pillow and the tension fell away from her fingers. 'Tired,' she panted. 'So very tired.'

'Then sleep, Little Mother. I'll be here when you wake.'

Clarice's eyelids drifted shut, and after a while Lulu retrieved Joe's letter so she could read it again.

'Is . . . from Joe?' Clarice's voice was sleepy.

'Would you like me to read it out?'

'No,' she sighed. 'Personal . . . private.' Her voice was fading and she seemed to shrink into the pillows.

'It's not, really, and I'm sure Joe won't mind,' said Lulu, smoothing out the thin paper.

'Will . . . go . . . back?'

Lulu's tears gathered in a lump in her throat. 'Probably not,' she admitted. 'I'm happy here in Sussex with you.'

'Are you in love with Joe Reilly?' Her voice was surprisingly strong, her breathing suddenly less erratic as she opened her eyes and regarded Lulu with piercing directness.

Lulu blushed and nodded, hope sparking that at last Clarice was rallying. 'I think so,' she admitted, 'but—'

Clarice's grip on her fingers was surprisingly strong for one so frail. 'Then go to him, darling girl. Tell him. Don't waste your life.'

'I'm not leaving you again, Mother.'

The grip weakened and her hand fell to the bedclothes as her eyes closed. 'Tasmania is where your heart has always been,' she said softly, 'and now the man you love is there too. Don't leave it too long, darling – he won't wait for ever.'

Lulu blinked back the tears. 'I don't expect him to,' she said, her voice unsteady.

'I wish I could have met him,' sighed Clarice. 'You will make a beautiful bride.'

'You'll meet him,' sobbed Lulu, fearful at how tired she sounded, how distant – as if she was fading, drawing away from her bit by bit. 'And of course you'll see me as a bride. Why, you're looking and sounding so much better already. It won't be long . . .'

Clarice's parchment skin became luminous in the winter light from the window, and her eyelids fluttered.

Lulu gripped her hand. 'Don't go to sleep, Mother. Please don't. I have so much more to say to you.'

'I must go,' she murmured. 'Eunice is calling me.' Her voice faded, and with a last sigh, Clarice left her.

Lulu climbed on to the bed and gathered her into her arms. She held her gently, her fingers running over the silver hair, her heart breaking. Her mother was gone, and she had never felt so alone.

Joe was sitting in his untidy office, Lulu's letter on the desk before him. He was sorry Clarice had died, and his heart ached at the thought of Lulu in deep mourning. Frustrated that he could do nothing to help her, he shoved back his chair and went to stand in the doorway, hands in pockets, shoulder against the frame. If only he could have taken time off to go and see her, but England was so far away, and he had responsibilities here that he couldn't ignore. It was an impossible situation.

His thoughts returned to her letter. At least she wasn't alone, for Sybilla had left Brisbane earlier than planned and had arrived to take charge of things until Lulu felt more able to cope. From what she'd written, Lulu was finding solace in her work, and she'd made great inroads on the commission pieces – but there had been no mention of her returning to Tasmania now she was free, and that was the hardest part of all.

'Joe?' Eliza appeared in the office doorway. 'I think you'd better come and look at this.'

'What is it, Eliza?'

'You'll see soon enough,' she said grimly. 'Come on.'

He followed her out of the yard and through the paddock to the leafy corner that had been fenced off many years ago when his grandfather was still alive. The family pets had been buried here, each little plot marked with a cross and their name.

'Why have you brought me here?'

'Look.' Her voice was unsteady as she pointed.

It was then that he saw the freshly carved markers and his blood ran cold. There were three of them, each adorned with an eyeless doll's head, the names crudely etched but all too legible.

Molly

Frank

Lorelei

Joe's skin crawled as he stared into those sightless eyes. Gwen Cole still sought revenge, and there was no telling what her crazed mind would think up next.

Sybilla had proved to be a stalwart help over the past three months, and although she remained acerbic and rather bossy, Lulu found she turned to her more and more for advice.

The house didn't feel quite so empty when she was around, and as they worked together in the summer house, or walked across the downs, their friendship deepened. But her true solace came with her sculptures. The commission pieces were almost ready for the foundry, and she'd begun to work on some of her own ideas, using the sketches she'd done in Australia.

'What do you think I should do, Sybilla?' They were in the summer house, the watery sun flooding in on a crisp March day. 'I'm sure I won't be able to finish anything in time for the exhibition, and I can't let Bertie down again.'

'You're perfectly capable of finishing at least three pieces by July,' she replied, 'and Bertie doesn't really expect much from you this year, so I wouldn't fret over it.' She eyed her thoughtfully as she put down her palette knife and ran her fingers through her tangle of hair. 'It really is time you stopped relying on me for everything, you know. I have a husband and a house in Brisbane to get back to.'

Not the least offended by her tone, Lulu smiled. 'Doesn't he mind you being away so much?'

'Alf gets along just fine without me,' she said briskly. 'He goes sea-fishing and bush-walking and spends hours messing about with his motorbikes. I reckon he doesn't know I'm not there half the time.'

'Do you have children?'

'Children are overrated, if you ask me,' she said with a sniff. 'They ruin your life by demanding every ounce of energy from you, and end up breaking your heart. Better off without them.'

Lulu remained silent as Sybilla picked up her palette knife and vigorously added dabs of burnt umber to the canvas. She suspected that behind that gruff exterior beat the heart of an unfulfilled woman who would have loved to have had children and a husband who took some notice of her – but she would never voice those thoughts. If Sybilla ever decided to confide in her, she would be happy to listen.

'I've had a thought,' said Sybilla a few moments later. 'If you do manage to put something together for London, I might be able to persuade the gallery in New York to take them as well. I'm due to exhibit there in September, and it would be a tremendous boost to your career if they agreed.'

'Do you really think they might?' Lulu felt a burst of energy and excitement.

'Only if you get on with your work and produce something they can show,' she said drily, 'and you won't do that by sitting there grinning like a fool.'

Lulu laughed and eagerly turned her attention back to the drawings, the energy building as her imagination soared. Sybilla was right. She was perfectly capable of producing several pieces in time. They needn't be cast in bronze, but fired in the oven – which would give them the rustic effect she'd been searching for.

*

'She's gone missing,' said Molly, her arms tightly folded as if to hold in the fear he could see in her eyes. 'The police say there's no sign of her at her place, and it looks as if it's been deserted for weeks. They managed to speak to that bloke she was living with, but he said she'd booted him out and sold off the horses a couple of months back. He hasn't heard from her or seen her since.'

Joe led her to the chair in his office and sat her down. 'I've doubled the guard at night,' he soothed, 'and every man has a rifle. She wouldn't dare come back again – not now she knows we're ready for her.'

'The thing with the dolls was bad enough,' Molly said with a shiver, 'and the slashed tyres were expensive to replace – but to leave a dead rat on my kitchen table and cut up all my photos of Patrick is sick. She's mad, Joe, utterly mad, and I'm terrified of what she might do next.'

Joe put his hand on his mother's shoulder, but he had no words to comfort her. Gwen Cole's campaign of terror had affected them all. He had the stable hands patrolling the house and stables every night with guns, the police making regular detours to scour the boundaries and the neighbours on alert for anything suspicious. The owners were getting jittery, making noises about taking their horses away, and if it went on for much longer she would ruin his business. He just thanked God Lulu was safe in England.

'We'll get through this,' he said, trying to instil some kind of assurance in his voice. 'If she is insane, then she'll get careless. It won't be long before she's caught and locked away for good.'

The London house had been sold long ago, so Sybilla and Lulu had booked into a hotel close to the gallery. Bertie was well acquainted with the gallery owner, and they had come to an agreement over Lulu exhibiting there. Now the gallery was alive with the chatter and laughter of the large gathering that spilled out into the manicured gardens beneath a star-studded July night. Waiters glided from group to group with champagne and caviar, cigarette smoke drifted up to the chandeliers and the mixture of perfumes was quite heady.

Lulu turned to Sybilla with a grin. 'They seem to like what they see, don't they?'

Sybilla smiled and tossed back her hair. 'I reckon you could say we've woken up London to Australia,' she drawled in her Queensland twang, 'and when we exhibit in New York in September, I think you'll find they'll like us there too.'

Lulu's eyes widened in excitement. 'They've agreed?'

'Of course,' she replied haughtily. 'I do have *some* influence, you know – and Bertie's marvellous at pulling strings.' She waved to someone on the other side of the gallery and bustled away – a billowing vision in red and purple silk.

Lulu couldn't stop smiling. New York. Who would have thought it? She eyed Sybilla's paintings on the white walls. The canvases brought the Outback to life with their searing colours and harsh beauty, and she could almost smell the eucalyptus. Her father's sister was a gifted artist who could replicate the debris of the bush floor with ease – who could paint a waterfall tumbling over red cliffs and capture the rainbow it created – and whose delicate touch could catch the glint of avarice in the eye of a tiny fairy wren as well as the ominous power of the great wedge-tailed eagle as it hovered over its prey.

Glad to have a few moments to herself, she moved through the crowd and inspected her own work. It was very different to her last exhibition, for there were fewer pieces, none of them as stylised as before, and certainly no large bronzes.

The life-studies were two feet high, standing on tall slender glass tables about the room. There was Joe in his broad-brimmed hat, saddle over his shoulder, dog at his feet – and here was Peter squinting into the sun from beneath his bush-hat, with a calf slung around his neck, his long coat falling almost to his boot-heels. The largest piece stood a foot higher. It was the trunk of a tree, with the bark peeling away and drooping like paper. At its foot sat a tiny rock wallaby, busy cleaning his snout, ears alert for danger.

Lulu moved on until she came to the child. She sat beside a bucket and spade, her tiny star-shaped hand holding a shell to her ear, eyes wide with wonder and curiosity as she listened to the ocean sighing within its depths. But her favourite piece was the foal, taken from the drawings she had done in Hobart on the night Joe had first kissed her.

It had been the hardest piece to get right, and had only been finished the day before, but it evoked such sad memories she felt the tears threaten. Without Clarice and Joe beside her, it all seemed rather pointless.

'I like the child with the shell. Is it supposed to be you?'

She turned and gasped with surprise and pleasure. 'Dolly!' she exclaimed. 'You didn't tell me you were coming.'

'Wouldn't have missed it for the world, darling,' she murmured as they embraced. She was dressed in an outrageous creation of silk and lace that left very little to the imagination, but her eyes were bright, her face glowing with health. '*Wonderful* exhibition. I recognise Joe and Peter – you're *so* clever – and I simply *adore* the foal. I'd like you to meet Jasper Harding.'

Lulu smiled and shook his hand. Jasper was handsome in a rugged sort of country way, but his accent was public school, his formal attire from Savile Row. She liked the look of him, and by the sparkle in Dolly's eyes, she did too. They talked for a while, and then Jasper wandered off to speak to Bertie and Sybilla.

'What do you think?' asked Dolly breathlessly. 'He's asked me to marry him, and I'm seriously considering it.'

'Congratulations,' said Lulu, 'but don't you think you're rushing things a bit?'

Dolly gave a shy smile, her cheeks flushing with colour. 'You know when it's the real thing,' she said, 'from the moment you meet.'

Lulu grinned with delight. 'If you say so.'

'Oh, but I *do*, darling.' Her eyes widened. 'And that's why you *have* to go back to Joe. You're *obviously* in love with him, so why hang about *here*?'

'I have an exhibition on, or hadn't you noticed?'

Dolly waved her hand dismissively. 'You don't need to be here, and Joe won't wait for ever, Lulu.'

Her words echoed Clarice's, and she felt a pang of sadness.

'Look, darling –' her bejewelled fingers encircled Lulu's wrist – 'I know it's been a *ghastly* year, what with Clarice and everything, but are you *seriously* going to rattle about in that *enormous* house and *bury* yourself in your work there for the rest of your *life*?'

She paused and took a quick puff of her cigarette. 'You can work *anywhere*, and with Sybilla and Bertie looking after you, you'll find your career will take off *regardless* of where you live.' She tugged the sable stole over one slender shoulder and waved her ivory cigarette holder to emphasise her point. 'Sybilla lives in Brisbane, darling – how far is *that* from civilisation, for heaven's sake? – and it hasn't done *her* career any harm, *has* it? Tasmania might be at the bottom of the world, but art is *global*,' she finished with a flourish.

Lulu hadn't really given much thought to her future since Clarice had gone, and had indeed buried herself in her work, incapable of making any serious decisions about anything else. The house was certainly too big for her, but she was loathe to leave it, for it held the essence of Clarice, had been in the family for generations, and she felt safe there.

But security and cosy familiarity had their own dangers. Sybilla would be returning to Brisbane after the New York exhibition, and she didn't know how she would feel about having only

369

Vera Cornish for company. The only family she possessed lived on the other side of the world – as did the man she loved.

Dolly's words had spiked an awakening in her. She'd tasted the thrill of adventure before – so why not again? 'Do you know, Dolly,' she said, with deep affection, 'there are times when even *you* talk a lot of sense.'

It was a week later that Sybilla solved the problem of what to do with Wealden House. 'If you're determined to go back to Tasmania, then you can't possibly sell this place,' she said as they sat in the garden enjoying the summer evening. 'The family ties must be continued, so I suggest you turn it into an artists' retreat. Painters and sculptors – and even writers and poets – could come here for courses, or just to work in peace and comfort. You would get to keep the house, and then if things don't work out in Tassy, you would have a home to come back to.'

'That's a brilliant idea,' said Lulu. 'Why didn't I think of it?'

Sybilla snorted. 'Too busy mooning over Joe, I suspect,' she said sagely. 'I suggest you write and tell him your plans, but keep the tone friendly and unemotional. You say you don't know how he feels about you, and it wouldn't do to corner him.' She smiled and lit the first of the two daily cigarettes she allowed herself. 'Ocean Child will be a good excuse for you to get to know one another properly – what happens after that is in the lap of the gods.'

Lulu nodded, digesting her advice, her thoughts drifting. 'How would I turn this place into a retreat?' she asked. 'Who would run it, look after it, make sure people don't abuse it? You know what artists are like. They can be very careless.'

'I'm sure Bertie knows some impoverished soul who would jump at the chance of taking care of it, and then of course there's Vera. She has nowhere else to go and is as attached to this place as you – she's bound to want to stay on as housekeeper.'

She blew a stream of smoke into the still air. 'Though how she'll manage with a bunch of wayward artists is anyone's guess.'

Lulu laughed. 'She'll revel in it. There's nothing she likes better than being disgruntled.'

'That's settled then. Shall we have a drink to celebrate? We can tell Vera what we've planned for her at the same time.'

Vera stared at them as if they'd gone mad. 'I don't know about that,' she sniffed, her arms folded beneath her bosom. 'Arty types can get a bit out of 'and.' She eyed Sybilla with her customary disapproval.

'I promise you will have the last word on choosing the caretaker,' Lulu pacified her. 'Please say you'll consider it. Clarice would want you to stay.'

'I'll think about it,' she muttered. 'Now, if you don't mind, it's my housey-housey night down the village 'all, and the vicar don't like it when I'm late.'

The next few weeks were exciting but exhausting. Lulu took it all in her stride, the prospect of returning to Tasmania and Joe keeping her focused. Vera approved of the caretaker, Phoebe Lowe – a friend of Lulu's from art school who'd fallen on hard times but could be relied upon to work with Bertie, who would oversee the accounts. A small part of Lulu's vast inheritance would provide bursaries for impoverished artists who otherwise couldn't afford to come, and there had already been lots of enquiries from potential clients.

The hardest part was packing up Clarice's precious things, but she and Vera attacked the packing cases and boxes and put them into storage until Lulu decided what to do with them. Wealden House was already taking on a new life, with all the bedrooms decorated and ready for the guests, the dining room set out for lectures and readings, the drawing room furnished with deep sofas and comfortable chairs, and the second reception room turned into a dining room. The summer house had been cleared of Lulu's work, the smaller pieces crated up to go by sea to Tasmania, the larger to be stored in Bertie's gallery until she was settled.

A week before she and Sybilla sailed for New York, they attended Dolly's wedding to Jasper. It was held on the last Saturday of August amid the splendour of the ancestral chapel that had stood on the Carteret estate for several centuries. Freddy attended with a pretty girl who bore more than a passing resemblance to Dolly, but whose demeanour was far less exotic – and Lulu suspected Dolly had deliberately thrown the bridal bouquet to her.

On the last day, Lulu wandered through Wealden House, remembering the years she'd been so happy here. She shed no tears, for there was an air of expectancy in the old place, a reawakening, as if it understood it too was on the verge of beginning a new life – and although the memories came at every turn, she knew she would carry them with her always.

Sybilla proved to be a knowledgeable and experienced traveller as they crossed the Atlantic, and it was she who showed Lulu New York during their three-week stay.

Lulu enjoyed the excitement of such a pulsating city, marvelled at the towering buildings and the racing, honking yellow taxis and was entranced by the lavish theatre productions and the size of the parks, the glittering shops and galleries. But despite the New York hospitality and the thrill of being exhibited, Lulu's thoughts were centred on Tasmania – and Joe.

The exhibition was successful, and as Lulu left New York with Sybilla she knew she had achieved more than she could ever have hoped for in her work – but her doubts over whether or not Joe loved her or not remained. As the ship drew ever nearer to Australia, Lulu kept those doubts at bay by writing him a long letter in which she told him about the artist's retreat, her time in New York and her decision to set up home in Tasmania. She gave him no dates for her arrival, nor did she mention future plans. Time and distance could make things seem more intense than they were, so she'd kept the tone light and friendly – and given no hint of her feelings or expectations.

She posted the letter in Brisbane, and after visiting Warrego Station for a few weeks she travelled down to Melbourne, boarded the *Loongana* and set sail for Tasmania.

18

It was a mild spring evening, the shadows lengthening as the sun slowly sank behind the hills. Joe had joined Molly and Eliza on the veranda for a beer while Dianne prepared the tea and, as usual, the conversation had turned to Gwen and the trouble she'd caused over the past months.

'She's been ordered back to Poatina and will be arrested on sight if she's seen within twenty miles of Galway House,' Joe said grimly, 'and as it's been over a month since her last attack, I reckon it's over.'

'You would have thought Arnie Miles could have done something to keep her under lock and key,' said Molly crossly. 'The flaming woman's a menace.'

'He's just a local policeman trying to do his job. She denied everything, and without evidence, they had nothing to hold her on.'

'Surely he could see she was lying?' piped up Eliza.

'I suspect Arnie knows the score,' said Joe, taking a long pull of his beer. 'He'll have the Poatina ranger keep an eye on her.'

Molly snorted with derision. 'She managed to get in here without anyone seeing her – who's to say she won't slip back again?' She folded her arms, her expression belligerent. 'If I catch her within a hundred yards of the place, I'll take the shotgun to her, you see if I don't.'

Joe shared her sentiments. He eyed the dogs, which were

sprawled panting at the foot of the veranda steps. They were good guard dogs, but Gwen had managed to get in without them raising the alarm. He could only conclude she'd found somewhere close to hide so she could watch and wait until the coast was clear. It was unsettling.

'I suppose we ought to be thankful she hasn't harmed any of the animals,' Molly said, 'but that hasn't stopped two owners taking their horses away. Word's out, Joe. I had another call today from the mainland asking if the rumours were true. I think I managed to persuade them the horses were safe, but what if they're not?'

'Let me deal with the owners,' said Joe briskly. 'You've got to stop worrying over this, Ma. It will make you crook.' He saw the dark shadows beneath her eyes and silently cursed Gwen for the trouble she had caused.

'I wish to God Lulu had never come here,' she blurted out. 'I warned you it would be a mistake.'

'That's not fair,' he retorted.

'I agree with Molly,' said Eliza coolly. 'If Lulu didn't have her colt here, and hadn't stayed with you, Gwen wouldn't have come near the place.' She eyed him thoughtfully. 'Perhaps you should think about sending Ocean Child to another yard.'

Joe frowned. 'I thought you liked Lulu?'

'We got on all right,' said Eliza with a pout, 'but I found her a bit stuck-up, if the truth be known. Dolly was far more approachable.'

'Well, I *did* like her,' said Molly, 'and she can't help having a mother like that.' She sighed. 'But you can't get away from the fact that Eliza is probably right. We should find another yard for the Child and be done with it.'

'Ocean Child is staying where he is,' Joe retorted. He exchanged a glance with his mother. 'The trouble we've had with Gwen probably has more to do with being thwarted by you and Dad all those years ago,' he said. 'With Frank and Lulu out of reach, we were the most accessible targets for her twisted revenge.'

Molly's expression was thoughtful. 'You may be right, but I don't think so. I'm glad Lulu and Frank are out of harm's way, but I do wish we knew if Gwen has given up her campaign for good, or if she's merely biding her time until we become complacent.'

'Complacency is a thing of the past from now on,' he said firmly. 'We will continue to be vigilant, and I'm already setting up a security system.'

He paused, knowing the reaction he would get to his next piece of news and steeling himself against it. 'I got a letter this morning from Brisbane,' he said. 'Lulu's up in Queensland with Frank and Peter.'

'What on earth is she doing there?' Eliza's eyes narrowed.

He noted his mother's shocked expression and ploughed on. 'She's planning to return to Tasmania and set up home in the Kirkmans' old place down by the beach.'

In the ensuing babble of protest and argument none of them noticed the figure melt cat-like into the deeper shadows at the edge of the homestead – but if they had, they would have recognised her immediately.

As the SS *Loongana* docked in Launceston, Lulu breathed in the familiar scents of a warm November spring day and knew she had made the right decision. She was home at last – and would stay, regardless of what happened between her and Joe, for this was where she belonged, and she was determined to make a good life here.

She gathered up her bag and coat and followed the other passengers down the ramp to the quay. As she'd kept her arrival date secret, there was no one waiting for her, but it didn't stop her searching the crowd for a familiar face. He wasn't there, of course, but the sight of horse floats and utilities lining the docks made her yearn to see him.

Resisting the temptation to drive straight to Galway House, she concentrated instead on getting her trunks and boxes safely loaded on to the delivery truck with detailed instructions on where to take them. Once the car she'd bought in Melbourne had been off-loaded, she threw her overnight bag in the boot and drove west.

After a brief stop in town to collect the keys and do some food shopping, she continued her journey in deep contentment. The perfect spring day's bright sun and clear sky were welcoming her – the solace and warmth that had been missing since Clarice's death returning as she caught tantalising glimpses of the sparkling sea.

The coastal lane had been metalled during her absence, but the trees still formed a beautiful dappled archway. Pulling up outside the house she'd admired since childhood, she stepped out of the car and leant against the bonnet. The elderly couple who had owned River View were long dead, and the new owners had leased it out to a succession of tenants. But someone had looked after the place, for the paintwork gleamed in the sun, the gardens were colourful and the lawns and monkey-puzzle tree were verdant.

With a rising sense of excitement she pushed open the gate, walked slowly up the path and slotted in the key she'd collected earlier. Opening the door, she stepped inside, and felt the house embrace her. 'Hello, house,' she breathed. 'Remember me? Remember how I used to walk past you on the way to school every day?'

She smiled at her silliness and began to explore – for although she knew the house well, she'd never been inside. The ground floor consisted of a reception room on either side of the front door, with bay windows overlooking the river, and a kitchen that led out to a walled back garden. Upstairs were three bedrooms and a bathroom. Everything inside was old-fashioned and sadly neglected, despite the care taken in the front garden.

Walking into the largest bedroom, she flung open the windows and shutters and stepped on to the veranda. She had never dreamt she would ever live in this house, but here she was, looking out over the busy river to the eastern shore, watching the gulls wheel and float against the lapis lazuli sky.

'Thank you, Little Mother,' she whispered, 'you have given me so much.' She blinked away the tears and wrapped her arms tightly around herself. This was not the time for tears or regret, but a time to acknowledge that Clarice would always be with her, watching over her as she had done throughout her life.

She turned her back on the view and regarded the room. The furniture was dated, too dark and heavy for her taste, but would do her for now. The walls were an unhealthy shade of green which would have to go, and the curtains were moth-eaten, but she had all the time in the world to make it homely – and if things went right and the owner could be persuaded to sell to her, then one day she might actually own River View. With a grin of delight she hurried down to the car and brought in her overnight bag.

The morning passed swiftly once the men had delivered her trunks and boxes. The sculptures and more precious items would come from the mainland after Christmas, each carefully packed to protect them from the rough sea-crossing, but she had already planned where to place them. She stood amongst the chaos of packing cases, trunks and boxes and decided she would unpack only the necessities for now and take her time with the rest.

By three in the afternoon she was tired, dirty, hot and ready for a stiff drink. She had made up the bed with fresh linen, beaten rugs and curtains, put photographs and books on shelves and hung some of her clothes in the wardrobe. There was still a great deal to do, but it would have to wait.

The kitchen and bathroom were antiquated, and the water gushed out in erratic rusty spurts for a while until the pipes cleared. Having washed and changed, she scrabbled in the box of groceries and pulled out the bottles of gin and tonic water. She raised the glass in a silent toast to the house – and the future – and after a satisfying gulp, took her drink into the back garden.

It was quite large, but set out in a way that shouldn't need the services of a gardener, and hidden away beneath a rampant tangle of overgrown ivy, rose and honeysuckle she found something that made everything perfect. The summer house was in a bit of a state, with a sagging glass roof, swollen timbers and some cracked windowpanes, but with love and attention it had the makings of a perfect studio.

Lulu grabbed the handle – which fell off – and tugged at the weathered door, which reluctantly screeched back on rusting hinges. The inside was full of junk and probably rife with vermin – but the size of it was just right, and once the vegetation had been cleared and the glass roof replaced, the light would flood in. She stood for a while, planning where she would put everything, and making a mental list of the tradesmen she would need to bring it to life again.

Contented and happy, she went back into the house and grabbed a light jacket. The wind was freshening and there were clouds on the horizon – Tasmanian weather was maintaining its reputation, and it would probably rain before nightfall. With the key in her jacket pocket, she closed the door behind her and drove back towards town. She had resisted long enough. It was time to see Joe.

Galway House looked wonderfully familiar, but she was unaccountably nervous as she knocked on the door.

'Hello, Lulu,' said Molly, 'I'd heard you were back.'

'I only arrived this morning how on earth . . . ?'

'This is Tasmania, love.'

She beckoned her in and led the way to the kitchen, where

Dianne was cutting up vegetables. The girl squinted at her from beneath her fringe and nodded at Lulu's greeting.

Lulu sat down at the table. It wasn't the warmest of welcomes, and Molly seemed to be feeling as awkward too.

'Ocean Child's out on evening ride-out,' said Molly, pouring a cup of tea and pushing it across the table, 'but they shouldn't be much longer. Ocean Child's really come on in the past few months, but Joe was wondering . . .' She fell silent, her gaze sliding away.

Lulu was deeply disappointed not to see Joe, but then she could hardly expect him to sit about here waiting for her when there was so much to do around the yard. 'What was he wondering?'

Molly fiddled with a teaspoon. 'The really important races are all on the mainland, and Joe was wondering if perhaps he should be trained over there.' She glanced up at Lulu and looked away again.

'But Eliza's horses are still here, aren't they – and the four that came while I was here?' Lulu regarded the woman on the other side of the table, her thoughts whirling. 'All of them will be racing on the mainland at some point,' she said flatly, 'so why single out my colt?'

'We've had a bit of trouble,' admitted Molly, 'and it would be better if the colt was moved.' She looked up. 'Len Simpson has space in his yard in Queensland and would gladly take him.'

Lulu felt a chill tingle down her spine. 'What kind of trouble?'

Molly bit her lip, and after a long pause told her about Gwen. 'We'd all feel easier if the Child was gone,' she finished up.

Lulu scrubbed her face with her hands, the chill burrowing deeper as she digested the full impact of what Molly was saying. If Gwen was wreaking revenge on Joe, then her own arrival could trigger off something far more dangerous. 'I'm so sorry, Molly. I never realised . . . Joe never told me any of this.'

'He didn't want to worry you,' she replied, 'and being so far away, you couldn't do anything.'

Lulu took her hand and dredged up a smile. Poor Molly was looking strung out and deeply worried, and her presence was likely to make the situation worse. She stood and buttoned up her jacket. 'I can hear them coming back from the gallops. I'll go and see Joe and try to sort out something.'

'He's down in Hobart with Eliza,' said Molly quickly.

Lulu had a sharp memory of the racetrack and all that had happened there the previous November. The thought that he was with Eliza shouldn't have bothered her – but it did. 'When are they expected back?'

'Next Tuesday,' she replied, 'and then on Friday he's off to Melbourne with her to see how Starstruck does in his big race.' She smiled, the colour rising in her face. 'Joe's planning to enter him in the Melbourne Cup next year if he qualifies,' she said, 'and I suspect we could have a couple of reasons to celebrate.'

Lulu frowned, not understanding.

Molly leant towards her. 'Joe and Eliza have become very close these past months,' she confided. 'I reckon it's only a matter of time before he pops the question.' She cocked her head, her eyes as knowing and bright as a robin's. 'Wouldn't it be lovely if we had a Cup winner and a wedding all in the same year?'

The shock and the pain were almost too much and Lulu excused herself as quickly as possible and hurried out into the yard. Joe and Eliza were getting married. She was too late. Too late. Too late.

She barely acknowledged Charlie's greeting and the cheerful g'days from Bob and the other jackaroos as she headed for Ocean Child's stall.

With a whicker of recognition the colt nuzzled her, and as she stroked his neck and fondled his ears the tears ran down her face. Shattered dreams were hard to mend – and until she saw Joe and spoke to him she must cling tightly to the hope that Molly had been mistaken – that it had all been wishful thinking.

But if Ocean Child was shipped to the mainland and Joe married Eliza, the future she'd planned for her new life in Tasmania would be smashed almost beyond repair.

Several days had passed but Lulu still had to unpack most of the boxes and crates. She had lost her appetite to make the house a home, and knew she couldn't settle until she'd spoken to Joe and learnt exactly how the land lay.

Feeling restless, she'd left the house at noon and was taking her daily walk on the beach. The gulls screamed overhead and the trees rustled in the gathering wind as the surf raced up the sand and crashed against the bluff. The boom of the blowhole was accompanied by great spouts of water shooting skyward, and the beach was rapidly clearing as children, picnics and blankets were gathered up and hurried home.

Her hair was whipped from her face, and she could taste the salt spray on her lips as she drank in the wildness of it all. She loved it. It sang to her.

Standing on the sand, she watched the ocean swell and heard it roar, feeling herself reborn and invigorated – ready to face Joe and whatever the future held. She turned away, walked back to her car and headed once more for Galway House.

She parked the car behind an enormous truck she didn't recognise, skirted the homestead and headed straight for the yard. She could hear voices and the ring of hoofs on cobbles, and steeled herself for the first sight of Joe.

She froze as she reached the corner of the stalls. Joe was walking away from the yard towards the paddocks and the steep hill that ran down to the river. He was not alone. His arm was around Eliza's shoulder, hers around his waist. He was drawing her close

– so close her head rested against him, and it was clear they were oblivious to everything going on around them.

Lulu didn't want to watch them, but somehow she seemed incapable of moving.

They stopped walking as they reached the brow of the hill. Eliza slipped into his embrace, her head against his heart as his cheek rested on her hair. His arms tightened around her, holding her as if he never wanted to let go.

Lulu fled. The tears blinded her as she rushed to the car, and her hands were shaking so badly she could barely get it started. Slamming the door, she rammed it into gear and hurtled out of the driveway and along the rough track. She didn't care that she was going too fast, or that the potholes and ruts might damage her new car. She just needed to escape, to get home, to close the front door, crawl under the blankets and blot out the sight of them together.

Joe was doing his nightly round of the yard after tea, checking that everything was locked away and the horses settled, when Bob came hurtling around the corner and almost knocked him over. 'Whoa there, mate, what's the rush?'

'Nothing,' Bob spluttered, clearly eager to be on his way.

Joe kept hold of his collar, deeply suspicious. 'What are you up to?'

'Nothing,' he replied, trying to squirm away. 'I gotta go,' he squeaked. 'Dianne's expecting me to help wash the dishes.'

'The dishes can wait,' he replied tersely. 'Come on, mate, something's bitten your backside, and I want to know what it is.'

'It's yer ma,' he muttered reluctantly.

Joe frowned and let go of his collar. 'What about her?'

'She'll kill me if I tell you,' the boy spluttered.

'I'll kill you if you don't,' Joe growled. 'Out with it, boy, before I lose my patience.'

'Yer ma's just given me a right ticking-off cos I told her I saw Lulu last week,' he said miserably, 'and that she was back again today. Molly clipped me round the ear'ole and said I was to keep me mouth shut and not tell you.'

'You're lying,' said Joe. 'Ma wouldn't do that.'

'Look,' said Bob, showing him a reddened ear.

'But if Lulu had been here, she'd have come to see me.' He glared at the boy. 'You're lying to me, Bob, and I want to know why.'

'I'm not a flamin' liar,' shouted Bob. 'She was here today. I swear.'

'When?'

Bob shrugged. 'I dunno what time it was, but she only stayed a minute.'

Joe turned on his heel and without another word to the hapless Bob stormed off to the homestead. 'Ma? Where are you?' he roared.

'What's all that noise about?' Molly came out of the kitchen, arms akimbo.

'Why didn't you tell me Lulu was back?'

'I haven't had the time to worry about her,' said Molly with studied calm. 'So what if she is?'

'What did you say to her when she came over last week?'

'I might have said something about the trouble we've been having,' she muttered. 'She agrees with me that it would be better to move the colt to Simpson's yard.'

'And today? Did you speak to her today?' Joe was hard-pressed to remain calm in his urgency.

'I saw her park up, but she went straight to the stables.' She eyed him steadily. 'She only saw what we've all witnessed over the past few months. I expect that's why she didn't stay long,' said Molly defensively.

'What the hell are you talking about, Ma?'

'You and Eliza,' she said, not quite so confidently. 'It's obvious you were made for each other. You have so much in common, and I'm sure it's only a matter of time before you and she . . .' She fell silent.

'And I suppose you told Lulu all this . . . this . . . nonsense?' he hissed.

Molly shrugged and turned away into the kitchen. 'Stop gawping, girl,' she snapped at Dianne, 'and get on with those dishes.'

'Did you warn Lulu that Gwen could still come looking for her?' he asked quietly.

'I didn't see the point,' replied Molly. 'Gwen probably doesn't even know she's back, and I doubt she'll risk everything by driving up here while the police are keeping an eye on her.'

Joe was about to reply when he heard a strange noise from the other side of the kitchen. He looked over and saw Dianne cowering in the corner. Her strange eyes were awash with tears, the sobs coming with every breath. 'What on earth's the matter with you?'

'I didn't mean to,' she babbled. 'I'm sorry.'

Joe slowly approached her, his large hands reaching out to her, his voice soft and coaxing as if trying to calm a startled foal – but his skin was icy, the fear clawing at him. 'What didn't you mean to do, Dianne?'

'She said she'd pay me two quid if I kept me ears open and told her if Lulu turned up.' The sobs turned to wails. 'She said she was a reporter, and I would get me picture in the paper,' she howled. 'But it was her, wasn't it? That Gwen?' She clung to him, her face ugly with fear and remorse. 'Oh Gawd,' she shrieked, 'I didn't mean no harm, Joe, really I didn't. I didn't know she'd done all them things otherwise I'd've never—'

Joe tamped down on his impatience. 'Did she come here today?'

Dianne broke into another loud wail as she nodded and put the grubby pound notes on the side. 'I wouldn't have taken it if I'd known,' she stuttered.

Joe gently pressed her into a chair and patted her shoulder. 'Look after her,' he ordered the wide-eyed Molly. 'I'm going to Lulu's.'

Lulu had locked all the doors and windows and pulled every curtain before she ran up the stairs and climbed into bed. The pain of losing Joe was almost unbearable, and she had cried herself into an exhausted sleep.

The dream was confusing and eerie. She was at Ascot, but they were running the Melbourne Cup. Ocean Child was in the lead and Molly was riding him. As they passed the winning post they were greeted by Dolly, who waved her ivory cigarette holder about and declared them man and wife. Molly had turned into Eliza, and Joe was putting a ring on her finger. He lifted the white veil to kiss her and Dolly waved her cigarette again and the stench of smoke filled the air as a terrible scream rang out.

Lulu sat up, fully awake, her heart pounding as she stared into the darkness. The smell of smoke still lingered, and there was a soft crackling sound coming from down below. Realisation hit and she scrambled out of bed. The house was on fire. She had to get out.

Grabbing her dressing gown from the bottom of the bed, she couldn't find her slippers. It was so dark she couldn't see a thing. And the smell of smoke was getting stronger. Disorientated in the unfamiliar room, she scrabbled along the wall in search of the door, sobbing with fear. She couldn't find it. Where was it? She had to find a way out.

The smoke filled the room, making it hard to breathe. She began to cough and dropped to the floor. Crawling back and forth she tried to find the windows. But her lungs were burning, and her heart felt as if it would burst through her chest. She collapsed on the wooden floorboards, and in the instant before she passed out she realised they were hot.

Joe saw the pall of smoke and rammed his foot down on the accelerator. As the ute careered along the road he prayed it wasn't the Kirkman place and that Lulu was safe. But as he screeched around the corner and almost sideswiped a ute on the other side of the narrow lane, he saw the flames leaping up the side wall. Sick with fear, he drew the utility to a slithering halt and leapt out.

He took it all in at a glance – the elderly neighbours in their nightwear, confused and frightened, clinging to one another on the other side of the lane; the sound of the fire-engine's bell in the distance; the orange glow in the sky as flames gorged on the timber and crackled with demonic fury as they roared through shattered glass and took hold of the interior. 'Where's Lulu?' he yelled at the elderly couple.

They looked at him wide-eyed and shook their heads. The fire-bells were nearer now and more people were coming to watch.

Joe's fear and frustration built as he eyed the flames. One side of the house was an inferno, the flames voraciously clambering up into the roof and the overhanging trees. The curtains were closed and there was no sign of anyone inside. Lulu could already be dead – he didn't have time to wait for the firemen.

Racing for the river he pulled off his coat, drenched it and dragged it over his head. The front door was blazing, flames spitting as they lapped at the paint, which gave them greater power. Joe eased through the gate and dodged the fingers of fire that reached out to him. The bay window had yet to catch light – it was his only way in.

He clambered on to the wide sill and kicked in the glass. Taking a deep breath, he climbed through and ran towards the door. It was ajar and the smoke was already pouring into the hallway and up the stairs. He gathered the hem of his sodden coat and pressed it against his mouth and nose. He could barely see anything, the smoke was so thick, and his throat and lungs were already burning from the heat of the flames that were running across the ceiling.

A timber crashed somewhere nearby, and he heard the explosion of shattering glass. He'd reached the stairs. Racing up them two at a time, he came to the landing. 'Lulu . . . !' he yelled. 'Where are you?'

There was no reply, just a line of doors barely discernible through the smoke. The first was a bathroom, the second and third empty bedrooms. He shoved open the last door, the smoke billowing in with him.

Lulu was lying by the bed, surrounded by tongues of flame that were licking up through the floorboards.

Coughing and gasping, eyes and throat stinging, lungs bursting, he gathered her up. She lay still and limp in his arms and he held her close, wrapping her in the wet coat. Now he had to get them out.

Back through the door to the landing to witness a beam crashing down in a shower of sparks which fuelled the fury of the flames that were now racing towards him. He backed away. They were trapped.

Returning to the bedroom, he slammed the door shut and put Lulu on the bed, still covered in the wet coat. Dragging pillows and a blanket together, he rolled them up and rammed them along the bottom of the door. Every second counted now.

He raced to the windows, opened them and looked down. The firemen had arrived. 'Up here,' he shouted. But they couldn't hear him above the fire's roar and the crashing timbers as the roof on the other side of the house began to collapse.

Joe yanked the moth-eaten curtains from their brass poles and tied them together with the sheets from the bed. Testing the knots, he kept an eye on the door. Flames were licking around it, the pillows and blanket already smouldering. Back to the window, and on to the veranda to fix the makeshift rope to the iron railing.

He looked down again – and then up. The fire was all around him. They had almost run out of time.

Grabbing Lulu, he hoisted her over his shoulder, swung a leg over the veranda railing and prayed the knots would hold. He slid down the curtains and sheets, hearing them tear, seeing the knots begin to unravel as fire began to lick at the railings above him. As his feet hit the ground the rope gave way and fell in a burning snake on top of him.

Hands beat out the flames, took Lulu and helped him stagger away. He ignored the firemen's praise and the applause of the crowd that had gathered, and raced to Lulu's side. 'Is she alive?' he asked the fireman.

'She's breathing,' he said, 'but she doesn't look too good. Some-one's called the ambulance.'

'There isn't time.' Joe scooped her up and bundled her into the ute, which miraculously was still running. Clambering in beside her, he spun the wheel, rammed his foot on the accelerator and gave a blast of the horn to clear the watchers. The hospital was minutes away, and he prayed he was in time.

Lulu woke, disorientated by the strong light and the white walls. The smell of disinfectant was all too familiar, and when she saw the white-coated doctor, she knew where she was. 'The fire,' she said, and coughed. 'I couldn't get out.'

'Don't try to speak,' said Joe, edging the doctor aside. 'You've taken in a lot of smoke, and you need to rest.'

She stared at him in confusion. His hair was singed, his face smeared with soot, his clothes charred in places. 'What are you doing here? What happened?' The coughing fit lasted longer this time and her lungs and throat felt raw.

'You're safe, that's all that matters,' he said softly. 'I'll leave you to rest.'

'No.' Lulu struggled to sit up. 'I want to go back to River View.'

'You must stay and rest,' the doctor said. 'We don't know what effect all this has had on your heart.'

'It's fine,' she said between coughs as she clambered out of bed. 'Joe, will you take me, or do I have to call a taxi?'

'There's nothing left to see.' His dark eyes were full of regret. 'Don't go back, Lulu. You will only find it upsetting.'

'I must.' She took in her nightclothes and tied the belt on her dressing gown before she staggered down the hospital ward. 'Where's the way out?'

'I really would advise you against leaving, Miss,' stammered the doctor.

'I'm a grown woman. I'm free to do whatever I want,' she croaked, bending almost double with a coughing fit.

'Please, Miss Pearson. You must rest – at least for tonight.'

'Joe?' She looked up at him, her lovely eyes ringed with weariness and sorrow. 'Joe, please. Help me.'

Joe exchanged a knowing look with the doctor and shrugged. 'I reckon the lady knows her own mind, mate.'

'You'll have to sign a release form.'

'I'll sign anything you want,' she rasped. 'Just let me out of here.'

With the form duly signed, she staggered towards the main door and would have fallen if Joe hadn't grabbed her arm before leading her into the chill night air. Once she was installed in the passenger seat, he wrapped her in a horse blanket and handed her the flask of water. 'Like it or not,' he said grimly, 'you're going back tomorrow for a proper check-up.'

'Just drive, Joe. I need to see what's left of River View.'

Lulu's breathing was still ragged as she slowly climbed down and stood in the lane looking at the charred, smoking remains. The chimney was intact, standing like a lone sentinel among the rubble, but everything else was gone.

'I heard about the fire on the two-way,' said Molly, coming to stand beside her. 'I'm so glad you're safe, Lulu. I don't know what I would have done if Joe hadn't got to you in time.'

Lulu stared at her, trying to digest the fact Molly was here. 'Joe rescued me? But how did he know I was in danger?'

'We'll talk about it when you're feeling better,' said Joe, giving his mother a stern look. 'For now, I suggest you come back to Galway House with us.'

Lulu glanced up at Joe and then turned her attention to a utility truck parked further up the lane. 'I recognise that,' she murmured. A cold tremor ran through her as realisation struck. 'Did Gwen start the fire? Is she still here?'

Molly took her hand. 'I've spoken to the firemen,' she said softly. 'They found a body and a petrol can where the fire must have started. He reckons she must have got trapped as she lit it.'

'The scream,' Lulu murmured. 'I heard a terrible scream. It was what woke me up.' Tears of fatigue and sorrow coursed down her face. 'What an awful way to die.'

'Come on, Lulu, let's get you home.'

Lulu felt the strength of his arm around her shoulders, the grip of his fingers on her dressing gown and knew she could never face Galway House again. 'Thank you for saving me, Joe,' she said, easing away, 'but I think I'll book into a hotel for a few days before I go back to England.'

'England? But I thought you were going to settle here?'

She looked up into his puzzled eyes, her heart breaking. 'I've lost the house I've loved since childhood, and the man I thought I would spend the rest of my life with,' she said sadly. 'There's nothing here for me any more.'

Joe looked down at her in puzzlement as his large hands gently held her shoulders. 'You're talking in riddles, Lulu. You might have lost the house, but if I'm the man you think you've lost, then you're very much mistaken.'

Hope surged through her as she saw the sincerity in his expression. 'But you and Eliza . . .'

'There's nothing between me and Eliza,' he said softly. 'What you saw the other day was Eliza grieving for Moonbeam. The mare broke her leg and had to be put down.'

'The big truck parked outside,' she breathed. 'It was the vet's?'

He nodded and pulled her closer. 'I have loved you Lulu Pearson from the moment I set eyes on you – but until this moment I never dared hope you could love me. Do you, Lulu? Do you really?' His brown eyes were warm and intense as he looked down at her.

'You've been in my thoughts ever since I left here,' she murmured. She softly touched his cheek, saw hope light in his eyes and felt a rush of love. 'Of course I love you, Joe, but we come from such opposite worlds, have such different ambitions – can it really work for us?'

His smile warmed his eyes and softened the lines of his face as his arms wrapped about her waist. 'I'm up for the challenge if you are,' he said softly. 'We have the rest of our lives to see what we can make of it – and as long as we continue to love one another the way we do at this moment, then yes, I'm up for the challenge.' Lulu sank into his embrace, leaning against him, feeling his heart race between them as he kissed her.

The touch of his lips was infinitely sweet, promising everything she could ever hope for. At last she was complete – and where she truly belonged. She was home.

ACKNOWLEDGEMENTS

This book could not have been written without the help of many people in Tasmania. Thank you to Tracey Wyllie for giving me so much of your precious time and for answering all my questions about breeding horses. Thanks too for the advice and information generously given by the Wishaws at their beautiful stud farm, and a huge thanks to Beryl Stevenson for her enthusiasm in opening up her address book. Her contact list was invaluable. To Jim Osborne and Bert Wicks I also give thanks for their seemingly endless knowledge of the Tasmanian Racing history.

Last, but never least, I wish to thank my lovely, loyal friends, Tony and Diana Zanus for their generous hospitality and enduring friendship